D0311414

THE SONS OF THE ZODIAC SERIES
BY ADDISON FOX

Warrior Ascended

WARRIOR AVENGED

THE SONS OF THE ZODIAC

ADDISON FOX

A SIGNET ECLIPSE BOOK

SIGNET ECLIPSE
Published by New American Library, a division of
Penguin Group (USA) Inc., 375 Hudson Street,
New York, New York 10014, USA
Penguin Group (Canada), 90 Eglinton Avenue East, Suite 700, Toronto,
Ontario M4P 2Y3, Canada (a division of Pearson Penguin Canada Inc.)
Penguin Books Ltd., 80 Strand, London WC2R 0RL, England
Penguin Ireland, 25 St. Stephen's Green, Dublin 2,
Ireland (a division of Penguin Books Ltd.)
Penguin Group (Australia), 250 Camberwell Road, Camberwell, Victoria 3124,
Australia (a division of Pearson Australia Group Pty. Ltd.)
Penguin Books India Pvt. Ltd., 11 Community Centre, Panchsheel Park,
New Delhi - 110 017, India
Penguin Group (NZ), 67 Apollo Drive, Rosedale, North Shore 0632,
New Zealand (a division of Pearson New Zealand Ltd.)
Penguin Books (South Africa) (Pty.) Ltd., 24 Sturdee Avenue,
Rosebank, Johannesburg 2196, South Africa

Penguin Books Ltd., Registered Offices:
80 Strand, London WC2R 0RL, England

First published by Signet Eclipse, an imprint of New American Library,
a division of Penguin Group (USA) Inc.

First Printing, September 2010
10 9 8 7 6 5 4 3 2 1

For Beth

My little sister, my dearest friend.

My partner in Grease dances and
basement Miss America pageants,
my nemesis in selecting the radio station
and riding in the front seat.

You know I've said it before—
my memories begin the day
you came home from the hospital.

What you may not know
is that all the best ones include you.

I love you and I am so blessed to call you mine.

ACKNOWLEDGMENTS

My deepest thanks to:

Kerry Donovan—you've taken on the Warriors and made them your own, and I am so excited to be working with you.

Holly Root—aka, the Bomb-digity. 'Nuf said.

To the amazing marketing team at NAL. Kathryn Tumen—I am so grateful for how you've helped bring the Warriors to readers. To the NAL art department—there are truly no words to describe how much I love the cover design you've developed for the series.

My family and friends—the amazing group of people I am fortunate to share my life with. All of you have supported me and cheered for me and told everyone you know I sold a book. You've touched me in a way I never could have imagined and your excitement and encouragement have made this journey to publication one of humble gratitude.

The Writer Foxes—Alice Fairbanks-Burton, Lorraine

Heath, Jo Davis, Tracy Garrett, Kay Thomas, Suzanne Welsh, Julie Benson, Sandy Blair and Jane Graves. You guys are amazing. Seriously.

And to Lorraine Heath—you can't imagine how much I miss our Café Amore dinners. For all its fabulous restaurants, New York can't touch Amore's stuffed mushrooms— or how wonderful it is to catch up over them.

Finally, the last year has brought an amazing group of women into my life—the 2009 Golden Heart class, the Ruby-Slippered Sisterhood. You ladies are awesome and I am so very lucky to know you. An extra-special shout-out to Liz Bemis from Bemis Promotions. You've created the most beautiful Web site for addisonfox.com. Thank you.

Scorpio Warrior

    Fierce and cunning, my Scorpio Warriors will execute their tasks—and their enemies—with swift and fearless justice.

    Those he battles will know the pointed sting of his scorpion's tail, the razor-sharp edge of his powerful claws.

    Intense and passionate, my Scorpio will not be easily satisfied. But once he meets his mate—that fearless soul who can match the emotions inside him—will his sharp sting be calmed, his restless heart tamed.

    Magnetically sexual, my Scorpio will attract many women, but will love only one. . . .

                       —The Diaries of Themis, goddess of justice

Prologue

The Golden Age of Man

"**Y**ou must protect him for me."

Adrasteia looked into Rhea's eyes, clouded with fear and anger, desperation and . . . something else she couldn't name. Could only feel. "Yes, mistress."

"He will depend on you. You must hide him from his father. Hide him from the wrath of Cronus."

"Of course."

Rhea whisked them from Mount Olympus into the land Adrasteia had heard others speak of. Greece, they called it.

Greece?

What an odd word. It stuck on the tongue, between the teeth when she tried to say it.

Greece.

She held the squirming baby in her arms, held him tightly to her breast as Rhea's sharp tone forced her attention back to the baby's mother. "This cave will protect you. My husband won't know to look for you here."

Panic rose up in Adrasteia's throat, clawing there, suffocating her as it took her breath. She was to live here? In a cave? With a wee babe?

"But where are we?"

"This cave is called Mount Ida. It is the highest summit in Crete. It will keep you protected. Keep you hidden."

"But, mistress, I know nothing of raising a baby." Adrasteia looked down at the red-faced, squalling infant in her arms. "Look at him. He reaches for you." She held the baby toward Rhea, hoping the action would soften the woman somehow.

"You will watch him and you will protect him. Those are my wishes, Nymph. I will send others in secret to help you along the way. Know that at the end of this trial, you will be justly rewarded for your service."

With that, Rhea abandoned them. Adrasteia found the most well-lit corner of the cave and sat with her back to the unyielding stone, the screams of the baby in her arms echoing off the walls of the cave until she feared she'd go mad from the sound.

As the years went by and the baby grew into a powerful young boy, then into an even more powerful young man, Adrasteia often reflected on the things that had kept her from descending into true madness that day.

As promised, Rhea did send her help, in the form of a sacred goat to milk for the baby's needs. She also sent the brothers, the Corybants, male soldiers dressed in heavy armor who spent their life in dance. Each time Cronus came looking for his son, the Corybants beat their drums with their armor, creating a diversion and drowning out the sounds of the baby's cries.

The second thing that kept Adrasteia sane that day was the promise, Rhea's vow to reward her for her service.

Over the years, Adrasteia's thoughts on this reward expanded and grew, until she'd pictured her life after her time as caretaker in exquisite detail.

A great and lovely palace on Mount Olympus, where she'd finally be reunited with her nymph sisters. A beautiful chariot to ride in so when she went by, all who saw her would proclaim that here was the glorious nymph who had protected the great god. Robes of spun gold to clothe her form and proclaim to all who looked on her that here was the woman who'd raised a god.

But all that was a mirage in the face of the gods' caprice.

For one day, when Zeus was old enough to defend himself, when he finally thrust off the mantle of protection, when he no longer accepted her mournful pleas to stay hidden away with her, he fled the cave and Adrasteia, heading for his destiny.

Adrasteia feared for him. She spent seventy days and seventy nights in frantic worry that she had somehow failed in her duties. Failed to protect Zeus as he had grown into manhood.

Was he strong enough?

Did he possess enough knowledge of battle and warfare?

Would he be able to fight the father who sought his death?

On the seventy-first morning, Zeus arrived at the mouth of the cave. Blood stained his chest and claw marks ran the length of his torso, but he carried a thunderbolt in his hand and wore a crown upon his head.

Adrasteia ran to the boy who had become the man, stretching her hands to reach his face, amazed as always when she felt the soft down of his beard under her fingers.

"You are alive! You have returned!"

Zeus pressed at her shoulders, shaking off her ministrations. "I have vanquished him. My father is imprisoned in Tartarus."

Relief swelled in her breast as the fears of his mother were finally laid to rest. "Then all is as it should be. We shall return to Mount Olympus. There shall be much rejoicing, this day and always."

"*We*, vile Nymph?"

Adrasteia heard the loathing in his voice, yet puzzled at its source. "Yes, Zeus. We. You have lived up to the promise of your birth. You have vanquished your father. It is time to leave this place and celebrate."

"This place where you kept me hidden? Where you kept me from my duty? Where you allowed my father to roam and stalk the skies as I lay hidden here, like a coward?"

Panic bubbled within her, like the small stream that ran at the base of their mountain. Why did he look at her as if she'd crawled from under a rock, like the snake who crawled on his belly?

"I have protected you, as I gave my word I would do. Your mother asked me to hide you. To keep you safe. I have done my duty, Zeus. Now it is time for my reward."

"Reward?" His voice thundered around the cave, echoing off the walls in harsh reverberations. "There will be no reward. There will be nothing for you!"

The great golden dreams that had kept her alive for years, decades, centuries, as she protected his growth into manhood, crumbled like dust. Rising to her full height, she stood toe-to-toe with him. Anger flooded her veins as all that she'd given up—all that she'd sacrificed—flowed through her mind's eye.

"I will have what is promised to me. My beautiful home, a golden chariot, and the adoration of my fellow immortals."

Zeus shook his head, the long length of his hair brushing his back. "The woman I met on my journey—the woman I love—she spoke to me of this. Spoke to me of balance. I should have known you wanted something. Should have known you were plotting against me for some gain."

Fierce righteousness settled in her breast. She would have what was hers. She would have her own balance. "I have never plotted against you. I simply want what is mine. What has been rightfully promised to me."

"Then I will make it so."

Before Adrasteia could reply, Zeus swept his arm in a bold arc, light flowing like a river from the end of his lightning bolt. "You will have what is coming to you, Adrasteia. Forever."

As light swirled around her, blinding in its intensity, Adrasteia felt pain slam through her. Muscle, sinew, bone all ripped apart from the ferocious claws of that horrible light. Skin stretched and pulled as great, agonizing cries fell from her lips.

Seconds . . . minutes . . . hours later, she knew not.

The light had died. The pain had dulled to a vicious ache. The stone floor was cold and harsh against her cheek.

Willing herself to move, she lifted herself from the floor of the cave, desperate for the warmth of the sun as it shined down over Crete. Movements stiff, she dragged herself toward the mouth of the cave.

Toward the generous, beautiful, life-giving light of the sun.

As Adrasteia stepped out of the cave, the scream in her head echoed through her nerve endings.

Invisible to the outside world, her screams were heard only by her.

As the sun's rays beat down toward the mouth of the cave, Adrasteia felt herself disappear.

Chapter One

May 15

The poison coiled, a living, writhing beast that skipped through his veins on spiked heels. The venom was an unmerciful taskmaster, lying in wait for the one day each year when it could dominate.

Control.

Kill.

Even now, silky threads of it wove through his bloodstream. Expanding, growing, pulsing with life.

Kane Montague, Scorpio Warrior of the great goddess of justice, Themis, ignored it. Ignored the whip-quick lashes that slammed through him from the inside out, as if his very organs were being rent in half.

Ignored the brutal assault on his muscle fibers, like the stinging prick of a million wasps.

Ignored the wicked, boiling sensation that filled his bloodstream like a flowing river of lava.

If you pretended long enough that something didn't exist, you could almost make it so that it didn't exist.

Almost.

He continued to bench-press a row of weights, his rhythm even and easy, his breathing focused and controlled.

Arms up, breathe in. Arms down, breathe out.

This cold-blooded, laser-sharp focus had been the hallmark of his life, even before he made his life-changing agreement with Themis. The selection for service as one of her scorps only sealed the deal.

Nothing got in the way of his militant focus and there was nothing that could pull him from his goals.

Not his Warrior brothers.

Not the poison.

And sure as fuck not a luscious brunette with endless legs and a gorgeous rack.

So why did she still dominate his thoughts six months later? The woman had gone by the name Ilsa. The double agent who had managed to seduce him, fuck him brainless and drug him to make her escape.

He could still smell her scent, could feel the mind-bending tightness of her as he filled her with his cock. The fact he hadn't ever felt a tighter passage was beside the point.

What *was* the fucking point anymore?

"You keep driving yourself like this and the poison won't need until the end of the month to kick your ass to the curb."

Kane grunted on an exhale of breath and didn't even bother to turn toward their Taurus and self-appointed leader as he walked across the weight room. "Get out of here, Quinn. I don't need a fucking babysitter."

"Since when don't you want a workout partner?"

Kane ignored the bull, although he could see Quinn

Tanner's hulking form move closer in his peripheral vision. "Since you've taken it upon yourself to treat me like I'm still in diapers."

Quinn dropped to a nearby weight bench and began lifting his own set of metal. "Concern, buddy. Nothing more."

Fuck concern. And the casual questions. And the slightly pitying looks they sent him like he had no clue.

The poison in his bloodstream leaped at the anger, giving it strength. Power. Fuel.

With a loud thud, he slammed the heavy bar into its rack and slipped off the bench. He'd be damned if he was sitting around listening to this shit like he was some invalid.

Kane ignored the sharp stabs in his gut as the poison twisted his intestines like rows of tangled-up Christmas lights and headed out of the weight room. If he could, he'd have just ported from the room to hightail it out of there as quickly as possible, but he had a meet later tonight in London and couldn't risk using up that much strength. He needed food to stay strong and not a whole hell of a lot wanted to stay down right now.

A rush of air greeted him as Quinn's large body took shape in front of him in less than a second, the bull's port from his own weight bench instantaneous. "You've got two weeks, Kane. And you're pushing too hard. Give it a rest, stay strong and once you beat it back, you can go after her again."

Whether it was his own anger or the added aggression of the poison, Kane wasn't quite sure. Nor did he care. He launched himself at Quinn, knocking the Taurus to the ground, where they fell into a heap of grunting, groaning testosterone.

Where Quinn was broad, beefy muscle, Kane's body

was long and lean, his muscles more sinew than heft. He knew they must not look very well matched from a distance, but his leaner form allowed him fuller range of motion and an ability to squeeze out of Quinn's hold.

'Course, it also meant he took a sizable hit from those meaty fists when Quinn finally laid one on him.

A satisfying zing ran up Kane's arm as he planted his own fist smack in the middle of Quinn's baby-faced mug. The satisfaction was short-lived as he felt strong hands latch on to his shoulders and pull him from behind. The black-silk-shirt-covered forearm gave his captor away before Kane even saw his face.

"Get off me, Grey. I don't need your help."

The strength of the hold didn't weaken, but Grey's voice held sly amusement. "What you need is a serious ass-kicking from both of us, but you're not worth the risk to my new Brioni slacks."

"Pussy."

The hold lessened, followed immediately by an open-palmed smack to the side of the head. "Right back at ya, Monte."

Before Kane could react, Grey was already leaning down to extend a hand to Quinn, whose mouth was on overdrive, as usual. "Ignore him, Grey. The scorp's wardrobe is even flashier than yours."

"Understated and elegant are my hallmarks," Kane added for good measure. This was an old argument and his protests were token at best. He'd figured out long ago clothes made the man. And when you iced bad guys for a living, it helped to look the part.

"Hardly." Grey dusted a hand over those black slacks he was so proud of. "Seeing as how I didn't actually come here to break up a dogfight, you want to hear me out?"

Kane felt the hot flare of annoyance rise off of Quinn. "Fine."

He still felt pissy, but curiosity quickly won out. "Fine. What's going on?"

"I think I got a line on that brunette you've been after."

A renewed flare of anger flooded his system, this time having nothing to do with the poison living underneath his skin. "How do you know it's Ilsa?"

"She's a blonde at the moment, either via dye job or wig. My call's a wig—I'm very rarely wrong about these things."

"Do you have a point somewhere in all this self-congratulating?" Kane rubbed his stomach, the center of his body the current attack point of the poison.

Kane saw Grey's eyes narrow to his torso, but his answer was matter-of-fact. "She's been paying an awful lot of attention to my club lately. Couple that with several jaunts up and down the front of this place, captured on the cameras, and it's a match with the photo Quinn turned up of her. I think we've got her."

Kane's stomach tightened again, this time having nothing to do with the toxin that filled his veins. He didn't want there to be any *we* in Ilsa's capture. He wanted her. All by himself. Shaking his head, he pressed through the selfish desires he had no business having. "She's clearly a highly trained agent. There's no way she'd be so stupid to get caught like that."

Grey shrugged. "Maybe she's not nearly as savvy as you think she is."

"She knocked me on my ass, Grey. She knew what she was doing."

Quinn rubbed at his jaw as he added his input to their little coffee klatch. "Grey's got a point, Kane. Something's always rung false for me. Top of the list is why she burned you in the first place. You've done nothing to make yourself a target. Hell, from the files I've hacked into, you're seen as an incredible asset within MI6. What would be the incentive to get rid of you?"

Kane had asked himself the very same question for the last six months. Banging his head against concrete would have produced better answers than what he'd managed to come up with in all that time. The only thing he kept coming back to was how they were introduced.

The director of his übersecret branch was the ever-capable Edward St. Giles. He'd worked for St. Giles for years and trusted the man more than he trusted any other mortal on the planet. Edward had asked him to attend a state dinner with Ilsa, where they were tasked to ferret out a scientist who'd caught MI6's attention for his excessive interest in uranium—and its potential sale to countries developing their weapons programs.

Straightforward. Simple. Easy.

Maybe he'd thought it was too simple. Hadn't kept his guard up as he should have. And maybe that was how she'd managed to sneak in underneath it and fuck him.

Literally and figuratively.

Grey held out his cell phone, a surprisingly clear image covering its glass face. "Is this her?"

Kane knew it before he'd even focused on the screen. Knew it as he took in the shape of her jaw and the aristocratic line of her neck. The blond wig couldn't disguise the pure essence of her face.

"It's her."

Grey was already in motion. "Then let's go. She's been outside Equinox every night for the past three. If she follows suit tonight, we'll intercept her outside the club."

Kane stopped Grey before the Aries hit the doorway. Before he reluctantly had to grip on to the calm-headed asshole for the port. A port Kane knew he wasn't strong enough to make right now. "She's mine, Grey."

"Don't worry, Monte. None of us is dumb enough to get in your way."

There were serious benefits to being a Greek goddess. Immortality, permanent youth, and a blessed lack of self-doubt all rode quite high on the list.

So when had she become so intent on second-guessing herself?

Nemesis hotfooted it down the lightly crowded New York sidewalk, the street growing increasingly full of humans as she neared her destination. She ignored the light spring rain as it clung to the pale hair of her wig, trying desperately to figure out when she'd lost her mental ability to kick ass, take names and move on to her next victim.

When had she become a sniveling bore like the rest of them? And why in the name of Hades was she even risking herself like this with these stupid jaunts past the Warriors' club?

Even the name she'd selected was stupid. Ilsa.

As in Ilsa and Rick from *Casablanca*.

It had seemed like such a great idea at the time—a cheeky wink at the Fates, if you will. Of course, somehow in her rush to make a joke of her original meet with Kane, she'd forgotten one small fact.

She'd watched that movie over and over, weeping each and every time for the ill-fated lovers.

And now she knew exactly how Ilsa had felt.

Torn between bone-deep attraction for one and duty to

another. Suddenly trapped inside a life she didn't actually want. Full of a love that drove her nearly mad.

It was true Rick's Ilsa wasn't actually a real human being, but rather an image on celluloid, Nemesis reflected. Of course, if you wanted to mess with technicalities, she wasn't human in the truest sense of the word, either.

So why, then, had that cold rock of a heart she'd ignored for millennia suddenly come alive with a vengeance?

Kane, her conscience whispered.

For six months, the answer had been the same. Six months that had lasted longer than any single one of her sixteen thousand years of life.

Kane. Always Kane.

The blocks flew by, the cacophony of New York traffic doing nothing to drown out her thoughts. For six months she'd barely handled her duties to Hades, had skated around her agreement with Emmett and had ignored the loud voices in her head telling her this was a very bad idea.

All so she could get a glimpse of him. A peek at his life and how he was doing. A sense of the man he was.

Ilsa remembered the first time she'd laid eyes on Kane. Emmett had infiltrated MI6 just as he'd promised her he would, assuming the body of one of the organization's top leaders, Edward St. Giles.

Emmett could hardly wait to introduce her to Kane, he was so anxious to put their plans in motion to capture one of Themis's Warriors. He'd found an opportunity quickly enough. The two of them would attend a state dinner, ferreting out as much information as they could from a well-connected scientist.

Or at least that was what Kane thought they were doing. Her real job was to keep an eye on the Warrior, searching for weakness.

Vulnerability.

Something—anything—that might give her an advantage.

In retrospect, Ilsa knew the dinner should have set off her instincts. Should have warned her, somehow. Her only defense, when she'd thought about it later, was that there was simply no way anyone could have prepared for the image of Kane Montague in a designer tuxedo. The suit jacket molded his broad shoulders, descending in a V toward the whipcord-slim hips that sat atop long legs. Legs that, she now knew from a later viewing, were all sinew and muscle.

She could still remember the feel of the silken threads of his tuxedo jacket under her fingertips as he'd maneuvered her across the dance floor. The bold stare of his onyx eyes, their endless depths fathoms darker than the black cashmere of his tux. The almost-harsh planes of his body as he pressed her against him.

No, there was nothing vulnerable about the man.

Nothing.

Ilsa snapped back to attention at the loud squeal of a silly girl dressed in a nearly nonexistent miniskirt as she barely sidestepped a puddle of rainwater. The rain had begun to come down in hard, lashing waves, but it made no difference to the legion of clubbers who wanted in. The line to get into Equinox tonight was a long one.

What am I even doing here? Especially since she had a big job for Hades tonight and she really should already be on her way to it. Duty called, and all that flowery responsibility shit. Yet here she was, doe-eyed and obsessive, walking past this stupid club.

Again.

What had possibly possessed her to walk when she

could have ported in and out to see if Kane was there to-night?

Bad decisions. Bad choices.

Continuing her streak, Ilsa kept right on going, walking past the club and toward the rear entrance of the building.

He's not worth it. Not worth what you'll have to sacrifice.

Ignoring the steady stream of internal dialogue, Ilsa had barely cleared the back side of the club when a harsh line of static burned a fiery path down her spinal cord. Although not fully immune to pain, her immortal body was vulnerable to very little.

But this?

The intensity of the heat was so jarring she fell to her knees in a puddle, rain running in rivulets down her back and neck, over the exposed line of her cleavage. Pushing the pain aside, ignoring the stinging heat by sheer force of will, she attempted to regain her footing. Surprise—and was that panic?—shot through her as a heavy weight bore down on her back, holding her in place as large arms wrapped around her in a bear hug.

Vaguely, a shout registered through the adrenaline lighting up her system and the heavy rush of blood in her ears. "Do you have her yet?"

A vile stench filled the air as a pair of wet lips rubbed against her ear, fetid breath coming heavy against her face. "Got her."

Forcing strength through her slight frame, she rammed her head back toward the heavy weight, trying to dislodge the asshole who thought he'd have his way with her. Just as she made contact—a deep, satisfying thud—another wave of heat assaulted her, wrapping her nerve endings in liquid fire. Her neck, already extended from the reverse head butt, swam with pain, as she choked in breath, desperate for air.

What in Hades's name is this?

Real panic flared, the sort she hadn't felt since Zeus's irreparable anger had descended upon her those many thousand years ago. Panic that twisted the gut and forced air in and out of her lungs in harsh bursts.

With it, another wave of resolute anger filled her. She'd vowed that day that she would never be weak again.

Would never surrender to another being.

Would *never* be beaten back.

With grim determination, Ilsa forged renewed strength in the fire of the pain. Straightening inch by inch, she pressed against the immense weight at her back. She felt it—knew it—the moment she had him. As her captor's resistance slipped, she used one final burst of strength to dislodge him.

Fists bunched, she lifted her shoulders, extending her arms in a sweeping arc against her captor's hold. Stumbling forward, she whirled around to finish the job and take the asshole down. No sooner did she have him in her sights—a large brute of a man with scars crisscrossing his face and a spiderweb tattoo covering his neck—when his head went spiraling off his body.

Ilsa blinked through the pouring rain.

What the—?

Kane Montague stood over the rapidly disintegrating corpse, his wolfish smile broad and easily visible through the torrents of rain. He held an ancient-looking sword aloft in his firm grip. "Hello, Ilsa."

She nodded and bit back an actual gulp. "Kane."

"I guess there's really only one thing to say."

Her gaze drank him in as he stood before her. Rain

poured off the short length of his hair, down over the gray T-shirt that now molded itself to every delicious inch of his torso. As if at a distance from herself, Ilsa heard her voice come out on a breathy moan. "What's that?"

"Of all the gin joints . . ."

Chapter Two

Ilsa hadn't actually ever had gin. The taste burned her tongue and sent a torrent of shivers down her spine as the overlarge sip struggled its way down her throat. Despite her reaction to it, she wouldn't cough.

Would. Not. Cough.

The well-dressed Warrior they called Grey spoke first. "What were you doing dragging that scum to my club?"

Ilsa recognized him from her earlier surveillance of Equinox. He was the owner and it was his office they'd brought her into. Sleek metal and chrome were the hallmarks of the room, matched to ocean-sized black leather couches. The overall effect was an effortless blend of power and male sanctuary.

Despite her ability to see deeply into men's souls, this one was closed up tighter than a drum. Just like the other Warriors. Just as Kane had been all those many months ago.

And still was.

Grey continued to stare at her in expectant silence, but

she let him wait. Ilsa—or Nemesis, damn it, her name was Nemesis—bowed to no one.

Letting the moment draw out, she diverted her thoughts to more important matters. She figured it was a small miracle they hadn't elected to restrain her, but the sandwich she made between Kane and the other one called Quinn ensured she wasn't going anywhere fast. Even if she tried to port, the fact their bodies touched meant they'd be locked in the port with her.

Not that either of them knew she *knew* how to port.

But the end result was the same. She was stuck there.

With Kane's long, slender leg burning a hole into the side of hers wherever their skin touched.

She glanced down at her own very naked leg, stretched out from under that stupid skirt she'd put on earlier. Why hadn't she thought of wearing pants? She hated the uncomfortable feeling of restraint the pants gave her but at least they offered a modicum of protection from the heat rising off that sexy male leg.

A strong, sexy limb that separated her from his very large, very long—

Grey's harsh voice interrupted one of her most favorite fantasies. "Perhaps I didn't make myself clear. I've got you on surveillance. And then I find you behind my club working with Des—serious scum. If you think a trampy skirt, fuck-me heels and your MI6 contacts are going to save you from us, you really don't know who you're dealing with."

And that was where he was wrong. She knew exactly whom she was dealing with. It was these boys who had no idea whom *they* were dealing with.

A spark flared deep inside, the pilot light of her fury that refused to go out. An anger that had refused to be squelched in any of the endless years of her existence. Oh, she knew all about Themis's Warriors. Her band of zodiac-inspired soldiers, made in a deal with Zeus during the fifth—and darkest—age of man.

All those present-day whiners who complained the world was coming to an end didn't know how good they had it. During the darkest ages, she'd been busier than she'd ever been before or since. And instead of living the life she'd been called to, she was stuck doing Hades's bidding for a mere chance at some semblance of a life.

No thanks to Zeus and that bitter bitch who had infected his mind.

Themis.

Themis was the real reason Zeus had turned on her. Ilsa was only happy the self-righteous pain in the ass had finally gotten her comeuppance when Zeus dumped her for Hera.

Justice.

A bitter taste swam on Ilsa's tongue, having nothing to do with the gin. It hurt badly enough when justice was turned back on you. It hurt infinite times worse when you hadn't done anything to deserve it.

No one knew that lesson better than she did.

With a mutinous glance up at Grey, Ilsa took another leisurely sip of the gin. And barely fought off the need to cough again. By Cerberus's spiked collar, that was some strong stuff. The time to stall was up. Besides, if she waited any longer, she might be tempted to take another sip of that nasty liquid.

Pushing bravado into her tone, and resolutely ignoring the heat of Kane's body where he sat pressed against her, Ilsa talked around the gravel that had taken up residence in her vocal cords. From the gin.

Yep.

It had to be the gin.

"I never saw those men before. And I didn't bring them. In the event it escaped your notice, I was trying to get away from them, not control them."

Grey ignored her plea and continued pressing her. "This is the fourth night in a row you've been hanging around here. What do you want?"

She almost glanced at Kane, but caught herself just in time, instead keeping her gaze trained firmly on Grey. "I thought this was a public place."

Kane took over the questioning and leaned in toward her so that she had to turn her head fully to look at him. "Fuck the innocent routine, Ilsa. You've got a problem with me and you already burned me once. You looking to do it again?"

That firm jaw was hard to resist, but it was the haunted, hollow look in his eyes—not to mention the deep grooves under them—that nearly stole her breath.

Completely.

Where was the unbearably strong man who'd made love to her until she'd nearly forgotten herself? Forgotten her mission? Forgotten her past?

The strength was still there, but so was pain.

Could Emmett possibly be right about Kane? Not that she hadn't believed him, exactly. But the incredibly virile man she'd spent those three glorious days with hadn't acted like anything weakened him, despite Emmett's claims to the contrary.

And now?

Now he looked like he was struggling against something that was slowly eating away at his formidable power. His body was still strong—she felt its strength in the long length of him pressed to her side—but it was the eyes. Those dark onyx orbs were filled with pain.

She felt an answering pain in the recesses of her soul. It

ate away at the cold shell she'd built around herself so very long ago.

And for the first time since she'd taken up the mantle of Nemesis, she felt *something*. Something besides the raw, pulsing need for vengeance.

For three hundred years, Kane Montague had hated the weakness that lived under his skin. The poison that, by his own admission, made him less of a Warrior.

Who'd have known—could even Themis have imagined?—that the tattoos she branded them with to aid them in their tasks could be manipulated? That the tattoos could be altered?

With dark magic and mindless obsession.

And he'd let it happen. He'd let his guard down over an excruciatingly beautiful woman and had loved her to distraction. And in return, he made a mistake he'd pay for with the rest of his days.

Oh yes, he'd had years to reflect on his mistakes. Years to castigate himself for what an incredible, arrogant fool he'd been.

Those years in Italy had been like a dream. Working in secret, as security protection, for the lingering lines of the Medici family. The time had served him well, allowing him to hone his skills as an assassin, while ensuring the Warriors were tapped into the highest sources of power.

It had taken only one sorcerer with the darkest of powers to bring it all crashing to a halt.

Ruined love. Ruined lives.

Kane forced his attention back to the woman who called herself Ilsa. Was he destined to repeat his mistakes over and over again just as the poison rose to power under his skin, year after year?

"Answer me." The fury in his voice surprised even him. Kane knew the woman had gotten to him, but his ability to stay calm, cool and in control had completely evaporated at seeing her again. Add to it the evidence she might be looking for him and any sense of reason had flown away on furious wings.

Her pert nose turned up in a snit. "I won't talk to you like this."

If he hadn't been so angry, Kane thought he might have actually laughed at her. "Why not?"

"You've seen me naked. You owe me some level of respect."

Respect? Seriously? "You fucked me and drugged me senseless. How respectful was that?"

She sniffed and turned her attention toward running her finger over a small freckle on her kneecap. Kane remembered that freckle. And the one that matched it on the back of her knee. And how he'd run his tongue over that sensitive spot, causing her to . . .

"Grey. Quinn. Out."

With a surprising lack of argument, the two of them left Grey's office.

Despite the additional room now available on the couch, Kane didn't move. Neither did Ilsa. She just continued to torture him with those endlessly long legs hanging out of that oh-so-short skirt. Heat rose up between them and it took everything inside of him not to reach out and touch her.

To demand she explain herself and make clear what had happened six months ago. Explain why she'd left and why she'd drugged him. Hell, why she'd targeted him in the first place.

The poison in his veins chose that moment to rear its

head, slamming a wave of fire through his stomach muscles. Kane nearly doubled over—the only thing keeping him straight was his own stubborn refusal to allow Ilsa to see him in pain.

"Why—" Kane felt the words forming before pressing down on them with tensile strength.

He would not ask.

And he never begged.

Another wave of pain washed through his abdomen, like a physical taunt from the poison in counterpoint to Kane's thoughts.

To his unwillingness to beg.

Focus, Montague. Focus. "Who set me up? Who are you working for and why did they tell you to burn me?"

"No one. And I didn't burn you."

"You drugged me."

"Right. I drugged you; I didn't burn you. I had no fire with me. Why do you keep saying that?"

Kane searched her face for some sense that she was playing him, the absurdity of her comment almost laughable if he didn't know better. Her sky blue eyes met his, surprisingly bereft of guile.

Of course, when he'd last known her those eyes were the darkest of browns, so perhaps searching for answers in their depths was a pointless exercise. Just another lie, only physical instead of verbal.

Besides, was it really possible she had no idea what he was talking about? "Burn" was common enough language in the spy community. Hell, they even made TV shows about it now.

"Burn me as in fuck me over for some hidden reason I'm still trying to figure out."

The confused look didn't quite vanish, evidenced by a

small telltale crinkle between her eyebrows. That ugly blond wig hung in a bob around her chin and it took every ounce of self-control he possessed not to rip it off to expose the luscious waves of chestnut brown underneath. Clenching his fist to keep from touching her, he continued to press her in her silence.

"Cut the bullshit. St. Giles wouldn't have ordered you to do something like that to me, so who put you up to this? One day we're following a couple of suspect scientists, the next we're having some seriously kick-ass monkey sex and a few days after that I'm waking up with the hangover of the millennium. Who put you up to it?"

"Monkey sex?"

Kane saw the confusion stamped on her face as that delightful little crinkle paid a return visit. *More common language she doesn't understand?* "You know. All-over-each-other sex."

"Um," she sniffed again and reached for the gin she was having trouble swallowing back. "I thought of it a bit differently."

"Oh, wait. You thought we made love?" The words blistered his lips as he spoke them, the joke of what they'd shared for three glorious days still haunting him in vivid detail.

He saw the grimace and the hurt look come into those diamond-bright eyes midsip of the gin. And watched as she promptly choked on the liquor as the words "made love" registered.

Instinctively, Kane reached over to swat her across the back. Even that, the mere caress of her slender frame through her tight-fitting sweater, sent shock waves of heat running through him.

What the hell was it about her? He'd enjoyed women

throughout the long, long years of his life, taking the pleasure they offered and giving it back to each and every one of them. So what was it about her—what was it about *this* woman—that was so unforgettable?

He'd slept with women more beautiful, although it was *her* face that haunted him. It was *her* voice that wouldn't let him go. And it was the recollection of their lost, seductive, blissful hours together he couldn't erase from memory no matter how hard he tried.

Why couldn't he let this go?

Another one of those delicate little sniffs. "Even I know we didn't make love."

Before he could reply to that, she shifted gears on him. "What was that man outside? You killed him as casually as if he were a bug."

"That's basically what he was."

"He disintegrated the moment you removed his head."

"Yes." The yes was out before he could stop it, her matter-of-fact questions lulling him into a false sense of security. For fuck's sake, she was a human. He had no business even letting her see him kill the Destroyer, let alone confirming that the guy actually disintegrated.

Time to do some damage control.

"Human bodies don't do that."

No, human bodies didn't do that. But soulless minions of the goddess of war did. The Destroyers were one of Enyo's nastier weapons in her ongoing battle with the Warriors. Full to the brim with an odd sort of electric energy, they looked human, but their bodies were actually just husks—an inhuman shell, really.

So why wasn't she more upset about what she witnessed?

Reining in his casual answers, he attempted to fix the

damage he'd already allowed to happen. As one of his duties was to keep Destroyers and any other evidence of Enyo out of the minds of humans, he leveraged one of Themis's handier gifts. The ability to cloud—and often erase if the memory was fresh enough—human minds.

Pushing as much mental energy at her as he could muster through the pulsing pain of the poison, Kane worked to change the course of the conversation. "He was just regular old street scum and he needed to be dealt with. Surely you, of all people, know there are people who need to be removed."

"But he wasn't a person."

Pushing harder, he added, "Of course he was."

Those blue irises stared back at him, but to his frustration, they didn't appear to haze with cloudy memories in any way. Which was odd, because her next words contradicted that assumption. "Thank you for coming to my rescue from that horrible man."

"You're welcome. Now. Do you want to tell me what you were doing out there?"

"No."

"Were you looking for me?"

"No."

Silence descended between them once again as Kane took in her words. It wasn't possible she simply happened across Equinox, and certainly not its back entrance. Nor was it possible she'd simply *happened* upon the Warriors' home on the Upper West Side based on the intel Grey shared earlier. How would she even know to look for him there?

He made London his home and that was the only place they'd ever seen each other. Unless her deception ran far deeper than he'd suspected.

Although he lived in Britain, he was a member of the North American Warriors. He'd joined their group a few centuries ago when they'd lost their own Scorpio. And yet Ilsa had been at both places.

There was no way she'd have made any other connection to both spots if it weren't for him.

Was it possible she'd acted on the wishes of someone else? All this time, he'd assumed her orders came from MI6. But . . .

The loud chime of a clock caught Kane's attention. The sleek, chrome timepiece on Grey's credenza rang the hour and he realized just how late he was. He had a meet tonight.

Well, he'd just have to skip it. The assholes had waited this long, they'd keep a few more days. Scientists selling uranium were a problem, but their sales activity had already been mitigated with a few well-placed e-mail interceptions by Quinn.

It would keep.

Even though he made it a rule never to miss a meet. Shoddy performance could make the suspect lose confidence in their relationship. It was a policy he applied to his commitments to his Warrior brothers as well and the only time he'd violated his rule had been because of Ilsa. He'd nearly left their Leo, Brody, and his new wife, Ava, at the mercies of an ill-timed Destroyer attack.

Fuck.

How was it this woman had managed to screw with his ability to do his job more in the last six months than anything he'd ever come across? Hell, he'd managed to sidestep Napoleon easier than this one single woman.

Summoning up the harshest expression he could, Kane turned the full force of his badass persona on her. And as his gaze took in the lush sweep of her lashes and the heavy thread of the pulse at her throat, he promptly remembered her naked instead. Annoyed at the sudden memory, his voice was even more clipped than he'd originally intended. "Come now, you don't expect me to believe that, do you? I think you're really here to finish the job."

"I'm not."

"And I should believe you because?" He let the question hang there, as visions of those gorgeous calves resting on his shoulders filled his thoughts.

Instead of a ready retort, those sexy blue eyes simply stared back at him in quiet mutiny.

Well, what should he have expected?

A loud banging noise outside the closed door of Grey's office caught their attention. The Destroyer attack still fresh in his mind, Kane took off for the hallway outside the office at a run. Slamming open the door, he caught sight of a band of pixies running single file from the women's room back toward the bar.

Grey raced after them down the hallway, Quinn on his heels. Although the main floor of Equinox hosted New York's most well-heeled and connected residents, the basement level hosted any number of supernatural creatures who made the city their home or simply a stopping-off point.

Quinn returned quickly enough, a disgusted look painted across his face. "Fucking pixies. That dust is flammable if they're not careful with it." Grey followed on the bull's heels, shooting the last pixie in their bathroom conga line a dirty glare that she answered with a flirty little wave and a jaunty smile as she passed.

Grey shook his head, then glanced meaningfully toward his office door. "You getting anywhere with her?"

"No. Although she had an incredibly odd reaction to the Destroyers."

Quinn cocked his head, already pushing toward the office. "Odd? Odd how?"

A sinking feeling twisted Kane's insides, the horrible pull a formidable rival to the poison already in residence. "She didn't seem all that surprised by their lack of humanity."

Rushing past Quinn, Kane hit the doorway first.

And saw nothing but an empty office.

Chapter Three

Molecules reforming, Ilsa completed the port into London's Hyde Park. The moon was low in the sky, and she could sense, rather than actually see, that the night was heading toward dawn. The May air lay heavy on her skin as she stopped to catch her breath.

Damn Kane Montague. Her heart thundered in wild, galloping bursts and she could still feel the imprint of where his body had pressed against hers.

Why had she thought peeking in on him was a good idea?

Where had the edge gone? Her razor-sharp attitude and focused dedication?

It evaporated right along with your virginity, her conscience taunted. *Mind-blowing orgasms have a way of doing that to a girl*, that miserable voice of reason added for good measure.

Blowing out a heavy breath, Ilsa struggled to regain her equilibrium and focus. Eyes closed, she cleared her mind and sought to erase the lingering effects of the port.

Gods, but she hated it. No matter how many times she did it, she'd yet to get comfortable with the whole concept of teleportation. Something about pushing every molecule of her being into the ether and reforming it somewhere entirely different just hadn't ever sat well with her. Alas, complaining was as useless as whining about any other aspect of her life.

It was high time she started remembering that again.

Heaving one final sigh, she prepared herself to meet with the nuclear physicists. The two men had cooked up this scheme—strategic theft and then black market sale of uranium—while still in college and their comeuppance was a long time in coming.

Opening her senses, Ilsa allowed her aura to search for theirs. Her gifts had been honed over millennia and she had the ability to track those wayward souls whose time had run out with the delicate precision of a tuning fork. Pushing her attention toward a deserted area of the Serpentine where they'd agreed to meet, she sought out the assholes who currently sat on top of Hades's list of incoming arrivals.

There.

She had a lock on one of them. And with it, her senses filled with the writhing, evil toxin his soul emitted into the universe. Opening her senses wider, she searched for the second man, his choices in inexorable lockstep with the other. Searching . . . searching . . .

Nothing yet.

Ilsa knew she couldn't wait any longer and moved closer. She'd barely made it on time as it was, her unexpected meeting with Kane nearly scattering her plans to the winds. Although, if the swirling pool of menace and greed that surrounded her target was any indication, a few minutes likely wouldn't change things. The lure of money she'd dangled to get them here ensured they'd be forgiving of her lack of punctuality.

She adjusted her skirt and smoothed it over her backside, adding a bit of sex to her movements to sweeten their dispositions even further.

As her hands ran over the sides of her thighs, her thoughts immediately reverted back to New York. And the large, virile man who had dominated her every thought for the past six months.

Kane Montague and his onyx fuck-me eyes and his long, lean body and the wicked heat of him had pulled at something deep inside of her.

Damn him.

Refocusing, Ilsa moved deeper into the park, the lure of the immoral pulling her toward her destination. "You shall avenge what is right and just," she whispered to herself. "Your wrath shall slay the wicked."

Zeus might have abandoned her, but his brother, Hades, had seen a very real purpose for her life. She was Nemesis—the goddess of retribution—and right now, these guys needed some divine justice real bad.

Even after taking so many souls she'd lost count, Ilsa could still remember her bargain with Hades in vivid detail.

Zeus had abandoned her, claiming she'd held him back from his true calling. From ascending to the high throne of the gods. If she'd thought the bleak, hateful look of reproach in his eyes was bad, his punishment had been even worse.

If she dared to leave the cave on Mount Ida—dared to

leave the very spot where she'd hidden him and raised him for so many years—she couldn't take corporeal form. To all who knew her, she was nothing but a ghost, a spirit of someone they remembered from long ago. A walking spirit. Dead to others, yet fully alive.

She'd lost the contact of others for endless years of her life, in her forced role as caretaker to Zeus. But she'd done it. She'd helped raise him into a strong warrior who would be able to defeat his father in battle.

And how was she repaid?

With a punishment worse than death.

How fitting, then, that the god of death should be the one to save her. Hades had defied his brother and, in doing so, changed her life.

Even now, Ilsa recalled every detail of Hades's arrival on Mount Ida.

"He doesn't appreciate your gift, but I do, sweet Adrasteia. It was your sacrifice, raising Zeus in secret, that allowed him to grow strong. Allowed him to defeat our father and set me and my brother and my sisters free. I owe you a debt of gratitude."

Tears rolled down her face, their wet warmth a welcome sign that she still lived. Existed. She stared at Hades as he filled the mouth of her cave. *"How am I to know this isn't yet another trick of the gods? Your mother, Rhea, forced me here. Your brother Zeus has ensured I can never leave."*

"My family does not understand the gifts of others, or the sacrifice others make. I will not make the same mistakes. Which is why I offer you a bargain."

She felt the interest pecking at her heart, like birds sought seeds on the ground, but vengeance still swirled in *an impenetrable mass, holding her curiosity at bay. Her arms remained firmly crossed over her breasts, but her tears dried as she looked at the great god of the Underworld. "Fine. Tell me if you wish."*

"I propose a new life for you, Adrasteia. A life beyond this cave, beyond your upbringing as a nymph, even beyond the lot cast for you by my brother and my mother. You've been called to so much more."

"Again, I must repeat myself. How do I know this isn't yet another trick?"

"I am offering you vast power, Adrasteia. I'd like you to become my goddess of divine justice. You shall see into men's souls and you shall bring me those who defy the natural order of things. You shall repair what is wronged and you shall be the great distributor of men's eternal fortune. You shall be the one from whom there is no escape."

Another wave of tears welled in her eyes. "That's where you're mistaken. It is I who have no escape."

"Bah!" Hades waved a hand. "My brother isn't all-powerful, nor is he all-seeing. I can offer you life. It is your choice if you wish to embrace it."

So Hades had laid out his plan—how he needed one who could roam the earth and bring the wicked and the small-minded to his door—and she'd accepted. Perhaps under duress, perhaps as one who could see opportunity when it was presented.

Either way, she'd long since accepted her duties.

Adrasteia was no more, replaced by a new name. One guaranteed to strike fear in all those who heard it. A name befitting the goddess of divine retribution.

A name she'd worn proudly through the millennia, until recently.

Until Kane. Always, her thoughts returned to him.

With a sigh, she allowed the malevolent stench of the physicist's soul to guide her toward him, pushing images of Kane to a place inside of herself the evil couldn't touch.

And as she wandered the length of the Serpentine, she prepared herself to face more of the world's dark and depraved.

Others for whom there was no escape.

She knew the evil in men's souls. Knew the depths of wickedness to which they could sink.

And she had the power to destroy each and every one of them.

Kane fell to his knees as the port ended, the wet spring grass of Hyde Park soaking through his jeans. Oh gods, he hated this clumsiness, an effect of the poison as it neared its zenith.

Although several of his Warrior brothers detested porting, he'd always had a fondness for it. The ability to come and go as he pleased—to go anywhere he chose—was one of the most awesome gifts Themis had bestowed upon them.

It also took a tremendous amount of energy, of which he was in short supply, using all of his normal strength to stave off the fiend tap-dancing its way through his bloodstream.

Fighting off a round of nausea, he ripped open an energy bar their housekeeper and all-around den mother, Callie, had made for him. She'd worked on the recipe for years and in the past it had helped sustain him as the poison's power grew. The bar was a concoction of oatmeal, vitamins and some ungodly thing that smelled worse than a gym full of his Warrior brothers.

But at least it stayed down.

May thirty-first. You just have to make it to the night Antares is at its zenith and then you're free for another year.

The poison punctuated that thought with a harsh battering ram to Kane's rib cage.

From the inside out.

Kane allowed himself a moment to catch his breath in privacy—allowed himself that small moment of weakness to collect himself—then swallowed the last bite of the protein bar. On one more deep breath, he shoved the wrapper into his jeans pocket and took off for the Serpentine.

There just wasn't any time to worry about the rapidly deteriorating state of his body. The scientist he'd been following since initially partnering with Ilsa had set the meet, after a long and arduous dance where they both sized each other up and tried to figure out how hard each was playing the other.

Three months ago, the little Hitler wannabe had changed the stakes by bringing his partner along on a meet, forcing Kane to pull back and reassess. New entrants into a setup always made him twitchy.

So where Kane had thought he was closing in on them, it had taken another three months of careful planning. He'd seeded information in bits and pieces—sensitive e-mails, realistic contacts for uranium sales—and also agreed to make a hit on one of their enemies to prove his worth—all so he could gain their trust.

No wonder he was so fucking tired he couldn't see straight. The deep concentration required for this level of cover along with his nonstop hunt for the elusive Ilsa had the edges of his carefully honed self-control fraying.

Still, he soldiered on.

Ignoring the increasing power of the venom that lived inside of him, Kane had taken his time, digging deeper into the new asshole's background. Sadly, the investigation had proved only what Kane had already suspected: The second scientist was as twisted as his partner and both were bound and determined to reach their objective.

Earlier meetings where Kane had posed as an enterprising, double-crossing British spy, ready to work for the highest bidder, had established how large a stash of uranium they currently had access to. Tonight's meet should confirm the list of terrorists they'd contacted to open up the bidding.

In his moments of pure honesty, Kane knew it was these times when he most questioned Themis's intentions. Throughout his service to her, he'd seen the depths of depravity humanity could sink to. Had witnessed the greed and selfishness inherent in their life choices. Still, Themis never relinquished her great, driving need to protect humanity.

Defend humans from forces beyond their control?

Hell, how'd you protect them from forces completely *within* their control?

Shaking his head, he continued on. Light was in short supply in this area, which was why they'd selected it for the meet, but he could still make out vague shapes ahead of him. Two figures, facing each other in the moonlight.

Kane's footfalls were quiet in the grass, muffled to a soft squish by the light dew. A soft call died on his lips as his gaze caught the silhouette of one of the two people standing there.

A woman?

It was definitely a woman, from the outline of her breasts and the arch of her backside.

Slowing, he mentally walked through the possibilities of what it meant. Yet another person involved from the scientists' side? Kane quickly discarded it as the scientists' ability to succeed in this venture required only a small number of people in the know. Not only wasn't there any honor among thieves, but there wasn't a hell of a lot of secrecy, either.

Was it an even easier answer? A late-night visit from an enterprising prostitute, perhaps? He'd lived long enough to know that dark, deserted places had a way of finding the most lost souls.

As Kane walked closer, voices rose in the night air.

"Where's your partner, Robert? You said you were bringing him." The sexy, whiskey-rough voice caught Kane's attention immediately, reminding him of Ilsa.

Was he so far gone he couldn't even hear a woman's voice any longer without thinking of her?

Kane recognized Robert's haughty manner immediately. "He's working on some things. You don't need to see both of us anyway."

The husky, seductive tones of her voice rose up in the night air, an unmistakably sharp edge underlying her words like a razor on velvet. "I don't like being purposely misled."

The large hands that went up in a gesture of innocence had Kane's gut tightening in response. He looked as if he were ready to strike the woman. "I didn't mislead you. I'm here, aren't I? What do you need to see Alex for, too?"

"We had an agreement."

Kane held his breath, desperately puzzling through the conversation. Was he being played? Was Robert? Who *was* the woman and what was she doing in the middle of his meet?

"Yeah, well, I changed it," the man said.

"And why'd you do that, sweet pea?"

"Alex and I agreed, something about you doesn't make sense, love. We both agree it's time to end our relationship with you."

"You know I can't do that, love." Even at his distance, Kane heard the sneer in her voice, the low, dulcet tones that couldn't hide steely determination. Before Kane could move another foot, the scene unfolding in front of him morphed into something far more sinister.

Robert lurched at the woman, his hands outstretched in a reaching motion, aimed for her throat. At the last minute, the woman sidestepped him, her movements effortless and full of a casual grace that belied the danger she was actually in.

Kane leaped forward, intent on closing the gap between them when her movements pulled him up short. The woman's back was to him, but he could see her shift, crouching slightly, bracing for Robert's attack. She extended her arms and blocked his advance as he ran forward, shoving him as they made contact. The feint knocked Robert off balance and she was on top of him immediately. With precise movements, she straddled him and had her hands on his throat, despite the fact the guy had her by six inches and at least a hundred pounds.

"Now, you're going to listen to me, Robert. You've been a very naughty boy." He made a heavy grunt, but she only leaned in closer. "Very naughty."

Kane felt the answering response in his groin as the woman lowered her head toward her victim. The sensuality of her movements as she leaned in—the way her face fell toward Robert's—had raw desire thrumming in his veins, strong enough to dislodge the poison's power.

Ilsa had straddled him in just that way, the curtain of her hair falling around him in abundant waves. She'd leaned over him, her lush lips stroking the length of his jaw as she detailed each and every thing she wanted to do to his body, her husky voice sending shivers straight to his cock.

Shaking off the memories, Kane moved into the small clearing where the woman still lingered over the scientist. His rock-hard state proved—without a doubt—he'd not forgotten a single second of those glorious hours he'd spent with Ilsa. He kept his footfalls quiet as he moved into a small circle of light where the moon shined down through the clouds and—

"Ilsa?"

She lay prone on Robert, her lips hovering just above the scientist, yet not touching. Her hands rested on the asshole's shoulders and long wisps of breath were visible between their mouths.

At the sound of her name, she lifted her head, shock etching her mouth into a wide O of surprise. "Kane?"

The loss of contact and momentary distraction was all it took. Before Kane could warn her, Robert's hands came up, throwing Ilsa off his body in one clean movement. With lightning-quick reflexes, he was on his feet and moving in the direction of a pathway almost invisible in the dark.

"Get the hell out of here, Kane! I don't need your help. You shouldn't even be here." Ilsa took off after her prey, the four-inch-heeled thigh-high boots she wore doing nothing to slow her down.

Kane took off after both of them, ignoring the throb of

pain in his abdomen as the poison heightened his exertion. What was she doing here? And what in the gods' names had she been doing to Robert?

More seduction to get what she wanted?

Pounding fists of fury assaulted his central nervous system as he chased after them. No way was he losing either one of them. And no way was he letting her put her body anywhere near a traitor and criminal with the ability to start World War III.

Like a sprinter chasing the lead in a race, Kane kept his eyes firmly on Robert. He'd deal with Ilsa later was anticipating it with a furious sort of excitement—but the scientist was his first priority.

It was high time he put an end to their charade of criminal brothers in arms and eliminate the asshole. But first, the little toady owed him some explanations and he was damned sure going to get them. Pushing his weakened body forward, Kane ignored the pain—the sharp stabs in his lungs and the tearing muscle fibers in his thighs—and kept running as the two silhouettes in front of him fell in and out of moonlight while he narrowed the gap.

Arms and legs pumping as his feet flew over the slick, dewy grass, Kane caught up inch by inch. Ilsa had shifted positions so they ran almost alongside each other, fanned out like big cats did to take down their prey. She had the length of one full stride on him, but he was narrowing her lead with each passing footfall.

Almost . . . there . . .

As his hand reached out and extended toward Robert, Kane felt the rush of air from Ilsa's direction.

Saw the quick disappearance of her form in his peripheral vision.

Heard Robert's scream.

Veering off just before toppling both of them, Kane watched in amazement as Ilsa reappeared from the air in front of Robert, absorbing the man's weight at full speed as he slammed into her.

Chapter Four

"**K**ane. I don't need your help. Go. Please go."

Robert writhed underneath her as he struggled to free himself. She kept her thigh muscles clamped around his midriff, her ass on his thighs and her hands on his shoulders. He didn't stand a chance.

"Let me the fuck up, you bitch!" Robert's eyes were wild and he kept making slight jerks from his hips in a futile attempt to dislodge her.

Ilsa ignored him. Ignored the struggles, the protests, even the smell of fear that emanated off him in pulsing waves. He'd earned these consequences fair and square. She wasn't the arbiter. She simply delivered the punishment.

Instead, all she could focus on was getting Kane to leave. The impulse pounded in her mind far louder than Robert's screams.

"You ported." She heard the accusation in Kane's voice along with his confusion and disbelief.

"Yes, I did."

"What are you?"

"You need to leave. You don't need to see this." At those

ominous words, Robert's struggles ratcheted up significantly, his body flailing against her like a panicked fish thrown on the deck of a ship. His desperation was palpable and hers was quickly growing to match it.

Kane reached for her, but she stopped him before he could touch her. "Don't."

"Who *are* you?"

"Go." Tears filled her eyes, hot on her cheeks in the cool early-morning air. "Please go."

He couldn't see this.

She couldn't *let* him see this.

And she couldn't let Robert go, either.

Kane didn't move any closer, but the wariness didn't leave his eyes as he loomed over her. His face held a mix of confusion and anger, etched in the lines around his eyes and the hard set of his jaw.

Had she ever seen anyone with such expressive eyes? His face belied nothing in the squaring of his firm jaw nor in the craggy lines around his mouth, set as if locked in granite. But oh, those eyes. Dark and fathomless, she wanted to fall into them.

Desperately.

"Who are you?" Kane asked the question again, much softer, his words penetrating her thoughts through Robert's screams. Then he reached for her once more, slowly, much as a person tries to move toward a wild animal. "You need to get off of him and let me deal with him. He's mine, Ilsa."

Robert stopped struggling, as if he inherently sensed he had a better shot with Kane than with her. His voice quivered, its cadence pounding out in gulping, fear-laced waves. "You've got to help me, man. She's a freak. I'll tell you whatever you want to know, but you have to help me."

Again, Ilsa ignored the man's struggles, not even offering him a glance. "He's not yours to deal with, Kane. Please just accept the fact I got here first and leave."

Without warning, Kane leaped on her, knocking her off Robert and onto the ground. Just as before, the scientist didn't spend any time waiting around, moving on the second opportunity to get away just as fast as he moved the first time.

"Fuck you, Kane! This isn't your battle. He's not yours and you can't. Have. Him." Ilsa struggled against him, pounding his shoulders and kicking her legs as he forced her back toward the wet grass.

Sweat popped out on his brow as they fought, muscle straining against muscle, male form to female form, struggling for dominance. Ilsa recognized she couldn't beat him in upper-body strength, so she refocused, using the power in her legs to keep him from holding her down.

Locked in battle, they tumbled over the ground, neither wanting to give in, both sensing that giving in to their physical battle could mean so much more.

On a grunt, Kane got the upper hand, pressing her back and using his weight to pin her to the ground. "What are you about? And what do you want with Robert?"

"He needs to be taken care of and the longer you do this," she ground out through clenched teeth, "the harder it will be to find him. But he's going down and it's got to be tonight. Those are my orders."

"Orders? What the hell does that mean? Who are you working for?" Kane's breath was hot against her ear as he spoke to her, the words a mix of frustration and confusion through gritted teeth.

If circumstances were different—perhaps if she had the time—she might consider telling Kane. Might consider sharing that part of her life. But there just wasn't any *time*.

Damn Hades and his perceptive nature. She could still

see the glitter in his eyes when he'd given her the assignment to retrieve the scientists a few days ago. Although she had no idea how he'd known what she'd been up to for the last six months, his wry order left no doubt in her mind he knew *exactly* how she'd been spending her time. If she'd had any doubts, his briskly worded order—"I'd like you to go pick up your new little friends"—confirmed it.

Now the god of the Underworld had made his request and she needed to deliver them.

She'd never failed before. She *refused* to fail, still so full of the constant fear that if she didn't live up to Hades's expectations, she'd be sent back to a life of invisibility.

Of nothingness.

All she needed was a millisecond and she could get away from Kane and complete her task. One single millisecond when she could separate their bodies so she could port after her prey.

The long lines of Kane's body pressed against her, his jeans-clad hips cradled in the vee of her thighs. The soft cotton of his gray T-shirt molded against her breasts from the heavy weight of his chest and she felt those sculpted muscles heave in and out as he lay on top of her.

"It's his turn, Kane," she sobbed. "You have to let me go. You have to let me do my job."

With another hard push, Ilsa pressed on his shoulders, willing him away. As her fingers made contact with the hard planes of his chest, she couldn't ignore the wash of pure, feminine need that filled her. Her body longed for him and this close proximity was a temptation she'd never expected to feel again.

How had she managed six long, torturous months without this man's body covering hers?

A loud sob bubbled from her throat on that last thought,

falling from her lips with a traitorous note of pleading. "Please. You have to let me go."

Without warning, he rolled off her. Shock flooded her veins before duty kicked in with a vengeance. Imagining her destination, her body began another port, the rush of air in her ears instantaneous.

Just as her body dissembled, Ilsa heard the growl low in Kane's throat and felt his grip on her forearm. "I'm not letting you go."

Emmett paced his office, boiling lava flows of anger coursing through his veins. Where the hell was the bitch? It galled him to think that he needed her this much, but fuck it all if it wasn't true. He'd waited too long. Had planned and plotted for almost three centuries and couldn't—no, *wouldn't*—lose it all when he was so close. And there was no way he would let her take this from him.

He gazed at his cell phone again, nearly dialing her number for the third time that day, but resisted the urge. He might need her, but groveling didn't sit well with him. She'd come through for him. And if she didn't . . . Emmett shoved the phone into his slacks pocket. Well, then, he'd just take care of her once they fought on even ground.

The darkened windows that surrounded him cast a mirrored reflection as he crossed the plush office of one Edward St. Giles. Cocking his head, Emmett took in the reflection that gazed back at him.

Trim physique, broad shoulders, a fair amount of distinguished gray at the temples. Other than an occasional penchant for neat glasses of whiskey and a few brazen puffs on some unfiltered cigarettes, St. Giles was quite the specimen.

A lifelong SIS man, Edward St. Giles had spent his days and years devoted to queen and country, rising to a status few ever saw within MI6. Of course, it had come at quite an expense. His teenage children barely knew him and his mousy wife had a piece on the side, after years of neglect by her globe-trotting hubby.

Actions and consequences, Emmett mused. It was a formula that never failed.

But even Emmett couldn't have guessed what a perfect mark St. Giles actually was until he'd immersed himself in his life. Not only was the man a conduit to Kane Montague, but his shitty family life ensured even his closest, most beloved family members had no clue something was amiss with their absentee loved one. Even on the rare occasions he needed to make an appearance at the St. Giles household during waking hours, no one thought anything of it when he forgot where the silverware was or how to get to Grandma's house.

Nope, St. Giles was perfect in so many ways. And the stupid, lifeless fuck hadn't known what hit him the day Emmett hunted him down.

It really was very easy to take a soul and assume the body, if you knew how to do it. Emmett had learned the darkest of black magics years ago from his incubus father and had spent his life putting them to good use. Although he hadn't been fortunate enough to get his father's full gifts, he did inherit an unnaturally long life.

Of course, as long as his mortality was intact, it would never be long enough.

But soon, even that worry would evaporate like poor St. Giles's soul. Once this plan was complete, Emmett would no longer have to worry about something as pesky as mortality. Or his age. Or even stupid bitch goddesses like Nemesis.

Oh no, he'd have immortality, just as he was always meant to.

The harsh ringing of the phone jarred the sleepy quiet of the room, interrupting Emmett's plotting and pacing. Surprise at the late-night call quickly morphed into something far more enjoyable as he recognized the encoded number flashing on his phone.

"St. Giles."

"You told me we'd be safe. That your man knew what he was doing. You double-crossing us?"

Emmett forced the snottiest tone he could down the phone line. The two scientists St. Giles's department had kept tabs on had proven themselves a more than apt diversion to throw Kane and Ilsa together six months ago, but they'd quickly become tiresome to deal with. "And whom am I speaking with?"

The scientist named Alex sputtered at him from the other end. "You know who the fuck I am and you also know we had a deal. So why did Robert leave two hours ago and still hasn't come back? And why did he just text me about some woman he thinks is following him?"

Emmett pushed calm warmth into his tone. He had no idea where Robert went, but these little clues of Alex's were likely tied to Ilsa. They had damn well better be.

Oops. He was British now. He needed to think like St. Giles would.

They had *bloody well* better be.

"Ah. Alex. How are you this fine evening? Bit late for social calls."

"He went out for the meet, just like your man asked him to. But he keeps seeing this woman. And, funny enough, he thinks she looks just like the lady your man took to an event six months ago."

Excellent. Emmett's attention went on high alert, even while he kept his voice level and calm. "I wouldn't worry yourself, Alex. The woman you're referring to is likely one of Kane's conquests, nothing more. If six months have passed, she's likely no longer his latest conquest and has decided to follow him."

"All I know is Robert left for a meet your agent set up and he hasn't come back."

"Are you still in the safe house?"

"Hell yeah. I'm sitting on a hundred pounds of uranium. Where the fuck do you think I'm going?"

"Calm yourself, Alex. Please. You can trust Kane, just as I told you." *Just like you can trust me,* Emmett thought with no small measure of glee.

"Then why hasn't he gotten back here yet? With Robert?"

"I'm sure it's only a matter of time. You know how these things work. All the dancing around the issues. Kane and Robert'll be back before you know it."

"I'm done waiting. Done letting you people call the shots. I don't know why Robert ever agreed to this fucking plan. You're not some rogue agent, helping us sell the stash. You're setting us up."

How perceptive of you, asshole. "Decisions made in the heat of a stressful situation rarely work out well, Alex. You made a decision. Chose a course of action. It's time to stick with it."

A ball of fire ran down the length of his arm and out his fingertips. As the swirls of light ebbed and flowed in front of him, Emmett calmed himself with the light display and the soothing tones of Alex's fear. Nothing like watching these useless, pathetic waste-of-skin criminal wannabes flounder once things got tough. Emmett tsked to himself as he lobbed the fireball from hand to hand.

No one really understood true wickedness anymore.

"Calm yourself, Alex. Everything will be all right."

The phone clicked off without a reply.

Emmett had to admit, his father really did know his stuff. Bad blood always rose to the surface. He'd said that often, clapping Emmett on the back when he did, winking and laughing that they knew the true meaning of a fulfilling life.

His father had sired exactly two children in all his years. Emmett and, one thousand years before that, his older brother, Merlin.

Dark and light. One who understood how to boldly accomplish his goal and the other who spent his life in service to another.

Oh yes, dear old Dad had been right. You got nowhere working for others. Work for yourself. Do things your own way. And always, always believe the worst in others.

Darkness always won.

Emmett sat down to issue "orders" to Kane, the Warrior moron who really believed himself to be an agent in the field. As Emmett typed the encrypted note, he felt the stirring down deep in his blackened soul.

Immortality was nearly within his reach. Ilsa was clearly in range of Kane which meant his wait was nearly over.

Once he had immortality, there would be no one he couldn't touch. Nowhere he couldn't go. Nothing he couldn't make his own.

Settling himself behind St. Giles's desk, Emmett hit Send on the encoded message.

SAFE HOUSE. DEAL WITH ALEX. HE'S BECOME A LIABILITY.

As the message floated into the electronic ether, Emmett opened the top drawer of his desk.

There. Nestled in a small box with a velvet bottom lay his bargaining chip.

A vial of blood from a Warrior of the Zodiac.

The blood of an immortal.

Reassured it was still where he'd put it, he ran his hand over the top of the sample to ensure the spells he'd employed to enchant it were intact. With one last look at the vial, he closed the drawer, satisfied that he would be victorious in his quest.

Twirling in his chair, Emmett again faced the windows. With one final glimpse at his reflection, he straightened his tie. It was time to hit the field and close this op once and for all.

Kane dropped next to Ilsa, flung off of her by the force of the port and his loose grip on her forearm. Her quick actions again stopped Robert's forward movement, the scientist's loud screams rending the air as she tackled him to the ground.

In an agonizing counterpoint, the poison in Kane's bloodstream jumped with glee at the sound of Robert's panic, punching sharp fists of merriment in Kane's stomach. An unpleasant side effect, that one, but one he'd experienced before in his line of work. Another's agony seemed to inflame the poison, making its feral bite extra sharp when it was in its rising stage.

Add that to the hard landing and his earlier depletion of energy from his port to London, and Kane struggled to right himself. Pressing down on the nausea, he followed the sound of Robert's screams, knowing full well what he'd see when he looked at Ilsa and her quarry.

This go-round she wasn't wasting time. Her face again lay over Robert and his screams disintegrated into a long, low moan as Kane saw the breath fly out of the scientist's body.

What the *hell* was she?

Clearly an immortal, that was obvious. But how had she landed in his world? And why hadn't she identified herself? And who in the Pantheon could kill with their breath?

He knew he should stop her—knew by rights Robert was his to question—but for the life of him he couldn't remove the image of her tearstained face and the pleading in her voice as she begged him to let her go.

So instead, he simply watched. Watched the avenging goddess as she lay prone on top of her victim, her movements almost sensual, and so deeply intimate, he couldn't stop the jealous stirrings that fought the poison for dominance in his bloodstream.

Jealous of a man losing his life?

As he observed, Kane wondered how he could reconcile this avenging angel with the woman he'd seen only moments before. The one with the pleading voice and teary eyes. It certainly wasn't the badass goddess before him, straddling a man on her knees, taking his life.

She wasn't death. He knew that—on some instinctive level he couldn't define, he was sure of it. But she was certainly its messenger.

What had she said?

"It's his turn."

"You have to let me go."

"You have to let me do my job."

She might not be death, but he also knew she wasn't one of the Fates. He'd met those clever mistresses of human life and death and he'd have remembered if any of them looked like Ilsa.

So what job was she tasked to do? And how did she know it was Robert's *turn*?

Robert's movements grew increasingly lethargic and his moans weakened with each passing moment. Ilsa never lifted her head, her concentration focused and intense as she drew the man's life from him.

On a last moan, Robert's body went still, his skin taking on an odd pallor in the moonlight.

"He's dead."

Ilsa sat back on her heels, her breath strangled. "Yes."

"You killed him."

"It was his time. He's due to pay for his crimes to someone else."

"Why didn't you tell me you were immortal six months ago? Why keep up this charade?"

"I didn't know who you were."

Kane took in Ilsa's words, searching her gaze, desperate to know if she was telling the truth. Was it really possible that what happened between them was simply a coincidence? *No, that was impossible.* "You seriously expect me to believe that?"

Her slim shoulders went up in a delicate shrug. "It doesn't matter what you believe. You didn't need to know. About me or what I'm capable of. You didn't need to know he"—she glanced down at the lifeless body—"was my mission."

"If he was your mission, then why'd you play me?" Kane's stomach muscles squeezed in tight, pulsing spasms, the poison he'd managed to keep at bay during the chase through the park returning with a vengeance as his adrenaline faded. "Why'd you burn me? There's no reason to. If you're part of the Pantheon, too, you could have told me."

"I didn't know you were immortal." Ilsa's eyes stayed on the body.

Is she lying? Much as it twisted Kane to think that she could lie to him so effortlessly, she'd given him no reason to believe anything but the worst.

In brisk and efficient movements, she lifted herself off of Robert's lifeless form. Getting to her feet, her gaze rose to meet Kane's. "Look. We just got in each other's way, that's all. We had a nice interlude and some hot sex. As you so quickly reminded me, we certainly didn't make love. So from my point of view, I don't owe you a damn thing." A wry smile painted her lips. "We're both adults well past the time for silly games."

Kane reached out for her, unwilling to end this so quickly. Desperate to not have her walk away yet again and leave him full of questions that had no fucking answers.

Her only response was a pointed stare at his hand where it rested on her forearm. "Now, if you'll excuse me, I've got a soul to deliver. Hades hates to be kept waiting."

Hades?

So *that's* who she worked for. The god of the Underworld and the keeper of souls. The mouth-to-mouth shit suddenly made a whole lot more sense. "Fuck Hades—he can wait. I want some answers."

"I don't have any to give you."

Ilsa fought for calm against the hot, luscious waves of need that flowed over her skin at his simple touch. Oh, she knew she should pull her arm away. Should just be off with it. But the alluring sight of Kane kept her gaze locked in place and ensured her feet stayed firmly planted.

Robert's soul curled around hers, a filthy suit that encased her very essence and painted her insides with corrosive fibers of evil. The familiar pit opened in her stomach as those icy fingers scraped her from the inside out. She *hated* this part. Hated holding the soul of another in her body. Hated the feel of another's life force pulsing within her.

Like a putrid slime living under the skin, each time it

made her feel as if she'd never be clean again. Never be free of the dark and ugly pull of immorality and sinfulness. Like every bad thing she'd ever done had coalesced in the deepest, most secret part of herself.

Was the feeling that far off the mark?

Guilt she'd tried hard to ignore rose up and pricked at her conscience. Six months ago, when she'd first met Kane, she'd stolen a vial of his blood. To this day, the act haunted her.

Driven by her need for vengeance against Themis, she'd felled this man with enough drugs to knock out an elephant, then stolen something from him. Something so personal— so essential—that she couldn't quite clean the stain of it off her own soul.

Pulling her arm back—in self-preservation or in embarrassment?—Ilsa stared him down. "Why do you persist in this? I haven't seen you in six months, Kane. Surely you haven't spent your days pining over a good fuck." The words sliced her insides to ribbons, the pain of it sluicing over her with far more devastation than the most evil of souls.

The agony of the truth filled her, the consequences of her actions all too evident.

We're not meant to be together. Not meant to breathe the same air. We're enemies, even if you don't know that or understand it yet. But once you learn what I've done, there's no way for you to feel otherwise.

Why, oh why had she made that horrible bargain with Emmett? Weren't her duties to Hades enough? But if she hadn't made her agreement with the sorcerer, she'd never have met Kane. Would never have spent those three glorious days in his arms, when she was just . . . herself. The woman she'd always wanted to be. Desperately.

In his arms, she was Ilsa.

She'd spent the time since then trying to determine how to fix it and, as always, she grew no closer to figuring out how to unwind herself from her poor decisions.

Her battle was with Themis. But now she'd involved the goddess's Warriors, too. Those nameless, faceless men she'd thought to use to get to Themis now *had* names and faces.

Now she knew Kane.

And unless she figured out how to unwind her agreement with Emmett, she'd already given her Scorpio a death sentence.

Chapter Five

S he was an immortal?

Ilsa stood there, moonlight cascading over the ugly blond wig she wore, color riding high on her cheeks. The eyes he'd originally believed to be darker than midnight flashed blue fire.

"You've lied from the first." The cell phone in his pocket buzzed, but Kane ignored it. Instead, he reached over and yanked the wig off, watching in agony as luscious waves of hair fell to her shoulders. "Even your eyes are a different color."

She shrugged, the small insolence doing nothing to calm his ire. "Colored contacts are an amazing thing. And so very versatile." Her gaze fell to the dead man on the ground. "Humans are far more ingenious than any of us want to give them credit for. It's sad so many of them choose to use their gifts for ill."

"Who made you judge and jury, Ilsa?"

A small sigh escaped her, like the slow leak of a balloon. "Powers far beyond either of us. And I'm not the judge and jury. I simply carry out someone else's decisions."

"You expect me to believe you're just a pawn?" The words fell from his lips in a rush. "Acting as an agent of someone else?"

Another one of those annoying, delicate little shrugs lifted her shoulders. "Believe what you want."

Kane's earlier thoughts, from the weight room, came back to him. Why did he even care? Why had he spent the last six months damn near obsessed with this woman? This cold, unfeeling monster who cared for nothing but herself and her duties.

Without warning, a trickle of sweat ran the length of Kane's spine, chased almost immediately by a line of shivers.

Not now. Oh gods, not now.

The rush of adrenaline that had allowed him to follow Ilsa through the park had nearly worn off, his body's instinctive ability to protect itself rapidly evaporating along with the immediate danger. In its place, his temples throbbed with the pain of a thousand battles as the poison raked over his central nervous system. The fucking Taurus was right. He *was* pushing himself too hard.

And now he was about to look like a swooning fool in front of Ilsa.

If her name even *was* Ilsa. To the best of his knowledge, there'd never been anyone with that name in all the Pantheon. It sure as shit didn't take the cunning of a master spy to figure out she'd made up the name.

"What's wrong with you?"

Kane's head snapped up. "Nothing's wrong with me."

"I can see it. Around your eyes. In your skin tone. Something's wrong. Are you ill?"

Kane barked out a short laugh and threw a pointed stare at Robert's lifeless body. "If you're gonna worry about someone's skin tone, you should worry about his. That's a nasty pallor he's sporting here in the light of the moon."

Ilsa's gaze dropped to the body. If Kane's tired eyes were to be believed, those shoulders she'd shrugged so carelessly only moments before seemed to droop. Was it possible she actually felt guilty?

He discarded the thought as soon as it came. She'd chased Robert halfway across the park, determination layered in each and every stride of those endless legs. The man might have had it coming, but Ilsa had hunted him down.

Predator stalking prey.

Immortal with power versus mortal with none.

It was murder.

And what would you call your vast library of hits, Scorp? A wee bit of target practice?

Kane knew he was a lot of things, but hypocrite wasn't one of them. Stubborn, lethal and full of attitude he'd own up to. But someone who couldn't acknowledge who and what he was? No way.

Using every ounce of willpower he possessed, Kane fought to push back the effects of the poison. With a deep breath, he focused on the woman in front of him and ignored the trail of cold sweat that covered his back in ice. "So tell me one thing. Why did St. Giles put us together? And how'd you manage to get in his good graces? He doesn't suffer fools and he'd have checked you out six ways to Sunday before bringing you on."

Ilsa's gaze returned to him. Although it passed quickly, even she wasn't fast enough to hide the stark fear in her eyes before shuttering those liquid blue orbs. "I have friends in high places."

Before Kane could respond, she continued on. "Look. This little catch-up has been lovely and all, but there's still a second scientist on the loose."

The cell phone in his pocket buzzed again, and Kane reached for the SIS-issued device in his pocket. The encrypted text was straightforward and to the point.

SAFE HOUSE. DEAL WITH ALEX. HE'S BECOME A LIABILITY.

"Let's go. We need to get to the second scientist. He's still sitting in an MI6 safe house, and if we don't get to him soon, there's the very great risk he'll flee. And when he does, he's going to take all that uranium he's preparing to sell right along with him."

Again, her eyes filled with a wariness she wasn't quick enough to hide. "We're not going there together."

"Yeah, we are. I've got my orders from St. Giles."

Her short laugh was harsh in the predawn air. "And you're telling *me* about them?"

"I don't exactly have a choice. This needs to be dealt with and I'm not letting you out of my sight."

A small smile tinged the corner of those luscious lips. "Doesn't that violate protocol?"

Not only did it violate about fifteen different protocols, but it was an enormous risk. She'd played him from the first. Giving her access to a top secret safe house was the dumbest move he could possibly make.

Of course, letting her go would be worse, so he wasn't veering from this plan. "This is what we call an executive decision. And I figure it's a good one, unless you've got another vial of drugs on you that you're planning to stick me with?"

His hands shifted to her waist in a mock effort to search for a syringe. What had started as a joke, morphed immediately into full-blown lust the moment his fingertips hit the smooth leather plastered over her ass.

Kane's body hardened immediately as his hands roamed over her soft, feminine curves. Memories of their three days together blasted through his system, so intense it felt as if he could reach out and touch the scenes that ran through his mind like an erotic film.

The curve of her breast as it molded to his palm, her distended nipple growing hard at his touch. The taste of her on his tongue as her body melted in the glory of her orgasm. The ecstasy as she rose over him, the hot, slick warmth of her encasing his shaft with the powerful waves of her body's response.

"What are you doing?" Breathless outrage colored her small shriek before she batted at his hands. "Get your hands off me."

Kane shook off the memories as he removed his hands, but even his famous ironclad control couldn't stop the shaking of his fingers. "Can't blame a guy for protecting himself."

"You were copping a feel."

At her outrage, he couldn't keep the cocky grin at bay. "Bonus points for me."

"Charming."

"Opportunistic," he shot back. When she didn't rise to the bait with another comment, he shook his head, trying to dislodge the remainder of his carnal haze. "We're wasting time. Let's go."

An answering grin met him, cheeky in the extreme. "And how do you propose to get us there, Casanova? It didn't escape my notice you needed me to port across the field."

"I followed you here from New York, didn't I?"

Ilsa cocked her head, that beautiful visage filled with both questions and answers. "Fine. Maybe you got yourself here, but I'm still not buying the idea that everything's okay with you. Something's hurting you and I don't think you have the strength for another port."

"I wasn't letting you go back there. That's why I grabbed on to you." Lame, but hopefully effective, despite the knowledge she was far more perceptive than he gave her credit for.

Ilsa held out a hand and waved it between them. "Well, then, by all means, let's go. To the safe house."

"Hang on, princess." Kane grabbed her waving hand with a solid grip, grit his teeth and imagined his body into another part of London.

He only hoped like hell he could get them to their destination.

Thunder screamed through the air and lightning rent the skies of Mount Olympus as Enyo, goddess of war, stalked out the front door of her parents' mansion. Zeus and Hera had been going at it for a while and Enyo took some small satisfaction from the fact she'd not only caused the fight, but that it lasted even with her departure.

At least she could still create chaos *somewhere* without fear of lessening her power.

That fucking whore Themis and her Warriors. The last battle had been bad and now she'd ended up one Warrior stronger at the end of it. How her father had allowed Themis to turn that simpering fool of a girl, Ava Harrison, into a Warrior was beyond her.

What had possessed Zeus to buy into Themis's logic for turning the mouse, anyway?

Annoyance scraped down her spine like nails on a chalkboard. It was knowledge she wasn't privy to, no matter how many times she'd railed at her father over the last six months. Finally, after long months of alternating between pleading with him and nursing her postbattle depression, she'd had enough of his frustrating silence.

She knew how to fight her own battles and she'd normally avoid her mother's interference like the plague of a thousand swarms of locusts, but at her father's stubborn refusal to give in, she'd finally pulled out the big guns. Just let him try to keep Hera in the dark about a decision.

Especially one that involved his ex-wife, Themis.

A small smile played at Enyo's lips as another round of thunder filled the air in harsh, resounding waves. She pulled her mother in sparingly, but when she did, she normally saw results. The shrewish screams Hera had thrown at Zeus for the last three days would go a long way toward keeping him from being so lenient with Themis in the future.

Enyo was sure of it.

Of course, what was she supposed to do now? Even she'd gotten tired of her own company, her endlessly morose thoughts hardly fitting for a woman of action.

Truth be told, she had underestimated the Warriors in this last battle. Had been so blinded by her lust for the Summoning Stones—and the lies she'd been fed about her ability to truly possess them—that she had missed some very clear signals before it was too late.

The comforts of her own home greeted her as she stepped through the door. The dark decor, enhanced with various torture devices scattered throughout the living room, never failed to soothe. The insistent buzzing of her cell phone pulled her toward the dining room table, where the device lay near a perpetually full bowl of ambrosia.

She glanced at the caller ID. Numbers that indicated London greeted her on the display.

"Yes?"

When nothing but the sound of labored breathing echoed through the phone, her suspicions grew. No one but her Destroyers had this number. And if it *was* one of her Destroyers on the other end, he'd already be making his point.

"I'm waiting, darling."

"Um . . . I was told you could help me."

"And who told you that?" A small spiral of irritation unfurled in her stomach, twined tightly with interest at the sheer audacity of the caller.

Did he have any idea just who he was talking to?

"We . . . well, my partner actually got your information. Wouldn't tell me how, just told me I should use it if I needed help."

"And why should I help you, sugarplum?"

"Do you know Edward St. Giles of MI6?"

Well, now, this was interesting. St. Giles directed the most secretive activities of MI6. She'd followed his division's activities with a great degree of interest, seeing as how his SIS agents were the most cold-blooded—and psychopathically soulless—branch of the entire organization. She'd even found a few of her Destroyers there and lured them away. Those cruel, enterprising souls who recognized the limitations of their mortality and who aspired to something more.

This sniveling bore on the other end hardly sounded like a cold-blooded agent.

And it still didn't explain where he'd gotten her number.

The quaver stayed in his voice, but the slight thread of impatience overlaid the fear. "Um. Hello?"

"I'm aware of St. Giles, yes."

"Um, well, he's been something of a patron to my partner and me."

"And now I think you're teasing me. MI6 isn't a patron of anyone."

"They are when you're sitting on a cache of uranium."

Interest flooded Enyo's veins, filling her up and making her feel as buoyant as Mercury.

Enyo added a distinct purr to her voice, a technique that had yet to fail her. "What are you planning on doing with all this uranium, lover?"

"W-we—" She heard a strangled "oh shit" before he continued. "We're going to sell it."

"I'll send someone right over to help."

"But I haven't told you where I am yet. I don't even know where I am. They blindfolded me when they put me in this safe house."

"Don't worry, lover. I know how to find you."

Enyo ended the call and rushed toward her home office. Although she'd been gifted with many supernatural talents upon her birth on Mount Olympus, Themis's beloved humans had added their fair share of toys to her life.

Satellite technology was one of the best. With a flick of her long nail, the location of the caller filled her mind's eye. She'd have the little weasel's location in no time.

Images of what she could do with the uranium filled her, even as she questioned how to play St. Giles. From all she knew, he might run the most devious branch of MI6, but he was loyal to queen and country.

What did he have up his sleeve?

And how to get what she wanted from him?

Excitement skipped through her breast on the lightest wings as her mind raced with possibilities. Oh, what she could do with that uranium and a senior MI6 agent in her pocket.

Thank the gods. It was time to get back in the game.

Ilsa knew the moment her knees hit the ground in a tangled heap of bodies that she shouldn't have baited him. She shouldn't have challenged him when she knew—knew—Kane wasn't one hundred percent.

"Shit." Kane groaned from underneath her where one of his long legs tangled with hers. "Are you okay?"

"Yes, I'm fine."

She could only blame herself for this mess. If he hadn't scrambled her brains so hard with the ass grab, maybe she would have had a clearer head. Instead, heat had flooded her, taking away any capability for rational thought. Her body throbbed in awareness, dark coils of passion unfurling down low at the apex of her thighs. She could still feel the imprint of his hand on her skin and the warmth of his body as he pressed in close.

How did Kane manage to do this to her?

Since she was young—even before the agreement with Rhea to care for Zeus—Ilsa had worried there was something wrong with her. She was a nymph by birth, raised with all her sisters who, from all appearances, seemed to have no problem with intimacy, desire or, to be quite candid, fucking their brains out with whomever—or whatever—made themselves available.

Not her.

Instead, she'd sat on the sidelines and wondered when she'd feel that way about someone. She had yearned for so much . . . *more.*

The desperate need that would grip her until she believed she'd simply die without her beloved. The awareness that his mere presence in her life made her better somehow. The knowledge that she loved and was loved in return.

Madly.

But it had never happened. Season after season, as her sisters flirted with anything and everything in the Pantheon, she'd been alone. Until meeting Kane, she might as well have been raised by an army of Cyclopes for all the sexual abandon and wanton need she'd experienced over her lifetime.

She had long stopped believing herself capable of feeling anything sexual at all. It was the single biggest thing that scared her about her bargain with Hades. Was her readiness to do his bidding and deliver souls to the Underworld a bitchy substitute for the lack of sex in her life? Did the violence she regularly spent on others replace her need to feel desired?

Or worst of all, had she simply been used so hard—by Rhea, then Zeus and, even though she went willingly, by Hades—that she was used up?

And then she'd met Kane and all her internal fears and insecurities vanished under his touch. Instead of focusing on the job, all she could focus on was *him*. It was all-consuming, this need for another person. For the first time in her life, she had needs. Deep, soul-stirring needs that consumed her with the unforgiving flame of desire.

Needs that had gone unsatisfied since she'd double-crossed Kane.

For six long months, she'd cursed herself for her own folly. In her vengeful insistence on going after Themis— attempting to harm the goddess through her Warriors—Ilsa seemed to have inadvertently set herself up for more heartache.

Yet another brilliant moment in a lifetime full of ignorant foolishness.

Kane's groan pulled her from the weight of her guilt, an ever-present state since she met him those long months ago. Concern stabbed through her as he struggled to right himself. Even if he wouldn't admit it, Ilsa could see he was fighting off something horrible. The pallor of his skin and the hollowed-out cheekbones she'd seen earlier in the moonlight looked even worse under the light of the streetlamp they'd landed beneath.

"Where do you think we are?"

Kane pushed to his feet, his movements so exhausted he looked as if he had weights attached to his limbs. "Can you smell the bread baking?" At her nod, he added, "We're behind Harrods. Which means I didn't take us very far from where we started."

"Do you want me to take us to the safe house? I can—" She hesitated, not sure how much to share, then decided it probably didn't matter. "I can sense where the souls are that I need to transport to Hades. I know how to get to Alex."

"I'll get us there. I just need a minute. Besides, you can't be feeling all that hot right about now." Kane swiped at his jeans in harsh, clumsy movements as those wicked, dark eyes raked the length of her body. "Isn't there a soul rattling around in there somewhere?"

"It'll keep for a bit longer. Getting to Alex is more important."

More important, maybe, but agonizing all the same. Robert's soul continued to scream, the noise her own personal symphony of the damned in her head. The rotted tendrils of his essence clawed at her in a vain attempt to free itself.

Clearly whatever sensual magic Kane managed to weave

around her couldn't keep the disgusting, soul-marring feelings at bay for long.

"Kane. Tell me. What is wrong with you?" She held up a hand before he could protest. "Before you go all manly on me, you look like you're going to fall over. Let me help you."

"The way you helped me six months ago?"

"That's beside the point."

"It is the fucking point!" Like aftershocks from a volcano, she felt the reverberations to the very marrow of her bones. "You don't have any right to ask me how I feel. Or what's wrong with me. And you sure as hell don't have the right to offer me help."

"But, Kane—"

He moved up into her personal space until their faces were so close they practically touched, his breath coming in harsh pants. "You. Don't. Have. The. Right."

Before she could reply, his large hand had wrapped firmly around hers and he dragged her toward the edge of the building. He might appear weakened, but there was pure steel in his grip. Ilsa fought the warmth wending its way through her body as they walked hand in hand. Fought the fact that her focus on their physical connection quieted the screams in her head.

With the hard-core attitude and tough-girl routine that were her hallmarks, she started her campaign to get rid of Kane. "Why don't you go on your merry way and leave this to me? It's clear you're not on your game. I can handle this."

Please, please take the hint. If you get mad enough, maybe I can send you far, far away from here. Away from Emmett's clutches. Away from that ridiculous bargain I made with him.

Please let me do what I can now to keep you safe.

"Alex is mine. And you and I have a few things to clear up after I take care of him."

Abandoning the bitch-on-a-mission approach, she softened her voice and opted for honesty. "He's already spoken for, Kane."

"He's not spoken for until he's caught."

Desperate for something—anything—to make her point, Ilsa pressed on. "You don't belong here. How many different ways do you need me to prove it to you? Add to that the fact that you're clearly sick. You need to go home to that nice, sleek black-and-chrome apartment of yours, curl up in that mile of silk sheets on your bed and sleep off whatever is eating away at you."

"You mean the bed you drugged me in?"

The bitter aftertaste of his words floated between them. Unwilling to cop to the bait, she simply lowered her voice another notch. "Are we really back to that again?"

"We keep coming back to it, because it's the only thing between us. And I'm not letting you go until I figure out why you did it. Mark my words, princess—you *will* tell me why you burned me."

"Why did you call me that?"

He turned to look at her. "Call you what?"

"Princess. I'm not royalty."

"It's a turn of phrase." Forehead crinkling, Kane added, "Haven't you heard it before?"

She shook her head in return, surprised to see his shoulders relax, the question altering the direction of their conversation. "No."

"Just like you never heard of monkey sex before, either. You might be some great big mystery of the Pantheon, but you're here. In modern times. How'd you miss out on basic colloquialisms?"

"Again you've lost me."

A slightly bemused expression replaced the lines that ran across his forehead. "My mistake."

How did this happen? This odd compatibility between them could defuse even the most challenging situation. She'd felt it in his bed, too. Had thought about those odd moments of warmth as many times, if not more, than she'd recalled the feel of his big body filling hers.

The moments spent in his arms, laughing or simply engaged in idle conversation. Those three days of carefree abandon in body, heart and soul.

Now, as then, the simple ease of being with another person comforted her, even as it puzzled her.

And just as before, she had to be the one to end it.

Ilsa allowed herself another moment to savor the feeling. To savor the time with Kane that did more to shut out the agony of carrying Robert's soul within her than anything she'd ever experienced.

And then she made her choice.

Although the scenes changed, the ending remained the same. Like the *Casablanca* Ilsa who had to make her dutiful choice of her husband over Rick, Ilsa faced the same thing. There could be nothing between her and Kane, because she'd already ruined their chance for happiness.

What a joke.

The very sin Hades punished—hubris—was now her own punishment.

Her earlier decisions had already set in motion their intertwined destinies and the only way she could save him was to let him go.

So she'd face his ire again, face the consequences of a

vow she made before she'd met him, by taking matters into her own hands.

Tightening her grasp on Kane's fingers, Ilsa imagined them in the safe house on the opposite side of London. As the port began and the air grew heavy, enveloping them, she let go of Kane's hand.

Chapter Six

The rush of air ended with abrupt finality as Kane landed, belly flop style, on the roof of a car. Lifting his head from its face-plant, he fought the urge to moan long and low.

And released, instead, a string of curses that would have turned Quinn's hair blue.

"Son of a fucking bitch, I don't believe this." Rolling toward the edge of the car—some government-issued piece of shit, if the metallic gray color was any indication—he did a mental accounting of his body parts.

Stomach on the verge of nausea. Check.

Back muscles screaming. Check.

Headache that could resurrect the dead. Check.

"Fucking beautiful job, Monte. You sure know how to manage an op." The scorpion tattoo on his right shoulder twitched its stinger in vague annoyance. "So glad to see you've finally woken up," Kane muttered. "Fat lot of good you've been doing me."

The tattoos—one of Themis's gifts to all her Warriors— were literally that. Ink that rode high on the shoulder, shaped in the sign of the zodiac the Warrior represented. In addition to identification, the tattoo served a far more serious purpose. It lived within each Warrior's aura, coming to his aid, fighting alongside him in the heat of battle.

One hundred fifty-six men in all had been marked. Twelve for each sign, with double that for Gemini.

Barely one hundred of them still existed today, scattered across the globe.

Some had defected for what they believed to be greener—and more lucrative—pastures, while some were killed in battle. He and his Warrior brothers had eliminated one of the traitors the previous November, when they discovered the believed-dead brother of their Leo had aligned himself with Enyo.

The bitch had dealt him a death blow before any of them had gotten there to do the job. Which had galled Kane's assassin's sensibilities to no end until he'd come to the realization that Enyo had done them all a favor. For a change.

She'd also proven—yet again—one of the world's universal truths. No one slept with a cobra and lived to tell the tale.

Ajax certainly hadn't.

Kane couldn't help noticing how the betrayal had changed their Leo. Brody was still his jocular, jovial self, but it was clear the family bullshit had gotten to him. His wife, Ava, had gone a long way toward helping erase the new shadows in his eyes, but they still showed on occasion.

As his scorpion twitched again, Kane had to wonder if he was heading down a similar path, albeit with better intentions than Ajax. Was he walking into a trap because he believed himself immune to harm? It had happened to him before and he'd paid the price for his hubris.

They didn't call good intentions the path to hell for nothing.

No one, not even Themis, had had any idea the tattoo could be turned against the Warrior. To the best of his knowledge, he was the only one who'd ever had it happen.

Of course, it wasn't like they spent a lot of time having group therapy about it, either, so maybe some of the others had suffered through their own problems over the years since their own changing. Problems that affected them that they were afraid to mention.

To talk about.

Just because they were an immortal band of warriors didn't mean they all knew one another. Trusted one another. Their deployment across the globe meant they didn't know all the ins and outs of each Warrior's life.

His brothers—the contingent he fought with—were the only ones who knew about the poison and they kept the knowledge to themselves. They had his back and they ensured he had someone watching out for him when the poison reached its zenith.

As if on cue, another round of pain lanced through his muscle fibers, a heated wave of stinging pain.

Fuck.

Each and every time he thought he could handle this, the damn shit managed to drive another spike into his central nervous system.

With agonizing movements, Kane deftly ignored the poison and reached for his cell phone. He shot a quick text to Quinn with his location, gritting his teeth through the pain.

Believe it or not, he had bigger problems at the moment.

It ate away at him, this need to call for help. Not for the first time, the thought hit him that the acid of his stubborn pride stung far worse than the poison ever could.

A rush of air stirred next to Kane where he lay sprawled on the roof of the car. And then Quinn's six-foot-five frame loomed next to him. "What happened to you? Where's the woman? And why the *hell* did you think you should go after her in your condition?"

Add Quinn's tactless, bullheaded questions to the mix and Kane's stubborn pride went from frustrated to explosive in less time than it took to blink.

"Shut up and help get me the fuck off of here. Ilsa's inside the safe house. I'm, as you can see, *outside* the safe house and I need to go inside to get her and the bad guy currently wasting the oxygen in there."

Quinn's hand latched around his biceps, pulling him forward like a freaking toddler. Shit. Had it really come to this? He wasn't even strong enough to see an op through to completion.

There was a clear dent in the roof where Kane's body had landed, a fact that didn't escape either of them once Quinn had helped him into a standing position.

"How'd you land here?"

"Ilsa took matters into her own hands." At Quinn's pointed stare, Kane added, "I tried porting us out of Hyde Park and landed us behind Harrods by mistake. I guess she got tired of our little tour of London because she ported us to the safe house before I could argue any longer."

"She ported you?"

"Yeah. That's the one wee little detail we didn't know. She's an immortal."

"Who is she?"

An involuntary shudder ran the length of Kane's spine. "She won't tell me. But she can absorb a human soul into her body and she has some agreement with Hades."

"No shit." Quinn shook his head; his mouth dropped in surprise. "I'll do some digging. She's got something to do with the Underworld. It doesn't make me feel any better about her, but at least we might begin to understand who she is. I still don't get her connection to you and MI6, though."

"She was with me at the first observation of the scientists."

"Yeah, but why drug you? I'm still not buying she's squeaky clean."

"Of course not." In his increasingly weakened state, Kane had started to focus on the things that were vitally important, leaving the rest to stew somewhere in his subconscious. Clearly he was worse off than he'd thought, because he was all too ready to give Ilsa the benefit of the doubt.

"I do have to give her credit," Quinn added. "She's level-headed and cold as ice. Truly frosty."

Except, Kane thought, when she was all hot and sexy for him. Then there was nothing cold about her. Nothing that even remotely suggested she had ice crawling through her veins.

Quinn spoke again, thankfully breaking into what was likely to become another trip down Fantasy Lane. "So if she ported you, how is it that you're outside and she's inside?"

"She let go."

Without warning, the usual hard-ass look on Quinn's face morphed into a broad, shit-eating grin. "Seriously?"

"She didn't want me along, but I never thought she'd

actually throw me off right into the port. I'd have held on harder."

Great, loud guffaws of laughter penetrated the early-morning London air as Quinn fought to catch his breath.

Kane balled his hands into fists, the urge to slug Quinn for the second time in one day rising up on him immediately. "So glad you're having such a blast at my expense."

"She's really got you torqued up, doesn't she?"

That was the hit to his pride that hurt most of all. In all his years of immortality, he'd never felt this bruised—hell, gut-deep wounded—over a woman. And now . . . now everything he did was tainted by these feelings for her. This idiotic, desperate need to be around her. To follow her. To find out who she was and what she wanted with him.

To maybe see if she wanted to stick for a while.

He really was a joke. Scorpio, the great lover of the zodiac, felled by the one woman he couldn't have.

"Just help me, would you?"

Quinn slapped him on the back. "'Course I'll help you. I always have your back, whether you want me to or not."

Kane nodded toward the far end of the alley they were in. "It's that split-level at the end of the street. On the far side of the house, there's a tunnel that'll run us into a secret basement. It'll give us the element of surprise."

With a nod, Quinn pulled out his own BlackBerry. "Hang tight for another minute. Grey's shaken himself loose from the club and he's got Drake with him. I need to tell them where we are."

"When did the Pisces show up? I thought he was discovering himself in the wilds of Wyoming?"

Quinn shoved the device back in his pocket. "Guess he found what he was looking for."

"I thought you had to think deep thoughts for a long time to make any sense of them."

"That approach work for you?"

"Hell no. I prefer action to sitting around *feeling* shit."

Quinn shrugged. "Guess it didn't work for Drake, either."

As if conjured up by their conversation, Drake and Grey appeared next to them in a rush of air, both landing solidly on their feet.

Drake extended a hand, his greenish gold eyes lit with wry humor. "You look like hell, Monte."

"Yeah, so everyone's been telling me."

Those genie's eyes narrowed, the humor fleeing along with his convivial tone. "How do you feel?"

"I'll feel better once we deal with the terrorist scum inside the safe house and I get my hands back on that woman. And I'll really feel better when you all stop asking me how the fuck I feel." With a glance at Grey, Kane added, "Did you fill him in on Ilsa? On the rules?"

Grey's hands went up in an "I'm innocent" gesture. "Yeah, yeah, yeah. She's yours. All yours. We know."

"He's selfish that way," Quinn added. "And just so we're all in on the great cosmic joke playing out before our fine friend here, he discovered this evening that his Ilsa is actually a mystery member of the Pantheon."

"She's an immortal?" Grey's jaw dropped, the move so uncharacteristically uncool of him, Kane felt the first stirrings of a laugh in more days than he could count.

Quinn reached for the Xiphos at his calf, the rest of them following suit. "That she is. So don't underestimate her."

Kane loved the feel of the weapon in his hand. The Xiphos, a lethal fighting weapon gifted to each of them upon their turning, was a blade a little over a foot in length, nestled in a hilt fit perfectly to each Warrior's grip. Worn at the calf, they were small enough to stay out of public view, and long enough to do some wicked damage.

Personal, wicked damage.

Quinn slapped him on the back as they moved in unison down the alley, in the direction of the tunnel. Unable to resist one more prick at Kane's pride, the bull added, sotto voce, "I'll give you one thing, Monte. Since you met this woman, your life is far from dull. If she weren't such a liability, I'd actually be pushing you toward a little white chapel in Vegas."

Moonlight reflected off the lethal edge of his blade as Kane held it aloft, while his breath caught in his throat at the image of Ilsa as his wife. "You do realize if you don't shut up, you'll get the business end of this, don't you?"

"I'd expect nothing less."

Faded yellow appliances greeted Ilsa as she dropped into the kitchen of the MI6 safe house. She could hear a blaring TV through the wall and contemplated how to play this. Storm in, guns blazing? Skulk in and do the deed? Present herself and tell him exactly why she was there?

The question of "how" dogged her each and every time she captured someone for Hades and it never got easier to decide. Oddly enough, despite her angst about it, the victim was usually the one who made the decision, their actions the true measure of how they'd leave this world.

A wave of guilt suddenly swamped her for letting go of Kane. Add in the sharp agony of no longer being in his company and it took every ounce of discipline she possessed to move forward and do Hades's bidding.

Why, why, *why* had it seemed like a good idea to let go?

Ignoring the mounting questions and the continued un-
certainty where Kane was concerned, Ilsa focused in on the
sounds from the other room. The sounds she could hear
through the noise of the TV. Lightning-quick tapping on a
computer keyboard. Heavy breathing. A heartbeat that raced
with uncontrolled adrenaline.

Obviously Alex didn't feel very safe here in the safe
house.

Slipping past the refrigerator, Ilsa stepped into the living room and took in the scene. A scrawny man who looked
like nothing but skin stretched over his bones sat before a
computer on a backless stool. A discarded pack of cigarettes lay next to his keyboard and a haze of smoke hung
over his head, filtering the light from the computer screen.
The T-shirt he wore had faded print covering the back.

As she stepped closer, Ilsa could read the washed-out
writing. WHEN I WAS YOUR AGE PLUTO WAS A PLANET.

Finally! A joke she actually understood.

She purposely kept her interactions with humans limited, which also meant she understood very little of what
they said. Usually, the deeper meaning of a comment was
just out of her reach.

Like Kane's comment about monkey sex. Her insides
had lit up at his mention of sex, for instance, but she had no
idea what he'd really meant.

Was it a compliment? An insult? Both?

Who knew?

A streak of affection slashed through her as she reread
the Pluto T-shirt, but she ruthlessly tamped it down. She
couldn't afford to see Alex as human, with needs and be-
liefs, a life and a mind of his own.

It made destroying him only that much harder.

On a deep breath, she shut out the internal voice of

compassion and stepped closer. Robert's soul was howling at her by now, as if he could make his friend hear him by virtue of all the racket.

But the room remained deathly still, the quiet broken only by Alex's breathing and tapping on the keys.

"I've come for you."

Alex whirled around, a half-finished cigarette dangling from his chapped lips. "You . . . you really did know where to find me."

"Of course I did."

"I know you said you knew where I was, but . . . from one phone call? That was all it took?"

"Well . . ." Phone call? What was he talking about?

Ilsa decided to play along. If there was one thing she'd learned in all her years of gathering those who most certainly didn't want to go with her, it was to sit back and listen. "It takes very little."

Alex's dull blue eyes lit with fervor as he hastily stabbed the cigarette in an ashtray next to the computer keyboard. "Robert said you'd be the answer and he was right."

At the sound of his name, Robert's screaming howls lit up inside her head like a pinball machine she'd seen once when she'd tracked a child molester to a gaming arcade. The shiny lights had intrigued her, but the sorry-ass soul of the man had diverted her attention before she could give the game any further thought.

"The answer?" Ilsa asked him softly, hoping to gain clarity from her own vague questions. "To what?"

"That you could help us. Help us get out of here. This was a bad idea and we never should have made that deal with St. Giles. If you can just get us out"—Alex's gaze darted across the room, then back to her—"I'm willing to make a payment."

Robert's soul quieted at Alex's words, as if he were anxious to listen to his friend's pronouncement. Curious, she pressed for answers. "And what payment do you offer me?"

"You can have our stash of uranium in exchange for my life. Please just remove me from this safe house and you're welcome to the trade with the arms dealers."

The resounding scream that reverberated through her skull indicated *exactly* what Robert thought about the proposed trade. As if somehow he could change things by his carrying on.

You're dead, evil one. Get used to it.

Why were all the truly evil ones unable to accept their lives were over? That whatever plans they'd made were no longer their concern.

Of course, the skull-headed boat she locked them into to cross the River Styx usually brought them around.

The finality of *that* journey was lost on precious few.

"That's a bold pronouncement. How would Robert feel about this?"

"He's gone and I have a bad feeling about this and, well . . . now that we're so close to the decision something doesn't feel right."

These were the worst cases. The repentant ones who came clean at the end. In Alex's case, it was even worse than usual, because he was penitent on his own accord. He didn't even know yet she was here to destroy him.

Alex got to his feet, shifting back and forth on his worn sneakers. His concave chest quivered but his eyes were bright with . . . lust? "You're as beautiful as your voice."

Her victims might dictate the terms of how they died, but this was a new one, as most didn't suddenly sport the urge to take a tumble around the floor. In fact, most could barely bring themselves to look at her. "Excuse me?"

"Your voice. On the phone. So sultry and"—Alex took three tentative steps toward her—"perfect. I haven't been able to stop thinking about it."

The ever-present screams morphed into something different as Robert's soul burst into loud, guffawing cackles. The disembodied reaction shot something far more toxic through her system. Alex had believed he and Robert to be the best of friends and the raucous laughter suggested Robert had felt something else entirely.

Superiority and conceit and a smug arrogance, maybe, but not friendship and devotion and belief.

Without warning, the thought of straddling Alex to kill him disgusted her in some way she couldn't quite define. This pitiful soul who, while not necessarily deserving of mercy, had been duped beyond measure. Dominated by a silver tongue and a devious mind.

Just as she'd been duped by Rhea, all those many, many years ago. And later, by Zeus.

As duty bore down on her, the weight of her choices brought on the hot well of tears. Ilsa felt her throat tighten into a hard knot and tried to swallow around it, desperate for air.

Desperate for life.

Movements stiff, she approached Alex and watched his eyes grow more addled with lust.

The woman that hopelessly craved the chance to be Ilsa knew she couldn't keep on. Couldn't continue to do this and stay sane. So she curled up inside of herself and shut out the call of duty, hiding her true self so deeply even the tainted soul that intertwined with hers couldn't touch her.

On legs that felt made of lead, she took the steps to close the distance between her and Alex. With simple moves, dictated by her victim, she pushed him to the floor and straddled his waist.

Leaning forward, her mouth so near to his their lips practically touched, she whispered, "You know why I'm here."

She heard his loud exhalation of breath. Saw the smile that spread across his face.

And the woman that was Nemesis took one long, slow, deep breath.

Chapter Seven

"Holy shit," Grey breathed as they entered the living room of the safe house from the basement stairwell. Kane came to a full stop just past the doorway and he felt the Aries slam into him from behind. Quinn and Drake had already fanned around him, positioning themselves in a fighting phalanx.

Raw, all-consuming hunger flooded his veins as Kane took in the sight of Ilsa, straddled across the scrawny scientist who lay motionless on the floor.

Through the lingering haze of cigarette smoke, Kane saw discarded food wrappers and heard the blaring TV, screaming about the latest car deals. He ignored all of it as his gaze laser-focused in on the pair on the floor.

Just as in the park, the sight of Ilsa leaning over her victim in such an—intimate—way shot a bolt of need through him.

She shouldn't be doing this.

She shouldn't be here.

She shouldn't be *tainted* in such a way.

Unable to hold back his ire and the horror of seeing her

do this a second time, he surged forward. "Get off him. I told you he's mine."

Ilsa leaped to her feet immediately, her eyes darting to each Warrior that stood before her, until finally allowing her gaze to rest on Kane. "I told you I had a task to complete."

"We would have dealt with him. I needed information and now"—he tossed a glance toward the evening's second dead scientist—"that won't be happening."

She shrugged, an oh-so-slight lift of the shoulders that looked as if it cost her great effort. "I already got the information you needed before . . . I took care of him. Over there." She pointed to a large metal trunk in the corner of the room. "The uranium is in there. Take it and give it to MI6 to deal with. The scientists clearly won't be needing it any longer and we don't want it to fall into the wrong hands."

Kane reached out for her arm, moving into her personal space at the same time. "And you think that makes it okay? You got my answers so you spared me the need to do my job."

Her gaze raked over him as scorn curled the corner of her lips. "You need all the help you can get right now, ace."

A loud series of coughs went up behind him as Ilsa's words registered. "I'm doing just fine, sweetheart."

"You can barely stand up straight."

"Don't you worry your pretty . . . little . . . head about it." A loud rushing hit Kane's ears as frustrated fury swam behind his eyes. Knees buckling, he stumbled forward, wrapping his arms around Ilsa for support.

The poison stomped a nasty two-step on his muscles, twisting the sinuous fibers under its evil spurs.

"Kane!" Ilsa tightened her arms around him, her slight body bearing his full weight without any noticeable effort.

"What is wrong with you? And why are you chasing after me when it's clear you're running on empty?"

Quinn moved up to the two of them. "Kane. She's right. Enough of the macho bullshit. You're pasty white and you look like you can barely stand. You need to go home and sleep for a while or the fucking poison is going to beat you this time."

Kane struggled to keep upright, the bull's words landing like a nuclear missile in the middle of the room. "Damn it, Quinn. Why'd you—?"

"Poison?" Ilsa's grip on him faltered and, despite his weakness, Kane felt his body stirring as his hand brushed the curve of her hip. "What poison? That's what's wrong with you?"

"He's not well." Kane felt Quinn's meaty paw grab him at the elbow. "That's all you need to know."

Ilsa's own grip held tight, but the tension in the room rose to boiling as Drake and Grey closed the short distance to stand with Quinn. Her voice was cold steel as they surrounded her. "I don't think so. He needs medical attention. Help. *Something*."

Quinn's grip didn't lessen. "Well, then, let's just zip him over to Lenox Hill. I'm sure they have lots of doctors there who majored in black-magic poisons and immortal vascular systems in med school."

Kane blinked once. Twice. Then he clenched his jaw and tried to focus on the room. "No one can help me, Ilsa. It's got to work its way through."

"But where did it come from? You're an immortal."

Blinking again, Kane fought to keep his attention on the room—fought to ignore the stabs of pain that were doing everything they could to wear him down from the inside—

but he knew he'd pushed too hard. The poison was too close to full strength and he just didn't have anything left. Gasping, he grasped at the right words. "Bad. Choices."

The room swam as Kane felt himself falling forward into Ilsa's body. Quinn let go, hollering for Grey and Drake to help him, but Ilsa didn't need any more than a millisecond to react to Quinn's lack of contact.

Before he felt his Warrior brothers' hands on him, Ilsa pushed them into the stratosphere.

Ilsa stroked Kane's hair as she sat with his head in her lap. She hadn't taken them very far, teleporting them into a small detached garage she'd seen behind the safe house when she'd arrived earlier. The string of garages that ran behind the block of homes appeared to be an old, renovated mews area, and the garage had a surprisingly warm coziness to it.

What had possibly possessed her to do this? Gods, she needed to get a grip. It was all she could do to try to get away from him, and yet somehow, here she was, with a very large, very dangerous man in her lap. An individual who kept the company of other very large, very dangerous men.

For reasons that weren't entirely clear, her need to protect him overruled every other thought in her head.

And your need to touch him had nothing to do with it?

Ilsa resolutely ignored the taunts of her conscience as she sat with her back against the wall, Kane stretched out to the side on an old picnic blanket. He'd been unconscious for almost ten minutes and she alternated between numbing fear that the port was too much for his system and relief that she had gotten him away from the other Warriors. She needed to think and there was no way to do that with four large men bearing down on her.

Well, three actively bearing down and one who just wanted her to go away so he could suffer in peace.

For all her bravado and ready knowledge she could handle herself, the lot of them were rather intimidating.

Okay. *Very* intimidating.

And, if she were honest with herself, she didn't want to just think. She could think alone. What she wanted was to have free access to Kane.

To ask him questions. To see his reactions. To simply drink him in.

Another minute ticked by in silence as Ilsa gently stroked his hair.

Poison?

And based on Quinn's flippant answer about Lenox Hill Hospital, a toxin that had its genesis in some sort of powerful black magic. How long had he suffered with this? When they'd last been together, his strength had seemed limitless.

Even now, despite the clear signs the poison ravaged his body, he was still a formidable opponent. The man's muscles were forged of steel. Although his body was in prime condition, she suspected it was sheer, stubborn will alone that kept the poison from completely taking over. A feat, she suspected, a lesser man wouldn't have been able to do.

"Where are we?" Kane mumbled.

"Not too far from where we started."

"But far enough you had to port me here." The words held a bitter flavor as they fell from his lips.

Well, if you weren't pushing yourself so hard. Those were words she wanted to say. A reprimand that would put Kane in his place and keep her firmly in control of the situation.

Only, as she sat there, stroking his hair and gazing on

that incredible face—strong jaw, high cheekbones that looked even higher with the slightly gaunt look he'd gotten from the poison, and black eyelashes so long they made spiky curls—Ilsa found herself asking something else entirely.

Something that caused the heat to pool between her thighs before she even uttered the first word.

"Is your strength tied to the same things as other immortals?"

Kane's eyelids never lifted, but his voice was more solid than when he first awoke. "Uh-huh."

"So the usual. Food and sleep are restorative."

A wry grin lit the corner of those firm lips. "If I could keep much of anything down, yes, food would be restorative. And I haven't been sleeping much, either, so same deal."

Did she dare do it? Did she dare ask the question she desperately wanted an answer to?

"And sex? Sex brings you back, too, right?"

This time, those eyelids did open and those dark onyx orbs fixed on her. "Sex, yes. Orgasm, specifically, brings me back to strength."

"I see."

"Do you?"

Was she mistaken or was there more to that question than his words implied? And could she risk more with him?

Oh gods, yes. A million times yes.

Then his eyes closed again and his voice held that same muffled tone as when he'd first awakened. "Yeah, well, now you have your answers. Answers to questions you wouldn't need to ask if Quinn didn't have such a big fucking mouth."

"I'm glad Quinn has such a big fucking mouth."

And then the decision was made before she could think for one more nanosecond about consequences.

Or what an inopportune moment it was to do what they were about to do.

Or her deal with Emmett.

Ilsa pressed her lips to Kane's and let herself go.

Freedom, sweet freedom, filled her, crowding out all the ugliness. It drowned out the souls she carried inside of her for their trip to the Underworld. It chased away the guilt she felt for her bargain with Emmett. And it made her feel whole.

It made her feel like . . . Ilsa.

With tentative, seeking movements, she pressed her tongue against Kane's mouth and was immediately gratified by his ready acceptance. Before she could explore further, he took over the kiss, his tongue sweeping up to meet hers, demanding immediate possession.

The sweet suction built between them as they explored each other, her light, breathy moans breaking the silence of the quiet room.

Long, glorious moments spun out, their reality almost more than she could have hoped for. She'd dreamed about this—wept for the insane longing she couldn't define and couldn't deny—and now, to finally *feel* him again, their lips pressed together in fervent need.

What was this madness? What was it about this man that made her forget all she'd believed in? All she'd hungered for, for so very long.

Hate.

Vengeance.

Retribution.

Emotions that had sustained her for millennia.

But none of it mattered when she was with him. None of it had any power over her.

As Kane's tongue tangled with hers in dark, powerful

thrusts that imitated the joining of their bodies, she felt her world tip. Everything she thought she knew—everything she thought she wanted—faded in the heat that lived between them.

Kane's hand reached up, pressing the back of her head so he could pull her closer and take even greater control of her mouth. Ilsa reveled in the feel, the possessive movement so sexy she felt it all the way down to the answering pull at the apex of her thighs.

Without warning, he pulled his mouth away and struggled to a sitting position, then stumbled to his feet on shaky legs. "We can't do this. I need you to take me back to my Warrior brothers and then we can figure out what to do with you. You're not seducing me again."

Seduce him?

With the sensual haze broken, she could only stare at him. "You want to leave? And what do you mean by seduce you *again*?"

"Oh, don't play the innocent, Ilsa. Six months ago you seduced me, fucked me and left me drugged in my bed." Anger, resentment and—was that hurt?—swam in the onyx depths of his eyes.

"*You* seduced *me*." Which was completely true. Her three days with Kane had come as a complete shock. Her intent had been to get close to him, drug him to get a vial of his blood to confirm he truly was an immortal and then get out of there. But the attraction that lived between them had taken her totally off guard, off her game and off on a journey she couldn't have predicted no matter how hard she might have tried.

A sneer dragged down the corners of his lush lips and his dark eyes grew even darker, if that were possible. "Funny how we have a vastly different recollection of the events."

"You know, how is it I'm the only one to blame for what transpired between us? I didn't exactly see you suffering in that big silk-sheeted bed of yours, Kane Montague. In fact"—she allowed her gaze to travel slowly down the front of his body, coming to rest on the front of his jeans—"you seemed to be a more than willing participant."

Those dark eyes were absolutely smoldering when she finally lifted her gaze back to his. "I was a willing participant in good sex. I was not, however, a willing participant in manipulation. You took care of that all by yourself."

"And what about your ulterior motives? What were you planning on doing with me after it was over? Send me on my way and ignore me? Act like nothing happened between us the next time you saw me at work?" Although Ilsa had no idea how this relationship stuff actually worked between men and women, she'd watched enough TV in the last six months to get an idea of what happened between men and women after they had sex. And not all of it ended very nicely.

If she hadn't left first, would Kane have wanted to keep her around? Or did the very fact that she chose to leave first cause him to think of her as some sort of challenge?

What would Oprah say about it?

"You're not an innocent, Ilsa. And lies don't become you."

Now what in the name of Hades was that supposed to mean? *Shit.* For all the TV she'd consumed and her desperate urge to learn the nuances of modern-day society, she really had no idea what he meant.

Sure, she'd lied about the syringe. But the rest of it wasn't a lie. The feelings he drew from her in his bed weren't a lie, either.

From his tone and the hard set of his jaw, however, she knew a losing battle when she saw one. He'd never believe she'd been innocent of sex before they'd met.

Never.

So why not meet his expectations, her conscience whispered, *and get a taste of him again?*

Just one.

More.

Taste.

With deliberate movements, Ilsa sauntered toward him, her gaze roaming the length of his body once more. "Why won't you let me give you what you need?"

"What I need is to get back to my brothers."

She reached out and laid a hand on his chest, her palm over the beat of his heart. "You need to get some strength back."

Ilsa felt his stomach muscles tighten in response, their ripple echoing through his skin and up to her palm, even as his voice stayed irritatingly firm. "We can't start this again. And we certainly can't start it here."

"You need this, Kane. And you need me. I know that galls your stubborn, pigheaded, I-can-handle-anything nature, but you need me." She couldn't pull her gaze away from his, and she couldn't stop the words. "You need me."

"Fat lot of good that did me before."

"You weren't sick before. This will go a long way toward regaining some badly needed strength."

"Oh, so you want to fuck me out of the kindness of your heart? How thoughtful of you."

At that, Ilsa jumped back, dropping her hand from his chest. Hurt and pain poured through her, like the slash of a thousand swords. "I won't be spoken to that way."

"Why not? You set the tone for what's between us six

months ago. It's a funny time to suddenly develop a sense of self-righteousness about it."

"You make it sound so . . . so dirty." She hated the taste of the word on her tongue. Hated what it implied.

"We had a good time. A few days of fun. That's all."

His words continued to slash at her, tearing any hope they could share something—however fleeting—to ribbons. Soul-deep hurt filled her, his rejection so harsh she felt as if she'd been slapped. "If that's all, then why are you so angry at me?"

"You left, Ilsa. And you left me in a drugged stupor. I won't play the fool again."

She whirled on him, the large room closing in on her as the air grew heavy with their circular argument. "Well, you won't have to if you keep doing this to yourself. The moniker "immortal" isn't completely true and we both know that. There are vulnerabilities. We all live with the knowledge that there are ways we can be killed. Whatever's living in your system is working damn hard to eliminate you and clearly you're going to let it."

Kane's shoulders set in a rigid line. "I'll fight it off. I've done it before and I can do it again."

"Before? You've had this happen before?"

He nodded, his voice quiet, even as the impact of his words hit her like a gunshot. "I've lived with it for three hundred years."

Her only reaction was a deep inhale of breath. Three hundred years? He'd lived with something this detrimental for that long? Something so devastating?

"I can help you."

"I don't need your help."

"You're not the one looking at you. I can see it in the haunted look in your eyes. This time's different, isn't it?"

"It's not different."

Ilsa tried again, the knowledge she was right increasing in power. "I can see it, Kane. In your eyes. Something's different this time."

He finally nodded, as if resigned, that luscious mouth of his a grim slash. "The poison. It's in its rising phase."

"Rising phase?"

"Yes. It builds day by day until it reaches peak strength."

"Let me help you."

The edges of his mouth formed a tight sneer. "Like you helped me before?" At her small moue of surprise, the sneer vanished, replaced by a look so bleak it reached straight out and wrapped her heart in an iron fist. "What can you do? Besides, maybe I'm beyond help."

Ilsa walked toward him and reached for his face. Settling her hands on either cheek, she leaned in closer. "Maybe we both are. Let me at least try."

At that, Kane nodded. And then there were no more words.

Kane closed his eyes and leaned in to Ilsa's touch. This was a monstrously bad idea. He knew it as well as he knew his own name, but he was beyond caring.

For a moment—just one moment—he could close his eyes and revel in her touch. Catch his breath. And try to gather up as much energy as he could to go another round with the merciless taskmaster haunting his veins.

It also meant he could have her. One more time. With full knowledge of what she was.

And full knowledge that they went to each other without pretense.

Eyes still closed, he willed himself to calm down. Willed the air into his lungs in a slow, even pattern. Inhale. Exhale.

Inhale. Exha—

"Ilsa?" His eyes popped open at the tug on his jeans. This was a seriously bad idea. He knew that. Knew it with the certainty of a man who'd lived an endless number of lifetimes.

So why was he trusting her?

And why did the feel of her pressed against him fire him in ways he'd never felt in any of those lifetimes?

"Shhh, Kane. Let me do this."

She tugged again, a small triumphant smile crossing her features as she managed to get the top button open on his jeans. He reached for her hands, holding them still. "Are you sure?"

"Yes." She slipped her fingers from his grasp, her movements deft and determined.

What the he—? His head swam as she got the zipper down, her fingers brushing over his penis. He groaned from the touch as his body went on high alert.

Near death to rock hard in three seconds flat. If he wasn't so desperate for her he would have laughed.

But he couldn't allow her to do it.

No matter how badly he wanted it.

"Ilsa. You have to stop. You can't do this. It's not right."

"Would you shut up and leave me alone?" She placed one hand on his hips as her other stayed inside his open fly. She was quick, he'd give her that. She already had a hand inside his briefs, clenched around him like a tight leather glove that hadn't yet been broken in.

"This isn't—" he panted, trying desperately to figure out how to stop her. And desperately wishing he didn't have to. "This isn't how it's supposed to be."

"The universe says otherwise."

"This is your big plan?"

She pressed her lips against his and he felt her smile as she whispered into his mouth, "Shut up and take it, big guy." Her hand fisted around the base of his shaft and with skillful movements she pumped his flesh. "You can argue with me later."

He knew it the moment he lost the battle. His head fell back and his hips moved to the rhythm she set as he pressed himself into her hand.

Waves of power crashed through his life force as she caressed him with long, smooth strokes. Somewhere along the way, she'd managed to lower his jeans and his briefs as he felt cool air hit the lower part of his stomach.

And then he felt a lot of air as the position of her hands shifted.

Opening his eyes, he realized she wasn't standing in front of him any longer with her lush curves pressed to him.

And then Kane couldn't think at all as her hot mouth wrapped around his cock, drawing every rational thought from his head. Although her movements weren't nearly as sure with her mouth as they'd been with her hand, the tentative, daring strokes of her tongue slammed sensation after sensation through him in blistering waves.

Mind-numbing pleasure crashed into him as her tongue wove a web of seduction. She might be on her knees, but he was the helpless one.

Powerless to resist her.

Utterly vulnerable and open to her.

Helpless to deny her.

Her tongue was like a brand as she worked it around his cock. Sharp little darts with her tongue at the tip, followed by wet suction as she worked her way down over the crown. Lapping waves of pleasure as she caressed down to the base.

Over and over, she drew on him with her hot, wet mouth, driving him deliberately toward his moment of greatest physical defenselessness.

He knew he'd gone around the bend. His already tight body grew even harder, the urge to spill himself something he couldn't fight any longer.

With determination that matched the generous woman before him, he gripped her shoulders, pulling her up. Ignoring her protests, he crashed his mouth to hers, reaching for her hand. Placing it on his painfully eager cock, he growled into her mouth, "I'm yours, baby."

In great, mindless waves of pleasure he pressed himself against her hand and as the very essence of himself spilled in her palm, his life force ignited fiercely in his veins. The life-affirming power of his orgasm offered a punishing blow to the poison, even if it would be only a temporary respite.

As he fought to even his breathing, Kane couldn't stop touching her. Face, shoulders, back—his hands roamed over her, seeking the reassurance of her warm, solid body.

And still she gave, her lips pressed to his, her hands following their own path in comforting strokes over his stomach, hips and back.

With gentle hands, Kane ran his fingers down her cheeks, over her jaw, to cup her face. And as his tongue took possession of hers, he knew he was in some serious trouble.

This woman was dangerous, with her doelike eyes and tender touch. She was dangerous to his peace of mind. But, most of all, she was dangerous to his fierce, ironclad control.

And he had no idea what he was going to do about it.

Every cell in her body hummed in pleasure as Kane's quivering body pressed against hers. She'd pleasured him. This giant of a man, who looked like a god and had the strength of three, had been pleasured.

Seduction, my ass, Ilsa thought fiercely. This went way deeper than seduction. This was a need that they both shared.

With the last few moments replaying in her head, Ilsa watched the awesome strength that grew from his moment of greatest vulnerability.

She felt it—no, saw it—happen before her eyes.

His stance became straighter. The fiber of his muscles tightened under her hands. The circles under his eyes lessened and the weight and strain that rode him lightened, as if by magic.

Kane's head fell into the crook of her neck, his eyes closed as his body calmed and his breathing returned to normal.

She shifted to pull back when his hands gripped her shoulders and pulled her body against him. He whispered against her hair, "Thank you, Ilsa."

"You're welcome."

They stood there for a moment as time spun out. Even though it was just that—a moment—Ilsa was loath to see it end.

Just a moment.

As she stood there in the quiet with Kane, Ilsa thought about how she felt in his arms. Thought about the feelings this man could pull from her with the simplest of ease. Thought about how she'd like to find some way to assuage her guilt for what had happened six months ago.

Could she do it? Could she actually risk telling him the truth?

Did she have any other choice?

"Kane." Her voice was whisper soft and even she could barely hear it in the silence.

"Hmmm?"

"I need to tell you something." When he made no attempt to move, she spoke louder. "I have to tell you something. About six months ago. When we were together the first time."

He lifted his head at that, the sloe-eyed haze of sexual satisfaction giving way to a different sort of interest.

"What?"

"Um. Well." Suddenly, them standing there disheveled didn't feel like a good idea. "Pull up your pants first."

His look was unreadable as he stepped back, quickly righting his clothes. "Okay. What did you want to tell me?"

"I took something from you. Before."

Sheer puzzlement covered his face, from the quick of his lips to the questions that rode high in his gaze. "You stole from me?"

"Not your possessions. Well. Not really."

Oh gods, why was this so hard? If this was what admitting a wrong felt like, she understood why humans did it so infrequently.

Ice coated his next words. "Come on, Ilsa. Out with it."

On a deep breath, she closed her eyes and leaped. "Six months ago, when we were together, after I drugged you, I stole a vial of your blood."

After several seconds of stone-cold silence, Ilsa's eyes popped open. She had to gauge his reaction.

Had he heard her?

One look in his lethal gaze and she knew the answer to that. What she didn't know was why she thought it was such a bright idea to say anything.

"Kane?"

When he didn't answer her, just continued to stare at

her with that cold, penetrating look, she pressed again. "Kane. What is it?"

She saw him struggle to form words. Saw him think about, then discard, whatever it was he was going to say.

And then it didn't matter as a piercing scream rent the air, distinctly coming from the direction of the safe house.

Chapter Eight

"Hang on to me." Her fear of recrimination vanished in the face of the threat back inside the safe house. When Ilsa looked at Kane, the guilt and self-loathing that had filled her was already cataloged to her subconscious for another time. "I'll port us back there to save time."

Kane nodded and laid his hand on her forearm. "To the basement. We need to assess the threat."

Pleased he didn't argue, she flashed the two of them to his specification, equally satisfied he kept his feet when they hit the basement floor.

He *was* stronger.

Loud thumps resounded on the floorboards above, indicative of a battle in full force. "Who can possibly be here?" she whispered to him, not exactly sure why she'd lowered her voice, as the risk of being heard over the loud shouts was nonexistent.

"Why don't you tell me? You were here first. More people you need to steal bodily fluids from? Oh, wait. Was that part of your little charade back there in the safe house? Grab a few swimmers while you were at it, too?"

The tone of Kane's words—layers of distrust and anger, stretched over a healthy core of suspicion—penetrated through the loud racket from above. Whirling on him, her hands went to her hips of their own accord. "Don't be crass. I was trying to come clean—trying to make up for what I did to you. You have every right to be mad, but don't you dare suggest I put your friends up there"—she pointed to the ceiling—"in danger."

"You've set me up from the first. I've just been too dumb to see it." Kane muttered into his hands as he scrubbed them over his face in tired movements, "Just like before. Will I *ever* learn?"

"Whatever you think I did or didn't do today, you can get rid of the thought. I wasn't here. Remember?"

"Yeah. You had your mouth latched on to my cock. Mighty diverting of you, sweetheart. Well done."

"Son of a fucking bitch." Anger—soul-deep, raw and entirely self-righteous—swelled in her breast. By the gods, she was done being judged without benefit of a fair hearing. She'd told the truth! As scary as it was, she'd told the truth.

And still she was being treated as she'd always been. Sentenced to punishment without even the benefit of her own voice ringing in her defense, explaining her cause.

With swift movements, Ilsa launched herself toward the basement steps, following the path Kane and his brothers had trod less than an hour before.

And landed in the middle of a fight like something out of a Highland battle from the Middle Ages.

Men fought wildly, their large bodies clashing, retreating and clashing again in combat. A strange, static electricity filled the room, crackling around her and standing the hair on her arms on end.

What was this?

She recognized Kane's Warrior brothers immediately. Quinn and Drake both fought off two men each, while Grey tussled with a burly man in a neon green T-shirt and bright orange workout pants. The garish counterbalance of Grey's elegance with the neon color highlighted the battle playing out between them.

Both grunted and groaned, using all their limbs to try and subdue the other. Legs flailed, arms thrust in repeated motion and both men seemed intent on strangling each other.

With morbid fascination, Ilsa watched as Grey gained the upper hand—literally—and clamped his long, tapered fingers on Neon's neck. Movements deft, and undeniably lethal, the man's head snapped under Grey's expert grip.

As usual, when this close to death, Ilsa waited for the soul to separate from the body. Even though he wasn't hers to deliver to Hades—or anywhere else—she was in tune with the process. And with this guy, she felt . . . nothing.

Where was that fleeting brush? The ethereal essence of another?

And then the reason became evident as Neon disintegrated into a puddle before her eyes, the skin that stretched over his body shriveling and shrinking, like there was nothing to hold him up.

Where was his skeleton? His muscles? His organs?

The sounds of the other battles faded away in her fascination with what was happening in front of her. Just like earlier . . .

Just like in the alley behind Equinox.

What *were* these men? And why were they so intent on Kane and his fellow Warriors? And how had they found this place?

The sounds of combat reengaged her consciousness as

Kane's battle cry resounded through the room. Grey had already moved to help Drake while Kane stalked unerringly toward Quinn's side, a wicked, daggerlike instrument in his hands, pulled from a hiding place at his ankle.

A hiding place she'd never even seen or thought to look for when they were together before.

Had this man really made her lose every instinct for combat and self-protection? She'd had her hands all over him, for the gods' sake. While she hadn't made an inspection of his lower legs and feet, she'd stood mere millimeters from a nasty-looking weapon and had never even considered the possibility he'd be armed.

And then even her self-recrimination was gone as she watched Kane move. He was all sinew and muscle, full of lethal and predatory grace.

Without any warning, shock slammed through Ilsa once again. Her throat tightened on a scream as a large black scorpion, nearly as tall as Kane, rode along his back, its deadly tail sweeping in a wide arc behind Kane.

"'Bout fucking time, Monte!" Quinn shouted. "You got a clean shot?"

Kane raised the weapon, while at the same time the scorpion's tail swept in another arc. With movements so defined they appeared choreographed, the tail knocked one of Quinn's foes off his feet as Kane slashed the wicked dagger along the man's neck.

A loud pop rent the air as a great flare of electricity lit the knife edge with a spark. Then that body began disintegrating, just like the first.

Again, no soul.

Nothing spiritual marred the room. Instead, the body of the man was quickly becoming nothing more than an oily pool that seeped into the beige rug. Soon, a large spot was the only thing left to show for his life.

Ilsa thought she understood Themis's Warriors. In her plans for revenge, she'd researched the Great Agreement between Themis and Zeus. Researched how the Warriors were empowered and how they protected humanity.

But this?

Foes who disintegrated into oily pools of grease? She knew nothing of it. Had never heard of a creature that looked human but who died in that way, like his body was merely a shell. An image of humanity that hid . . . well . . . nothing.

In all the sixteen millennia of her life, she'd never seen anything such as this. Were they men? What filled them with life? Which god or goddess did they belong to? Or did they even belong to a member of the Pantheon?

Before Ilsa could think on it any longer, Kane and Quinn were already in motion, the greasy mess of no interest. Although his weariness was rapidly returning, shadowing his every movement, Kane fought valiantly with his brothers, his movements keeping pace with theirs.

As he parried and thrust toward Quinn's opponent, the room's overhead light gleamed off the edge of his blade now slick with the same oil that soaked the carpet. Kane kicked and punched when he couldn't get a clean thrust, his battle skills personal and almost intimate in the closed-in space.

The creature—the scorpion—had folded itself in on Kane's back once they were in close proximity to Quinn, disappearing into nothingness, as if it had never even been there.

Ilsa knew she should jump into the fray. She should help these men, but for her very existence, she couldn't understand what was unfolding before her.

Who were these men Kane and his brothers fought?

And why weren't they truly corporeal? Where was the blood? The proof of their humanity?

Had they suffered the same sort of curse Zeus originally levied on her? But if they did, how did they have physical mass and strength?

And what of that scorpion?

A movement from the direction of the second set of stairs drew her attention away from the battle and from her thoughts. Stairs rose at the far side of the room, with a landing at the top that was visible from below. A wooden railing framed the landing, preventing anyone from toppling to the first floor. A sixth man by her count stood at the top of the stairs, his gaze focused on Kane. Time slowed as, without warning, the man leaped over the railing, hurtling himself toward the fray below.

The scream built in her throat, rushing from her vocal cords with a painful blast of sound.

The predator landed squarely on Kane's back, a long dagger gleaming in his hand.

Kane felt the unbearable pressure as a heavy weight rode his back. A foul, fetid stench filled his nostrils as waves of static bombarded him from all sides. Add up all the clues and it didn't take ten thousand years of battling the same opponent to figure out a sixth Destroyer had joined the party.

Fucking shithead has a grip like a monkey's. Smells like one, too.

The only good thing about his current predicament was that the asshole was too close to lob a fireball at him. Those great rolling balls of energy that flew from a fully charged Destroyer were a challenge for any Warrior when he was at his normal strength. The energy pockets stung like a bitch and too many allowed the Destroyer to weaken his opponent.

It killed him to admit it, but in his weakened state, Kane knew he'd be flat on his ass in about three nanoseconds if he were hit with one.

Large forearms wrapped around his windpipe and Kane reached up with his free hand to tug at the grip, while with his Xiphos in the other hand, he swept a longways cut down the asshole's forearm. The Destroyer didn't let go, but the movement loosened his grip. The slight easing of pressure was just enough for Kane to wedge his free hand between his neck and his opponent, pushing for more air.

The weight added a few additional problems, including a decided lack of vision. Funny how one hundred and seventy-five pounds of asshole on your back had a way of doing that to a person.

Kane couldn't see Grey, Quinn or Drake, so he could only assume their battles were as challenging as his. But damn it all, he sure would have loved some backup. He didn't even have his scorpion, the writhing horde of energy covering his back ensuring the animal stayed locked inside his aura.

A loud scream broke through the grunts and groans flying all around him. A streak of color and long, luscious legs streamed past him and then Kane felt a second, lighter weight drop onto the first.

Ilsa. His little deceitful warrioress had decided to join the fray.

Gritting his teeth, Kane bent his knees, attempting to support the added weight. It nearly worked, his balance surprisingly even, until the two weights on his back launched into their own battle, twisting and turning.

Well, this is fun. What the hell was he supposed to do with three hundred pounds on his fucking back? At least the stranglehold on his windpipe was gone, but they also had him at a disadvantage because the Destroyer wouldn't drop his leg lock. Nor would he shift far enough to allow the scorpion out.

The instinct to slam the weight against a hard surface had Kane stumbling drunkenly toward the wall closest to him. Putting every ounce of strength he had into his movements, he rushed backward for the wall, desperate to dislodge the weight.

Almost . . . just nearly . . . bloody hell!

Kane pulled his landing and stopped just short of impact at the sudden realization that Ilsa would take the brunt of a crash against the wall. The combined weight and force of two full-sized men slamming into her would put her through the wall if she were lucky. Seeing as how this structure had stood the test of time—and World War II bombings—the plaster would be the likely victor and she a mere spot on it.

The poison, which had been blessedly silent since Ilsa's generous ministrations, reared up to further weaken him.

Long, sinuous waves of pain coated his chest, making it hard to breathe as he fought the Destroyers.

Fuck. Fuckfuckfuckfuck. How did the damn poison know? It was like whatever organ he needed most at any given time was where the shit struck.

Tightening the grip on his Xiphos, Kane fought the poison and the soulless monster currently attached to his person. He slashed at one of the legs wrapped around his midsection. Just as the forearm slash had given him much-needed air, the leg lock lightened enough to free the intense pressure on his rib cage and proved to Kane he might actually have a chance of getting the asshole off without hurting Ilsa in the process.

Even if she had brought this on all of them.

He slashed again, this time at the other leg, the sharp edge of his blade making a loud sucking noise as he pulled it from the Destroyer's body, full of that slick oil that made the minions of Enyo so lethal.

Pure, semiconductive energy. Their human appearance covered a liquid core that carried the electrical power of a lightning storm.

As Kane plunged the Xiphos again, something nagged at his subconscious.

Had Ilsa brought this on them? Despite her confession about stealing his blood, she had seemed as surprised by the melee going on in the house as he had once they'd ported back into the basement. And the hurt anger he'd seen in the depths of her eyes at his accusation was real.

Wasn't it?

And what did it matter anyway? He knew, sure as he knew the sun would rise tomorrow, he didn't have the balls to kill her.

It wasn't rational and it wasn't smart, but it was the truth.

Ignoring the new reality of whatever he shared with the woman, Kane forced his full attention back to the fight at hand. With skills honed over thousands of years of battle, he took a deep breath. His movements slow and deliberate, he took a moment to make sure he had his full balance, planting his feet and bending his knees to ensure his lower body held the writhing weight on his back.

There would be one chance to do this. One opportunity to do it without killing either himself or Ilsa in the process.

Holding steady, Kane attuned himself to the rhythm of

the fight above him. She obviously knew enough to go for the head, because Ilsa struck repeatedly at the Destroyer's face, ears and neck. Her blows were steady and true, and each was met with a back head butt from the Destroyer as he worked in counterbalance to subdue her.

Willing himself into a state of calm, Kane shut out the battle cries of his Warrior brothers. Shut off the jovial spikes of renewed pain the poison pressed to his organs. Even blocked out the pain-filled moans that Ilsa uttered when the Destroyer struck her, despite the fact they racked him with angry fury each time she took a hit.

He had one shot and he had to do this right, or he risked hurting her as well.

Steady . . . steady . . . and . . . now!

With an aim born of well-honed battle skills, Kane slammed the Xiphos into the Destroyer's head. A loud sucking sound accompanied the force of his movements. The pressure and weight on his back stopped and the battle ceased immediately as the large man fell to the ground, clutching his head. Ilsa tumbled after him, falling on top of him in a heap.

Kane whirled to finish the job, but the Destroyer had already rolled out of immediate range of both him and Ilsa.

Scrambling to her feet, Ilsa shifted into battle stance, proof she was as engaged in this skirmish as the rest of them. "Kane. What can I do?"

Leaping toward the Destroyer, Kane shouted instructions as he went. "His neck, Ilsa. It's all in the neck. You have to snap it."

He'd nearly closed the gap when Drake and the Destroyer he was battling fell into his path. The momentum of two men engaged in mortal combat stopped Kane's forward progress and forced him to his knees. Frustration clenched his stomach in knots, the tight pain a suitable rival to the poison's clawing hold.

Drake's voice was barely winded as he tossed off directions. "Monte, give me a hand. Underneath me."

Without needing any further direction, their movements already in sync with each other, Kane shifted himself into position. Drake used that to his advantage, pushing the Destroyer toward the stumbling block made by Kane's body.

Kane felt it as the Destroyer fell down over him. A wave of static electricity washed over every inch of his skin in prickling awareness.

Drake took advantage of the downed Destroyer immediately. Swinging his Xiphos in a deadly arc, he slashed the Destroyer's throat. The body deflated immediately, disintegrating into a large greasy pool.

Kane struggled to regain his feet, but Drake's weight, combined with the slippery, oily substance that now coated them both, slowed his movements. As he and Drake worked to free themselves from the slimy mess, the Destroyer who'd leaped on Kane's back moved toward them, a dagger held high in his hand as he ran.

"Kane!" Ilsa screamed, as her body evaporated in a port, reappearing almost immediately at his side.

Despite the speed of the port, Ilsa wasn't fast enough.

The moment spun out in front of Kane in slow motion.

Drake leaped as Kane did, his attention focused on the Destroyer, his stance further proof he was fully prepared to take the brunt of the attack. Although their Pisces managed to shift the asshole's momentum, shoving him off balance, the dagger that was aimed at Kane's throat brushed in a straight line across his collarbone.

Kane felt the dagger slice through his T-shirt into flesh, an arc of liquid fire branding his skin like an iron.

Great, gulping waves of heat consumed him from the inside out as the venom that lived under his skin rose up in happy waves of agony.

What was this?

Kane fought for consciousness. Fought to gain some perspective on a world that was rapidly tilting on its axis.

Although he could feel pain as an immortal—and a dagger thrust was never pleasant—it generally held no power over him. Even the poison, for all its deadly potential, had its limits. But this soul-searing agony was something . . . different.

Black spots swam before his eyes and all the noise in the room grew very far away, as if he listened through the opposite end of a megaphone.

"Kane!" *Was that Ilsa?*

"Stay with me, buddy!" *Drake? Or was it Grey?*

Kane felt the action going on around him, but he had no control over his body. The poison that lived under his skin cackled, tap-dancing great, happy circles on his nerve endings.

The thought hit him that he should make his limbs move. Should run after the Destroyer with the dagger. Should try and help his Warrior brothers with their own battles.

Instead, he let the black spots fold in on themselves until there was no more light.

Only the warm welcome of darkness.

"Kane!" Ilsa screamed his name again, but got no response. His body slumped to the floor in a heavy sprawl. Drake was already in motion, reaching for his fallen brother and hollering for Grey's and Quinn's assistance.

Her heart flopped over at the sight of his still body. Torn,

Ilsa wanted to be at his side, but she also wanted to take down the man—thing—who'd done this to Kane.

But what, exactly, had the thing done?

Kane was an immortal. A knife slash shouldn't have such power over him. She'd even seen humans withstand more, especially in the throes of an adrenaline rush.

Was he *that* weakened by the poison in his veins that a nonfatal knife slash could fell him?

The guy with the dagger was already across the room, heading for the door. She watched as he tossed a last, sneering glance at the room, his gaze roaming over the various greasy spots embedded across the floor.

So much for brothers in arms, she thought. *More like no honor among thieves.*

With one last glance of her own toward Kane, she imagined herself outside, allowing the port to take her across the room, out the door and directly in the guy's path as he departed through the front door.

Air rushed through her ears in loud swells, the sound of the leap consuming her for a brief moment.

Unerring and precise, Ilsa slammed into the guy as he cleared the front door. "Gotcha, asshole."

He'd had the upper hand in the house because of their positions, her hold from behind tenuous at best, but she wouldn't give it to him again. Ilsa felt his large body heave great breaths under her hands as she pressed him against the brick wall next to the front door. Early-morning light rose up behind them and birds twittered their greetings to the sun.

His first thrust she anticipated, as well as his second, but Ilsa held her ground, her hands wrapped on his neck and her body flat against him, holding him still against the wall.

Although they didn't look well matched, the size of her body was absolutely no indication of her true strength.

"Get off me, bitch." He grunted, thrusting himself forward for the third time, attempting to push her off balance.

"No such luck, dickhead. I want to know who sent you."

His voice had the refined cadence of the English, but his words were pure gutter. "Fuck off, bitch. I don't owe you anything."

"Hmmm." Ilsa painted a thoughtful look on her face, before leaning in toward his ear. Her voice like velvet in the cool air of early morning, she whispered, "While you're in corporeal form, are you as vulnerable as the rest of them? Hmmm . . . I wonder."

Before he could even process her question, her hand snaked between them. With swift movements, Ilsa reached down his pants and her fingers clamped around a decidedly male form.

With one hard yank, she twisted his balls in a tight squeeze.

The resounding scream gave her the answer she was looking for. "Just as I thought. You're as vulnerable as a human male."

His dead eyes stared at her, full of one emotion.

Hate.

"Now. Let's discuss again what you owe me."

When the mutinous expression on his face didn't change— nor did any answers seem forthcoming—Ilsa squeezed again and was greeted with a long, low scream.

"Who sent you here? And how did you know we were here?"

Still, nothing.

Ilsa shook her head and clucked her tongue. "My, my,

my, aren't you a brave one? I've been nice so far. But I'm only asking one"—she clenched her fingers in a tight grip—"more"—harder still—"time."

His eyes bulged and his lips quivered. "I can't tell you."

"Sure you can."

His lips continued to tremble, but he finally spoke, his voice a harsh, grating whisper. "This is a walk in the fucking park compared to what awaits me if I tell you."

"I want a name. And I've got all day, sweetheart. All night, too, as a matter of fact. And did I mention I've got strength, immortality and a skill set awarded me by the lord of death on my side?"

She squeezed one more time, frustration building at his stubborn unwillingness to tell her who he worked for. "If this isn't cutting it, I can dig up a few more goodies from my magic grab bag." She laughed at her own joke. "Grab bag—get it?"

The hatred in his eyes grew deeper, stronger, but he still remained silent.

"Well then." She flicked one long nail against the sensitive, thin skin of his balls, then dug in with a sly, steady thrust.

"Who do you work for?"

Agony flooded his features, but he held in his scream.

Barely.

"E-E—"

Complete and utter shock replaced the waves of frustration. "Emmett sent you?"

The asshole nodded, the sneer fast returning to his lips.

Emmett? Emmett sent this . . . creature? Creatures, if she counted the grease spots inside the house.

But how?

She knew for a fact Emmett didn't have anyone else working for him. That's why he'd found her. Bargained with her. Asked for her help.

Help she'd given willingly in a bargain she never should have made.

"What did he tell you to do?"

The guy's eyes darted wildly in their sockets. "Take them down. We were supposed to take them down."

That strange nothingness filled the air around Ilsa, reminding her this man she held wasn't really a man. No whisper of a soul—good or bad—assailed her. The silence was odd.

Unreal, even. And it only added more deeply to the puzzle.

What was he and the others who'd already perished?

And what was she supposed to do with him now that she'd captured him?

Chapter Nine

Hades glanced at the large hourglass that sat in his throne room. Nemesis was late.

She'd had an appointment with two monumental pieces of shit and was due back with both of them more than an hour ago.

With a small, distracted pat on one of Cerberus's heads, he paced the room. In almost sixteen thousand years, Nemesis had been an unfailing employee, quick to do her job, with an impeccable record of on-time arrivals.

And then everything changed.

Hades knew of her secret bargain with Emmett. Had worried over it, especially as Emmett had been on his list for quite some time. Not yet ready for delivery, but on the list all the same.

Not that she knew that, but still.

If only it were simpler. If only he could just have Nemesis grab Emmett, bring him down and be done. But unlike the scientists, who weren't big enough to matter, Hades knew he couldn't play with the order of things. A soul as dark as Emmett's had to be properly dealt with while alive or he'd risk leaving a void for someone else to take his place on earth.

Darkness that black—that deep—drew others of a like mind.

Fuck, why was it all so difficult?

Had he and his siblings ever thought they'd have this much trouble with humans? This many complications?

Speaking of complications . . . Ilsa. Shit, why did he feel so responsible for her?

Truth be told, he had always worried over her, that forlorn soul who'd been so callously used by his mother and tossed aside by his brother.

But despite his concern—and the horrible feeling that her choices would end very badly—he couldn't say anything. Couldn't warn her or keep her from such foolish actions.

His curse as an all-seeing god.

He sighed, the sound resonating through the room. Despite his concerns, the girl made her own decisions. Lived her own life.

And it was that life, he'd begun to suspect, that was getting in the way.

"You can't expect her to avoid attachments forever," his wife, Persephone, had scolded him when he'd discussed it with her. "Zeus's punishment of her was unfair and for that he will pay. But you haven't exactly offered her work that embodies a spirit of forgiveness."

"I've put her talents and her energy to good use. It's honest work, Perse."

"Bah!" She'd waved her hands, those lovely long, tapered fingers waving around as she got going with her argument. "You found a convenient answer to a problem you were having. You needed someone to grab souls and she needed a real body and time out of that hideous cave. Admit it."

"I will not."

"Ah, as stubborn as your brothers, I see. I thought I married the kind one, my dark lover."

Annoyance had swelled in his breast at that. He'd hated the inevitable comparisons with his brothers—Zeus and Poseidon—all his life. Hated the sudden judgment that always accompanied the pronouncement of his name.

He did very respectable work, after all, and ensured a place for all after they died. An afterlife.

A *continuation* of life, to his way of thinking.

Why did everyone get so wound up about it? Earth certainly wasn't all it was cracked up to be most of the time.

Persephone turned down the lights and snuggled against him under the covers, those beautiful fingers of hers gesturing in a far more . . . pleasurable fashion. With a soft whisper against his cheek, she reminded him of a fact he'd always known. "Nemesis is entitled to a life, my love. She's entitled to love."

"Assuming she wants to reach out and take it. Risk herself for it," he'd grumbled in return.

At that, Persephone had shifted again, lifting herself up on one elbow. Her concerned face glowed in the candlelight that flooded the room with a warm glow. "You think she won't?"

"Perhaps it's too late for her."

At that, his beautiful wife let out a deep, rich laugh and fell against him. "Is that all that worries you?"

"What's so funny?"

"Oh, darling. A woman can't decide when she's going to fall in love. It just happens."

He didn't think it was a silly concern. Nemesis had

never shown any interest before. Perhaps she was past her prime. Past the point of ever caring if love happened for her. "But she's been here so long."

"So? When it's right, it's right."

"And what if she decides to leave me? What then?"

"Aha. So that's the real concern, now, isn't it?" At his silence, his perceptive wife pressed harder. "You want good things for her, don't you?"

"Of course I do. It's just—"

"Just what?" Persephone's voice grew quiet in that way he loved so dearly. The way that told him she truly listened—and heard—what he told her. "What bothers you?"

"She makes dangerous choices in this quest for vengeance. Has perhaps made one from which there is no turning back. I question if she can escape the path she's set for herself."

"That, my love, is beyond your control. Beyond the control of any of us."

Ilsa belatedly realized she still had her hand down the jerk's pants.

Eew.

Funny how when she'd dreamed of Kane, the long, powerful length of him and the glorious strength that made his body so different from hers filled her thoughts with happy abandon.

And this man's—this thing's—body was a revulsion.

With quick movements, she removed her hand and saw a noticeable easing of the lines around his mouth.

He might not die like a human, but he lived like one. Had some vulnerabilities, which was good to know in the event she ran into more of his ilk.

Of course, what was she supposed to do with him? She didn't have any backup. And did she dare bring him back inside?

With a decided lack of options, she figured that was the best course of action. Kane and his brothers likely knew how to dispose of these things. And she wanted to get to Kane and learn what was wrong with him.

Decision made, Ilsa prepared herself for the port back inside when a shiver ran through her organs.

The scientists.

Their renewed caterwauling as they gripped her soul reminded her—in long, loud, ungainly wails—of her dereliction of duties.

Shit.

Hades didn't like to be kept waiting. And he wanted this pair straightaway, as he'd informed her when she was given this assignment. Added to that, she'd never held on to a soul for this long. A distinct coldness had settled inside her body, filling her veins with ice.

Without warning, the door opened and it distracted Ilsa from her prisoners, both external and internal. That small moment was all the external jerk needed—a wave of electricity erupted all around her for the brief moment when she broke bodily contact between them.

The edges of the man's mouth transformed into a broad, leering smile as he danced out of her reach. With one final act of gloating, he hollered over his shoulder as he ran, "Have fun figuring out what I did to him."

Quinn let out a string of ungainly curses, struggling to squeeze between her body and the doorway to go after him. Ilsa grabbed his arm as she watched the man—thing—disappear into a port before he'd reached the end of the property. With a firm grip on Quinn's arm, she struggled to hold him in place, impatient for him to register his quarry had evaporated. "How's Kane?"

His gaze shifted from the empty air toward her face and his voice was grim. "Not good."

Without waiting for further details, Ilsa ran through the door and into the living room. And stopped as she came to Grey and Drake, huddled on the floor around Kane. "What's wrong with him?"

Grey stared up at her with dull eyes, real fear evident in his gaze. "We don't know."

"Let me see him."

Drake moved back to allow her access. Ilsa crouched down next to Kane's prone body, but what she really wanted to do was sit down and pull his head into her lap. Just like in the garage. Somehow, she sensed the three men surrounding her wouldn't take kindly to that presumptive move, so she opted for running her hands over his brow instead. "Has he said anything?"

Quinn's voice was harsh behind her. "He's mumbled a few words, but that's it."

"Have you seen him like this before? Is it the poison?"

"The poison doesn't affect him like this. Even at the very end it's not this bad. This paralyzing." Grey spoke, his tones even. Modulated. Kinder, somehow, than Quinn's terse barking. "He's just under two weeks out. It shouldn't even be possible for this to happen. Yet."

"What did you do to him?" Quinn's voice held nothing but accusation toward her, his question an arrogant demand.

Whirling, Ilsa sprang to her feet. "Excuse me? I didn't do anything to him. What makes you think this was my fault?"

"You bring Destroyers to the club. Then you bring them here. Hell, just now out there"—Quinn tossed his head back, gesturing for the front door—"you held one captive. Was he your whipping boy? Set up to take the fall?"

Whipping boy?

Fall?

What was he possibly talking about?

"I was trying to get information out of him. And before tonight, I'd never even seen one of these"—she gestured, struggling for the proper word—"*things*. Destroyers, you call them? What are they? Because they're certainly not men."

Quinn's terse bark turned hostile. "Don't play the innocent. You've set Kane up from the first. Why should we believe this was anything but more of the same?"

Fire burned a raw path down her throat to her stomach. How could she fight this and get them to believe her? She *had* drugged Kane, stolen a vial of his blood and left him behind. It made all the sense in the world the other Warriors would take his side over hers.

So why was she so frustrated and so determined to prove them wrong?

Why did it even matter?

These men were her enemies, simple victims of their association with Themis. It was Themis, her sworn enemy, who would pay. Kane and his Warrior brothers were simply collateral damage.

The internal pep talk almost had her convinced when Ilsa glanced again at Kane's still form. A sheen of sweat covered his face and a grayish pallor rode high on his gaunt cheeks.

Vengeance and justice.

Ilsa knew she'd earned both. Her life was carefully crafted with those two intertwined goals in mind.

But she seemed unable to leave this man.

Why?

A long, low moan interrupted her thoughts as Kane thrashed his arms. She barely missed a sideswipe of his hand as she leaned forward to put pressure on his shoulders, holding him still. Heat seeped through his T-shirt, a fire beneath her palms.

Without any further thought for the nasty glares and unpleasant attitude, Ilsa issued orders, a general marshaling her troops. "Ya know what, Quinn? You can bitch at me later. Right now, we've got a bigger problem. He's spiking a fever and none of you morons seems to know what's causing it."

"He's vulnerable," Grey interrupted her. "The poison weakens him. This is a likely complication we weren't expecting."

As Kane's thrashing stopped under her firm hold, Ilsa shifted into a sitting position next to him and ran a hand over his brow. The fever rose off him like heat off the desert floor. "How does the poison work, exactly?"

Grey knelt down on the other side of Kane, rolling his sleeves up as he settled in. "It lives inside of him, gr—"

"Grey!" That harsh bark of Quinn was back. "We're not telling her anything. She doesn't need any further ammunition to hurt the scorp. Or any of us," he added as an afterthought.

Decision riding high in his eyes, Grey ignored the large Warrior who seemed to think he ran the show, continuing his tale. "It's tied to the venom in his scorpion."

Scorpion? Was that what she'd seen?

"What do you mean, his scorpion? That huge animal that fought next to him for a short while?"

Drake nodded, adding, "It's an aid in battle. We all have them and they're specific to our signs."

Ilsa struggled to take it all in. They were warriors with animals that lived inside of them? "So why didn't any of you fight with yours? I only saw the scorpion."

Drake resolutely ignored the continued glare and loud harrumphs that came from Quinn's direction. "They come out when we're severely threatened." His shoulders lifted in a light shrug. "Guess none of us felt all that threatened before."

Thoughts jumbled in her mind faster than she could keep up with them. "So if the scorpion is his protector, how can it poison him?"

"The venom has limits to its power because the spell that released it had to be tied to something," Quinn interjected, clearly frustrated with the discussion but evidently unwilling to stay out of it. "The poison grows stronger day by day, until Antares, the brightest star in the Scorpio constellation, hits its zenith."

"And when he makes it through?" Ilsa pushed.

"Then the venom recedes for another year," Quinn confirmed.

"Who did this to him?" Ilsa reached for Kane's hand as he began thrashing again. Deep, dark anger burned in her belly, so forceful it drowned out everything else inside of her—the scientists, the unresolved anger for Zeus, even the need for vengeance against Themis—in a writhing hatred for the one who had done this to him. "How?"

Acid coated every word Quinn spoke. "A sorcerer with the darkest of magics. Powers no one—mortal or immortal— should possess."

Her stomach twisted as another long, low moan sounded

from Kane's throat. "Who is this sorcerer? Does he still live?"

"That he does." Grey nodded. "Kane's hunted him for three hundred years, but Emmett's eluded him all this time."

The bottom fell out of her stomach as the name Grey uttered washed over her. "Emmett?"

"Emmett the Dark," Quinn clarified. "Have you heard of him?"

Chapter Ten

Screams echoed in his head as Kane desperately tried to claw his way past the fury writhing inside his body. Sought to focus on what was happening outside of himself, instead of the maelstrom that swirled inside.

Focus.

Pushing against the pain with every ounce of willpower he possessed, Kane searched for quiet.

Focus.

He fought for calm. For an end to the screaming, ranting, clanging voice of the pain.

Focus.

Slowly, as if coming from far away, Kane heard the voices around him. Recognized Grey's levelheaded calm, heard Quinn's territorial snapping and sensed Drake's soothing presence.

But it was Ilsa who captivated him. Just as she had from the first, her voice coated his senses like a fine wine on the palate.

Only this time, the sound of her was *different*. Was that

concern in her voice? Caring? Was it possible? Or was it all a lie?

As he listened, unable to respond, unable to get out of his own head, her voice calmed him further. Eased the pain. And made him feel emotions he had no business having.

Made him feel something that ran . . . *deeper*, somehow. A feeling that was less sexual, although he felt that, too. Less of a physical need than an emotional one.

Why did it feel so damn good?

Tuning in to her voice again, Kane allowed those sweet, sexy tones to wash over him. "I've no idea who this Emmett person is."

Why was Quinn asking her that?

Before he could further analyze it, Ilsa was already pressing his Warrior brothers with dogged determination. "Quinn? What did that thing mean when he escaped outside?"

"I don't know." Ire coated Quinn's words. Kane knew the bull's frustration would have brought a smile to his face if he could have reacted to what was happening around him.

"Outside? The Destroyer who ran out? What did he say?" That was levelheaded Grey, always keeping them on point.

Ilsa's voice was quiet, her tone heavy. "He said, 'Have fun figuring out what I did to him.'"

Quinn's typical approach—jump in and demand answers—played out yet again. "Did anyone see what happened to Kane? What, exactly, the Destroyer did to him?"

Drake and Grey grunted their denials, but Ilsa's matter-of-fact manner held the certainty of recent memory. "The guy he was fighting slashed him with a knife."

"It had to be something else." Quinn's ready reply was

dismissive. "Knives can't harm us unless they're used on the jugular."

"No." Ilsa's stubborn reply suggested she wouldn't budge. "The rest of the fight was all basic combat. The only shot the guy got on Kane was with the knife."

"Drake. Remember that fight we had a few years back?" Grey probed. "The one with the killer in San Francisco? Didn't he pull a knife on the scorp?"

"He did. And Kane was even closer to the poison's zenith. Nothing happened to him. He healed a little slower, but it wasn't anything like this."

Gentle fingers pulled at the neck of his T-shirt as Ilsa's dulcet pitch washed over him yet again. "Look here. The gash is red and gaping. Raw. Immortals don't react this way."

Again, it was Grey whose voice remained steady. "Quinn. We need to get him out of here. Get him home so we can try to help him. We can't do that in this shithole."

"What do you want me to do with *her*?" Quinn demanded.

The soft touch abruptly ended and he felt the shift of Ilsa's body away from his side as her voice lifted and moved farther above him. "You're not taking him away. I won't let you take him."

Quinn's voice projected down at him from above. "You don't have a choice, sweetheart."

A scream of protest echoed in Kane's head. He'd finally found Ilsa. They weren't leaving her behind.

What if he never found her again?

Grey's answer held his typical directness and broke through the battle of wills brewing in the middle of the safe house living room. "She comes with us."

The air shifted around Kane, the movements of Ilsa and his Warrior brothers yet another frustrating sign he had no control of his body. A large hand settled on his forearm as the grip of Ilsa's gentle fingers latched on to his other arm.

A loud whoosh of air filled his ears.

"I gave specific orders to you and your brethren. I wanted you to take down whatever Warriors showed up at the safe house where that little cell phone call originated to me." Enyo lifted herself from her perch on the velvet chaise lounge in her residence on Mount Olympus and sauntered toward one of her Destroyers. "You followed directions, but where are the others?"

Enyo knew the answer before she asked it, but was curious to see his reaction. Withering fear or snotty superiority?

It was always one or the other with the scum she recruited as her minions.

"Grease spots." A sneer turned the edge of his lips. "Excuse me. Incompetent grease spots. All five of them." Enyo stared into his soulless eyes and bemoaned the need to ask questions. Resented her dependence on these imbecilic creatures of her own making.

What she really resented, though, was the increasing weakness she told no one about, yet which drove her every decision. Her recent battle losses to the Warriors had weakened her farther than she'd admit to anyone and she no longer had the strength to carry out her plans all on her own.

Nothing like having to play by the rules, set with ironclad formality by the goddess of justice and her father. Fucking balance. It was always about balance.

Her nephews, Deimos and Phobos, danced around the

Destroyer with their usual abundance of energy. Like evil, demonic puppies, they bounced over and around each other, shoving and clawing at the other when the urge struck.

Which was more often than not.

Pulling her gaze from the gods of dread and fear, Enyo continued her interrogation. "Where was the misfit who called me?"

"Dead upon our arrival and laid out in a corner of the room."

Enyo glanced down at her manicure, secretly pleased at the crisp, militant answer. He might be cocky, but this Destroyer knew his duties. Understood his priorities to the one who'd created him. "How was he killed?"

"No idea. But I did remove his cell phone for you." The Destroyer pulled it out of his pocket and handed it over.

With nimble fingers, Enyo hit the required keys to reach the dead man's call list. A London number displayed on the screen, the time stamp only a few minutes before the call that came in to her.

So simple, these modern devices. So clever. So *easy*.

Gods, she really would miss humanity once she'd destroyed all of them. She well and truly loved human ingenuity. From cellular technology to cosmetics, she found joy in so many of their inventions.

Deimos danced around her. "Let me see it, Aunt Enyo."

"I want it." Phobos shoved him so hard Deimos flew across the room.

She was blessedly prevented from having to interfere when Deimos raced back across the room to tackle his brother to the ground, the two of them striking each other in repeated blows that would fell even the largest human.

Ignoring their display, Enyo returned her attention to

the brightly lit screen of the cell phone and tapped one long red nail on the number dialed prior to hers. In moments, the conversation that took place to that number came to life in her ear.

Humans didn't have the corner on inventiveness. Life on Mount Olympus had its little ingenuities as well. With a yawn for the boring parts, Enyo waited for a useful bit of information.

"Robert left for the double meet your agents set up and he hasn't come back."

"Are you still in the safe house?"

"Hell yeah. I'm sitting on a thousand pounds of uranium. Where the fuck do you think I'm going?"

"Calm yourself, Alex. Please. You can trust Kane, just as I told you."

"Then why hasn't he gotten back here yet? With Robert?"

"I'm sure it's only a matter of time. You know how these things work. All the dancing around the issues. Kane and Robert'll be back before you know it."

"I'm done waiting. Done letting you people call the shots. I don't know why Robert ever agreed to this fucking plan. You're not some rogue agent, helping us sell the stash. You're setting us up."

"Decisions made in the heat of a stressful situation rarely work out well, Alex. You made a decision. Chose a course of action. It's time to stick with it. Calm yourself, Alex. Everything will be all right."

Enyo tapped the phone again to end the recording. So it was Kane, then? She scrolled through her mental Rolodex until an image of a lean, broad-shouldered man hit her mind's eye.

Oh yes, he was a yummy one. Kane Montague. She

never remembered their signs, but what did it matter? She knew what he was and what he was capable of.

Of course, all of Themis's boys were rather dishy, if she did say so. Ajax certainly had been quite the lovely diversion. Broad, gorgeous and relatively clueless.

Just how she liked her men.

She didn't regret killing the former Warrior six months ago. The first of Themis's boys Enyo had turned to her cause, Ajax had become a liability. She did miss the sex, though. He'd been good for very few things, but a screaming orgasm was one of them.

But Kane . . . well, now, wasn't this a small world? The Scorpio was one of the Warriors who'd battled her for the stones. One of the Warriors who'd helped Themis's Leo and his bitch girlfriend destroy the stones.

Stones that would have restored her powers and ensured her dominion over humanity.

The warm, tingly feelings she'd had for Kane died in the face of the bitter memory. Enyo returned her attention to her Destroyer, the sour taste of defeat on her tongue. "Who is the woman?"

"An immortal. Definitely an immortal."

Since when did Themis's boys work with other immortals? "Are you sure?"

"Yes." Enyo didn't miss the dark look that shaded his eyes, although he hid it well. Even the soulless could have a moment, apparently. "She seems to think someone named Emmett is involved. I didn't disavow her of the notion."

Emmett? As in Emmett the Dark? The sorcerer who'd left quite a mark on a few of the lesser members of the Pantheon a few centuries back.

"Very nice work." Enyo allowed her gaze to roam over

the Destroyer in one long, appreciative glance. This one was certainly useful. "Are they still at the safe house?"

"Likely. I left them with a bit of a diversion."

"Diversion?" Intrigue unfurled in her like a flower opening to the sun.

"Rumor has it, before Ajax died, he'd figured out a few things about our opponents."

"Such as?" Enyo had suspected Ajax's bragging and boasting had gone rather deep within her organizational structure. This little tidbit proved it.

"The Warriors may be immortal, but there are ways to harm them beyond the standard decapitation that can kill all of us."

"Do tell."

"Poison. Poison on the edge of the blade can do some damage."

"Nonsense. Their bodies can just fight it off."

"It worked from my vantage point. The Warrior they called Kane fell almost immediately at the touch of my blade."

Kane smelled the familiar comforts of the Warriors' main residence first. The warm, soothing fragrance of leather couches, the massive bouquet of seasonal flowers that sat in the front hall and the ever-present meal cooking on the stove.

The comforting aromas quickly gave way to the loud, jumbled protests of Grey, Drake and Quinn.

"Set him down gently."

"Is he bleeding from that wound? Callie will kill us if we mess up the couch."

"Put something under his head."

Kane heard them and wanted to reply, but he was trapped inside his body, with no way out. No matter how hard he tried, he couldn't make a sound. Couldn't move his limbs. Couldn't even force his eyes open.

Frustration swam in his veins, but even the simple autonomic reaction to adrenaline eluded him. The thud of his heart remained steady and even, without the slightest spike.

In the three centuries since the sorcerer's curse, the poison had never done this to him. Even in the throes of battle, when the venom of his scorpion reached its peak strength each year on May thirty-first, he still had some control over his body.

Kane felt additional jostling as he was wrapped up in a blanket on one of the leather couches in the main living room. Despite an inordinate number of rooms in the Warriors' brownstone—a home that straddled a parallel plane of existence between Manhattan and Mount Olympus—most of their activity centered on a few key rooms. The well-worn leather underneath his body attested to the heavy use of the living room.

The voices receded as a memory struggled to the surface—the first time he visited New York, when he made the decision to join the North American division of the Warriors in the mid-eighteenth century.

The European group he was a part of had lost several Warriors to Enyo and he'd grown disillusioned with the infighting among those who remained. Unlike the fairly friendly division in the seventeenth century that had split a group off and sent them to North America, these issues ran far deeper. And they were based on far more sinister problems, rooted in a cesspool of distrust.

Quinn was the first to welcome him to New York.

"You have a place here, if you want it. And we'd encourage you to maintain your residence and your contacts in Europe if you'd like. In fact, I'd like to leverage your

connections and your knowledge of the Continent and the European Warriors."

"We've known each other for a long time, Quinn. Fought with each other when the world was quite a bit younger."

"To think we thought we had it so hard all those years ago after our recruitment by Themis. There are days I long for the relative quiet of the Middle Ages."

Kane laughed at that, the thought one he'd shared often enough. The human population continued to grow by leaps and bounds and with it, their increasing role in keeping the peace. "Somehow, I don't see things getting any easier."

Quinn nodded and smiled. "Me, neither. It's good to have you on board."

After joining the North American contingent, Kane managed to conceal the effects of the poison for a few decades. Kept the knowledge from his new band of brothers as he struggled through the bouts at the end of each May, hidden away in London.

It had been easier then, although it had seemed all so complicated at the time. Finding ways to avoid his brothers as May shifted from spring toward summer.

He'd be toast if he attempted that shit now. There was something to be said for the lack of modern devices. Nowadays, a text message that went unanswered for longer than an hour drew concerns.

But back then?

Oh, he'd hidden it pretty well.

Memories that hadn't crossed his mind in years tripped across Kane's conscience.

Enyo was a royal pain in the ass during that era, mixing herself up in the war between Britain and the Colonies. She fed information to each side when it suited her as a way to extend the war and the bloodshed. She stole weak soldiers from either side to become her minions, part of her legion of Destroyers. And she manipulated the events in the misbegotten hope of destroying two countries—one well established, one with great potential—in the process.

It was Drake, their intuitive Pisces, who'd discovered Kane's deception. While he appeared calm and dreamy at times, Drake could go all piranha on a whole horde of Destroyers in the blink of an eye.

Although Kane had never once made the error of equating the deep, and often quiet, nature of their Pisces for lack of awareness, he'd also never figured Drake for a font of intuition.

As his Warrior brothers spent a late night carousing at a tavern in Boston, celebrating their victory, Kane stumbled to an old barn at the edge of town. The poison was three days away from full strength and already making its vicious effects known. Drake had followed in the shadows.

"Game's over, Monte." Drake pushed open the abandoned stall door Kane hid behind. *"You're dying inside and I want to know why."*

The venom swarmed in his veins with the sting of a million wasps. Sweat covered his face in a heavy sheen and his stomach rolled with the unmistakable pitch of sickness. "Bugger off, Drake. Don't need you here."

"I beg to differ." Drake rounded up blankets from the barn and made a pallet in the corner of the stall. With surprisingly gentle movements for such a large man, the Pisces helped settle him in the corner. *"You're too weak to move, so I'm going to port and go get Callie. I'll be right back."*

Kane drifted in and out of consciousness, only to be awakened by the cool touch and crooning voice of their care-

taker, Callie. Small and petite, she ordered the lot of them around with military precision. Positioning a warm flask at his lips, her voice was firm, but gentle. "Drink this down."

The bland broth stayed down—the first of anything to do so in days—and he fell back to sleep within minutes of drinking it.

And so it had gone.

For three more days, he drifted in and out of consciousness. And for the first time since the poison invaded his body, he didn't have to walk through the fire alone.

Kane knew he would have gone on that way, hiding his annual trip into hell. The way he figured it, the poison was a punishment for his folly. A penalty for falling in love. A lifetime sentence for his hubris.

Thankfully, his family thought otherwise.

Chapter Eleven

Emmett?

How could Emmett be responsible for Kane's condition? For the poison that raged inside the Warrior's body, slowly killing him?

And she'd gone and made a bargain with the man. A very specific bargain with a very specific target. Emmett? The man she'd secured the vial of blood for?

Oh gods, this was very, very bad.

Ilsa paced a long, wood-paneled study filled with floor-to-ceiling bookshelves, each shelf bursting with books. Quinn had shoved her in here with the promise he'd return shortly, threatening to follow her to the ends of the earth if she left.

The gruff warning meant nothing—she'd come and go as she pleased—but the image of Kane fighting for his life in the next room ensured she'd stay put far more effectively than an idle threat.

It had become increasingly clear to her since first meeting Kane, the bargain she'd made with Emmett was a mistake of momentous proportions. But this?

This news meant Emmett had used her and her anger toward Themis as a weapon against her.

She'd been duped.

Her pulse pounded and her stomach clenched in undulating waves as the horrible, bitter truth of the matter sank in. With unfailing regularity, she seemed completely incapable of dealing with others. Obviously Rhea and, later, Zeus had only been the beginning.

How had she missed it? How had she possibly missed the manipulation in Emmett's true intentions? How could she have been so stupid, allowing the need for vengeance to overshadow something so obvious?

So calculated?

Emmett knelt on the floor of her cave on Mount Ida in supplication, his eyes focused on the floor as he bowed his head. Despite her initial desire to run from the cave and never look back, she had an odd attachment to it.

It was home.

Yet he'd found it.

"You are the goddess Nemesis. And you are the only one who can help me."

She'd determined from the start that she'd not use her immortality to simply kill whatever got in her way. The gifts bestowed upon her by Hades had value—they weren't to be used for personal gain. She'd lived by that code—believed in it—but there was something about this man, this mortal, that put her senses on high alert.

Her fingers curled into fists at her sides as she stared down at him.

"Help you? How did a mortal like you even find me? You are lucky I don't kill you now for your impertinence."

"It is a risk I am willing to take. You are a legend, my

goddess." His eyes lifted. "And you are the only one with the knowledge—nay, the abilities—to help me."

"And why should I help you? Why should I believe you when you say Emmett is your name?"

"I don't lie to you. I am Emmett, born in Florence in 1628. Although my body is mortal, my soul expands the boundaries of my life. It is the great power that lives inside of me that has enabled me to live to nearly four hundred years, now."

"You're a sorcerer, then?"

"Yes. And my quest is so important to me, I will give up even that to possess it."

The question of how he'd found her still caused concern, his answers slightly too vague for comfort. She stared down into his eyes, which swirled with a hunger he couldn't conceal. Keeping her voice bland, she pushed at him, questioning his sincerity and determination. "You bore me, Sorcerer. Leave now and I'll allow you to live."

His gaze never wavered as those eyes remained fixed upon hers. "I will offer you something great in return for your help. Something far greater than what I ask of you."

"What do you seek?"

Seeds of doubt sprouted in the back of her mind. How did he find her? And what could she possibly gain from dealings with a mortal?

And why did he look so sure she'd agree?

But all her doubts were forgotten in his next words.

"I seek the Scorpio Warrior of the Zodiac. He ruined my sister nigh on many years now, and I seek my vengeance against him."

Interest slammed through her, filling up the endlessly empty chambers of her soul. She knew of the zodiac Warri-

ors. Knew of their origins in the Great Agreement between her archenemy, Themis, and her betrayer, Zeus.

With false bravado, she stared at Emmett. "And what matter is this to me?"

"Your desire for vengeance against Themis is legend, my goddess. Whispered by those who know of these matters. I've heard of the great betrayal that caused Zeus to punish you."

Ilsa had simply stared, unwilling to reply for fear she'd give herself away.

As if sensing her interest in hearing more, Emmett continued. "Her betrayal of you. Themis. It was she who whispered in Zeus's ear, with her endless prattle about balance and justice. She who forced you to this life."

"You speak boldly, Sorcerer. Who would dare whisper of me? Whisper of the great god, Zeus? One who cares little for his life, no doubt."

"The truth has a way of being found out, Goddess."

When she didn't reply, the man rose to his feet, his penetrating gaze as fixed as a steel cable. "I simply bargain with what I know you desire, Goddess."

"Just because you possess information, Sorcerer, doesn't mean you have any power with which to negotiate."

The sorcerer stood at his full height. "But I do have something to bargain with, and the power to make it happen."

"What is this you speak of?"

"I know when Zeus punished you he decreed you to be unable to retain corporeal form outside this cave."

How could he possibly know the great consequence of Zeus's unimaginable betrayal?

At that she'd leaped forward, taking his throat between her hands. Despite his height advantage, the sorcerer stood before her, his hands at his sides, that steady gaze still un-wavering.

"You take liberties, Emmett the sorcerer. Great liber-ties. You speak of things you should have no knowledge of."

A sly smile hovered at his lips. "So am I wrong?"

"Yes, you are."

The swirling gaze stilled, his eyebrows narrowing over the deep green of his irises.

"I leave this cave and I walk in sunlight."

She took momentary satisfaction in obviously tripping him up. Clearly he didn't have quite the cache of informa-tion he'd believed.

Words sputtered at his lips as he struggled to find a re-ply. "This is not true. It cannot be true."

"Aye, it is. I exist in the world, just as much as you do."

Emmett moved away from her and seated himself on an animal skin she kept on the floor, near her fire pit. Her normal ability to see into men's souls eluded her, his es-sence cloaked behind an iron will.

The fact he even knew how to do that was fascinating and she moved toward him, taking a seat on a skin opposite him. It took great strength—great understanding of one's essence—to cloak the soul.

"I came to offer you a great bargain, Goddess. I can see I was mistaken."

"What did you hope to receive in return, Sorcerer?"

His voice was quiet in the cave, the tone so low his words didn't echo around the walls. "I hoped to avenge my sister."

"What vengeance do you seek? And why?"

"The Scorpio betrayed my sister. Scorned her and left her behind, not caring what happened to her. Not caring if she lived or died."

Ilsa felt immediate sympathy for this nameless, faceless sister. She knew the pain of abandonment, especially for one deeply cared for. "Why do you seek me?"

"You, too, seek vengeance. Against Themis." Emmett's eyes searched her face. "I know this is true. I know it."

Ilsa nodded, unable to deny something she hated on a visceral level.

"I need you to get something for me from one of her Warriors. If you do that, I can help deliver you Themis."

She refrained from laughing at his earnest words. As if this mortal could deliver a goddess and her Warrior. "You need me to get you something? And in return you'll hand me Themis. And just how do you propose to do this?"

"I know how to reach the Scorpio."

"That's a bold statement."

"Goddess. As I stand here, I tell you, I can reach him for you. Connect you to him."

"And what is it you'd like me to do?"

"I need you to secure a vial of his blood."

"And then?"

"With that, I will find a way to capture him. Weaken him. Themis will come for him. She'll know he is in danger and will not be able to resist providing her aid."

Ilsa nodded, weighing the truth of his words—and his ability to deliver on them.

"When she arrives, you may have Themis. All I ask is that you leave the Warrior for me."

"And if I agree? How long do you propose this to take?"

"It must be done in stages."

"Stages?"

"The Warrior has protection. His own strength as well

as the strength of his brothers. You'll need to earn his trust.
Work with him. Spend time with him. Once you have him in
your grasp, you will have the access you seek. The access
to Themis."

The memory of her conversation faded as the souls inside of her began their caterwauling again. How had she
been so blind to Emmett's motives?

And was it possible the screams of the souls were getting louder? What had been mildly irritating before had suddenly grown to a great clanging throng in her head.

Diligently ignoring them, she focused on the puzzle that
was Emmett. How had he gotten past her defenses?

The straightforward answer was because she was so
blinded by vengeance. It was that simple. But how to fix it
now?

The MI6-issued cell phone she carried boasted several
text messages from the miserable traitor in the past two hours.
She ignored them all, desperate and frantic to find a way
out of this. Desperate to come up with a plan that would
keep Kane safe.

A cold line of sweat crawled down her spine as the
screams of Alex and Robert played a demonic counterpoint
to her dismal thoughts of Emmett. She desperately needed
to get the two of them delivered to Hades. Their constant
banging and ramming against her insides felt like they were
trying to rend her very soul in half.

But she couldn't leave Kane.

Why? It wouldn't take any time at all to port away, deliver the souls and port back.

So why was she so reluctant?

He'd gotten along just fine without her so far.

Without warning, the erotic images of what they'd shared

in the garage behind the safe house swamped her. The hot moments overwhelmed her and locked her firmly in place, in spite of her dereliction of duty to Hades.

Quinn stepped into the study, with a pointed look at the open door. "I can see you were smart enough to stay put, unlike last evening at Equinox. You didn't even close the door behind me earlier."

A combination of worry and fury burned like steady fire, low in her stomach. The pure, undiluted panic twisted and churned with each minute she spent away from Kane. Add in the increasing pain she felt from carrying the souls of the dead scientists long past an amount of time that was wise and Ilsa figured she was entitled to her raging headache and equally raging bad mood.

"I know you have a problem with me, Quinn, but I'm not leaving until we figure out what's wrong with Kane."

Quinn paced the study, his impressive height easily reaching one of the upper rows of the floor-to-ceiling bookshelves. "You've got one thing right. You're not leaving."

Despite her desperate desire to stay with Kane, Ilsa was no one's fool. She'd protected herself for almost sixteen thousand years and the Taurus didn't scare her. "I'm not some helpless girl you've dragged in here. Don't think you can threaten me and I'll go curl up in the corner, ready to do your bidding."

"You don't have any choice."

An angry retort nearly spilled from her lips, but Ilsa stopped herself, opting for a different tactic. She was always on the defensive, always trying to explain herself and her actions. Quinn already thought the worst of her.

She was done defending herself now. There'd be plenty of time to do that later, when the truth about her bargain with Emmett came to light.

It would come to light, of that she was certain.

She'd spent her entire service to Hades capturing those who'd thought themselves above the rules of humanity. And had she learned anything from them? Obviously not, if she'd gone and made the exact same mistake.

An act of hubris of colossal proportions.

Quinn broke the silence first. "Tell me again why you think the knife fight caused Kane's condition."

"I watched as all of you fought with those *things*."

"Those things are Destroyers. As if you didn't know."

Another brilliant flare of anger washed over her, but Ilsa settled for a dark glance instead. "Okay. Destroyers." At his expectant glare, she kept going. "As I told you before, the two of them fought but the only contact made was the knife to Kane's collarbone. What else could have harmed him like this?"

Quinn nodded, seemingly satisfied with the answer.

Of course, who knew with him? She'd been in his presence for less than a day and it was easy to see he was difficult to please, his stubborn, suspicious nature prone to question everything from multiple angles.

Seeking answers to some of her own questions, Ilsa shifted the conversation. "Kane and I were outside when we heard a scream. Who was that?"

"One of the Destroyers squealed the first time Drake got him in a choke hold. Which brings me to a more important point. Would you kindly explain why you ported Kane outside in the first place?"

Ah well, so much for leading the question-and-answer period. "He needed air. Open space. And I knew I could help him."

"Like you've helped him so far."

Ilsa thought of those glorious moments in the cozy garage, when it was just her and Kane. A long, beautiful stop in time that belonged to no one but the two of them. She refused to taint what they'd shared by discussing it with Quinn.

"We heard the scream and ported into the basement so we could assess the situation. I went first because Kane was in no position to enter the fight on his own."

She omitted that it was anger—and Kane's own lack of faith in her—that had sent her barreling into the fight.

"I entered the living room and waited for a moment to jump into the fray and then I stopped looking and simply stared. Other than the attack outside the club last night, I've never seen a Destroyer and I was fascinated by the battle, especially when the first one to die disintegrated into a greasy spot."

Quinn's eyes stayed focused on her in his persistent disbelief, but he refrained from saying anything, his mouth set in a stubborn slash.

"After I got past the weirdness of the fight, I began to see patterns emerge."

"What patterns?"

"Battles have patterns. They have energy. Experienced fighters have moves they depend on. Moves they've honed over time. The older the fighter, the stronger their patterns."

"Patterns?" His voice tapered off in amazement and for the first time, Ilsa saw an expression on Quinn's face that, for once, didn't contain harsh slashes of anger.

She pressed her point, trying to find the words to explain something she intuitively knew. "I watched the patterns that emerged throughout the fighting and I had a sense the neck was the key to everything. Kane confirmed it for me."

Suspicion again filled Quinn's eyes and his lips resettled into the harsh line he seemed to reserve only for her. "How could you tell that?"

"The fights had an intimacy to them."

"Intimacy?"

"Oh yes. A fight to the death has that. Couple the stakes with the careful, deliberate maneuvering toward the neck and it was easy to see. After I watched the first guy fall, I put it together."

"How convenient."

A wave of nausea knocked her for a loop as Alex and Robert screamed, the sound echoing through her soul like spiritual nails on a chalkboard.

Gods, she was in one hell of a mess.

"How do you understand battle so well?"

Ilsa didn't trust the questioning tone, or the sudden outreach. Wrapping her arms around her stomach to stem the tide of nausea, she tossed back a glib answer. "I've had a lot of years to learn."

"Kane said you work for Hades. Do you battle for the god of the Underworld?"

Although her work for Hades wasn't exactly a secret—and it certainly didn't need to stay secret from fellow immortals—she wasn't interested in getting into it with him. "I don't see why it's important. You don't believe anything I tell you, so why waste the breath?"

"If you really work for Hades, then what was your purpose in drugging Kane six months ago?"

"What happened between Kane and me isn't any of your business."

Quinn stalked toward her, his face looming over hers. She knew the tactic—felt it each and every time she removed a soul. There was something about being on the receiving end, however, that chafed.

Badly.

Feigning nonchalance, she met him glare for glare. The urge to squirm was nearly impossible to resist, Quinn's glare filling her vision and the screaming scientists filling her head in long, low moans punctuated by bouts of high-pitched screaming. But resist she did. "Look. I'm not sure why you dragged me here or what you really want to discuss, but I'd like to get back to Kane."

"He's being taken care of."

Any sense of bravado fled at the idea of someone else tending to Kane. "By whom? What are you doing to him?"

"Callie thinks she can draw the poison out. She's creating a poultice now."

Ilsa recalled the woman's name mentioned when they'd arrived at the mansion. An unholy knot of jealousy gripped her chest—just below her heart—at the idea another woman tended Kane.

Touched him.

"Who's Callie?"

"Our housekeeper." Quinn's mouth quirked up in a wry grin. "Of sorts."

Was this another nuance of modern society she didn't understand? Or was he mocking her and her anger that another woman comforted Kane?

Whatever it was, the tone of his voice when he mentioned Callie suggested the woman demanded respect from the Warriors.

Clearly, she was a healer as well.

"I'd like to go see him."

She expected some angry retort, full of belittlement and the stubborn, willful ire the Taurus seemed to exhibit at every turn.

What she got was a simple question.

"Why?"

She knew she wouldn't be able to explain it to him. Explain how she'd come to life the day she met him. Hades might have made her corporeal all those years ago, but Kane had made her whole.

"Quinn! Come on!"

Drake shouted from the hallway, startling her and Quinn and drawing their attention.

Ilsa rushed for the door. "Is it Kane? Is he worse? Better? Callie's poultice? Is it working?"

Drake smiled at her—the first genuine reaction she'd gotten from any of them save Kane—and took her hand. "Come on. I think you need to see this for yourself."

Ilsa followed the Pisces back through the winding hallways, his gentle voice a constant companion as they walked. "He asked for you."

"Me?" A warm, dreamy sensation flooded through Ilsa, drowning out the voices of the dead scientists and muting the voice of her conscience as it replayed her agreement with Emmett.

Hope—bright waves of it—lapped at her ankles. Maybe there was a way out of this.

Maybe they'd find a way.

Drake led her back to the living room and as they stepped through the doorway, Ilsa saw that a small woman sat on the couch, her back to them, ministering to Kane.

This must be Callie.

She tamped down on any sense of jealousy—refused to give such a negative emotion room to grow inside herself. Instead, Ilsa moved forward boldly, savoring the fact that Kane had asked for her.

Quinn's heavy treads fell behind her as they walked farther into the large, cavernous room. Grey stood sentinel at the head of the couch and Drake walked over to stand next to him.

Those gorgeous dark eyes of Kane's caught hers from across the room. Although still filled with pain, there was a clarity—an alertness—that went a long way toward helping her believe he would be fine. His voice was husky when he said, "Ilsa?"

"How are you feeling?"

"I've been better."

Tears pricked the back of her eyes in sharp little darts and her throat closed on a hard knot. Even if the power of the poison had been stemmed by Callie's medicine, Kane still suffered.

Still lived with the pain of the poison that had him in its clutches.

The woman sitting next to Kane lifted his hand to place it against the poultice that rode high on his chest, keeping the wound covered. Turning, she stood to introduce herself, a large smile across her pixielike face.

With swift, vicious justice, Ilsa felt her past sweep out and kick her in the stomach with unrestrained merriment.

The small woman named Callie—Callisto, as Ilsa well knew—dropped the hand she'd extended in greeting. The smile on her face died with equal swiftness.

As Callie's mouth hardened into a straight line, she uttered words Ilsa had never expected to hear again.

"Hello, Sister."

Chapter Twelve

"Sister?"

Kane knew he'd just woken up from a nightmarish reaction to the Destroyer fight, but there was no doubt in his mind he'd heard Callie correctly.

She and Ilsa were sisters?

In what universe was *that* possible?

One glance at Ilsa's face and the tightening of her shoulders and he recognized the truth with startling clarity.

Before he could say anything, noise erupted throughout the room. What had been deathly still and quiet was suddenly full of a barrage of questions, shouts and a whole lot of confusion.

Quinn, of course, was loudest, his words directed at both women. "Your sister? Why? How? And, Callie, why in the hell did you keep this from us? That your sister is some sort of avenging goddess with a bad attitude and a vendetta against the scorp."

Callie's small form huddled before all of them, her arms crossed in a protective gesture while her eyes swam with tears. Kane wanted to feel more for her. This was their Callie, after all. The woman who tended them, ordered them about and took care of them. Their *Callie*.

But all he could see—all he could focus on—was Ilsa. Pain etched across her beautiful features in haunting script. Her lips pressed together until they were a small slash on her pale face. Her slight shoulders quivered under the strain of discovery. Her legs—still encased in the four-inch thigh-high boots—trembled.

In the end, it was her eyes that got him. That pale blue color, such a contrast under the dark eyebrows that matched her hair. Eyes that filled with tears and the frightened look of the hunted.

It was clear, Ilsa had no more expected to see Callie than the other way around.

As usual, Grey's calm voice broke the melee, his stubborn refusal to back down in the face of Quinn's heavy-handed attitude what it took to get the discussion back on track. "Callie. You first. How can this woman be your sister?"

"She is a nymph, like me. Her given name is Adrasteia, though she obviously no longer uses that name, if Kane's constant muttering of the name Ilsa is any indication."

The urge to protest welled up in his throat, but Kane held his tongue. He needed to hear the truth from both of them.

Callie continued her story, as the room fell utterly quiet. Even Ilsa's tears were silent, her upset evident only by the steady stream that rolled down her face.

"I haven't seen her in nearly sixteen thousand years. When she left us all," Callie told them.

Ilsa moved forward then, wiping at the tears with the sleeve of her sweater. "I didn't leave you. I was sent away."

"Your choice."

Callie's dismissal was quick, but it was Ilsa who surprised them all. "It wasn't my choice! I was forced to help Rhea."

"You cared for the mighty Zeus. Of course you chose that over your family."

Ilsa moved forward, but stopped at Callie's withering glare. "No, no, no. Rhea didn't allow for any arguments. She simply ordered me to take the baby—to take her son—and go. I struggled for years to understand why she picked me and, still, I don't know. All I know is that there was no choice in the matter. I wasn't allowed to deny her. Couldn't say no to the mother of the Titans."

"Then why didn't you come back once Zeus defeated Cronus? Once he was returned to his place as rightful leader, why didn't you return to us?"

Kane watched as every pair of eyes in the room turned toward Ilsa. Callie's question hung over Ilsa like an executioner's blade.

Ilsa's hands fisted at her sides, but she said nothing further. Stamped on her face, evident in her regal bearing, was the same answer she'd given from the start.

Rhea had given her no choice.

Kane saw it. Felt it. Understood, finally, that there was something in this woman's past that gripped her and wouldn't let go. Something that, all these millennia later, still drove her.

Still haunted her.

Finding out what that was would be his task. And he *would* find out.

Her voice a mere whisper, Ilsa uttered her defense once again. "I had no choice."

And then, without warning, Ilsa's pale visage went stark white as her legs buckled, forcing her to the ground.

Enyo sat in a recliner in the far corner of the safe house's living room and waited. The large case of uranium sat across the room, seeming so innocuous as it sat there.

She knew better. Knew what raw terror existed inside that box for those who had the key to unlock its power.

It tempted her.

Called to her.

Teased her with its possibilities.

She was the goddess of war, after all.

Despite her absorbed fascination with the uranium, she left it where it stood. Its lure was strong, but her desire for a fair fight was stronger.

She'd take down humans, but she wanted control over the process. And a handful of crazies with a bomb didn't suit her methods.

Or her plans.

Oh no, she wanted power before she got rid of everyone. Wanted them to know they were controlled. Wanted them to know they were doomed.

It was the great, glorious dream of hers. To take Themis's precious humans—these abject, pathetic creatures the goddess of justice loved above all others—and torture them with their pitiful humanity.

Fortunately, she didn't have to resist the uranium for long. A far sweeter diversion walked in the front door.

Emmett the Dark.

"Who the fuck are you?"

"One would think you'd have more respect for a woman who can fuck you over faster than you can blink." With lightning-quick reflexes, Enyo shot a flame of energy at

Emmett's windpipe, his eyes going wide at the contact and his body doubling over in immediate agony.

She knew it was petty, this delicious fascination with pain, but gods help her, she wasn't likely to stop anytime soon.

Pain and vulnerability.

Oh how she loved to revel in another's defenselessness.

With brisk movements, she took the few steps to stand over him. "Come now, there's no more electric current. You can stand up, you know. Breathe like a good boy."

Dark, hooded eyes glared at her as the man regained his feet.

"Now, Emmett. Come in. Sit down. Let's chat."

"I'm afraid you've mistaken me for someone else. My name is Edward St. Giles." The man straightened to his full height, his broad shoulders and trim waist an appealing package.

Enyo doubted, however, the body standing before her was the physical package Emmett the Dark had been born with.

"*Tsk, tsk.* Nice try, but you can't fool the gods, Emmett." She flung a hand at him, the motion tracing his form from top to bottom. "No matter who you have on."

The man had the nerve to swagger forward and Enyo couldn't help but notice, yet again, the fine physical form he'd chosen this time around. His voice was raspy from her earlier attack, but bold as he questioned her. "Funny how you seem to know my name yet I'm not fortunate enough to know yours."

"Ah, and here comes the bravado. Oh yes, as I live and breathe, it *is* Emmett the Dark."

"Again, my lady, you have me at a disadvantage."

And disadvantaged was just where he'd stay. Of course,

she didn't see any need to mention that little tidbit. Men got so surly and upset when you pointed out the fact they didn't have the upper hand.

"Surely you have some idea who I am, you with your extensive knowledge of the Pantheon."

His brows dropped into a slash at that news. "And what knowledge would that be?"

Enyo stood up and closed the remaining distance between them. Her smile might look all peaches and cream, but her voice was pure ice. "Cut the crap, Emmett. You've made it your business to collect a number of specimens, as it were, over the years. Various members of the Pantheon that you seduced into your clutches so you could learn all there was to learn about the power of the immortals."

He held his hands up, his eyes going wide. "I have no immortals in my possession. I'm merely a lifelong SIS agent, assigned to protect queen and country."

"You're a dark wizard, born of an incubus, brother to Merlin. You were born in Italy in 1628. You practice all sorts of dark magics, but you have a particular affinity to the *Strega*, that dark magic passed down through your mother's family."

"As I said, you have me at a disadvantage. Clearly you know all about me."

"That I do."

Enyo saw the quirk of his lips. Acknowledged the dark look that passed through his bold stare.

But even she was surprised by his next words.

"Then tell me, Enyo, goddess of war. What would you like to discuss?"

The screams echoed through her body yet again, a wicked cold feeling seeping into every fiber of her being.

The scientists.

The parasitic souls clamored and fought, shooting waves of pain through her body. What had been contained to her soul slowly spread outward, affecting her body like a disease. The shivers had started a half hour ago and didn't seem to want to stop, no matter how hard she held her arms wrapped around her body.

Had they found a way out of their containment? Had she done something wrong this time? Or was it something more?

Even she had to admit, while she'd spent a lifetime ferrying rotten souls to Hades for punishment, she'd never held one this long. Perhaps there was some sort of expiration date.

As a wave of nausea filled her stomach, her newfound conviction grew stronger.

She had to get to Hades. Had to deliver Robert's and Alex's souls before they ruined her.

"Ilsa."

She heard her name coming from far away and tried to focus around the screaming that filled her head.

"Ilsa."

Thoughts jumbled fast and furious through her mind as she sought something—*anything*—to grasp on to. Anything that would overpower the screams.

Was that Kane's voice? He spoke. Could speak. Was he all right?

Yes. Yes, he was all right. He was fine. He had woken up on the couch, the poultice Callie administered effectively able to pull the poison from his knife wound.

Callie. Callie? Callie! Oh gods, her sister was here. Worked for Kane, or was part of the Warriors, or *something*.

Her sister was *here*.

"What's wrong with her?"

Large hands held her shoulders and that dark, husky voice spoke her name again.

"Ilsa!"

With fierce determination, Ilsa focused on Kane's voice. Like a lifeline, she listened to him speak, allowing his voice to lead her from the darkness that threatened to consume her.

To devour all that she was.

"Come on, Ilsa. I need you to wake up. I need you to tell me what's wrong."

Focusing on her body, Ilsa thought about her eyes. Her lips. Her voice. Ignoring the screams as best she could and concentrating on that warm, husky voice, she thought about using her eyes.

Open.

Light flooded her eyes as she took in the room around her. It was a bedroom, she could tell that much. Could feel the softness of the mattress under her back and the pillow under her head. Although the lighting was dimmed, bright, warm sunshine flowed through a crack in the heavy drapes across the room.

Daylight.

The warmth of the sun.

Kane's dark gaze, his eyes the color of the richest, darkest chocolates, stared down at her.

"Welcome back, Ilsa." His smile was broad as he added, "Or should I call you Adrasteia?"

With a slight shake of her head, she offered up a small protest. "Il-Ilsa's fi-fine. Preferred."

His voice was gentle as small crinkles edged those deep pools of brown. "Good. I don't think I could call you something else, anyway."

The shrieking in her head threatened to take her under again, and it combined with the horrific guilt that consumed her. If he only knew. The name Adrasteia was the least of her problems. No one had called her that for sixteen thousand years. Until Callie had mentioned it, she'd not even thought of herself in those terms in more than five thousand years.

But she *had* thought of herself as Nemesis. *Did* think of herself in that way. Present tense. Immediate. Real.

No matter how hard she tried to pretend otherwise—no matter how often she thought of herself as Ilsa—she had chosen a life at Hades's calling.

And she *was* Nemesis.

The goddess of divine retribution. The punisher of man's selfish folly. The one from whom there is no escape.

Excessive pride would always be punished by the gods as the greatest offense of all sins, the worst of all wrongs.

And she was the great righter of those wrongs.

"What's the matter, Ilsa? I know seeing Callie was a shock, but that's not why you fainted. What is it?"

Her throat was on fire, but she squeaked out, "The souls. Of the scientists."

Knowledge covered Kane's face and the warm gaze shifted to something else. Something harder. Something implacable.

Before her eyes, she watched as Themis's Scorpio Warrior came to life.

"Tell me how to take them from you."

She shook her head, the slight movement enough to send waves of pain darting through her skull. "You can't. It's not yours to do."

"Come on, Kane," Grey muttered from the doorway. "There's no way you could do that even if she would let you. You're lucky to even be standing right now."

Kane never looked back, never turned his head toward his brothers. "She needs those souls removed."

"Then she's going to have to do it herself," Quinn added. "You can't take this on. Even if you wanted to, you heard her. This is her task."

She struggled to sit up, but gave up when Kane's hands pressed her back against the bed. "He's right, Kane. I have to do this myself. The souls are inside of me. I have to deliver them to Hades."

"Then I'll go with you. You need a companion and I want answers. Two birds and all that shit."

Four protests went up around him, hers louder than any of the others.

"Are you crazy? I won't let you do that. You couldn't speak an hour ago—that fight you had with the Destroyer weakened you so badly. You're not going with me."

"I'm fine. The poultice worked and you're not going alone."

Drake. Sweet Drake stepped forward. "Kane. We can't support you on this. She lied to you and, as far as any of us can tell, hasn't come clean about anything. And now this news between her and Callie. She's a threat. You can't go with her."

Hot waves of shame prickled underneath her skin, crawling up her neck and onto her face.

Ilsa supposed she earned that—deserved it, even. But to hear it out loud hurt. Especially when the comment came from the kindest of these Warriors. Drake sat at the top of her list for warmth and a caring nature that belied his physical size and strength.

Even he thought the worst of her.

Kane's voice was firm. "I'm going with her."

Smug satisfaction filled his voice as Quinn pointed out

the obvious from the far side of the room. "And just how do you think you're going to get there, Monte? You're too weak to port and it looks like Ilsa is, too."

Kane shifted, lifting himself off the bed where he'd sat next to her. Ilsa watched as he stalked across the room to stand toe-to-toe with the Taurus.

Quinn's grin faded at the direct challenge. His powerful shoulders hunched forward in battle stance as he prepared himself for Kane's advance.

Instead of fists, Kane's voice resonated through the room with its strong, deep pitch. "Quinn. I don't ask you for much. I never even wanted assistance as I dealt with this"—he waved a hand at his body—"annual shit I deal with. But I'm asking you now. I'm asking you to port Ilsa and me to the Underworld so she can deliver those souls to Hades. She needs to be rid of them. I want to see that she delivers them safely, with no further harm to herself."

Ilsa watched the dynamics playing out before her. What had begun as hurt feelings and wounded pride at Drake's lack of faith in her had morphed into something entirely different.

As she watched Kane and his Warrior brothers, she noticed something that went far deeper than a Warrior's pride.

She saw caring and support and family. The hard decisions and the difficulties that came when the ones you cared for did something you didn't agree with.

"Kane—" Grey broke off, as Quinn held out a hand.

"Fine. I'll take you to Avernus and no farther. After that, you're on your own."

Ilsa felt her own protest rise up, but Kane beat her to the punch. "Avernus is still a long hike to Hades's chambers, Quinn. A long way to the River Styx. She's in bad shape."

Quinn's voice was implacable. "That's as far as I go."

Kane held out a hand, but Quinn wrapped him in a large bear hug. Despite the show of affection, Kane's disappointment was unmistakable. "You mean that's as much as you'll give."

Ilsa swung her legs over the bed and struggled to her feet. How could he have missed this before?

How could all of them have been so blind? And how could she be so careless? And why was he worrying about her at all when he should be furious with her?

She'd betrayed him. Terribly.

But she needed him. Terribly.

"Why'd you do it? The blood?"

Those large eyes of hers met his gaze, the slight whisper of hope dying at his question. "I didn't know you then."

"That certainly didn't keep you from sleeping with me."

Her gaze dropped away as her words sharpened with a distinct edge. "Don't use sexual intimacy as an excuse. It wasn't like you were looking for a long-term commitment. You took what was offered." A small, triumphant smile edged the corners of her mouth. "Took it willingly, as I recall."

"We *are* going to talk about this."

"The answer isn't going to change, Kane." A small sigh escaped her lips. "All I can do is help you get it back. Now, if we're done with this, I need to leave."

"Let's go find Quinn, then."

"I can do this. Alone."

Regardless of his best efforts to stay angry, he'd already made his decision. He was going with her to the Underworld. They could worry about retrieving his blood once they got back.

"What's the longest you've held a soul inside of you?"

Busying herself with straightening the covers on the guest bed, Ilsa didn't meet his gaze. "An hour. Maybe a little more."

"And that's one soul? What about two?"

"I very rarely carry more than one soul."

Well, shit. Didn't that just make him feel all warm and fuzzy like Christmas morning. "So why do you have both now?"

"I didn't want to waste the time it took to get Robert to Hades and then go after the second. Besides, if I'd waited, you'd have gotten to Alex first. If he'd laid there dead for too long, his soul might have seeped away, allowing him to roam the earth as a ghost. It's hard to capture them once they reach that state."

So this was about him? It was *his* fault? Like hell it was.

"So you put yourself at risk like this?"

"I needed to get to both of them last night. They were on Hades's list and I had to get them before they did any further damage. I did my duty and I'd do it again if I had to."

"And look where it's gotten you. You can barely stand up."

Those blue eyes, currently dulled with pain, lasered in on him. "You've got some nerve, bitching at me for over-doing it. Last time I checked, you had something far worse living inside of you, waiting to fuck you over six ways to Sunday."

Kane gritted his teeth—the truth of her words was not lost on him. With an odd moment of clarity, he thought of his Leo brother Brody, who'd fallen in love with a mortal woman. Although Themis had granted Ava immortality after the battle for the Summoning Stones due to her ability to use the stones for the greatest good, their relationship had developed when Ava was a mortal.

At the time, Brody had been upset about it, concerned about living the majority of his days without her.

While Kane understood that—understood the bone-deep panic at the idea the one you loved would be taken from you—he couldn't help but envy the Leo his relationship with a levelheaded woman.

"I can handle it, Ilsa."

"Kane, you don't need to go with me. I need Quinn for the port and that's all. I'll be fine after that."

"For the last time, you're not going alone. And with Quinn dropping you off at Avernus, fucking miles away from Hades, you've got a long trip. The payment to Charon to cross the first river is only the beginning. I don't want you dealing with the little shit on your own."

"He's not that bad."

Kane thought of Charon, the little demon they'd face first. Once they paid him the toll, he'd ferry them across the River Acheron, drawing them deeper into the Underworld. Throughout the journey, souls of the not-quite-damned were allowed to stand on the banks of the river, screaming their judgments.

Kane had seen it only once, shortly after his agreement with Themis to become a Warrior. As part of their training, each Warrior was instructed on the various leaders of the Pantheon. While Themis diligently avoided Zeus and Hera, she'd ensured her Warriors spent time with all the remaining Olympians. The gods were willing teachers and Hades was one of the best. Although Hades had been a warm and open instructor, Kane had needed only one lesson on the Underworld to know he had no interest in returning.

He'd not known of Ilsa then. Or that Hades had some-one in his service, doing his bidding to fetch souls from above and take them directly to his throne for punishment.

"After Charon ferries us down the river, what's next?"

"I usually skip that part and port directly to the River Styx. I'm involved when a soul is being delivered at the request of Hades instead of through natural death. The soul is placed in a locked boat decorated with skulls. I lock them in and send them on their way across the river, the final leg of their journey until they meet Hades and their final pun-ishment."

The poison that lived inside of him chose that moment to jab a new round of spikes underneath his skull. The hun-gry taskmaster had been surprisingly calm for the past hour, but the renewed pain indicated it had simply been lying in wait.

Kane ignored the pain and focused on the fact he had thirteen more days until Antares was at its zenith.

Thirteen.

More.

Days.

On a muttered expletive, he bore down on the pain and refocused on Ilsa. "This is bullshit. I'm going to convince Quinn to take us right there."

"He won't do it, Kane. Not if you come along."

As Kane looked at her, the poison screaming in his head and her words ringing in his ears, he knew she spoke the truth.

Damn, why did it have to be the fucking Taurus who was his only choice? Drake and Grey had made it more than clear they agreed with Quinn on this and Kane knew he didn't have enough time to contact one of his other Warrior brothers for help.

Shit.

The answer was simple. Unacceptable, but simple.

If he stayed behind, he could convince Quinn to do what needed to be done. Could convince him to take Ilsa directly to Hades.

Quinn would take them only to the entrance of the Underworld if he went along.

A sane man would have allowed her to do her job. Would have trusted she could manage her way to Hades's throne room without further assistance.

But he'd be damned if he let her go without his protection.

Chapter Thirteen

Avernus, the entrance to the Underworld, was buried in the countryside of Campania, not far from Naples, Italy. A crater, formed as the earth's crust cooled, Avernus had been the doorway to the Underworld since the dawn of existence. The far side of the crater held the entryway and it was near there that Quinn landed them out of the port.

The familiar scenery came back to him as Kane looked around. So like his first visit almost ten thousand years ago. The mid-May sun rode high in the sky and a bright forest rimmed the edge of the two-mile-wide crater, a portion of which had filled in to form a lake. Birds flew overhead, but no sound reached his ears.

Nothing, not even the bright blue of the sky, could diminish the cold that crept into his veins.

"This is the place of death. You can feel it. Nothing can penetrate the dark, stale stench death leaves behind." The words fell from Quinn's lips as he gave the spot his own look around, his hands on his hips. "I still think this is a seriously bad idea, Monte."

Kane glanced over at one of his oldest friends and felt the steady anger he'd attempted to squelch at the house leaping up to swat at him. "If you cared that much, you'd take us all the way to Hades, so you've lost the right to comment on the matter."

Never one to take a slap, verbal or otherwise, lying down, Quinn swatted back with his own retort. "You put yourself in unnecessary danger. For her." Quinn shot a glance at Ilsa, who had moved a few yards away, apparently to give them some privacy. "I can't be party to that."

Maybe it was the poison. Maybe it was the residual anger he felt at the lack of support. Maybe it was just the place itself. Regardless of the reason, Kane lashed back. "No, you *can* be party to it, but your stubborn Taurus pride prevents you. Why don't you just go on home? We're fine."

"What's wrong with you? You were always the first to fight with us. The first to stand up, Monte."

"And now that I choose something you don't, you remove your support. Turn the mirror on yourself, Quinn. This isn't about me."

The bull backed away, his features harsh and craggy in the bright light of the sun.

Without another word, he disappeared into the ether.

Ilsa returned to his side, her steps slow, but steady. "I'm so sorry, Kane. I know that was hard for you. This won't take long. I'll get these souls to Hades and port us back to New York. And then we can concentrate on getting you well."

Her cheerful tone did nothing to lighten his mood, nor could it penetrate the gloom that descended over a person in this place.

Maybe it was the dismal atmosphere or the sheer truth of their situation. Despite coming clean about some things—

namely the job she fulfilled for Hades—Kane realized he still knew practically nothing about Ilsa.

He didn't know why she'd drugged him six months ago. He understood how she did it and now he even knew about the blood vial, but he still had no idea why she'd targeted him in the first place.

He'd ignored that simple fact in the rush of seeing her again, but why *had* she left?

And why wasn't he busy getting the answers he'd sought for the past six months?

Kane looked at Ilsa, trying to force some much-needed objectivity into the situation. Nothing but bright, guileless eyes stared back at him.

Voice low, he kept his gaze level with hers, seeking answers from her body language. "Why did you burn me six months ago? Who put you up to it?"

While he'd originally believed himself burned by all of MI6, nothing had changed with his freelance employer. They continued to call him for jobs and it was as if Ilsa had fallen off the radar.

Even St. Giles had left the subject alone. He'd simply given him other assignments as they'd come up. It was as if Ilsa was a ghost who'd flitted in and flitted out, never to be seen again.

"Burn?" The bright gaze was quickly replaced with the wary fear of the hunted. "Why did I drug you and leave you, you mean?"

"Yes."

"I know you won't believe me, but there are no answers for that."

"There are always answers."

"Please let me do this. Let me deliver the souls. Can you give me that?"

He wanted to say no. Wanted instead to rail and holler until she told him why she'd left. But the slim set of her slumped shoulders and the bleak wintery gaze that dulled the bright blue of her eyes suggested defeat.

What piece of the puzzle was he missing? What elusive piece of knowledge would solve the mystery? And why, despite the fact he'd still not figured it out, was he unwilling to leave her alone?

Taking Ilsa's hand, Kane turned them in the direction of the entrance. Hidden from human eyes, the portal was accessed by stepping onto what looked like an immovable boulder.

Although few humans ever tread there—the depressing and ominous atmosphere usually a large enough deterrent to keep a person out—human behavior wasn't absolute.

As his gaze traveled the vast edge of the crater, Kane had to acknowledge the gods had hidden their lower realm well.

Ilsa stepped upon the boulder first, shifting her weight to make room for him next to her.

As the boulder descended into the earth below, Kane had the fleeting concern that he might never see blue sky again.

Ilsa stepped off the boulder and felt Kane fall in behind her. They moved through a long, narrow passage, the walls damp with moisture.

She placed her feet carefully as she passed through the small enclosure, the dirt floor full of rocks and sediment. The limited light and the rocky pathway made it necessary to proceed with caution in the best of situations, but it was her increasingly exhausting internal battle and Kane's weakened state that demanded a slow, steady pace.

Ilsa knew most people associated the Underworld with heat and fire because they didn't truly understand it. Although the five rivers that converged down there were filled with boiling water, making it very humid, the heat wasn't some sort of endless fire that waited to gobble up souls.

Hades's realm was a plane of existence, just as Poseidon ruled the sea and Zeus the heavens.

It was earth and her inhabitants they all fought over.

Although there were those who wanted to compare Hades to the devil, or even to death, he was truly neither. He simply ruled over the Underworld, ensuring order and process met all upon the start of their postlife existence.

Over the years, Ilsa had come to realize that Hades was a benevolent god. He wasn't evil, nor was he an unjust punisher. He simply had the job very few others wanted to touch. She'd often thought of him as one of the kindest, warmest members of the Pantheon. His love for his wife, Persephone, shined from him in great, harmonious waves and he genuinely grieved over those he was called to punish.

She had watched tears rim his eyelids whenever she delivered what Hades called an *unredeemable*. A soul who had no goodness or light and who was forced into the darkest realms of the Underworld to serve out the remainder of his or her days.

At those moments, when Hades's grief was so expansive, Ilsa always wondered what he'd seen in her when he'd offered to help her and give her a place in the world. She wasn't sure if he knew about the deep desire for vengeance against Themis and his brother Zeus, which beat in her chest with the sound of war drums.

"Can you see up there?"

Kane's question pulled Ilsa from her thoughts. "It shouldn't be too much farther and the path will open so we can walk together." In fact, she could see the opening to the path about one hundred feet in front of them.

Once on that path, they'd walk for another mile or so, before meeting Charon at the River Acheron. Ilsa hadn't seen the ferryboat master in quite a while, as her usual delivery method brought her far closer to the end of the journey.

Would he remember her? And how would he handle the fact she brought a companion with her?

Charon had always been a wee bit touchy, his devotion to his job legendary. It was that very devotion that concerned her.

As they walked in companionable silence, Ilsa found her thoughts shifting toward a subject that held endless fascination.

Kane.

His life. His interests. *Him.*

"Have you ever tried to get rid of the poison?"

"Hmmm?" Kane took her hand again as they came into the widened pathway, their footsteps falling in sync with each other.

"The poison. In all the years you've had it, have you ever tried getting rid of it?"

At that, a broad smile broke across Kane's face and he laughed in a way that suggested he saw some funny memories in his mind's eye.

In an instant, she was captivated. Breathless, almost, at the warmth that filled her from his smile.

"Oh, I've tried. Or I should say we've tried."

She cocked an eyebrow at him. "Doesn't sound very successful."

A cheeky smile greeted her in return. "I've still got the poison in my veins, don't I?"

"Touché. How could I forget?"

He rubbed at his stomach and made a great show of limping the next few feet. "I'm not sure."

"Okay. So the poison's still there. Tell me how you've tried to get rid of it."

"Experiments, potions, you name it. We scoured the texts of the ancients we keep in the basement of the Manhattan house."

"And?"

"Nothing. Unless vast lessons on Greek history, dry enough to put me to sleep through the poison's zenith could be considered a cure."

She giggled at that, aware of the texts he spoke of. Early on, when she still thought there was hope for her situation, Ilsa had read the old volumes herself, hoping to find some way out of her predicament. Some explanation for the punishment from Zeus or even the agreement with Hades.

Both were ironclad.

And the texts that told her that put her to sleep more than once.

"Anything else?"

"Okay. So after the research angle went bust, we felt sort of stumped. Then, in the early part of the last century, Callie hooked up with some white witches."

"Witches?"

"Yep. We've got a few who live in the neighborhood in New York and Callie made friends with them at the market."

Ilsa's stomach muscles clenched at the mention of her sister, but she worked to keep her face open and curious as Kane talked to her. Whatever anger existed between her and her sister wasn't Kane's problem. It wasn't any of the Warriors' problem.

And she was the only one who could decide how she was going to fix it.

Or if she even wanted to.

"What happened?"

"They tried everything they could think of, but nothing worked. Spells during a full moon, a waxing moon, no moon—they couldn't find a single thing that would work on me. Everyone looked so sad and pitiful after that, too, like they'd let me down."

"None of their rituals worked?"

"Nope, but it sure was a lot of fun to see three women all sky clad every night for a month."

"Sky clad?"

Kane wiggled his eyebrows. "Naked."

"Kane!"

He just laughed again, his voice rolling with hints of humor and lots of teasing. "They were very upset, and all I could think was, 'All things considered, did you enjoy the play, Mrs. Lincoln?'"

Mrs. Lincoln?

Was that one of the witches' names?

Gods, another one of those expressions she didn't understand again.

Did she dare ask?

When Kane continued on, she kept the question to herself, unwilling to look stupid.

"The worst one was Brody's attempt."

"Which one is Brody?"

"You haven't met him. He's our Leo and he's been on a six-month honeymoon with his new wife, Ava."

At that word—"honeymoon"—Ilsa felt a great wave of longing fill her. Her skin prickled in awareness and warmth suffused her cheeks. She imagined what it must be like, six breathtaking, glorious months with the person you loved and chose to spend your life with.

How wonderful.

Ilsa shot a quick glance toward Kane, her pulse ratcheting up in its predictable way whenever he was near. This involuntary response to a simple view of his profile confirmed— as if she had any doubts whatsoever—that she'd love to do the same with him. Oh yes, she'd take any number of trips for Hades, carry any number of souls, to get a honeymoon with Kane.

She'd bet they'd get to have a lot of sex on one of these honeymoons.

That cheeky grin was back again as Kane looked down at her. "You with me?"

With him?

Oh *yes*. Yes, yes, yes.

"What? Sorry. Yes, I'm here. So what happened?"

"Brody was convinced he could try a few ancient rituals on me. I put up a good fight for quite a few years, but he kept bringing it up so I finally gave in."

"What happened?"

"Let's just say the Egyptians might have been a wily, superstitious lot, but clearly none of them had ever had to actually *live* with a black-magic-induced poison in their veins."

"What did Brody do?"

"Several chants and a bloodletting with these really huge ceremonial knives."

"Oh gods! How long did it take to recover?"

"Not as long as I made them think. Besides, everyone felt so bad for me, I actually got off pretty easy. The guys and Callie got stuck cleaning up a sizable mess in the workout room and then had to disinfect a bunch of bloody ceremonial swords."

"And what did you do?"

"Recover in bed, moaning all the while."

Her mouth dropped as images of him lying like that haunted her. The agony he must have suffered. "Were you in horrible pain?"

"Enough that I didn't get my ass downstairs to help them." Another laugh spilled from Kane and Ilsa reveled in the carefree attitude and the knowledge Brody's attempt hadn't truly hurt him.

It was obvious Kane loved his Warrior brothers, despite their natural bickering and infighting. It was equally obvious how much he cared for Callie. How much they all did, if the deference they showed her and the warmth with which they looked upon her were any indication.

The laughs stopped and Kane's face sobered as the path beneath their feet widened even more. "Thank you, Ilsa. This place. It disturbs me. Saddens me on so many levels. The laughter did me good. The memories are a comfort. A reminder that this year's bout with the poison *will* pass."

"You're welcome."

They continued on and Ilsa knew they'd reach Charon in a few more minutes. The sound of the lapping waves of the river was already audible above the crunching of stones under their feet.

Screwing up her courage, she took a deep breath. "Can I ask you one more question?"

"Sure."

"Who is Mrs. Lincoln?"

That bright shout of laughter was back. "There really are modern things you don't understand, aren't there?"

She shouldn't have asked. But the easy camaraderie made her feel she could be honest with him. Could ask him anything, really. "So she wasn't one of the witches?"

Kane stopped then, tugging on her forearm when she would have kept going, her footsteps already speeding up to move on ahead of him. Turning toward her, he reached for her hand, pulling it up to his lips. The humid air swirled around them as a warm lethargy filled her senses.

That dark, chocolate gaze focused on her and his lips were soft as he pressed them against the back of her hand. Warm breath fanned over the sensitive skin and Ilsa felt an answering call from every part of her body. Her nipples tightened in response, a flush raced up her neck and she felt a distinct, feminine warmth at the junction of her thighs.

She *wanted* this man.

Desperately wanted to *feel* him again. Feel his large body pressed to the entrance of hers. Feel those glorious lips as they explored every inch of her skin. Feel the answering response of her own body as she flew into a million tiny little pieces.

"Ilsa, I'm not laughing at you."

Her gaze dropped to the middle of his chest, embarrassment whirling through her in great tornadolike gusts of air. "Okay."

One long finger found its way under her chin and he pulled her head up to look at him again. "I'm not laughing at you. It's just a surprise—a pleasant one—when you don't understand something I'm telling you. I just made a little joke. A silly saying, really. And not a very good one at that."

When she still didn't respond, he prodded her chin again to force her to look at him. "Most of the time, the guys don't laugh at my dumb jokes. You don't need to, either."

From the small place where she pushed any and all emotion, she opened the door a fraction of an inch. And allowed him to see what lay beyond the door.

"I'm so behind. Always behind everyone else. It was like that with my sisters. Even before Rhea took me away, I was behind them and what they knew. What they understood and what mattered to them. Then I was forced to that cave with Zeus, no contact beyond our small little life. And now—" She broke off, not sure what to say. Not sure what to tell him.

Unsure how to truly explain how she felt.

"I'm not like anyone else. And I don't know how to be."

He bent his head, his lips moving to press against her ear, the hot fan of his breath sending shivers down her spine. "You don't have to be anyone else. You just have to be you."

"But I'm not enough."

"You're more than enough."

Then he shifted, moved closer and kissed that narrow gap between her earlobe and her mouth. The warmth of his lips, so sensual as he ran them over her hand only moments before, were a million times more intoxicating as they meshed with hers.

Fleetingly, she thought of the scientists. Wondered why they'd grown quiet throughout her and Kane's journey toward the river.

But the simple thought fled as quickly as it came, as want unfurled inside of her. That pure, feminine need for Kane kept all the ugliness—even the mere thought of it—at bay as the kiss spun out between them. Although Kane initiated the contact, she quickly responded, opening her mouth at the seeking pressure of his tongue. Liquid desire pushed its way through her body with insistent, potent need.

She leaned in to him as his free hand reached up to cup her breast. Searing pleasure unfurled in her stomach as his fingers plied her flesh. Wanton, reckless heat filled her as he captured her nipple in the V between his thumb and forefinger.

Ilsa felt his knee wedged between her legs; the heat of

his body burned the inside of her thighs where they rested against his jeans. Kane leaned into his stance, his thigh pressing against the most sensitive part of her, barely covered through the thin material of her panties.

His lips devoured her as he used his leg to exert exquisite pressure against her. "You are so hot. So beautiful. So incredible."

Ilsa soaked it all in and marveled they were together again. She was actually in his arms and the feeling was so much better than she'd remembered.

There were the long, hard lines of his muscular body. The musky smell that rose off of him, so masculine, so . . . Kane. The pure heat of him, how it wrapped around her, a sexy enticement to press her body against his.

Gods, she wanted to crawl inside of him, hold him and never let go.

Kane rained a fiery path of kisses down her neck, over her heavy pulse points until his lips hit the vee of her sweater. His free hand still cupped her breast under the thin cashmere and he seemed undecided at what to do next as the material made an obstruction for the continued trail of his kisses.

"Kane." She heard her own breathless moan and wanted desperately to tell him to continue. Even as she knew it was impossible. "We have to stop."

As if unwilling to break the contact of their bodies, he shifted again, his thigh pressed so intimately against her she couldn't keep from crying out at the incredible, intense pressure. "Kane!"

Frantic breaths of air filled her lungs as Ilsa gave up her protests and allowed the sensations to unfold. She welcomed the pressure that built inside of her, matched to the increasing ministrations of his thigh where he pressed it against her core. Magnificent waves of pleasure built within her as Kane assaulted every inch of her body.

She gloried in the insistent, mind-numbing bliss of his clever fingers as they caressed her nipple. And the hot kisses as his tongue thrust into her mouth, in matched rhythm to the pressure of his thigh against her. And the sexy whispers against her lips.

"Ilsa, my beautiful Ilsa. So sweet." His tongue thrust again as his mouth consumed her once more. As he withdrew, the words spilled from his lips on a groan. "So incredibly responsive to me. So *necessary*."

Necessary.

That one word, above all the others, penetrated through the sensual haze. It burrowed deeply within her soul, lighting her up from the inside, filling up each and every empty corner.

As Kane's thigh muscles pressed yet again in exquisite pressure on her clitoris, she let herself go.

The world exploded around her until all she knew— everything that she was—was encapsulated in the man who stood before her.

Chapter Fourteen

Enyo paced her home on Mount Olympus, the usual adornments and decorations of death that surrounded her ineffective at easing the raw, mind-numbing anger.

Her pulse thundered and her deep-set anxiety scattered each and every thought that whirled through her mind.

How did Emmett know who I am?

Like a master chess player, he'd put her in check and she'd never seen the move coming.

Nor did she have any response.

After he dropped his bomb of knowing exactly who and what she was, she stamped on her trademark haughty-bitch glare and wrapped up the conversation.

But he knew.

"Darling!"

Lovely. Just a glorious, fan-fucking-tastic time for her mother to show up.

Hera breezed into the room with her usual glowing demeanor. Her robes were inlaid with thick strands of gold, her dark hair coiled in an elaborate updo. While she loved her mother truly and completely—the only immortal in her entire existence Enyo could claim those feelings for—this was so not a good time.

"You look upset, darling. What's wrong?"

How to play this one? Her mother could sniff out a lie faster—and more accurately—than anyone she knew.

"Work's been a bit challenging lately." Not a lie. In fact, rather accurate, if the truth be known.

Hera took a seat on the couch and patted the empty cushion next to her. "I know you hate when I say this, but you really need to find yourself a man."

"Mother. I realize you're the goddess of marriage. And as such, you believe it's the answer to every ill." Enyo took the seat next to her mother, leaning over and laying her head on the shoulder that always waited for her. Always soothed, no matter how far away from the cradle she got.

"Yes, but maybe if you took the focus off your job."

She held back the sigh, attempting reason in the face of such implacable belief. "It's the definition of my life, Mother. I *am* the goddess of war."

"Yes, darling, but look around."

Enyo followed her mother's hand as she pointed to various decor choices around the room.

"A guillotine, Enyo? Really? Must you advertise what you do like that? How quickly do you think a man is going to warm up in here if he knows there's an instrument of death sitting in the corner?"

"It's a human instrument of death, Mother. Besides, you only want me to see immortals."

"That's beside the point. It's creepy."

"It's *me*, Mother."

"That it is."

Enyo resettled herself against Hera's shoulder and considered how to broach her questions. Although Emmett had caught her off guard, she wasn't completely without intel herself.

"Mother, do you remember that time—? Oh, it's been years now. There was a sorcerer who captured several immortals."

She felt her mother stir, felt the slight head nod as her mother's body shifted with the movement.

"Yes, I do. It was a dark, dark time for us. Your father wouldn't let me off Mount Olympus. You remember it too, don't you?"

Sadly, Enyo remembered very little of it. She'd gained back quite a bit of power during the Middle Ages, the plagues and terrors of that time putting several win marks in her favor in her ongoing battle with Themis's Warriors.

And then it had all come to a crashing halt. The Renaissance period had begun, humans flourishing each and every place she looked. With it, Themis's boys had gotten their shit together. By the end of the Renaissance, Enyo was in worse shape than before the Middle Ages, her power so diminished she had begun to feel rather panicky.

For almost a century, she'd curled up right here, enjoying the calming effect of Mount Olympus. Oh, she'd stayed busy, planning and plotting strategy. But she hadn't concerned herself with much of what took place outside her four walls.

"I really don't, Mother. I was a bit out of it then."

"That's right. I forgot. Your wallowing period."

And leave it to her mother to call them like she saw them.

Hera's tone grew frosty. "I swear, I absolutely hate that stupid bargain your father made with that hag Themis. She tricked him into it and got you roped into it in the process."

Enyo did sigh this time and sat up, shooting her mother

a harsh stare. "A conversation we've had more times than I can count. Yes, Themis is a bitch. Yes, she had Daddy first. Yes, you hate her. Did I miss anything?"

Now it was Hera's turn to sigh. "No, darling, you didn't miss anything."

Even though she thought she knew Emmett's history, Enyo continued to question her mother. Pushed to confirm that she had her story correct. "So. The sorcerer? What did he do?"

"Well, I got most of this secondhand from your father, but apparently the sorcerer convinced himself he could harness the power of the Pantheon if he captured enough immortals, that once he had them, he could figure out the secret to immortality."

"Who did he capture?"

"Oh, he managed to secure a sizable cross section of gifts. Seven, in all, I believe. A nymph, a Cyclops, one of the Horae"—Hera held up a hand and finished ticking off the list—"a centaur, an Argonaut and he even managed to capture a giant."

"Who was the seventh?"

The delicate sniff told Enyo all she needed to know. "One of Themis's Warriors. He was the one who freed them all."

One of Themis's boys had been captured by the sorcerer? "Which one?"

"Who knows? She has so many of them."

Although Hera saw no difference between the men, Enyo knew, without a doubt, it was Kane.

It had to be.

He was already involved in this and that was no coincidence.

"How did the sorcerer get so powerful? Especially if he wasn't an immortal himself."

"The darkest of magics. His sire was an incubus. The incubus who sired Merlin, in fact."

"But Merlin wasn't a dark wizard."

"Well, his brother is. The darkest of the dark."

In an even tone, Enyo pressed with one final question. "Surely he was killed when the immortals escaped?"

"That's the hope. But the immortals were so drained—so near death—they simply fled when the opportunity presented itself."

"And the Warrior? The one who freed them?"

"It's said that when they battled, the sorcerer lost a great deal of his power. That he *relinquished* nearly all his power."

Enyo couldn't believe this. How had she never heard the specifics of this story?

Were there really mortals walking the earth with this much power? This great an advantage over their brethren?

Nearly breathless, she pressed her mother with one final question. "Victory? The sorcerer was victorious?"

"Of sorts. The sorcerer left the Warrior with a terrible curse."

"What kind of curse? He's an immortal. How bad can it be?"

"The worst of punishments. He is an immortal who battles his own death."

"Ilsa," Kane whispered in her ear, "we need to keep moving."

What was he thinking? He and Ilsa were within screaming distance of the cruise director of the Underworld and he was so crazy for her that he'd practically torn her sweater apart.

Movements gentle, Kane disengaged himself from her. He pulled his hand from beneath her sweater, settling both hands at her hips before he stepped back from her body.

She was truly amazing.

Responsive. Warm. Beautiful.

And if given the opportunity, he'd have stood there all day, just staring at her.

A loud, insistent droning from the direction of the lapping river had pulled him from her arms. Now that he actually focused on it, the sound grew more intense, like a swarm of locusts coming closer and closer.

"Ilsa. Come on, sweetheart. We have to get going."

At the word "sweetheart," her gaze met his—and her blue eyes were deep, luscious pools he could fall into.

"Come on. The river isn't that far away and we need to get there."

A small smile hovered at the edges of her lips and her voice was husky when she spoke. "Why did you do that?"

"Because it gave you pleasure." A hot warmth filled his face and Kane almost laughed at his schoolboy reaction.

Almost.

"And because, at that moment, all I could see was you."

The bright blue of her eyes darkened and her lids went all heavy on him. "I'm so very glad you did."

Kane nodded, fighting the image of her as she came apart in his arms. They still had a lot of ground to cover and he'd barely be able to make it three steps if he didn't calm down and focus on . . . *something* . . . else.

Like her wiggling behind as she adjusted her skirt.

His already overheated body tightened in response to that tight ass covered by the thin stretch of material.

Fuck, he had it bad.

Reaching for her hand, Kane tried a little trick he'd used the last time they'd been together. As the letters of the Greek alphabet ran through his mind—backward—he focused on the road ahead of them. Despite his very best intentions, all the omicrons and epsilons in the world couldn't erase the feel of her pressed against him, the searing heat of her feminine core as she rode his thigh.

Gods, they'd shared pleasure twice since she'd come back into his life and he still hadn't even gotten her into bed. Hadn't driven his body into hers with long, mindless thrusts of pure bliss. Hadn't spent hours showering her with pleasure, lavishing attention on each and every part of her body.

What was it about her?

They'd just had the sexual equivalent of teenage groping in the back of a darkened movie theater and he was hotter than he'd ever been for a woman.

Ever.

The thought humbled him, even as it made him harder, ready to go off with the finesse of a Fourth of July firecracker.

Hopeless.

This woman made him hopeless. But she also made him strong.

On a sigh, Kane tried again to divert his thoughts. Right, left, right.

Movements precise, Kane concentrated on lifting his feet. On the effort it took to take one step after the other. The deliberate moves were designed to ignore the painful erection and the writhing poison that had come roaring back to life in his veins.

As if the poison would forget about him or leave him alone.

Nope.

Not a chance.

Ilsa's voice penetrated the fog in his head. "Kane. Are you okay?"

"I'm fine."

"You look mad."

"I'm strung out, not mad."

"Oh."

He could practically hear the wheels in her head turning in rhythm with the buzzing noise that grew louder from the direction of the river.

Stopping, he took a deep breath and turned toward her. "'Strung out' means that I've got a serious hard-on and I want to lay you down and give you so much pleasure you can't even remember your name. Just in case you were wondering."

A broad smile broke out across her face, the only bright light in this dark, dank place. "That's what I hoped it meant."

The urge to kiss her again gripped him with its madness. Bending down, Kane shifted his body closer to her to steal one more kiss before they closed the final yards of their journey without Underworld accompaniment.

Their lips almost touched—the contact nearly complete—when a low, ethereal voice echoed from behind them.

"What passage do you request of me?"

Ilsa heard Charon's disembodied voice and immediately pulled out of Kane's embrace. The little demon stared at them in interest, his gaze dark and sinister as it roved over their joined bodies, his long ferryman's staff held firmly in his scaly grip.

Robert's and Alex's souls began screaming inside of her, the cacophony raging through her head in a disharmonic symphony. They'd lulled her with their quiet, brooding silence as she'd navigated her way toward the river, but the continued silence wasn't to be.

Oh, how she longed to be rid of them.

Their renewed screams echoed through her body, and the mental pain from earlier flooded back in full force, in counterpoint to a sharp, stabbing pain in her rib cage.

Ilsa had no words to describe what happened while she was a host. The internal process was often so miserable, she just sped her way through it so she could be rid of the offending essence.

But this.

This was beyond anything she'd ever experienced. The mental pain had become a very real, physical pain, as if a hole was being rendered in the fabric of her soul.

Straightening away from Kane, Ilsa gritted her teeth through the throbbing torture and turned toward Charon. "We seek passage through the River Acheron."

"Do you have the toll?"

Kane shot her a questioning glance, but she nodded and patted her pocket. "Yes, I have the toll."

The loud buzzing she'd heard on their walk rose up in loud complement to the lapping waves of the river where it slapped against Charon's ferry. The souls of the unjust stood along the river, fiery torches held high in their hands, screaming at them in judgment.

Ilsa paid two tolls and took her place in the boat. Kane took the seat next to her, his back stiff and straight as Charon pushed off from shore.

They floated for a few minutes, Kane's discomfort growing with each passing second. He shifted restlessly on the bench seat next to her and his hands tapped a rapt tattoo on his legs. "Are you okay?"

"Fine."

Clearly not, but she avoided saying so. Changing tactics, she leaned over, whispering, "Is it the poison?"

Kane turned toward her, the slashes of his brows framing an eerie luminescence in his onyx eyes. His irises were so dark, their color reflected the torches waving along the shoreline. "It's not the poison."

"What is it, then?"

"It's the boat. This place. I can't see the stars. Or the daytime sky above me."

"We've been down here for a few hours now. Did it bother you before?"

"Not like this. Before I could have turned back. Now we're trapped."

She followed Kane's gaze as it skittered across various elements of their surroundings. The hot, boiling river they floated on. The dark cave Charon rowed them through. The dock where they'd boarded, now a small dot in the distance behind them.

"Why do you seek the sky?"

"Themis gave her Warriors many gifts, but the ability to communicate through the stars is one of them." Kane lifted his left arm, pointing to a tattoo that covered his inside forearm. The tattoo was an intricate circular design, with various markings on it.

"But you've been inside before. You even said you've been here, to the Underworld before. What's different now?"

"I'm too weak to port. I'm trapped."

The truth of his words struck her as well, her situation equal to his. The ability to port from place to place was an unconscious gift. Like breathing, it was just something she took for granted and never thought about *not* having.

Sure, there were ways the body weakened, making an immortal unable to port, but none of them severe enough to keep the gift at bay for long. All easily remedied with natural cures.

But now, as they rode slowly through the Acheron, Ilsa was forced to agree with Kane.

The loss of a gift felt stifling.

Unwilling to dwell on the unpleasant imagery of being trapped, she refocused on Kane. "So tell me about this tattoo. And here I just thought it was some sexy ink."

At the slight nudge he gave her with the leg pressed to hers, Ilsa nudged back. The increasing fear that there would be some damage if she didn't dispel the souls soon—a fear she couldn't explain but that grew with each passing hour—eased at the easy camaraderie between them.

How could a simple touch do so much?

Kane's voice was instructional but he kept his tone low, avoiding an above-world lesson for Charon. The less the little demon knew how things worked up above, the better they all were and she was glad Kane understood that on some innate level. "Although we communicate with modern technology now, it wasn't that long ago we used these tattoos to reach each other if necessary."

Unable to stop herself, Ilsa reached out to touch the ink on his arm, fascinated by the intricate interlocking pattern. "Does this move like your scorpion?"

"No. I use it by touch." A wry smile crossed his lips. "I can see the confusion on your face. I'll show it to you later. Once we're out of this place."

At the suggestion they'd be leaving, Charon's pointy ears quivered. "In a hurry, Warrior?"

"Just anxious for the lady to do her job."

"How *understanding* of you."

Charon's voice floated over them, even as he kept his stare firmly forward.

As the moment with Kane was lost, Ilsa couldn't help wishing the circumstances had been different. If she had ported in and out, they could have avoided Charon.

Avoided the need for secrecy.

Of course, if they had, she wouldn't have experienced those amazing moments in his arms along the shore.

Paths chosen and the ones not taken.

Odd how she'd lived for so many endless millennia never understanding that. And now, since Kane had entered her life, it was all she could think about.

All she could see as she navigated the strange waters of worrying about another.

Kane's voice interrupted her thoughts as he nodded his head subtly toward the crowd that lined the riverbanks. "What are those people on the shore?"

"The souls still awaiting their fate."

"But they have bodies. How can that be if they're souls?"

"Here in the Underworld, their souls have corporeal form. Every human does. Unlike immortals who can move between the planes of existence, once a human moves to a new plane, they stay there."

"How long will they wait?"

Ilsa shook her head, surprised at how closely his questions mirrored the same ones she'd asked Hades millennia ago.

In all that time, the answer had never changed.

"As long as it takes. Until their time is decided, they live in a purgatory of sorts. And while they wait, they stand on the banks and shout their judgment of those who pass down the river."

"Seems rather hypocritical, don't you think?" Kane leaned in toward her. Despite his lighthearted attempt, Ilsa saw something bothered him. Strain lined his mouth and he didn't relax the harsh set of his shoulders.

"That it is. But it works. By judging the souls in the boat, they're able to see others' sins and determine if they wish to atone for their own."

"Sort of a preview plan?"

Charon continued rowing them through the murky waters, the blaring screams coming from both sides of the river growing worse with each minute that passed. "Exactly."

"It's clearly not a heck of a lot of fun to sit on the receiving end. And we're not even the ones under judgment."

Ilsa glanced down at her hands, images of all the people she'd held in place so she could remove their souls, staring back at her. Their faces—and their last moments of realization—ran through her mind's eye like a movie reel.

"Hades's intent is that the ones who can truly learn from their mistakes will atone before their own journey, anxious to have a smooth trip." A long, low roll of anxiety skittered through her body. The screaming souls of the scientists continued to grow in intensity and the rocking boat didn't help matters. She felt well and truly sick now, nausea slapping against her stomach lining in matched rhythm to the water hitting the sides of the boat.

"They're screaming for the souls you carry?" Kane probed, his voice urgent.

She nodded, lifting her gaze from the imagined blood on her hands. "Aye."

The scientists' actions in their human lives ensured a scream-filled trip to their final meet with Hades.

Shouts and hollers flowed over them from the angry mob on the riverbank.

Traitor! Thief! Murderer!

Those and so many other epithets, directed against the two scientists who'd devoted their lives to greed and the most supreme form of self-indulgence.

Ilsa took several long, slow deep breaths, trying desperately to pull something fresh from the heavy, humid air into her lungs.

Although the derision wasn't directed at her, something about the taunting spirits on the riverbanks filled her with shame.

Didn't she blithely march forward with her own plans for revenge, ignoring the consequences to others?

Hadn't she accepted Emmett's bargain, uncaring what it meant to the Warriors who fought on Themis's behalf?

Without warning, a harsh cramp clenched her stomach as frantic screams rattled in her head like buckshot. Ilsa fell forward, clutching her midsection and gasping for air like she was drowning.

Nothing could stop it.

Even those glorious moments with Kane before they reached the river—the pure joy he could pull so effortlessly from deep inside of her—couldn't keep the increasing pain at bay.

Ever since Zeus delivered his harsh punishment, Ilsa had always had some greater sense of her physical form. The horror of losing her body—even if it were for a brief period of time—had never left her. But for the first time in all those years, she actually resented her body.

Long, low moans—were they coming from her?—fell from her lips as misery dragged at her, body, mind and spirit.

Ilsa felt Kane shift next to her as his arm swung around her back. With a scream, she shook him off, agony and terror filling her as her skin heated with flames and stabs of pain ripped through her rib cage as though she were being shot from the inside out.

She heard Kane call her name.

Even though he sat right next to her, the sound came

from very far away. All she could sense was the screaming inside of her and the desperate, clawing need of Alex and Robert to be free of her.

The sudden understanding the souls were trying to escape filled her with bleak certainty.

What to do?

Where could she go?

How could she ensure their delivery to Hades?

Kane reached for her again, but she shook him off, her gaze flying wildly as she sought an answer.

An idea took root as she looked at the boiling water that lapped against the boat, sizzling as it hit the ages-old wood of Charon's boat.

With no other options, she leaped into the swirling waters.

Chapter Fifteen

Kane rushed to his feet, almost going over the side of the boat to follow Ilsa when scaly fingers sporting long claws stopped him.

"I will get her."

Kane stared into Charon's eyes. The dark depths held no emotion—no sense of life—and Kane debated the wisdom of allowing the demon to rescue Ilsa.

"I will get her, Warrior. In your condition, you won't make it in the churning waters. The heat will boil you before you can even reach her."

"How can I know you'll help her?"

"I will get her or else Hades will be mad with me for losing one of his favorites."

Without waiting another moment, the little demon dived into the roiling river, swimming toward Ilsa in bold, sure strokes.

Kane watched, his pride a mass of bitter embers that curled into ash. *He* should be the one swimming to save Ilsa. And instead he sat in the boat.

Waiting.

The poison aimed to kill him through physical torture, but Kane would have taken the pain of infinitely more venom rather than have to stand one more minute waiting helplessly by as someone else did his job.

He was a Warrior.

And right now he felt like a helpless kitten.

The screams of the damned grew louder and louder as Charon swam for Ilsa's bobbing form. Her arms thrashed and each time she fell beneath the water, a silent scream echoed through Kane's head.

What if the little demon couldn't reach her? What if he was too late?

The screams grew louder still, deafening in the dark cave that surrounded the river. The souls waiting their judgment screamed and chanted, almost as if they wanted Ilsa to drown.

Wanted her to pay for some great sin.

And then, in a moment of striking clarity, Kane understood what was happening.

The chanting wasn't for Ilsa. It was for Robert and Alex. The souls on the riverbanks were passing their judgments, one harsher than the next, and they were all directed at the evil souls Ilsa carried inside of her.

Kane drew his first easy breath as Charon got a firm grip on Ilsa, dragging her through the choppy currents. She writhed and twisted in his grip, but the ferryboat captain clearly knew what to expect. He dodged her flailing arms as he pulled her toward the boat.

The screams intensified as they drew near, Ilsa's wild-eyed stare and thrashing arms growing worse with each stroke of Charon's arms.

As soon as the demon was in range of the boat, Kane reached out toward the boiling waters, grabbing at Ilsa to drag her into the boat, before helping Charon. Cradling Ilsa in his lap, it took all Kane's strength to hold her still, wrapping his arms around her in a tight hold.

"Let me go! I have to hold them. I have to get them to Hades."

Hold them?

Ilsa screamed and cried, her head turning and twisting. Pain rode her face in harsh, craggy waves.

For the first time in his life, Kane felt utterly and completely helpless.

Squeezing her tighter, ignoring the scalding water that soaked through his clothes, he crooned in her ear, "Shhh. Shhh, Ilsa. It's okay. You're safe."

Turning toward the demon, Kane barked out instructions. "Charon, we need to get to shore. I need to lay her down."

"I can't, Warrior. I must take her to Hades."

"Fuck that. We don't have time. I need to find some way to calm her down. I can't do that in this rocking boat. Over there. I see the shallows along the shore. Pull up there."

Surprisingly, Charon refrained from further argument, rowing them in the direction of the shore. As soon as he saw shallow ground in the water, Kane leaped from the boat, Ilsa in his arms.

If it was odd when the souls crowding the shore parted for them, he paid it no heed. In his heightened state, Kane's only thought was to get Ilsa on the ground and calm her down.

As he trudged the last few feet from the searing water, the heat soaking through his shoes and pant legs, the chanting ebbed, quieting abruptly. Ilsa's thrashing ceased as well, her resistance to his hold clearly weakening.

Laying her on the firm ground of the Acheron's bank, Kane leaned over her.

"Ilsa. Sweetheart. What's wrong?"

Her head swung from side to side as her eyes darted wildly to his face, then to the souls gathered around them, then toward the domed roof of the tunnel that housed the river.

"Ilsa! I need you to listen to me."

Still nothing.

The chanting had stopped altogether, and with it, Ilsa's body stilled.

Kane sat back on his heels, desperate to figure out what was wrong with her. Anxious to find some way to calm the seizurelike state that gripped her.

Without warning, Ilsa's entire body shook, her back coming up off the ground in an arching motion as a shriek tore from her throat.

As the scream flew from her vocal cords, a dark, opaque flash of breath followed from between her lips. The black flashes shaped into form a few feet away, immediately taking the outline of human bodies.

While the odd body-shaped outlines filled in, two men came to life before him. When the last bits of flesh filled out, Kane tried to process what he was looking at as scrawny arms and legs, concave chests and greasy hair stared down at him.

The scientists.

Robert and Alex stood for a moment in line with the other spirits that stood along the shore.

And then they ran.

Kane was on his feet and stumbling along the riverbank—over, around, through—and the horde of souls encamped there. There was no fucking way he was letting Robert and Alex go.

No way were they blending in with the mangled mass of humanity on the shore.

They didn't deserve to escape their fate.

And Ilsa didn't deserve to lose them.

She'd suffered too much—had come too far—to lose them now.

Kane ran, the heat rising off the river coating his body in a sheen of sweat as he kept an eye on the dynamic duo.

The only thing in his favor was the same crowd that made it difficult for him to get to the scientists kept them from getting too far ahead. The chants that had assaulted them in the boat while Charon rowed along the river grew louder and louder as the spirits passed judgment on Robert and Alex.

From the screams, Kane knew the verdict was bad, indeed.

His lungs burned with the exertion but still he kept on. As he ran, Kane tried to assess his enemies and gain a sense of their abilities.

His scorpion itched on his shoulder, that long tail sweeping back and forth in an impatient arc.

Did he dare let the animal out here, in the middle of all these bodies?

Was it even possible to hurt anyone in this realm?

Damn it, why hadn't he paid a bit more attention on his visit to the Underworld all those years ago? His infernal Scorpio need to control everything had ensured much of the lesson was lost as he focused on ways to get back aboveground.

Robert shoved and pushed his way through the crowd of writhing bodies, Alex increasingly falling behind him. Although the crowd slowed Robert down, his sheer determination and whatever passed for adrenaline in the Underworld had clearly given him an advantage.

Kane had suspected all along Robert held the power in the duo's partnership, and watching him push and shove his way through the bodies only reinforced that. What Kane hadn't expected was Robert's complete disregard for his friend.

Ignoring the aching screams of his muscles, Kane pushed harder, closing the gap by a few additional yards. What felt like endless miles of shoreline passed by as they navigated the stream of dead humanity.

Just . . . a few more . . . yards.

The poison slammed through his body, intent on destruction. He was winded, when normally the scenery flew by on a run. His muscles ached when they'd normally take the abuse and ask for more. And worst of all . . . air wheezed in and out of his lungs like an old man on oxygen.

Ignore. Ignore. Ignore. The word beat through Kane's mind with each footfall.

Great, searing shoots of pain filled his muscles as he ran. While the poison didn't literally have a voice, he could almost imagine it taunting him.

Die. Die. Die.

Pressing on, Kane couldn't deny his body's needs. Couldn't fully ignore his lungs' need for air.

A few more yards and he would be close enough to at least grab Alex.

Run.

Reach.

Push *harder*.

Run. Reach. Push harder.

RunReachPush—

Without warning, Ilsa landed on top of Robert in a chaotic port, a round of cheers greeting her tackle. Alex screamed, his frail body crumpling in on itself as he slammed into the two of them.

Relief filled Kane at Ilsa's seeming health and vitality, especially if her body was already able to port again. The sensation followed quickly on the heels of bone-shuddering anger.

This time, the scientists were *his* collar.

"Ilsa!" Kane ran the remaining distance that separated them, snagging a hand on the back of Alex's shirt to lift him from where he sprawled next to Ilsa. His little goddess had already regained her feet, steely determination filling her movements as she struggled to keep her hold on Robert. For his part, the newly embodied scientist was doing his fucking level best to decimate Ilsa, his arms wrapped around her as he struggled to grab her neck.

Rage pumped through Kane. Great, galloping waves of it. Like a horror movie unfolding before his eyes, Ilsa struggled against Robert as he attempted to subdue her.

He watched her gasp for breath, still weak from nearly drowning in the river, and all conscious thought evaporated.

Every shred of reason and clarity Kane possessed fled at the sight of his woman in danger.

His woman.

A war cry erupted from his throat as Kane dragged Alex along in his wake, throwing the protesting rat bastard toward the writhing souls gathered around them in a screaming mob.

And then he let his scorpion out.

Ilsa fought against Robert's hold—the skinny bastard stronger than she'd given him credit for. Pain continued to pummel her body; the tear the scientists had ripped through her soul was a gaping wound inside her that throbbed in agony.

She *would* heal. Ilsa knew the gifts of her immortal body well enough to know that.

But she'd be damned if she'd let this asshole get away while she waited to heal.

Robert's arms came around her neck again as he attempted to pull her into a choke hold across her windpipe. Unwilling to go gently, Ilsa slammed a fist toward the side of his face, satisfied when the direct hit snapped his head back like a punching bag.

Despite her ability to get a few good jabs in defensively, she couldn't get an upper hand. Couldn't find a weak spot. Couldn't get an advantage over him.

As she shifted and struck out with another punch, a loud scream echoed off the arched, caved walls.

Kane.

Robert's attention, momentarily diverted by the Warrior's scream, gave her all the chance she needed. Sliding out of his hold, Ilsa dropped to all fours, scrabbling away to gain some ground and work through her strategy.

But it was all for naught.

Like a feral ballet that played out before her eyes, Kane swooped in on Robert and began to attack. The magnificent black scorpion battled next to him, man and beast in perfect harmony as they fought the evil little man who resisted death with everything he was.

Alex huddled on the shore, curled up in a ball, ignoring the screams and shouts of the souls as he lay there.

As before in London, Ilsa couldn't help but feel some sense of sympathy for him. Yes, he'd done wrong. But he'd been betrayed, led along by someone he trusted.

Just like her.

She'd been betrayed by Zeus. Someone she believed in. Someone she thought had her back.

Was Alex all that different?

The reality hit Ilsa so hard her knees buckled and her

already-exhausted body fell to the ground at the sudden loss of strength.

Was she really any better than Alex?

Where Alex was led astray by ignorance, she lived with a far darker emotion.

With a far deeper wound.

And it would never heal as long as vengeance ruled her choices.

Look at what she'd wrought already. Her choices had put Kane in the gravest danger. Her agreement with Emmett ensured it.

The cries of the Warrior filled the air as Kane attacked, retreated, then attacked again. Robert put up a good fight, but he was weakening, his body slowing under Kane's rapid assault.

As the balance of power shifted, Kane got a firm hold on Robert's neck, using his height advantage to lift the scientist off the ground. Robert's feet dangled several inches above the shore and loud, gurgling sounds fell from his lips.

"You will not touch her."

Robert's frantic gaze darted toward her. "That thing?" he gasped out. "You mean her?"

"You will never touch her again." Kane's voice was low, the dead calm more menacing than if he screamed with the power of a thousand voices.

"Do you even know who she is?" Robert gasped out. "I lived inside of her and I know *exactly* who she is."

Ilsa's stomach dropped at Robert's words.

Was it possible?

Did he truly know her thoughts?

Had he heard them?

"Your little whore, ready to spread her legs for you. Right there on the shore," Robert ground out, gasping for breath as his lips turned a dark shade of purple. He lowered his voice to a whisper, his evil, soulless eyes filled with calculated cunning. "Don't you want to hear what I know?"

Slowly, Kane lowered him to the ground. He never broke physical contact, but Robert now stood on firm ground and the scorpion stilled, in a battle-ready position behind Kane.

"Do you know who she is?" The words slid out in an evil purr as Robert's lips returned to a more normal shade.

"Robert! No!" Alex screamed from where he lay. "There is no chance for you if you do this."

Dark, dead eyes shifted from Kane's face to focus on his partner. "There's no chance for me. There never was. So I'm going to ensure there's no chance for her, either. Isn't that right, Nemesis?"

Kane shook his head, as if the motion could dislodge Robert's words. Although he maintained a firm grip on the scientist, Kane shifted his attention toward Ilsa.

"Is this true?"

Ilsa's stomach dropped again, the cold tone of Kane's voice telling her all she needed to know and more. When she didn't answer his question, Kane pressed again, undiluted fury riding his tongue. "Is this true?"

Tears rimmed her eyelids, but Ilsa held her head high. "Yes. It is true."

Kane's voice was quiet now, the low tone almost harder to bear than the shout. "You didn't tell me. Even here, as we came down here, came to understand each other better, you didn't tell me."

Robert's calculating purr returned. Ilsa felt his gaze slip away from Kane, those dead eyes shifting to meet hers.

"Ever the whore, eh? Playing your lover with the greatest of ease."

Kane's justice was swift, his scorpion striking out in a deadly arch with its front pincer. The open claw severed Robert's head before he could make any further accusations.

Even if they *were* true.

Waves again lapped at the side of Charon's boat as they rode down the river.

Although they were tighter on board with the addition of one passenger, Kane hardly noticed. His bewilderment left room for little else.

Nemesis?

Ilsa was Nemesis? The goddess who lived in constant vigilance over men's souls?

Should he even call her Ilsa any longer?

Her name hovered on his tongue, but he ignored it, instead focusing straight ahead as Charon ferried the boat to Hades's domain.

Alex sat between him and Ilsa, huddled into a weeping mass of humanity. Now that he'd escaped his bonds, his body had corporeal form in the Underworld as he awaited his judgment.

Kane almost felt sorry for him, but held the urge in check.

The bastard didn't deserve any lenience.

None.

The race to capture Robert hadn't done him any favors, either. The poison had him in its claws with a vengeance, ripping his stomach lining to shreds.

Kane gritted his teeth but it wasn't helping. Nothing was. Combine the pain with the fact he'd been played the fool and it made for a bad fucking afternoon.

"Kane. Are you okay? You're awfully quiet. Is the pain back?"

He maintained his focus on the water ahead of them, unwilling to make eye contact. Unwilling to face the woman who had betrayed him.

Again.

"It's not the poison."

"But you haven't moved. I knew this was a bad idea. You've barely recovered from the knife wound. Damn Quinn for let—"

"Quinn?" He turned toward her then, uncaring they had an audience. "How the fuck can you think this has anything to do with Quinn?"

"He forced you"—her voice faded out to a whisper— "down here."

"Wrong answer. You forced me down here. You and my concern for you. Clearly I need not have bothered. It's obvious you know how to take care of yourself. I'd expect nothing less, after all, from the great goddess of vengeance and retribution."

"That's not fair! You knew I was immortal."

"There's immortal and then there's immortal, Ilsa. You're the freaking goddess of vengeance. That's quite a handle."

"Oh, so when you thought I was simply Hades's errand girl, I was fine?"

"How are you even related to Callie? She's a nymph, for fuck's sake. You can't be sisters."

"It's a long story."

"I'll just bet it is. And I'll also lay odds you'll keep that from me like you've kept everything else."

Charon's pointy little ears stood on high alert and even Alex sat up straighter as the argument escalated. Acknowledging the need to pull it back, Kane returned his gaze straight ahead and wondered when he'd lost his edge and become such a simpering, stupid fool.

And then he didn't need to remember.

He already knew.

The day he'd gone and fallen for a fucking goddess.

Chapter Sixteen

Hades greeted Kane, Ilsa and Alex as they were escorted into his chambers. "The host of many," as Kane had often heard him referred to, was a congenial man, with surprisingly strong vigor for a god who spent the majority of his days in the Underworld.

Their seemingly endless trip on the Acheron was blessedly over, and even though his deepest desire was to simply go home, Kane knew they'd not leave the Underworld until they partook of Hades's hospitality.

Despite the constant stream of arrivals, it turned out Hades and Persephone had surprisingly few guests.

Kane familiarized himself with the palatial surroundings. His last—and only—trip to the Underworld hadn't included a visit to Hades's judgment room. An oversized throne sat at one end, elevated upon a dais. A long red velvet runner ran the length of the room from the dais, bisecting the chamber in half.

Other than the slash of red, the room held minimal color. Sconces ran the entire length of the walls, the rows of candles providing the only light.

Alex's judgment would be private, but clearly Kane and Ilsa wouldn't receive the same courtesy as Hades began his inquisition.

"Took you long enough to get here. Where's Robert? And why is Alex in corporeal form?"

Kane's anger hadn't lessened since learning of Ilsa's true nature. Instead, his anger had morphed into something more raw—more *basic*—as shock faded into acceptance.

While not technically a lie, Ilsa had had no problem deceiving him through omission. From her real name to her true purpose, she'd kept herself hidden.

What he couldn't fault, however, was the authority with which she did her job.

"We had some challenges on the Acheron." Ilsa's pose was respectful, but her gaze stayed firmly on Hades.

"Challenges?" One lone, authoritative eyebrow rose at the suggestion. "What of them?"

Ilsa continued her report, her voice terse and stilted. "Robert and Alex found a way to escape their bonds. We dealt with Robert immediately as he was clearly a flight risk."

"Their bonds? Attached to your soul?" Hades's gaze shot toward Alex, who had resumed the kicked-puppy stance he'd adopted on the riverbank and zeroed in on the high points of the tale. "You did this?"

Alex's eyes remained focused on the ground. "Yes."

"How?"

"Physics."

"You what?" Kane felt the unexpected rush of surprise, the feeling matched by the dropped mouths and eye-popping gazes of Ilsa and Hades.

Physics?

"Sure. It was easy." Alex shrugged. "Her soul had limited space. Through careful calculation and an understanding of the limitless application of our souls, Robert and I created an antimatter calculation to break through. Well, I did the calculation. Robert agreed."

"Excuse me?" Hades pressed on, clearly at a loss for any other response. The details of particle physics were as lost on one of the most supreme gods in existence as the rest of them.

"We traded a bit of our souls to cancel out hers." Alex pointed toward Ilsa. "That gave us a hole to escape through."

"How do I get it back?" For a woman who had just stared down the god of the Underworld, Ilsa spoke in a tone that was decidedly panicky.

Alex shrugged again, his tone matter-of-fact. "You can't."

The blue eyes that had widened in surprise glazed over in fear. "What do you mean, I can't get it back?"

"It's gone. Destroyed. Matter and antimatter. If it makes you feel any better, a part of mine's lost, too."

"No, it doesn't make me feel any better." Her slender form quivered as Ilsa confronted Alex. "And I want you to find a way to put it back."

Alex focused on some point across the room as if unable to look at Ilsa directly, but the note of pride in his voice was unmistakable. "I can't put it back. It's gone. It wasn't all that hard, either. You had several weak spots we found when we looked for the proper place to break through."

"What's that supposed to mean?" she demanded.

Alex shrugged. "I don't know how they got there. It's not like I spent a whole helluva lot of time roaming around in other people's insides. My guess is they're weak spots from where you've got a lot of issues. I could see Robert's soul when we were inside of you and it was full of them."

"Did you know about this?" Kane turned on Hades. "Did you know this was possible?"

"I had no idea."

Yet again, score one in the column for humans.

Kane knew the venom that lived inside his body—an unexpected result of a sorcerer's dark magic—had been a surprise, too. A consequence Themis had never expected, or even knew was possible, when she created her Warriors and identified all their gifts.

Clearly Hades hadn't thought through all the angles, either, if Ilsa was now required to walk around with a hole in her soul.

A hole that would allow others captured in the future to escape.

A fact that was fast-dawning on Hades if the red face and sputtering voice was any indication. "You're human. You have no abilities in these matters."

Kane stepped forward. He was done with the bowing and scraping, the underlying trap of eternal gratitude he and his brothers were expected to endure.

They fought the battles and they lived with the consequences of the gods' choices.

Maybe it was time to start speaking up and speaking out to the gods who ruled their lives. Time to use his voice and the lessons he'd learned over more than ten thousand years of life.

He'd earned it, and so had his brothers. So, apparently, had Ilsa.

"Perhaps it's time we started giving the humans a bit more credit."

"You can't destroy souls," Hades muttered, walking in a circle around Alex, examining him like a rare specimen.

"You do." Ilsa shot back at him. "You do it all the time."

"That's different," Hades muttered, still shaking his head as he made another rotation around the scrawny scientist.

"How?" Ilsa pressed. "If souls are the only immortal part of a human, how is what they did any different than what you do?"

"I'm a god."

"Well, then, you need to figure out how to get rid of the loopholes. Because until you do, you're fresh out of an errand girl."

Ilsa paced the guest room in Hades's mansion, wrapped in a heavy, oversized, fuzzy pink robe. A large four-poster bed dominated the room, its royal blue duvet and mound of pillows beckoning with the promise of sleep. It would be so easy to just lie down and forget about all of it.

The deal with Emmett.

The damage wrought by the scientists.

Even Kane and this crazy, mind-numbing love for him that consumed her.

But it wasn't to be.

At this point, she wasn't even sure a visit from Hypnos would be effective. Finding out you had an irreparable hole in your soul sort of kicked the god of sleep's ass for mindshare.

Claustrophobia had set in hours ago, but Ilsa had no desire to put on her happy face and go sit through dinner with Hades and Persephone.

Had absolutely no interest in being a dinner companion, pleasant or otherwise.

How could this have happened? And what did Alex mean by weak spots?

What weak spots?

Had the thirst for revenge well and truly eaten a hole through her soul on its own?

Or was it something else?

Something far worse.

Her long-held fear that she was irreparably damaged resurfaced. Was that why she'd never found love? Why she'd so easily rejected the companionship of her nymph sisters? Was that why it had been so easy to live all these years alone?

Until Kane.

It had all changed with him.

"Ilsa, open up." A rough knock came on the heels of the command.

Kane.

Like she'd conjured him up.

Opening the door, Ilsa stared him down. He'd changed into formal wear for dinner with Hades and his wife—one of Persephone's odd requirements—and looked positively luscious in a perfectly cut tuxedo.

Even the shadows under his eyes—a perpetual reminder of the poison ravaging his body—gave his face a dark, sexy, craggy look that sent her pulse skyrocketing.

"You left me down there to deal with them all by myself? I thought you were coming down after freshening up."

Ilsa shrugged. "I didn't feel like coming down to dinner."

Kane closed the door behind him as he came into the room, unknotting his bow tie and tossing it to the floor as he walked toward her. Was it her imagination or was his gait slower? Less smooth? "Shit. Persephone talked my ear off for an hour. Do you know how lonely it gets down here in the Underworld?"

"No."

She watched in fascinated awe as he placed a hand casually on a hip, the tuxedo jacket opening to reveal his broad chest where it narrowed into his slim waist.

A truly perfect male form.

"Well, then, ask me."

"Okay. How lonely does it get down here in the Underworld?"

"So lonely that if she didn't have Hades and his godlike stamina in the bedroom, she'd have killed herself years ago."

A burst of giggles erupted. "She did not say that."

Kane held up a hand, the jacket falling back into place. "Yes. She did. I promise you, nowhere in my own mind could I have made that one up."

An awkward silence descended between them as her giggles evaporated as abruptly as they began.

Kane was standing right there.

In her bedroom.

And then the spell was broken. "Why didn't you tell me you were Nemesis?"

"There was nothing to tell."

"Damn it, Ilsa. Or should I call you that?"

"It's the name I prefer." *Especially when it falls off of your lips.*

"Fine. Ilsa. You should have told me. Should have explained. And what the hell are you doing at MI6? How'd you come to be there?"

And there it was. The question she'd dreaded since Kane came back into her life. Dreaded for the past few days as they'd spent time getting to know each other.

Up to now, she was guilty only of omission. But if she lied about her role at MI6, then she well and truly would cross a line.

She couldn't tell him yet.

And she didn't want to tell Kane a lie.

There *had* to be a way to deal with Emmett and get out

of their bargain. A way to give the sorcerer something else in place of Kane or his Warrior brothers. A way to satisfy Emmett's desire for more power that didn't come at the expense of Themis.

She couldn't tell Kane yet. She simply couldn't.

"It's classified."

"Bullshit."

"That's all you're getting from me."

"Fuck classified, Ilsa. I want answers."

"I don't have any to give you."

Those dark onyx eyes bored into hers, a mix of anger and—was that hurt?—whirling in a perfect storm.

"I'm in this with you, whether you like it or not. Why won't you trust me?"

"No one's in this with me. I am alone!" The words ripped from her chest with such force, it was a wonder she didn't fall down.

The truth of the statement—the horrible, embarrassing truth—stunned her to hear it out loud.

She was alone.

Had always been alone.

And due to the poor choices she'd made in her quest for revenge, she'd always *be* alone.

Always.

Legs trembling, Ilsa backed away from Kane. "Leave. Please. Just go away."

Kane ignored the request, his long, long legs closing the distance between them. "No."

Hot tears pricked the backs of her eyes and spilled over without warning, a rush of frustration that she was incapable of damming up. "Please!"

He reached up and brushed one heavy tear away with his index finger. "I'm not leaving."

Ilsa took another step backward and let out a slight "oomph" when the backs of her legs hit the side of the bed. "You can't stay. And I can't tell you what you want to know. And I am damaged."

"We'll find a way to fix the hole the scientists made."

"No, Kane. You don't understand. I'm damaged. I'm no good. The scientists were successful in their escape because they found a weak spot. Inside of me. On my soul."

"No, Ilsa, Robert and Alex found a loophole. Just like the sorcerer found mine. We're immortal, Ilsa, not infallible." He closed the remaining space between them. "That's the great cosmic joke we all operate under. That somehow, because we're immortal, nothing can ever happen to us."

"Nothing *should* happen to us."

"But it does. You and I are both perfect examples of that."

She wanted to believe him.

Desperately.

Kane wiped another tear away, then lifted his finger to his mouth. He pressed it to his lips and licked off the drop of moisture, his eyes never leaving hers. "I'm not leaving, Ilsa."

"Good. Because I don't want you to."

The salty taste of her tears covered his tongue as Ilsa's words registered. Unwilling to wait a moment longer, Kane reached for her, wrapping her in his arms and pressing his mouth to hers.

Tears still ran down her face and her lips tasted slightly salty as his tongue sought entrance to her mouth. As she opened for him, he dipped in gently, drawing at her tongue and sucking lightly.

Ilsa allowed him to lead the kiss, her tongue tangling with his, her response free of any restraint.

Oh gods, she felt so good in his arms.

So right.

He felt her hands settle at his waist where she tugged his shirt from the waistband of his dress slacks.

Breaking contact, he pulled back, dragging the heavy jacket from his shoulders, the dark silk sliding into a pile on the floor. Ilsa reached for the studs of his shirt, snapping them off one by one, allowing them to fall to the floor where they scattered on the hardwood as they fell.

Her hands were cool on his skin as she ran smooth fingertips down the center of his body. His stomach muscles responded under her touch in a shiver of need only for her.

His Ilsa.

Reaching for her, his hands sank into the fuzzy pink of her robe. Anxious to see the beautiful curves of her body, he pulled at the tie at her waist. The heavy pink terry cloth fell away, revealing her naked form underneath.

Kane's breath caught in his throat. "Gods, you are so beautiful."

When she didn't respond, he leaned in, pressed his lips against her ear and whispered it again.

She shivered in response to the warm breath he feathered over her ear, her own voice whisper soft as she replied, "It's you who is beautiful."

Stepping back, Kane stared down at her. "You *are* beautiful, Ilsa. Inside and out."

With a swift shake of her head, she reached for the open folds of her robe, pulling them tight against herself.

He reached for her hands, stilling her movements. Anger built in his veins at her unwillingness to either listen— or believe—what he told her. "I don't lie, Ilsa."

"I know."

"Then what's wrong? Why are you covering yourself and why are you turning away from me?"

"I can't see past it, Kane. Can't see past what I am and what Alex told me."

"What Alex told you? When?"

She nodded, her eyes bright, a sob catching in her throat. "Before. In front of Hades. That there were weak spots they used to tunnel through my soul. That's *me*. That's not particle physics or scientific theory or evil humans looking for an out. It's just all me. A damaged soul that's now even more damaged."

She slammed a hand against her chest, her blue eyes bleak and empty. "It's all broken in here."

How did he fight this?

How did he convince her?

And then the answer presented itself, so simple it took his breath away.

"Lie down." He patted the oversized bed.

"Come on, Kane."

"Ilsa, I'm serious. Please lie down."

She did as he asked, shifting to sit on the center of the large bed.

"Now, lie back."

One eyebrow quirked up, but she acquiesced, the pink of her robe in distinct contrast to the deep blue of the duvet.

"Open your robe."

"Kane."

He sat down on the edge of the bed, enjoying himself as she struggled with his direction.

"I promise you, I have a point."

"You want monkey sex."

A broad grin he couldn't stop spread across his face.

"Well, yeah. I'm a man. I always want monkey sex. But that's not what I'm driving for at this particular moment."

Her eyes narrowed in suspicious disbelief, but she complied yet again and opened her robe. The lush curves of her body spread out before his eyes like a feast and he couldn't keep his gaze from roaming over every exposed inch of her.

Leaning over, he pressed his lips under her breast, his tongue trailing over the hard crest of her ribs. A small squeak resounded in his ears as she squirmed underneath his mouth. "Kane. What are you doing?"

Lifting his head, he smiled up at her. "From what I can tell by the way you doubled over, Dr. Jekyll and his sidekick broke through right around here. Am I right?"

She nodded. "That's right. I can't explain it, but it just feels . . . empty there."

"Then I need to kiss it and make it all better."

Chapter Seventeen

Then I need to kiss it and make it all better.

Ilsa locked Kane's words deep inside her heart, allowing them to settle there. Years from now, when she was quite alone, she'd take them out and remember them. Savor them.

She'd remember this moment and this incredible man who rained kisses down her rib cage, murmuring soft words of praise and encouragement.

His tongue continued its gentle ministrations, lapping softly at her body as he interspersed a series of kisses along the slender ridge of bones.

Ilsa stared down at him from where her head lay on the thick pillows. She reached for him, his name a whisper on her lips. "Kane."

He didn't lift his head; instead, he shifted slightly and ran his tongue over the underside of her breast. "Hmmmm?"

Her head fell back as a wave of sensation followed the path of his tongue, the vibrations of his voice.

She knew she should say something. Should stop him or divert him or try again to make her point. But "should" suddenly had no meaning in the face of his sensual ministrations.

She wanted him. And that was enough.

As if he sensed her surrender, Kane shifted again, taking a nipple between his lips. Her body responded immediately to his touch, the long, sucking drags of his mouth pulling an answering response from deep within her. Wetness pooled between her thighs and her legs shifted restlessly underneath him.

"Ahhh." He stared up at her, a broad smile on his face. Reaching for her hand, Kane linked his fingers with hers. "Now you're with me."

"Yes," she whispered on an exhale of breath.

And then there was nothing else to say and everything to feel.

The lazy, languid moments evaporated as something more urgent—more forceful—took their place. His mouth returned to her nipple as his fingers reached for her other breast, plucking at the tip. Her back arched in pure, feminine pleasure while he laved his attention over her.

The hot, wet darts of his tongue spurred sensation after sensation, her body coming to life under his mouth and hands.

Lifting himself up on his forearms, Kane smiled down on her. "It suddenly dawns on me, we're both wearing far too many clothes. And while I definitely like the open-robe look"—his eyes roved over her body where it lay half in and half out of the pink terry cloth—"I need to feel you. Skin to skin."

A broad smile spread across her face. "Absolutely."

It took moments for her to drop her arms from the sleeves of her robe and for Kane to do the same from his open tuxedo shirt. As he shifted to the edge of the bed to stand on the floor, she watched with hungry eyes as he doffed his slacks. His briefs quickly followed to the floor and her entire body tightened at the sight of him.

Magnificent.

There was simply no other word for him.

The long, lean lines of his body captivated her as nothing in her life ever had. A light dusting of hair grazed his chest, tapering down to a thin line that ran into the male core of him.

His heavy cock stood proudly and she warmed at the sight of his arousal—and desire—for her.

That's for me, she thought with delight.

With disbelief.

All for me.

Extending her hand, she reached for him. Again, his fingers linked with hers—so simple, so easy—and she tugged him toward the bed.

Kane's body met hers as the urgency flared again, rising up between them. Their breathing grew heavy as their mouths met and meshed, tongues tangling in the urgent, desperate need to mate.

Heat rose off their bodies as he climbed back on the bed and nestled himself between her legs. His mouth settled over hers as he suckled her tongue into his mouth for another deep, drugging kiss.

Ilsa felt her body respond from deep inside her womb, and her legs shifted restlessly against his hips and the outside edge of his thighs.

She was here. Tonight. With Kane.

Just as she'd dreamed for six long months.

Finally—*finally*—they were together again.

Ilsa ran her hands over the broad width of his shoulders as deep, feminine appreciation for the hard muscles beneath her questing touch filled her with awe. Kane shifted beneath her, his fingers plying over her skin and leading a sensual path for his mouth to follow.

Another long, deep drag on her nipple, then the hot heat of his mouth as he placed more fiery kisses over her stomach muscles, stopping along the way to nip at her belly button.

And then there was no thought. No analysis of what was happening to her. Only sensation.

Only heat.

His mouth covered her throbbing center, his tongue dragging over her clitoris in long, sweeping arches.

She moaned, long and low, as Kane drove her to the brink of madness and back. He knew just how to please her, driving her body to the absolute edge of sensation, her muscles aching for sweet release, before pulling back. Holding her in his grasp, desperate for relief, teetering on the edge of orgasm's sweet oblivion.

Over and over, he pleasured her. Over and over he pushed her even closer to that edge, then pulled her back.

"Kane, I need you."

He worked his way back up her body, his mouth beginning a reverse path.

Impatient for him, Ilsa pulled on his arms. "Now!"

A broad smile met her insistent demands. "As you wish."

He centered himself over her, but she couldn't wait any longer. Reaching down between their bodies, Ilsa ran her fingers over the long, hard length of him, satisfied when he closed his eyes on a low moan of his own.

Wetness covered the round tip of his cock, and she ran her fingers through it, using the bead of moisture to paint the crown. Her efforts were rewarded with another moan, before Kane reached between them and stilled her hand.

"Ilsa."

She laughed, the sound a glorious wellspring of life filling her chest and falling from her lips. "Don't like the tables turned, eh?"

Pressing his lips to her neck, he positioned himself at the entrance of her body. "I need you."

Reaching down once more, she guided his body into her wet, slick channel. He filled her, stretching her in the most delightful, wonderful way as he buried himself to the hilt.

"I need you, too," she whispered before giving herself up to the moment.

Kane took control of the rhythm, pulling nearly all the way out of her body, then plunging back again. She met him thrust for thrust, rising up to meet him, the sounds of their joined bodies sweet music between them.

The glorious pressure built once again, her body throbbing with need, her muscles aching, desperate for release. Moments spun out, grew more frenzied, the rhythm faster and more intense.

More. Want. Need.

Just *more*.

And then, like the most incredible magic, Ilsa's world exploded, her body on fire with its release. Kane emitted a loud shout and followed her, shuddering with his own orgasm.

As the moment spun out, their bodies in lockstep with each other, their hands entwined in a tight grip, Ilsa felt the emptiness inside of her fill to bursting with the sweet light of life and love.

Kane absorbed the pure joy of being held in her arms, his body still quivering with its release. Lifting himself slowly from her, he pulled her into his embrace.

He hadn't felt this good in weeks—good sex went a long way toward fighting the poison and its effects.

Although the poison typically resisted the usual remedies that got a warrior back to full strength—sleep and food—it couldn't deter him or keep him from enjoying the third remedy.

Orgasm.

It might only be a temporary solution, but he'd take all the ammunition in the internal fight he could get.

"Tell me about the poison."

"Funny you should mention it," Kane whispered in her ear where she lay, pillowed against his chest. "I was just thinking about that and how I feel better than I have in weeks."

"It debilitates you."

"Yes."

"Is it really horrible?"

Kane pressed a kiss to her head. "Come on. Surely you don't want to talk about this."

Shifting, Ilsa lifted her head to look him in the eye. As always, the deep blue of her eyes distracted him, their endless depths a fascination. "I do want to talk about this. Maybe if we do, I'll see an angle someone else has missed."

"I've lived with it a long time, Ilsa. And I told you about all the tests we tried to get rid of it. I've come to accept it was an oversight in Themis's creation. Now that I am this way, I have to live with it."

Those blue orbs filled with anger. "Why? Why should you have to live with it? If something can be created, surely it can be reversed."

"Perhaps. But sometimes something changes and that's all. It just . . . changes." He stopped, at a loss for words.

"What if that isn't good enough?"

"What if it has to be?"

"That's awfully accepting of you, Kane."

"I'm feeling pretty good at the moment. I'm not sure it's acceptance so much as it's the pleasant afterglow of mind-blowing sex."

He got a smile out of her at that, but it didn't quite reach her eyes. Unfortunately, Kane didn't know how else to explain it.

The acceptance.

He'd struggled for so long—had hoped for a cure for so long—that one day he'd simply woken up and realized he had to live with it. Make a life with the hand he'd been dealt—a hand he'd earned fair and square.

He knew the risks he took each and every day.

The calling he'd accepted from Themis didn't promise a life free from pain.

And the poison. Well, it had taught a valuable lesson about the consequences of letting his guard down.

Some things just were.

As the moments spun out in quiet contentment, his mind ran through the events of the last few days. Of all he'd learned.

Of all they'd discovered about each other.

"How did you come to be Nemesis if you're a nymph? As Nemesis, you have the full powers of a goddess."

Her shoulders stiffened slightly. The movement was so small—so fleeting—he probably wouldn't have even noticed if she weren't wrapped in his arms. "I accepted the role at Hades's request."

"You weren't born to it?"

"No." She traced a circle on the upper part of his stomach. The light circles were oddly soothing, even as some part of him also registered the erotic feel of such a simple touch.

When it came from Ilsa, even the simple was complex.

Everything seemed deeper somehow.

Refocusing, he concentrated on his questions. Kane knew his reaction to her. Thinking too hard about her touch would put them right back to sex. Later, he promised himself. They'd have all the time they needed later.

"Why did you accept it? Hades's offer?"

She was quiet for several long moments, the pattern she traced the only indication she was even awake. Finally, on a soft exhale of breath, she said, "Because I had no choice."

"There's always a choice. Always."

"Perhaps. But personally, I think desperation colors choice. When you feel there's no way out, you will take anything that's offered to you. Anything."

Desperation?

Kane's stomach muscles tightened. What had happened to her? Or worse, what had been done to her? "Did you feel you had no choice?"

"Do you recall the history of the Titans?"

A history lesson?

"Of course. It's the root of who we are. It's what shaped Themis and, in turn, what shaped her Warriors."

"Then you know Zeus was hidden as a baby."

"Of course." Kane glanced down at her, placing a finger underneath her chin to pull her gaze level with his. "Ilsa. What does this have to do with you and your role as Nemesis?"

"I was the nymph who hid Zeus from Cronus."

"What? But that's not . . . What?" Kane struggled to a sitting position.

She raised Zeus?

The great god and leader of them all?

Raised by Ilsa?

It just wasn't possible.

"Ilsa. You were the guardian who protected Zeus? You are a legend. The entire Pantheon reveres the role you played in keeping him safe. In seeing him to adulthood."

A harsh snort escaped her and further surprise filled him when she leaped from the bed, reaching for her robe on the ground. "Legend? I hardly think so."

With long strides, she paced the room, wrapping her robe tightly closed, nearly ripping the tie as she moved.

"But you are. You're the missing heroine. The one who created a future for all of us. Everyone knows you existed, but no one knows who you are. That you're still alive is a miracle."

"I was betrayed! Left to rot in that fucking cave on Mount Ida by Zeus, ungrateful bastard that he truly is."

What?

What was she possibly talking about?

"Ilsa. I don't understand. You are the lost nymph. You are to be celebrated. Venerated by all who look upon you. If the Pantheon only knew you've been here all along. Alive. All this time."

Kane wasn't sure why, but his words had the exact opposite effect than he'd hoped. Apparently his attempts to convince her were doing anything but.

"Venerated? What a joke."

Ilsa stalked over to the closet, ripping apart the ties she'd just tied and tossing the robe to the ground. He watched as she shimmied her long, lithe body into another skirt and sweater set. His body tightened as his gaze roamed over her, but at the moment, he knew sex wasn't what she needed.

She needed to vent.

At the same time, getting to the bottom of whatever was wrong with her was the priority. Leaping out of bed, Kane stalked to her, unconcerned with his nakedness and semi-aroused state.

"What has you so upset?"

"Venerated? Revered? I'm anything but. I'm here because Zeus hated me. Turned on me. *Cursed* me, Kane."

"What do you mean, he cursed you?"

Ilsa dropped onto a couch in a sitting area on the far side of the room. He followed, taking the seat next to her. "Rhea gave me Zeus and hid us away in the cave on Mount Ida. She promised me I'd have my reward. This veneration you're talking about—I lived with the promise of that for all those long, lonely years."

When she stopped, he pressed her on. "And?"

"And once Zeus was grown, he left and headed off to battle his father, promising he'd return. Promising he'd bring me back to Mount Olympus when he was done."

Kane waited as she paused, her eyes filled with memories of years long past.

"How long did it take him to return?"

"Seventy days passed, with nary a sign of him. And then, on the seventy-first day, Zeus reappeared. Only he was no longer the boy I raised. In just over two months' time, he became someone else. Someone I no longer recognized." She sighed as a lone tear ran down her cheek. "And I was no longer someone he recognized. All he saw was the woman he believed betrayed him."

"But you raised him and kept him safe."

"Ah, there it is. The great irony of my life, Kane. On that day, the god I'd devoted my life to—the god I'd given up my life to—betrayed me with the worst punishment imaginable. A fate truly worse than death."

"But why?"

"He believed I'd kept him from his destiny. Kept him hidden away in my own selfish desires to keep him safe."

The anger that had filled Kane along the banks of the Acheron returned on swift wings. Raw, pulsing rage filled him as he imagined her, a young nymph, exposed to nothing for years on end but the endless responsibility of raising the young god.

She'd been used.

And discarded.

"What did he prescribe?"

"I was bound to the cave on Mount Ida for all eternity. If I attempted to leave the cave, I would lose my corporeal form, roaming the earth as a spirit."

Her tears flowed freely now, spilling over in great, gulping waves.

"He betrayed me, then punished me for some perceived crime he manufactured in his head."

"But you're here." Kane ran a hand down her arm, the motion darkening her eyes with desire. He gained a small measure of satisfaction to see she wasn't so far lost in her dismal memories that she couldn't still respond to his touch.

That she could still *feel*.

"I'm here because of Hades. He was newly released from his father's evil and had heard what his brother did to me. He arrived with a bargain."

Clarity rushed through him at her words.

Of course. It explained her role for him and it explained how she could be both nymph and goddess.

She was *created* a goddess by the power of an Olympian; she wasn't born one.

"And it was that choice you referred to earlier."

Ilsa laid a hand over his where it rested on her thigh. Movements deliberate, she lifted her gaze to his and kept their eye contact solid.

Unwavering.

"Do you see now why I scoff at the idea of choice? Choice exists when either option is viable. When either option offered is valid. It isn't choice when one of the options is a life of misery. Not even a life, really, but a half life. A trapped life."

The truth of her words struck him in a way nothing else had. He'd entered into his agreement with Themis willingly, the life she offered an enhancement, but not an escape.

Never that.

But for Ilsa, what Hades offered was escape.

She stood, her long legs carrying her swiftly across the room toward the door. "Where are you going?"

"I need to talk to Hades. Need to tell him we're taking our leave of this place. It's time I got you home."

"I can try to port right now. I'm strong enough and I can leave when I'm ready."

"I promised Quinn I'd bring you home. I won't break that promise. Won't give him one more reason to hate me."

Even though it galled him, he could admit he still needed help to port. His body felt better than it had for weeks, but still wasn't anywhere near full strength.

"I'll be back shortly."

She was nearly to the door when a thought had him stopping her for one more question.

"Ilsa, where did Zeus get those ideas? About you and your loyalty? Why would he turn on you as he did?"

Venom tinged her words. "He got them from one person. The woman he devoted his life to."

"Hera? But that's not possible. They met years after his defeat of his father."

"Not Hera, Kane. Themis. His first wife. Themis changed his mind and it is she who turned Zeus against me."

Themis watched Ilsa and Kane through her viewing mirror. The Mirror of Truth stood in the center of her small living room. Her quarters were sparse, her comforts on Mount Olympus easy to accommodate.

She needed her mirror to ensure balance. Beyond that and her bed to sleep in, her life was about movement.

Action.

Constant vigilance.

It galled Zeus that she lived in the simple dwelling and she'd be lying if she didn't admit it was a small side benefit that it irritated him so badly.

Petty, yes.

But they were her feelings and she was entitled to them.

Themis directed her thoughts back to the mirror and the woman whose visage was reflected there.

Ilsa.

Nemesis.

Adrasteia.

So many names. So many confusing roles. One woman, caught in the middle of all of it.

Although Ilsa's heart held no love for her, Themis's felt quite the opposite in return. The young nymph had been snatched from her home and given a challenging existence, followed by an untenable one in Zeus's punishment.

While Themis admired Hades's willingness to make right the actions of his brother, his solution smacked of far too much self-interest for her comfort.

But Ilsa *had* chosen. Just because that action was steeped in desperation didn't make it any less a choice.

Gaze roaming across the mirror, Themis shifted her attention to Kane.

Her proud Scorpio Warrior. He had suffered terribly at the hands of the sorcerer Emmett. Would likely suffer further, with the poison an ever-present trial to his body. Much as she'd longed to help him through the ensuing centuries, she was bound by her agreement to Zeus and the limits to how they were allowed to interfere.

Bound by her commitment to balance.

She'd never imagined one of her Warriors could be turned on by one of his gifts. And even though his Scorpio tattoo protected him and fought by his side, the scorpion's venom was a constant enemy.

An endless threat.

The mirror winked out as Themis considered the dilemma both of them faced. There were trials and challenges ahead—obstacles to them giving themselves wholly to each other.

Could they overcome those burdens?

Or would the crushing power of circumstance bury them both?

Chapter Eighteen

Ilsa's knees quivered and her stomach twisted in anxious knots as she walked to Hades's private chambers.

How had it come to this? And what had possibly possessed her to pick a fight with Kane?

Well, not a fight, exactly. But it certainly wasn't pillow talk, either.

And yet again, you fuck it up. Your one chance at a sexual encounter in all these months and you end it by talking about punishments and choice.

Ilsa shook her head as she headed down the last hall to Hades's chambers. She sure knew how to leave 'em begging for more.

The door to the private chamber was open when she arrived. The god of the Underworld sat at a large desk, a mountain of paperwork in front of him.

"Come in, Ilsa."

She moved into the room, surprised to see him signing his name to the top page on the stack. "What are you doing?"

"Paperwork." At her questioning gaze, he added with a

smile, "Yes, even in the other realms, paperwork is a necessity. From what I've gathered in my discussions with my brothers, we certainly produce more than our fair share down here." He shook his head. "Souls are serious business."

"Yes." She nodded, thinking of her own damaged one. "They are."

"I'm sorry, my dear. Poor choice of words." He stood, walked around the endless length of teak and motioned her toward a small library down the hall. "Persephone has set up tea service. She figured you'd find your way down here at some point."

Ilsa followed him down the hall, Persephone's feminine touch evident as soon as they walked into the library. Not only was there a tea cart set up and service already laid out, but a small plate of petits fours and cookies sat next to the teapot.

Hades shook his head. "That woman does know me." He popped a chocolate petit four into his mouth, his eyes closing in a moment of pure bliss. "Knows me so well it's scary."

Truth be told, Ilsa thought it was sort of wonderful. Amazing, actually, that someone could have a love so great—so deeply entrenched—that they'd make such small gestures.

Simply to give the other a moment of joy.

"We missed you at dinner."

"I am sorry to disappoint, but I wasn't up for company."

"You could have sent word."

Ilsa reached for the teapot, grateful for something to occupy her hands. "I thought you'd understand. Assumed you'd figure it out when I didn't show up."

"Of course we did. It doesn't deny the need for basic courtesy."

Ilsa slammed the teapot against the cart. "Damn it, Hades.

I had a lot on my mind. And at the top of the list"—she grabbed a teacup and handed it to him, her hands surprisingly steady as she moved the steaming liquid—"is the fact I'm missing a part of my soul. It's not exactly breaking a nail, if you know what I mean."

"No, it's not minor. Not at all."

"Did you deal with Alex?"

His mouth slashed into a harsh line as he stirred his tea. "You know I can't divulge punishment."

"I sort of figured I had a dispensation with this one. Especially seeing as how the little worm was the one who bored the hole."

Hades's eyes shuttered with finality, yet his tone remained even. Soft, almost. "I'm sorry, but on that I can't accommodate you. My rules are fixed."

"Can I ask one question, then?"

"Go ahead."

"Was he right? Is it irreversible?"

Hades took a sip of his tea, his warm brown eyes locked on hers. "I believe so."

"But how can that be? I've carried souls for you for millennia. Why now? Why was this different?"

"I suspect it's a variety of circumstances that all coalesced into one. There were two of them. And you carried them for quite some time before delivering them to me. And they had a particular set of skills that allowed them to figure it out."

Anger rippled through her stomach, highlighting the gaping emptiness that sat just below her ribs on the right side of her body. She leaped up, the tea in her cup sloshing toward the floor. With deliberate movements she settled the fragile china on the tea-service cart before she ruined Persephone's carpet. She didn't want the soothing brew anyway.

Whirling on Hades, she demanded, "So now it's my fault?"

"You jump to conclusions. I didn't say that."

"And how would you have me take it?"

"Shift your perspective. Look at this through a new lens. Perhaps this is a good thing. A good thing, indeed."

A harsh bark erupted from her throat, unbidden. "Good? And how, exactly, have you come to that conclusion? Is it just something to make yourself feel better?"

The storm clouds gathered in his eyes as his brows rose. "You take liberties, Nemesis. Even for you, this is a bit much."

"And why's that? You're not the one walking around with the hole, Hades. You're not the one who is suddenly out of a job. Or out of a life."

The outburst drained her, had her falling back onto the couch.

"You have a life. I gave that to you. You're the one who has chosen to avoid human contact, instead living in your world of vengeance and retribution."

"What choice did I have?"

"Ah. There it is again, that stubborn belief you cling to."

"What of it?"

Hades stared down into his cup, his voice grave when he finally replied. "Our circumstances are all unique. It is our choices that distinguish us."

There it was again. It was as if the entire universe conspired against her, pressing on her the idea that she must get over what had happened to her and move on.

Nature or nurture?

She never remembered which it was or which side she fell on, but either way, the message was the same.

Get over your fucking circumstances.

Rise above them, young woman, and be strong!

Be better than what is expected of you.

"Well, then. I can see you've made your decision on the matter. Seeing as how I am no longer able to carry souls for you, I will take my leave of you. It's time you began seeking a replacement for me. I hear there is a disillusioned group of nymphs in Eastern Europe. Maybe you can find one of them to give you a hand."

"You are always welcome here. I will always care for you."

Ilsa nodded, unable to respond. Unable to see past the gaping emotional wound, even larger than the physical one she carried within her life essence.

"Before you leave, there is one other matter I'd like to discuss with you."

"Yes?"

"This matter of a life. Or the perception you don't have one." She nodded her assent to continue, but couldn't stop the surprise at his next words. "Your love for the Scorpio offers you a life. A rather wonderful one, if the way you look at him is any indication."

"I don't love him."

The benevolent father figure evaporated. In its place, a snapping, defensive ruler. "Lies don't become you. And I won't tolerate them in my presence."

"Fine. What of it? Nothing can come of my feelings. And I . . . I've made choices that have the potential to harm him. I can't expose him to that. I must let him go."

He nodded at that, his acknowledgment of her words a revelation. *Of course* he knew about her bargain with Emmett. How could he not? Surely Emmett had secured a spot on Hades's hit list quite some time ago.

"Those we love can't share our burdens with us if we

don't allow them to." Hades's words were firm, leaving no room for argument.

It didn't really matter as she was all out of arguments.

With a final glance at the only security she'd known for these many long, lonely years, Ilsa turned and walked slowly for the door. Hades's voice stopped her just before she exited.

"Ilsa?"

"Yes?" She didn't turn. Wouldn't let him see the tears already making twin paths down her cheeks.

"While I can't tell you the specifics on Alex, I will tell you that he's paid for his crimes. Both to humanity as well as to you."

She nodded, then slipped through the door.

It wasn't enough.

But at least it was something.

He was done with waiting.

Emmett threw the book against the wall of his study and watched as the old text crumbled at the impact.

Fuck it.

He knew the text forward and backward anyway. It all lived in his head. Like a god with power he wasn't able to unleash.

His last meeting with Enyo had bolstered him for a few days, but the delicious joy of one-upping her had abruptly vanished on the wings of impatience.

He wanted action.

He wanted the Warrior.

Nemesis—or Ilsa, as she called herself, likely some dumb homage to *Casablanca*—thought she had one up on him, but he knew she was up to something.

Emmett knew her better than she knew herself, most likely. Because he made it his business to know.

The Scorpio had no doubt lured her in. The most sexually magnetic of the zodiac, that outcome was as inevitable as the sun rising tomorrow.

It was that sexual magnetism that had done his half sister in.

The whore.

Emmett had made it his life's work to understand those he wanted to capture. His Pantheon collection was a perfect example. He'd researched each and every legend, created a plan of action and then went in search of his creatures.

The centaur, the giant, the Cyclops and the nymph had been the easiest captures. Those four already existed in nature, their basic needs forcing them out into the open. Once he'd mastered the process with the low-hanging fruit, he'd shifted gears, focusing on more difficult foes.

The Horae and the Argonaut had been much harder, as he'd had to find a way to trap them.

Lure them out.

Although, even they had proven easier than he'd anticipated. The Horae was more of a natural creature than he'd originally given her credit for. And the Argonaut just wanted a battle.

As always, immortal or not, one truism remained constant.

Find your enemy's weak spot and pound on it.

And then, as he sought his next capture, the simplest joy of discovery. To find that his sister had delivered one right under his nose in the form of the man she claimed to love with wild devotion.

It hadn't taken much to secure the Scorpio after that.

A few dark words spoken to his sister in her sleep. That weak mind of hers so quick to do his bidding when he planted the seeds of doubt about her large, overbearing Warrior who killed for the Medicis.

She'd jumped in fear and acted quickly. From a woman desperately in love to a woman who scorned her lover faster than if he had the pox.

His plan had come together so beautifully and in no time Kane Montague was his.

And then, the greatest of pleasures.

His dark spell, designed to separate the Warrior from his powers.

"My brothers will find me."

"No, they won't. My sister has sent them on a merry chase to the farthest corners of the globe with her mad ramblings of your whereabouts. By the time they figure out they've been duped, I'll have what I need from you. They won't even recognize you."

He saw the Warrior glance down at the tattoo that sat on his forearm. "I know you can communicate with that. But you need the night sky to do so. As you can see"—Emmett flung a hand with pride at his surroundings—"you're two stories underground here. No night sky in sight."

The clamoring and screaming from the other cells was deafening as it echoed off the hard stone walls, but Emmett ignored it. He was preparing for his battle with the Warrior.

Already he was imagining the Scorpio's great power, vested within him by the goddess Themis, charging through his own veins.

"You will not succeed."

"Actually, I will."

Emmett had left him then, to make his preparations for the final spell. The spell that would release the scorp's powers and his immortality to him.

What Emmett hadn't counted on was the Scorpio's determination and unwillingness to fail. Nor had he counted on the Warrior's ability to port through time and space.

It was a gift not embedded with all immortals. Emmett had learned too late that Kane not only had the gift, but could use it without limitation.

When he'd returned to the basement, each cage stood empty, including the last. At the end of that long row of cells, Kane Montague awaited him, a small, sharp sword held aloft in his hand.

"You miscalculated, Sorcerer."

"Think that if you'd like. But these"—he waved a hand at the now-empty cages—*"immortals don't matter to me as you do. Their gifts aren't as robust—their understanding of immortality something they take for granted. But you. You received the gift. It is you who understand my longing."*

"I know not of what you speak."

"Oh, surely you don't think me that ignorant, do you? I see the flash in your eyes at the mention. You received immortality and you know the meaning of that gift."

Emmett approached the entrance of Kane's cell, the glory of what he planned to do beating through his system like the finest drug. The sweetest wine. The most intense orgasm.

"You understand the great joy of knowing your body will never age. Your years span out before you with the glory of endless life."

Before the Warrior could speak again, Emmett conjured the prepared words, pulling strength from all that surrounded him. The latent power of the earth surged into his feet and up into his legs. The age-old stones built into the walls sang to him, their lifetime of secrets unfolding in the power of his dark magic. Even the slight moisture that puddled in the corners of the cells, weeping from the humidity of the underground walls, sustained him as he drew power from the water.

All swirled around him in a pattern growing—coalescing— into the darkest spell he'd ever performed.

> *Power mine, power thine, all power rests with me.*
> *Power mine, power thine, take all he will ever be.*
> *Earth and air, water and wind,*
> *Become one with me, his power rescind.*

The air grew dark around them, heavy with the power he conjured from it. Dark, roiling waves suffused his frame and Emmett felt his body respond, heavy jolts of power— mental, emotional and sexual—rippling through him in tsunamilike waves.

Lightning flashed in the tight space, sparking off the metal bars and slamming around the room in bright arcs.

Emmett felt it all. The power of nature, building inside of him.

Turning toward the Scorpio, he extended his hands, willing himself forward, focused on the man's heart as the base of his power.

Kane's focus never wavered, his eyes steady as his body lay coiled in wait.

With a harsh flick of his wrist, Emmett flung the raw, writhing power toward the Warrior. Kane sidestepped a sparking arc of electricity as a large scorpion unfolded from his back, shifting to stand next to him.

"You do fear me if you release the animal," Emmett screamed at him, the power so great, so magnificent, he saw a spectrum of colors spread out before his eyes. Deep indigoes and rich purples flared with the brightest oranges and reds.

Power.

In his body, outside his body, coming to life through his body.

He saw it all.

The only thing that didn't brighten with color was the Warrior and his scorpion. They stood before him, dark as night, absorbing the colors that flew around them in a dizzying whirl.

"I will have you." Emmett flung more energy at the dark form.

Kane parried, the heavy knife in his hand reflecting the flash of power and sending it shooting back on Emmett, its force doubled on the return trip. A scream left his lips as Emmett fell to the ground.

What was this?

This ability to fight off his magic?

Fury joined the power, the two growing and expanding to cloud out everything in the room—even the joyous colors— until the only thing that remained in Emmett's line of focus was Kane and the animal who fought by his side.

"I will have you."

"You will never beat us. My brothers and I protect the world from men like you. From your evil actions, the evil you pull from the world around you. You are the dark and we are the light, come to stop you."

As Kane shifted, preparing for the next thrust, Emmett saw his plans—his grand vision—floating away on the air.

The colors that tinged the black form in front of him faded and the air was losing its heavy, expectant feel.

He would not lose. Would not surrender.

And as the black shape in front of his eyes shifted and moved, Emmett changed his plans.

The strength he pulled from air, earth and water weren't enough to defeat a god.

But he had other talents.

Other skills.

His incubus father had left him with many gifts, and one was the willingness to use any means at hand.

The Strega *his maternal ancestors used had its own belief. Its own ritual around curses and their power.*

Emmett might not have the natural power to beat the man standing before him and all he represented. But he did have the ritual power to weaken him.

To control him.

To tie their lives together.

With startling clarity, Emmett honed his focus down to a sharp pinprick of light, calling on his knowledge of the Strega.

The Italian phrases fell from his lips as he impressed the curse on the Warrior.

With each word spoken, the air around them filled with expectation. With excitement. With inexorable change.

A scream penetrated the air as Emmett watched Kane fall, the animal crumpling in on him.

As Emmett continued to chant, the scorpion rose, separated itself from the Warrior's aura, and scrabbled over toward Emmett.

Hands shaking with the most awesome power, Emmett directed him.

"Strike your master. Envenomate him with the poison."

The scorpion hesitated, his stinger held aloft, his focus still on Emmett.

As if he could hear the animal's question, the knowledge of what he must do flowed through him.

"I will sacrifice as well. I will sacrifice my magic until

that time when we will meet again. When we face each other anew. Other than my most base gift—the ability to create fire—I will it to be."

Little could anyone imagine, it wasn't really a hardship. Oh, he loved his magic, but he'd found so many other avenues for protecting himself.

He'd created potions and charms he could use without having to add any further magic to them. And for the really dark stuff. Well . . . there were always ways around a promise if you were clever enough.

The scorpion appeared to nod, then followed Emmett's orders, shifting quickly to slam into Kane's body. As the Warrior writhed on the ground, Emmett felt an answering pull in his body, his limbs freezing into immobility.

What was this?

He'd promised. He'd sworn. Was this what it felt like to be without magic?

Or was it something else?

The words of his grandmother came back to him. Her teaching on curses and how to issue them properly.

The curse is only effective when something is exchanged.

Okay—check—he had done that. His power for Kane's.

The curse must have limits and parameters. No one curse has all-seeing perpetuity.

Shit.

He'd forgotten that one.

"By the power of the Strega, *I vow to control the poison. It will have limits to its dominance."*

The stiffness in his limbs receded slowly. He was definitely on the right track.

In bold Italian, Emmett completed the curse, the answer coming to him on a rush. The perfection in the stars the ideal balance for a Warrior of the Zodiac.

"*I call on the patron star of the* Stregheria, *Antares, one of the four wardens of the western gate. When the star—the brightest in the Scorpio constellation—is at its zenith, the power of your scorpion's venom will ascend to its greatest height. It is at those moments when the Warrior and I will be in greatest harmony, our bodies in tune with each other.*"

The scorpion folded back in on itself, reassembling into the Warrior's aura.

As Kane slowly regained consciousness, Emmett watched from across the length of the jail cell, his own body returning to normal.

He had his Warrior. The Scorpio could not escape him, the poison in his veins like a lodestone that paired them.

And until he figured out how to expand his skills to take the Warrior's power forever, this was a satisfactory start.

Oh, the glory of that day, Emmett thought, as he walked the perimeter of his study, examining the various tomes and texts on the shelves. Of course, like his joy at one-upping Enyo, it had been short-lived. While he could track the Warrior when the poison was at its height, reaching him was another matter. He was protected by the other Warriors, preventing Emmett from final domination.

But no man could deny a beautiful woman. Through Ilsa, he could draw the Warrior out. And once she was part of his trusted circle, she could persuade him—lure him out—during the time he fought the worst of the poison.

Through her, he'd finally get the Scorpio.

Emmett was tired of living his half life, assuming bodies of various humans so he could sustain some level of his power, feeding off the latent energy each human produced but which very few—if any—attempted to channel into true power.

So he used it.

Assumed it.

Stole it.

He was nearing his final goal. This sacrifice had tested his limits, certainly. But now, as his goals moved ever closer into reach, he acknowledged the sacrifice had been worth it.

Now that he was *so* close, it was *all* worth it.

Whether she liked it or not, Ilsa would deliver the Warrior to him.

And he would finish what he'd begun so many years ago.

Chapter Nineteen

Kane heard the loud, boisterous cries from the dinner table as he and Ilsa landed in the front entry hall. The dining room wasn't far off the hall and clinking plates and loud laughter greeted them as they arrived.

He knew his brothers' attitude toward her, Quinn's especially. Knew this had to be the last place on earth she wanted to be, with her sister right down the hallway.

But as they stood there in the foyer, like two teenagers standing awkwardly after a high school dance, he was loath to let her go.

Did teenagers do that any longer? It happened on TV and movies, but he'd never experienced it. They sure as hell didn't do it when he was that age.

He'd spent more than one delightful evening groping with a girl from the next village over in a darkened corner of the woods that divided their homesteads.

Fuck, he was old.

"Kane?"

"What? Oh. Sorry."

She shuffled, the slight movements causing the tap of

her heels to echo lightly around the immense marble foyer. "I need to leave."

"Where will you go?"

"I have a place. I need to deal with a few things. Get my life in order."

"That sounds awfully cryptic."

"Fine. I need to deal with my contact at MI6. Resign my post." She hesitated for a moment, then looked him square in the eye. "I'd suggest you do the same. It's no kind of life running around killing people. It's . . . no kind of life."

"Even if they deserve it?"

She nodded. "Even then."

Another awkward moment slid past them before Ilsa stood on her tiptoes and pressed a kiss to his cheek. Warm heat assailed him as her body made contact with his. Then, as she stepped away, he reached for her, pulling her close, crushing her to his chest.

Every word that failed to rise on his tongue poured forth in the kiss. Powerful and forceful, yearning and needy, an emotional connection spun out between the two of them.

Lips met and merged. He felt her nip at his lower lip with her teeth and he dragged her tongue into his mouth, the hot suction a reminder of earlier.

A reminder of all they'd shared.

Gods, but he didn't want to let her go, even as he knew he had to.

She made him vulnerable.

And he had a life he needed to get back to.

"Well, this is a surprise. I'm not sure if I should grab a hose or a video camera."

Ilsa leaped away from Kane like a scared cat while Kane leveled a harsh stare at Drake. "You're a funny guy."

"Glad to see you made it back." Drake turned his focus toward Ilsa. "Did you make your delivery?"

"No thanks to you assholes," Kane added before Ilsa could say anything.

"You're the one with the death wish, Monte. Quinn simply pulled his pack-leader bullshit."

"And you went right along with it."

The words clearly hit home, if Drake's scowl and ready fists were any indication. Their normally placid Pisces went from resolute to feral in a heartbeat.

"What the fuck?" Kane felt the punch almost as soon as he saw it, Drake's lightning-quick reflexes knocking him for a loop as a fist slammed into his jaw.

All the anger—at himself and the poison, at Ilsa and her circumstances, at the forces that conspired to keep them apart—came out in a rush. Kane punched right back, his fury quickly giving him the upper hand.

"What the fu—?"

Kane felt large hands dragging on him as shouts echoed around him. Quinn held Drake as Brody, their Leo, held Kane by the shoulders.

"Seriously, Monte? Only you could pick a fight with the Pisces." Brody's voice growled in his ear. "So nice to have you home, by the way."

Neither Brody nor Quinn let up their grips, instead dragging Kane and Drake toward the dining room. Kane saw Ilsa slip toward the door, only to be intercepted by Brody's wife, Ava.

He missed what she said, but it had to be fairly persuasive as both women entered the dining room a short while later.

"You want to tell me what's going on? My bride and I return from Egypt to find all hell's broken loose here."

Kane nodded to Ava, then made quick introductions between Ilsa and the Leo. It was obvious she'd met his new wife already. Ava's recent turn to an immortal at the hands of Themis certainly seemed to agree with her. Her already-creamy skin glowed pink and a look of deep satisfaction and happiness rode high in her warm brown eyes.

After a few polite words, Brody went straight for the throat. Kane wasn't sure if the comment was directed at himself or at Quinn. "So why'd the two of you go to the Underworld alone?"

"Work needed to be done. Ilsa had a delivery to make."

"So you went with her, having no real working knowledge of the Underworld and being less than two weeks out from the poison's zenith?"

Why the fuck had everyone crawled up his ass? It pissed him off because it was his choice.

Not theirs.

With a shrug, Kane reined in his anger, refusing to show how much it bothered him. "Ask Quinn. He's the one who stayed behind."

"His common sense is gone. Which is typical this time of year. The poison takes over and he still thinks he can fight it. Still thinks he's at full strength," Quinn said.

Unable to stay silent, Kane interrupted the bull's litany of sins. "You know, Quinn, I'm still here. What the hell is this, a parent-teacher conference?"

Before the comments could escalate any further, Ilsa jumped in. "Look. I really should be going."

"You're sitting down for dinner." Ava stopped her and pointed to a chair. "You both look dead on your feet. Eat something and get your strength back and we can decide who is leaving after that."

Callie picked that moment to enter the room, an enormous, steaming tray of lasagna in her hands. Its twin already sat empty on the other end of the table.

"Um, Ava," Kane added, but it was too late.

"Callie, we need some more plates," Ava said with a smile.

"Ava—"

All conversation stopped as Ava prattled on. "Kane brought a guest for dinner. This is Ilsa and she'll be joining us. I'm sure we have enough food."

The words floated off in a hum that rose above the room.

Kane watched the drama unfold before his eyes. Quinn and Drake had grown abruptly silent at Callie's entrance. Brody's gaze had gone speculative and Ilsa had made definite steps toward the swinging door into the room.

But it was Callie who really caught his attention.

Her small frame quivered with attitude and she slammed the heavy tray onto the table, the motion causing a loud crack as it hit two ceramic pot holders.

"I will not break bread with that bitch. If she eats with us, I'm leaving."

Oh gods. Ilsa had heard the expression "crawl through the floor," but had never experienced the sensation.

She now realized she could have happily lived her life without ever learning how that actually felt.

Heat flushed her face and she added a few more steps to the light, tentative ones she'd already taken toward the door.

"What's the problem? She's our gue—" Ava was halfway through her next thought when Callie's words penetrated. "Am I missing something?"

Callie's shoulders went up in a huff, her finger point unmistakable. "Ask my sister."

"Your sister? You two—?" Ava's glance swung toward her before shifting back to Callie. "You have a sister?"

"Yes. I have many sisters."

"Really?" If Ilsa wasn't mistaken, the eager look that suffused Ava's face indicated some deeper level of interest.

Was Callie secretive with them?

While Ilsa wouldn't have expected to be the first name on her sister's tongue, they came from a large brood of nymphs. It would have been natural for Callie to talk about some of them, especially if she lived here, with the Warriors.

Ava looked as if the news was a delightful surprise.

"Look, I really do need to leave. I'll just be going." Ilsa took a few more steps toward the door before her body betrayed her with a long, low growl from her stomach.

Ava went into order mode. "You're not leaving. You're hungry." With a turn toward Callie, she added, "Ilsa and I will eat upstairs. I'll just fix us a few plates. We'll leave the boys to their discussion."

Ten minutes later, Ilsa sat before a heaping plate of lasagna and garlic bread at a small table in what looked like yet another library.

"I was in a library the other day. On the first floor. And now here's another. The guys sure do have a lot of books."

Ava smiled as she tucked a napkin on her lap. "They have a lot of subjects to keep up with. A lot of interests. Each one's different, you know."

"Well, of course. They're all different people."

"Yes, but each has a different role within the whole, too." Ava poured two glasses of wine, handing one over. "My husband, Brody, he's the group's archaeologist."

Dinner passed quickly as Ilsa listened to Ava talk. Fascinated, she was interested to learn that not only was Ava incredibly warm and engaging, but she was very new to this world of the Warriors.

Ava poured out the rest of the wine and Ilsa watched the dark red liquid fill the deep red bowl of the glass. A lovely sense of calm had settled over her, the wine and a full stomach doing an incredible job of mellowing out some of the desperate urgency she'd felt earlier.

"So"—Ilsa leaned forward—"in the short time you've been with Brody, what have you learned about them?"

"The Warriors? They're a true band of brothers, willing to help one another when the need arises. But . . ." Ava tapered off as she looked deep into her glass, then back up, her gaze direct. "They struggle. More than any of them would like to admit."

"Struggle how?"

"All of them are very dominating personalities. Each knows how to do his job. How to be a protector."

Ilsa nodded in agreement. Memories of the past few days ran through her mind's eye.

Kane as he helped her catch Robert in Hyde Park.

Kane as he ran after the escaped scientists on the banks of the Acheron.

Kane as he stood by her during their report to Hades.

He was a leader.

"That's so true."

"Because of that, I don't think they always know quite what to do with one another."

"How so?"

"It's hard to explain. When they're all focused on a task, they band together and nothing can pull them apart. But it's the day-to-day life." Ava waved her hand, as if searching for the right words. "It's like they don't know how to interact with one another as regular people. So they keep their distance much of the time."

"Quinn did that. The other day. He wouldn't help Kane if he insisted on going with me to the Underworld."

"That's exactly what I'm talking about. And Quinn is definitely the worst of the bunch. He's so intent on his stubborn, bullheaded ways, he can't see past the end of his nose most of the time."

Ilsa tried to read Ava. Tried to understand the nuances that added to what she actually said. "You don't like him?"

With a broad smile, Ava let out a small giggle over the rim of her wineglass. "Oh. I love him. He's wonderful. He's just a pain in the ass."

Ilsa wanted to ask more. Wanted to know how you loved someone who you called such a derogatory name, but didn't know how to do it.

She was so bad at this and their conversation only highlighted, yet again, how inept she was in dealing with others.

"Ilsa." Ava's voice was quiet as it broke into her thoughts.

"Yes?"

"Why are you so sad?"

"I'm not." Ilsa shook her head as hot tears pricked the back of her eyes. "I'm really not."

"Because you can tell me. You know, if you want to."

"Really. I'm fine."

Ava nodded and her face held the wisdom of the ages. "Tell ya what. I believe you. Really, I do. But I'm going to open another bottle of wine and we'll keep chatting. And if you decide you want to talk about anything, well"—she shrugged her slim shoulders—"I'm here to listen."

"You just spent the last day and a half in the Underworld? No shit!" Brody's eyes were wide with questions.

"Ilsa needed to return some souls to the Underworld," Quinn added as he poured their third round of scotch from the sideboard in the dining room. "Kane felt it was his duty to accompany her on this journey."

"Fat fucking lot of help the bull was, too," Kane added, his second scotch already working a number on his tongue. "Wouldn't even take us. Had to ride the ferryboat with the little demon."

"You met Charon?" Now it was Drake's turn to question, his surprise comparable to Brody's.

"What did you miss the other day, Pisces? None of you would take us to Hades. The only way in if you can't port is through passage on the river. Who did you think was going to take us?"

"Yeah, but you're not dead," Drake persisted. Whatever ire—or guilt—that had plagued him earlier in the hallway had evaporated, his current mood calm as he pressed his questions. "I thought you had to be dead to ride the boat."

"Obviously not. And so glad you just thought about that little tidbit, by the way." Kane offered up a mock salute. "Fuck you twice."

Brody's gaze flipped from Kane to where Drake and Quinn sat next to each other on the opposite side of the table. "Okay. What did I miss?"

Kane caught him up on the last several days' events, including his brothers' unwillingness to travel with Ilsa and their further unwillingness to support his own decision to do so.

"I didn't say I wouldn't travel with her." Quinn gestured with his glass. "I said I wasn't taking you, too."

"Wasn't your call, buddy." Brody gestured strongly with his own glass.

Quinn's eyebrows pulled close as fire flashed in his eyes. "I'm not responsible for death wishes, Talbot. And that's what he wanted."

Kane objected to the pointed finger and accusation, but was too comfortably numb to make a fuss. He did manage to toss a slightly annoyed "I don't need a fucking babysitter," which was his annual litany during the poison's ascension.

Poison that had been slowly tightening his muscles since he and Ilsa had left the Underworld.

"Bullshit. This isn't about the poison and you know it," Quinn ground out. "You've got no objectivity when it comes to that woman."

"No." Kane shook his head. Somewhere inside, a small part of himself knew he should keep his mouth shut. But the pleasant numbness had no problem shutting down the voice.

None whatsoever.

"I don't have any objectivity when it comes to her. She's got me so fucking torqued up I barely know my own name. And you know what? I don't exactly care about it all that much."

Brody held up his scotch and they clinked their matched leaded-crystal glasses to each other. "It's fantastic, isn't it?"

Was it?

Kane thought through the insecurity. The frustration. The mind-numbing fear when he worried something had happened to her on the Acheron.

Was that what it meant to care for someone?

That you were so fucking scared to lose them, you died a little bit each time things didn't go smoothly for them?

The thought was quickly followed by another one. Ilsa wrapped in his arms, her unique scent filling his senses. "Yes."

It was Drake's turn to gesture. "Besotted fools. Both of them."

"Yeah, well, at least Brody knew what he was getting with Ava," Quinn added. "Ilsa's got too many secrets for my comfort."

Kane nodded, unable to get mad at Quinn for the comment. "That's true, too."

Drake shook his glass to dislodge the last of his drink. "You any closer to figuring her out than you were a few days ago?"

"I know a bit more than I did."

"Will any of it change our opinion?" Typical Quinn. Direct and pointed and pulling no punches.

Kane shrugged. "Will you change your opinion?"

"If you give me a damn good reason to."

"She's the missing nymph." The room grew so quiet Kane could practically hear their heartbeats.

"Adrasteia? The nymph who cared for Zeus?"

Kane nodded. "That'd be the one."

"What's she doing taking souls to the Underworld?" Brody probed. "As her job?"

"Uh-huh." Kane nodded, swallowing the last of his drink. "She's Adrasteia and she's Nemesis and she's my Ilsa."

"Your Ilsa?" Drake asked. Kane wasn't sure if the Pisces's voice was actually slurred or if he'd missed something in the translation of the comment back to his brain.

"Mine."

Three pairs of eyes stared at him from around the table, holding a mix of concern, good humor and a fair amount of teasing. Even Quinn had the decency to look slightly impressed at all the information Kane had managed to glean on the trip south.

Brody reached for the half-empty bottle of scotch and

laid it on the table between the four of them. "A little possessive there, Monte?"

"Nope. Just engaging in a bit of modern-day territory marking."

"Don't worry," Quinn added dryly. "I may be the asshole who wouldn't take you to the Underworld, but even I wouldn't horn in on my friend's girl."

Ilsa fought off a wave of giggles as she flopped back onto the bed. She wasn't going to stay the night. Hadn't even wanted to stay for dinner.

So how did she end up staying?

Oh right.

Ava.

Very persuasive woman, that Ava. And sweet and kind. And fun. And for such a demure-looking woman, with her soft blond hair and warm, teacherlike brown eyes, she certainly liked to talk about sex with her new husband.

Ilsa giggled again. Who knew women did that? No wonder most of the nymphs spent the majority of their days giggling with one another.

It was fun to talk about sex.

And very illuminating.

She had absolutely no idea you could squeeze a man's cock to prolong his pleasure. But the tips of her fingers certainly itched to give it a try on Kane.

Maybe it was good she was staying the night here.

Maybe Kane would want to have sex again.

And maybe she should tell him about that other thing. Ava said it was important, but she didn't know.

Ilsa sat up, the room spinning in a weird circle as she looked around.

A large armoire dominated the far wall and the bed she

lay on dominated another. A small love seat ran the length of the wall with the door and the fourth wall was a bank of windows from one end to the other.

How did she end up here again?

In Kane's bedroom?

The bed was soft under her back and she ran a hand over the cool silk of the bedspread, listening idly to the sound her fingernails made as they swooped and swirled over the material.

She felt so nice. So loose and limber and . . . liquid.

She felt like the problems in her life weren't really all that bad.

Which was funny, really, since the problems in her life had never been this bad. Ever.

With her fingers, she made more swoops and swirls on the coverlet, liking the soothing sound it made, the repetitive action allowing her to think.

The door opened on a whoosh of air.

Ilsa sat straight up in bed, surprised by the loud sound of the door as it slammed against the far wall.

She was even more surprised when Kane slammed it closed, then staggered to the bed and flopped down, facefirst.

"What's wrong with you?"

"Shit-faced," mumbled back at her from the direction of Kane's mouth.

"Me too," Ilsa said, flopping backward so her head lay next to his. Another round of giggles she couldn't stop floated up and out of her.

More mumbled details. "Whaz so funny?"

"Everything."

"Oh."

They lay there like that for several minutes. Every so often, Kane emitted a low moan and mumbled something about his head, then the room grew silent again.

What was that she wanted to ask him again?

Oh.

Right.

"Did you know if I put the proper amount of pressure on your cock when we're having sex, it prolongs your pleasure and will keep you from coming?"

Kane lifted his head, groaning as he used his elbows to push himself up. "What did you just say?"

"Doesn't it work?"

An odd, strangled gurgle escaped his lips and his dark eyes did this cute sort of roll. "Well. Um. Where'd you hear about this?"

"Ava told me."

"She did, did she?"

"Oh yes. She said she does it to Brody and he loves it."

Kane groaned and slapped his hands over his ears. "Oh gods. Fuck me swinging. Don' need an image of that."

She shrugged. "S'kay."

Kane lifted himself onto his elbows again, his face delightfully close to hers. "Anything else you found out tonight?"

"Well, we discussed what an ass hat Quinn is. Even though Ava loves him very much."

Kane's laugh erupted around them even as his upper body sort of wobbled. Or was that her eyesight? "Ass hat?"

"It was Ava's term."

Kane leaned in and pressed a quick, hard kiss to her lips. "I'll have to start using it. Immediately."

Silence fell between them as Kane's gaze captured hers.

She felt all warm and gooey inside, sort of like the brownies Ava had hunted up after they finished off their second bottle of wine.

"So is there anything else I need to know? Besides sex tricks and new variations of dirty words."

Ilsa dropped his gaze. "Um. Sort of."

"Well, don't keep me in suspense. My attention span's gotten fairly limited since the image of you squeezing my cock has taken up all the space in there."

"Well, um, there's something I never told you."

"You've got another name?"

"What?"

He grinned, the lopsided tilt of his mouth doing funny things to her heart. "It was a joke. So what did you want to tell me?"

"When we had sex. That first time six months ago? Do you remember?"

That smile got a little bigger. "Yes. I think I remember."

"Well." Ilsa took a deep breath. Should she say it? Shouldn't she?

Might as well go for it.

"I was a virgin."

Chapter Twenty

A virgin?

Was it really possible?

Kane knew it was a stupid reaction. If nothing else, he'd always—*always*—prided himself on his innate respect for and belief in women. Their interests. Their lives. Their sexual choices.

But the caveman impulse clearly wasn't dead, either, as his body filled with white-hot desire at the idea he was the only man who had ever had sex with Ilsa.

Had ever lain between those luscious thighs.

Had ever brought her to orgasm.

"Why didn't you tell me?"

"Tell you what?"

"Then. Six months ago. You didn't tell me you were a virgin. I'd have—" He broke off.

"You'd have what?"

"Um. Well. I'd have done it differently."

A delightful little wrinkle pulled up her nose as her pale blue eyes filled with questions. "You can do it differently?"

"I mean the *way* I did it. I'd have gone slower. Been more gentle."

"You were wonderful."

Damn, but she was too good for his ego.

Kane ran a hand over his face, trying to scrub some sense into his brain. The scotch—which had seemed like a raging good idea at the time—was wreaking havoc with his common sense and every word that came into his head was quickly discarded as he searched for the right thing to say.

"Are you upset?" Ilsa asked him, her voice as soft as the down pillows they lay upon.

"No."

"Well, you look upset. Your face is all crinkled up and your eyes are all squinty."

"The squinty's from about three glasses too many of scotch."

"Really? Do I look like that? I had quite a lot of wine."

Kane scrubbed his face again, running his fingers over his eyes in deep, soothing circles before opening one to look at her eager, flushed face.

How to handle this?

How to make her realize what an amazing, incredible, beautiful gift she'd just given him with her words.

Rolling over, he laid his head on the pillow next to her and pulled her into his arms. "I'm not upset. At all. In fact, I'm so incredibly flattered and honored, I'm sort of at a loss for words."

"Oh."

"What I meant before is that, had I known, I would have made sure to be extra careful and make your first time something really special. I'd have gone slower and allowed your body to adjust to sex for the first time."

She let out another one of those cute drunken giggles.

"I realize I don't have anything to compare to. But I thought that first time and all the other times since were perfect."

"Flattery, my dear, will get you everywhere. But I'd like to think of myself as an overachiever. Perfection can always be improved upon."

With deft movements, Kane lifted her, pulling her on top of him to straddle his body. Reaching down, he slid his fingers underneath her panties, a growl of pure male satisfaction rumbling in his chest when he felt her already slick and ready for him.

Ilsa's head fell back, her high, pert breasts thrust toward him, her nipples visible through the thin sweater she wore. Before he could help her, she had her hands at her waist, lifting the sweater to expose herself to his hungry gaze.

Tossing the sweater to the side of the bed, Ilsa bent over him, a sexy smile spread across her face. Her eyes were dark with arousal, her voice husky with need.

"Well, then. Overachieve away."

Ilsa slipped into the library early the next morning, her head throbbing with the pain of a thousand jackhammers. This was a hangover?

The ache in her head confirmed that's *exactly* what it was.

Ignoring it, she focused on her task and prayed the dull edge of sickness would work its way through sooner rather than later.

Didn't it take humans all day to get over these things?

She could only hope her immortal body would shed the pain sooner.

Of course, her immortal body wasn't what it once was, especially with the tear in her soul still causing its own fair share of pain.

Ilsa did a quick scan of the shelves as she crossed the

room. The memory had come to her sometime early that morning, as she lay in the circle of Kane's arms, unable to sleep.

Over dinner the evening before, as Ava explained the various roles of all the Warriors, she mentioned why there were so many books strewn around the mansion. Ava had pointed out how they'd organized the categories and how to search for information, anywhere through the house.

With swift keystrokes, Ilsa tapped out what she was looking for on the laptop that sat in the far corner of the room, on a small table in front of the floor-to-ceiling shelves.

She tried several subjects, including MAGIC, CURSES and COVENANTS.

Each directed her to the same section, shelved in a room called the first-floor library.

Must have been the room she and Quinn had argued in the other day.

With swift steps, Ilsa navigated the hallway to the stairs, on her way to the first floor.

The library was where she remembered, the room double the size of the one upstairs. She moved down the stacks, reading the labels until she found what she was looking for. Securing the book from a high shelf, she tucked it under her arm as she hunted for the other title she wanted to review.

"What are you doing in here?"

Ilsa muffled a scream as she whirled toward the door. "Callie! You scared me."

"What are you doing in here?"

"Looking for a book."

"You have no right to touch those." The pinched face and clipped voice had a harsh quality Ilsa would never have expected for her sister.

"Why not?"

What had happened to her? Why was she so callous?

Or was the attitude a special sort of anger directed solely at her?

Was this how *she* behaved?

Was she this implacable? This harsh?

Yes, her conscience whispered. *You're exactly like this. Likely even worse.*

Her drunken conversation with Ava came back to her. The woman had survived some terrible horrors, including watching her father die in her arms after he had been shot when she was a child. Ava's entire life had been one challenge after another and even recently—even after she'd met Brody—her grandmother betrayed her. Had set her course and sided with Enyo.

And yet she chose life.

Love.

For the first time since Zeus walked out of the cave, his curse still echoing off its walls, Ilsa stopped to think about her role in what happened. She didn't deserve his wrath, that's certain. But she did make all the choices that had come after.

She chose Hades's offer. Presumably because she *did* want a life.

She elected to live her life alone.

She had made the agreement with Emmett.

No one else.

Callie marched toward her, her hands outstretched in expectation. Ilsa didn't bother to argue, holding the book in her hand out for inspection.

"What do you need books on magic covenants for?"

"I have some things I need to deal with."

"Does Kane know about this?"

"No."

"He should."

"Why? This doesn't concern him." Ilsa brazened her way through the lie. The covenant did technically concern him, but she was correcting that and there was no reason to drag him into it.

She'd fix this. It was her only choice. The only way she could keep Kane safe.

"What are you playing at?"

"Callie. I know you don't have a very high regard for me."

"I have no regard for you."

Ilsa ignored the remark, but it stung. Way down deep, it stung. "Fine. But know that I have a very high regard for Kane. And my only priority is keeping him safe."

Her sister's eyes narrowed, but her tone softened. "What are you going to do?"

"I'm going to see the sorcerer who put the curse on Kane."

Callie's eyes widened at that. "You know who he is?"

"Yes."

"And you think you're going alone?"

"I am absolutely going alone. Kane's weaker than he wants to admit and no one here cares what happens to me. I need to take care of this on my own and I won't drag others into it."

"Kane will be mad."

Ilsa sighed. Callie was right. No matter how much she wanted to deny it or believe she could talk her way out of it, Kane would be mad when he found out.

It was a risk she was willing to take to keep him safe.

Emmett looked around the small café. He had no desire to be here—and he didn't want a fucking latte—but he sat still and waited. Nemesis's message had been clear about that.

She slid into the booth opposite him, her hair windblown and her eyes bright.

"You're looking well, Goddess."

"As are you, Emmett. Thank you."

Polite niceties out of the way, he nodded. "You wanted to see me?"

"Yes. I know we haven't seen each other in a while and I wanted to address our arrangement."

There it was. The moment he was waiting for.

"Yes. Go on."

"I fear the original agreement can no longer be upheld."

He deliberately arched one eyebrow, but kept his tone neutral. "And what has changed your mind?"

"My reasons for vengeance have changed. The assumptions I operated under when we made our agreement are no longer valid. Basically, my needs have changed. Surely you can appreciate a woman's right to change her mind."

"Actually"—he leaned forward across the table, reaching for her hand and covering it with his own—"I can't."

"I had suspected as much. Which is why I'm prepared to make you a deal. I do understand your plans are equally important to you. But I believe I have an alternative you might appreciate."

Emmett did have to give her credit. At least she arrived with a bargaining chip.

Or what *she* thought of as a bargaining chip.

"Tell me more."

"When you suggested a bargain between us, your rationale included a way to get back at Themis. I no longer require that. I've decided to approach the goddess a bit differently in my quest to resolve our differences."

Ah, so his little Nemesis *had* been busy. Just as he suspected.

"You do realize my reasons for approaching you last year haven't changed."

"Yes. Your desire to capture an immortal."

"Exactly."

"I'm proposing a trade, actually. So you can still get what you want."

"A trade? I'm not sure that will work. Themis's Warriors are fine specimens. They are the immortals I am most interested in."

"I understand that. But surely, after your review of the Pantheon, you understand they're not gods."

Emmett gave her a slight nod, unwilling to look too eager, but his interest was definitely engaged. What was she driving at?

Although he was quite certain he wasn't interested in whatever it was she was peddling, Emmett couldn't stop the curiosity. If anything, the one skill he'd always had in spades was his enterprising nature. If there was something better she could offer, perhaps he'd been too hasty to simply demand a Warrior.

"Yes, Nemesis. I'm aware of that."

"I'm prepared to offer you a god in place of a Warrior."

"And who would that be?"

"You can have me instead."

"She went where?" Kane turned his head in the direction of Callie's voice, watching her from his position on the weight bench.

Although it galled him to admit it, he was grateful for the reprieve. The poison was doing a number on him this morning, using his hangover and the decreasing time until the Antares zenith to tighten each of his muscles into long, inflexible ropes.

"To see the sorcerer."

"Callie. I know you don't like Ilsa, but this is a bit much."

Storm clouds filled her eyes as she marched forward. "Just because I don't like her does not mean I'm lying to you. I've spent the last hour trying to figure out how to tell you."

Kane wiped the sweat from his forehead and sat up. "How the hell would Ilsa know how to find the sorcerer?"

"She claims to know where he is."

Well, didn't that just beat all?

How was it possible Ilsa knew where to find the sorcerer who cursed him? He and his brothers had searched for the man for years—and they still had no leads.

"What did she say? What exactly did she say?"

"That this didn't concern you and that she'd take care of it."

Damn it!

How did the infernal woman manage to build him up one moment only to emasculate him the next?

And why—*why, why, why?*—was she insistent on dealing with her problems on her own?

Was she immune to what they had built together?

Or had he blown all of it out of proportion?

"Kane, I'm sorry."

"Yeah. I am, too."

A shout came from some far part of the house and Callie bustled out into the hallway to holler back.

"It's Ava," Callie informed him. "Ilsa's home."

Kane grabbed a towel on his way out of the room, his steps quickly outpacing Callie's as he raced down the hall.

Ilsa stood in the foyer, the blue of her eyes in stark relief to the pale color of her face.

"What happened to you?"

This last lifting session had left him weak and his legs felt made of spaghetti as he stalked toward her.

Quinn, Drake, Brody and Ava stood around her in a circle as Ilsa chattered with abandon.

As soon as she caught sight of him, Ilsa smiled. A real smile, broad and true.

One that reached all the way to her eyes.

And then it faded in the onslaught of his words.

"Why did you do that? Why did you go to him?"

Ilsa shot Callie a glance, but it didn't hold anything other than acknowledgment. "I wanted out of our bargain."

"Your bargain?"

She nodded, the small edges of a smile still visible on her lips. "It's the final piece. The final part of my old life I need to be rid of. So I put the wheels in motion."

"What are you talking about, Ilsa?" Quinn's question echoed off the marble. Kane listened to the resonating sounds that matched the echo in his head.

Bargain? With a sorcerer? With *the* sorcerer who'd captured him and then later poisoned him?

Endless questions filled him, but the most important—the most insistent—came first. "Did he agree?"

"Who knows?" Ilsa's shoulders went up in a delicate shrug. "Probably not."

"What?" Ava pressed her. "Tell us what happened. Here. Let's go into the family room and you can fill us all in."

Kane stood at the doorway, not sure of his exact place.

He wasn't sure why the thought of her going alone to visit the sorcerer angered him so badly.

Her visit had introduced a sense of hope into his situation that he hadn't dared feel in years.

Was it possible she'd be successful in getting the curse lifted? Where the rest of them had failed repeatedly, would Ilsa be the one to find success?

A cure? Or more likely, an antidote.

As if on cue, a wave of fire shot through his bloodstream. Cold sweat joined the sheen of his workout and one of his knees buckled. Kane grabbed the wall for balance, struggling to keep his feet. He was unwilling to have the others see him and come running back to help him.

When he felt strong enough to walk the few short steps to the living room, he joined everyone. Ilsa had settled herself in one of their leather club chairs while the rest of them assembled in the various couches that made up the conversation area. Kane remained at the door, not trusting his legs to carry him across the room.

Ilsa smiled at him one more time before she began her tale. That lone action—a simple smile—went a long way toward bolstering the hope in his soul the poison was hellbent to destroy.

"Several months ago, I made a bargain with the same sorcerer who released the poison into Kane's system."

"How convenient." Quinn's dry input wasn't enough to derail her.

"Stupid," Ilsa added. "Monumentally stupid. But if I hadn't, I wouldn't have met Kane, so I'm trying to focus on the positive. On the future."

Again, it was Quinn who pressed her. Quinn who had

the harsh words of recrimination. "You don't deserve a future. You've lied to us. Lied to Kane."

Kane moved into the room, suddenly quite sure of his place.

Quite sure of where he wanted to stand.

Moving into the room, he stood next to the chair Ilsa occupied. "This is your chance, Ilsa. I want to hear everything. It's your choice. Tell us and we all deal with it. Or you're on your own from here on out."

Chapter Twenty-one

Phobos hopped from foot to foot, his frenzied dancing nearly driving Enyo back to Mount Olympus.

"Phobos!" She whispered for what felt like the hundredth time in the last five minutes. "Put your hat back on so no one sees your horns. I know this is London, but they're going to get attention. And stand still for one fucking minute."

Her nephew stilled, but the air practically shimmered around him from the energy coursing through his body.

Two Destroyers stood sentinel, flanking either side of them where they stood and waited in Trafalgar Square.

"What are you looking for, Aunt Enyo?"

"I told you. We're waiting for someone."

"Waiting's boring."

Enyo sighed, her nephew's dense inability to grasp the most basic of concepts another reminder of his inane simplicity. He knew how to incite fear in a target. Nothing more and nothing less. It often surprised her when she was again faced with the single dimension in which her nephews operated their lives.

And then she forgot about it until she needed them again.

Shifting her attention from her nephew, Enyo turned toward one of the Destroyers. "You understand how I wish to have this handled?"

"Yes. At any signal from you, we'll take care of the sorcerer."

"That's correct. However, I don't think that will be necessary and I'd prefer to keep him alive if at all possible. He's got the potential to be useful."

"Of course, my queen."

Emmett walked up a short while later, precisely at the time he had proposed. "Thank you for coming."

"You suggested that things were ready to move."

"Oh, they absolutely are. But we've had an interesting development."

"Oh?" Enyo allowed the word to hang in the air.

"Nemesis found me several hours ago. Let me know she wanted to change the terms of our agreement. Demanded it, really."

"I suppose you laughed her from your presence."

"I heard her out."

"And what did you discover?"

"She's prepared to sacrifice herself for the Warrior."

As the words hung there, blowing on the light spring breeze that filled the square, the deeper implication of what he suggested became clear.

"She's in love with the Scorpio."

"I'd say so."

Oh, this was delicious. Truly, wonderfully delicious. "Does he feel the same?"

"I can only assume he does."

Enyo turned that one over in her mind. Even if Kane didn't love Nemesis, he likely had some feelings for the woman. And the fact he wasn't with her when she visited Emmett was another mark in favor of that.

"She came to you alone?"

"She did."

More interesting news. The goddess hid her visit from the Scorpio.

Was she unwilling to expose him? Or unwilling to tell him of the bargain in the first place?

"What did you tell her?"

"I suggested I needed some time to think and that I'd like a follow-up meeting. She agreed immediately."

"Where did you suggest?"

"Where it all began."

"What changed your mind?"

Kane and Ilsa were the only two left in the family room, the others all leaving for various parts of the mansion.

Ilsa focused on Kane's words. "You mean about the bargain? Or telling your family about the poison? Or going to Emmett at all?"

"All of it."

"You. And Ava. The two of you convinced me."

The last hour had gone far better than Ilsa ever expected. All the Warriors had taken the news of her alliance with Emmett and subsequent actions with surprising equanimity. She was still reeling from that turn of events, in between trying to figure out why.

"How so?"

"I can't have a life—can't move forward—if I don't take care of this. If I—"

As the silence expanded, he prodded gently for her to continue. "If you what?"

How did she explain what now seemed so very, very clear? "Last night was special to me."

"It was to me, too."

She smiled. "The part between us was wonderful. Perfect. But I mean the whole evening."

A desperate urgency overtook her as she sought to find the words that would make him understand. Leaving her chair, Ilsa sat next to Kane, perching on the edge of the cushion next to him. "I spent several hours talking to Ava. Learning about you and your brothers. Learning about this place. And learning about her."

His dark eyes twinkled with merriment. "So that's why you had so much wine."

"We had girl time." Awe filled her at the thought.

"Did you enjoy it?"

"I loved it. It was fun and funny. And I had someone who understood when I tried to explain how I felt about things. And . . . I think I made a friend."

Kane nodded. "As much as I'd like to murder them where they sleep on occasion, that's how I feel about my Warrior brothers. They're my battle companions. They have my back. And they're my friends."

"I never expected that to be so comforting. But it is."

His dark gaze captured hers and he leaned in for a kiss. His mouth pressed, soft and lush against hers, his tongue running a lazy request for entrance against the seam of her lips.

This was so right.

How could she have ever thought there was any other emotion in the universe to compare?

Under the light of his love and affection, the need for

vengeance that beat in her soul had no room to sustain itself.

"What the fuck, Monte?" Quinn paced the computer room he used as command central. Monitors covered the desks and hung from the ceilings, dictating a variety of information and shooting live feedback from an assortment of cameras around the globe.

Their bull might be a stubborn, know-it-all pain in the ass, but he sure as shit knew his technology.

And he used it to their advantage, as another weapon in the Warriors' arsenal.

Drake added from the far corner of the room where a book lay on his lap. "Why didn't she tell us about the blood? Before? Why didn't you tell us?"

"I've been working through that one."

"In between fucking her?" Quinn snorted.

Kane whirled on the bull. "I am so done with you. You either need to decide you can accept her, or you lose me. You can pull your stubborn-as-shit routine all you want, but she's staying. I made a call so I could handle it as I saw fit. She gave me some fucking respect by telling me, Quinn, which is more than I can say for you."

Quinn's large form unfolded from the rolling leather chair he sat in. "What the hell is that supposed to mean?"

"It means you've put strings on your aid and on your friendship. That crap the other day about not taking us to the Underworld. A fucking power play. You had nothing to lose—hell, it wouldn't have taken you more than five minutes start to finish—but you used your power to screw me."

Quinn's fists clenched and unclenched at his sides and the start of sentences bubbled up on his tongue only to be discarded. Finally, he spoke. "I didn't agree with your choice.

And knowing what the poison is doing to you, I couldn't help you make the trip."

"Is the view nice from your glass house? Because the best I can tell, you're sitting in there all by yourself."

Kane turned on his heel, anger and frustration riding his ass like a demon.

He should have expected this response. Should have expected all he'd get from the bull was a lot of "I told you so" and "Why should I help you?" questions.

What Kane never expected was the large hand that wrapped around his biceps as he hit the halfway point of the hallway.

As he whirled, his scorpion flicked its stinger where it rode high on his shoulder. He held it in, but wasn't surprised when its tail flicked in annoyance. He bit back the words that hovered at the tip of his tongue, instead forcing Quinn to talk first.

"When do we leave for London?"

"As soon as we put together a battle plan."

"Then let's get to it."

Enyo had been back on Mount Olympus for hours and still her conversation with Emmett replayed continuously in her mind.

Something didn't sit well with her. His ready acquiescence. Nemesis's ridiculous expectation that she'd get out of the bargain. Even Emmett's willingness to tell her about it.

No. It was abundantly clear something wasn't right.

Tigers not changing their stripes and all that. There was no way Emmett would change gears and give up his quest for a Warrior.

She needed a backup plan.

But what?

The meeting on Mount Ida was scheduled for the next day. Emmett was likely bathing himself in whatever dark magics he could still conjure up and probably a few more incantations for good measure.

Enyo paced her quarters, testing various solutions, discarding most of them as fast as she thought of them.

Send Deimos and Phobos.

Absolutely not.

Kidnap Emmett and attend the meeting herself?

Not ideal. It was time to test the sorcerer's loyalty and compatibility with her own goals and objectives.

Lightning lit up the room, followed quickly on its heels by a dark roll of thunder.

Her father was mad at someone.

So what else was new?

As another bolt of lightning lit up the room, fast on the heels of the first, an idea struck with the same degree of force.

Could she pull it off?

It wouldn't be that hard, would it?

She'd sneak in and sneak out, with no one the wiser.

As a third bolt lit up the room, Enyo had her backup plan.

Kane pointed out various elements on the architectural drawings for Vauxhall Cross, also known as MI6 headquarters. He knew Ilsa was insistent on going after Emmett and convincing him to rescind their bargain, but there was no way it was happening.

And in the meantime, they needed that vial.

"No. It's there." Ilsa pointed to a small square, depicting an office.

"That's St. Giles's office," Kane reminded her. "It can't be in there."

Ilsa pointed again. "It is, Kane. That's where Emmett's been hiding."

"In St. Giles's office?"

"As St. Giles."

Air doubled up in his lungs like he'd taken a punch to the gut. "What do you mean, *as* St. Giles?"

"That's what I tried to explain before."

"I thought you meant he was impersonating St. Giles."

"No." Ilsa shook her head.

Drake held up a hand. "I'm sorry. I know you both know this place and this St. Giles guy, but it looks like a rabbit warren from here. Ilsa—start from the beginning and help us understand what we're dealing with here. Even if we get into the building undetected, there's no way he's just got a vial of Kane's blood lying around."

"I don't know how he did it, but Emmett assumed St. Giles. His body and his life."

Kane shook his head. "The sorcerer's a mortal. How could he do that?"

Drake remained the voice of reason. "You've dealt with him, Monte. Didn't you get a sense for him? That's some powerful stuff, assuming a body. It hasn't been done since the Dark Ages, best as I know."

Kane tried to remember back all those many years ago. Much as he prided himself on his battle skills, memories did have a way of fading and three hundred years was a long time. "I suppose. But it's not like his power is scrawled across his forehead in Magic Marker."

Callie hovered outside the door to the study. Although she wouldn't join them, she'd stood there for some time, her gaze missing nothing. Kane nearly forgot about her all the way over there, until her soft voice broke through their discussion.

"He's hiding himself, and presumably the vial of blood, with very dark magic. You need someone who can over-power it."

"Overpower it? How?" Kane demanded.

"It can be done with white magic." She held up a heavy book, its leather cover cracked and worn. "It's in here. White magic can overpower the dark if done properly."

A flare of interest flashed brightly through Kane at her words. "So there's a way to reverse his magic?"

Callie nodded. "If you know how."

Quinn gestured Callie into the room. "Do you know how?"

"No. A reversal like this requires a very powerful witch."

Sarcasm rang out, and Kane was surprised that the words came from Drake. "And where would we conjure one of those on short notice?"

Callie pointed toward the direction of the windows. "I don't know about conjuring, but we can talk to the witch next door."

Kane glanced toward the bank of windows that framed the far end of the room. "Since when do we have a witch living next door?"

"You remember the witches I got to help you? Hip-polyta, Muriel and—"

"And Maeve. Yeah"—Kane nodded—"I remember them."

"She's Hippolyta's granddaughter. Would you like me to call her?"

"Callie, I'm sure she's great and all, but it's not like her grandmother had any success with my situation."

One delicately carved eyebrow shot up. "You got any better ideas?"

Kane glanced around the room. His brothers and Ava all nodded their agreement.

As his gaze settled on Ilsa, he saw her agreement as well. Saw the hope and belief shining forth from her bright blue eyes.

The hope he'd felt earlier came back in full force. That was all it took.

She was all it took.

His Ilsa.

"Make the call."

Whatever Ilsa had expected, the woman who swept into the room an hour later was so not it. Although she'd never had any dealings with white witches—the purity of their souls ensured they never found their way onto Hades's hit list— the mere term "white witch" conjured up a certain set of images.

Flowing robes. Titan red hair. A soft, sweet glow to their features.

Emerson Carano was none of those things.

Her pixie-sized frame was clad in black leather, not flowing white. Her jet-black hair stuck up in fashionable spikes all over her head. And while Ilsa wouldn't call her hard—her physical presence had an oddly feminine bent to it—the intricate tribal tattoo that ran along her inner arm didn't suggest a soft, sweet glow.

Emerson looked at all of them, her gray gaze slowly engaging each person in the room after Kane and Ilsa took turns explaining their situation. "This is some seriously dark magic. What a person has to give up to do this? It's beyond dark. It's evil."

"Yes, but can you help us fight it?" Quinn pushed, his tone flat. "Can you tell us how to break it?"

A wry grin spread across her face, showing small, even white teeth. "I can do it, ace. But you guys can't."

"Of course we can. It's a simple matter of showing one of us how."

It was clear Emerson wasn't pleased with Quinn's stubborn response. "You call me over here and tell me this is a matter of grave importance and then blithely think you can handle it yourself. You don't know jack shit."

Drake inserted himself, his calm, reasonable voice going a long way toward stemming the ire building in the room. "We're empowered by the goddess of justice. Surely that sense of balance can help in this matter."

Ilsa was fascinated to watch as the power in the room shifted again. Emerson walked toward Drake, her attention fully focused on him. "I don't care what goddess you serve, sweet cheeks. You certainly aren't going to be able to conjure the power required to counter this sorcerer's magic."

A distinct hint of red crept up his neck, but Drake's voice stayed firm. "Even if he's weakened?"

"Even then."

"What do you suggest we do?"

Emerson moved in close to Drake, their bodies near enough a whisper of air could barely pass through. He towered above her by well over a foot, even with the high-heeled boots that covered the lower half of her legs. Face tilted, her voice dropped into a range that could only be considered low and sexy. "Stay the hell away from him, for starters."

The red spread farther up his neck, but to Drake's credit, he held his own. "That's not possible."

"Then it looks like you're taking me along."

They spent the afternoon building their battle plan. First, Ilsa would port them into MI6 so they could retrieve the vial of blood. While they all wanted to catch Emmett, the need to capture him had to take second place to the retrieval of the blood.

Once that was secure, Ilsa would contact Emmett and draw him out with the promise of giving herself up.

Only then, when they had Emmett out in the open, would they attack, Emerson weaving a counterspell on him to pull him from St. Giles's body.

All Ilsa could see were the potential risks of the plan, but as they'd yet to come up with a better one, it was the working model.

"I still don't like it. We're vulnerable to attack. Here"—Quinn pointed to the map of MI6—"here and here."

Kane reached for the map, rolling it into a tube. "We can't prepare for every emergency, Quinn."

"But we don't have a true sense of what we're dealing with."

"I don't agree. We don't know what he can throw at us, but we know all we need to know about Emmett. He's a dark, evil man with dark, evil plans. And he's got it out for me."

"What about the magic?" Drake interjected. "We have no idea what will happen with the countercurse. Is it safe to take Emerson along? Or Ava? Or even Ilsa? We're trying to pull a human from the body of another."

Kane wrapped a rubber band around the floor plans. "We have to accept we're flying a bit blind on this. It's time to act."

Although he meant every word—and he knew they fought at their best as a unit—privately, Kane couldn't help but wonder what their trip to London would bring. He thought through all the angles as he headed for his bedroom to prepare for dinner, imagining the timeline they'd mapped out and the choreography of the battle.

They had to subdue him.

Had to catch him off guard.

And they couldn't make the mistake of assuming that because he was mortal, he would be an easy mark.

Kane opened the door to his room and slipped in, every thought in his head fleeing at the sight of Ilsa in a towel. Her hair fell in thick wet waves down her back and a light flush covered her body from the heat of her shower.

Long, firm legs met his gaze as he looked below the end of the towel and saw that cherry-red nail polish covered her toenails.

She was a vision.

And she was all his.

As he moved forward, his hot, hungry gaze never left hers. As he moved close enough to brush up against her, he leaned over and laid a kiss on the edge of her shoulder.

"You're very clean."

"I thought it might help me relax. I'm so nervous. I don't know why, because I never get nervous. But . . ." Her voice tapered off as he continued his kisses, trailing a path toward her neck, then on up to a delicious, sensitive spot behind her ear.

Reaching around her body, he felt the bump where one edge of the towel was secured against her chest and flicked it open, the indigo blue terry cloth falling to the floor in a rush.

Turning her around, he allowed his gaze to roam over her body. "I want you. Always. It lives under my skin and calls to me. I want you." He bent his head to capture her lips, whispering against them as he reached for one of her breasts. "Always."

He heard the small moan that came from the back of her throat. Felt the way she pressed her body against his hand. Smelled the distinct musky scent of her arousal and Kane knew he was lost.

Hopelessly, utterly lost.

The only good thing, he reflected, as he bent even farther and captured one pink nipple between his teeth, was that in the losing, he had finally found his way.

Chapter Twenty-two

Ilsa gloried in the warmth of his mouth, the sweet pressure of his lips, and lost herself to the sensation.

With an urgent tug on his shoulders, they stumbled across the room to fall onto the bed. Ilsa pulled him down so his weight rested fully against her.

She loved this feeling. Taking his weight. Feeling the bold strength of him, under her fingers, pressing into her stomach.

Allowing him to surround her.

"You know," she whispered against his cheek. He continued to lave his tongue over one of her nipples, the sensation shooting sparks through her body with each long, languid stroke. "Something dawns on me."

Kane lifted his head as a warm smile spread across his face. "What's that?"

"This is a beautiful bedroom. But I sort of miss your cold, icy apartment in London."

"You do?"

"Yeah. I do. I've thought of it often. Walked past your building, even."

His eyes widened as he looked up at her. "The guys hate it. Tell me it looks colder than a meat locker."

"I don't know. I think it's sleek and sexy." She leaned down for a kiss. "Like you."

His dark eyes filled with concern. "I'd like to take you there, but I'm not going to be able to port until the poison is past us."

"A little over a week?"

Kane sighed, his eyes clouding over with past memories of what it meant to deal with the poison. "That's it."

"Would you mind if I ported us there? Now?"

"You really want to go there?"

Ilsa ran a hand through the hair at his temple, nodding her ascent. "Yes. I really want to go there."

"Then by all means."

Ilsa pictured Kane's London apartment. Pictured the acre of black silk that covered his bed. And sent them on their way.

Air rushed around them before dropping them in the exact same position, over three thousand miles away.

"You know. Every time I think this is a rough life, I need to remember I never—ever—have to get on an airplane."

Ilsa giggled at the thought. "The horror. Sitting inside that thing. Ew."

"Brody had to do it. Last year, after he met Ava."

"Why?"

"She didn't know what he was and he couldn't tell her. The whole secrecy thing we all live with."

At his words, a question she'd often thought of when alone popped into her head. The glory of actually being able to ask it of another was too wonderful to pass up. "Do you really think humans have no idea? About us, I mean. Immortals."

"I think they're smarter than we give them credit for. And as their technology continues to evolve, they're bound to find out about us. Heck, Quinn uses a variety of infrared sensors and nanotechnology to test for the presence of immortals."

"Does it work?"

"I think so. I let him geek out on all the specifics, but where I'm going is that there are tools. All it takes is the right person to figure them out."

His words hit their mark, one she knew Kane wasn't aiming for. "Like the hole inside of me."

"Aw, Ilsa. I'm sorry."

"No. It's true. The scientists figured it out. All on their own. We have to stop assuming humans don't know anything and don't know how to protect themselves. Ignorance like that ensures we're the ones who are paying for it."

Kane ran a hand over her stomach, rubbing the vicinity of where the scientists broke free. "I'm still sorry."

Reaching up, she ran her hand through the short hair at the nape of his neck. "You live with damage every day and have managed to thrive. I'll figure it out."

As she said the words, Ilsa had to acknowledge that she meant them. Each and every one.

She was done blaming others for her circumstances.

Done dwelling on them.

She chose life. Enormous, splendid helpings of it. With a broad smile and a light push on his shoulders, Ilsa took the first step. "Roll over."

Kane did as she asked.

"I didn't notice before. When did you put on the black slacks and a silk shirt?" When he blushed, Ilsa couldn't keep the laugh from bubbling up in her throat. "And why do you look embarrassed by the question?"

His gaze slipped from hers as he focused on a point somewhere below her chin. "I didn't feel like wearing jeans and a T-shirt any longer."

With dexterous fingers, she flipped open three buttons, curious delight filling her at his clear discomfort. "Is that really all?"

"Unlike most of the guys, jeans aren't my favorite."

She pressed a kiss against his chest, where it peeked out of the black material. "We all have things we like."

"Exactly."

"*Nice* things." Ilsa opened a few more buttons, allowing the shirt to fall away, pooling to either side of his body. "Of course, this isn't any old outfit." She pressed more kisses down his chest, over his rib cage and on to his stomach, where her path was blocked by the top of his slacks.

His heart thudded under his skin, his pulse heavy under her mouth. "You don't think?"

"Oh no." Her fingers slipped under the material of his slacks, making quick work of his belt and the button at his waist. "This is the outfit of an assassin."

Kane reached for her, stilling her movements. "You figured that out."

"Well, yeah. You look like an ass kicker in this. It's seriously sexy."

"Sweet music to my ears, darling."

"Now," she whispered against his stomach, "let me make you *feel* the music."

And then there were no words. No banter. Nothing but the sounds that rose up between them in the pleasure.

Kane sat up, removing the rest of his clothes in a few quick, clean strokes, then lay back under the pressure of Ilsa's hands.

Her conversation the evening before with Ava came back to her. All the things she was dying to try on Kane.

With the surety born of love, she roamed over his body, exploring the terrain with soft fingers and a questing tongue.

She ran her tongue over his nipple, pleased when his low moan greeted her ears. Clearly, he had some sensitivity there, just as she did, and the knowledge made her bold.

With deliberate movements, she continued down his body, the sharp jut of his penis against her belly like a promise of what was to come.

She followed the trail of hair that ran down the center of his stomach, tracing it farther until she reached the pulsing length of him.

All this was for her. This man wanted her. Needed her.

Was completely vulnerable to her.

And it was in the vulnerability that Ilsa saw the gift. That this proud Warrior would lay there before her, naked to her gaze and barren of any of his defenses.

He trusted her.

And he desired her.

Warm heat suffused her as she realized what a precious treasure lay before her. How this man had changed the way she saw the world.

The way she saw herself.

Her every thought—about what she wanted from her life and about who she was—had changed since Kane's arrival in her life.

And at that moment, she knew the path held no return.

She could reach out and take life. Joy and heartache, moments of pure magnificence and moments of deep grief.

Or she could set herself apart from it all and feel nothing.

Leaning down, she enveloped the very essence of what made him a man between her lips.

And chose life.

When Ilsa took him inside her mouth, need swamped him.

Unable to stop the deep moans she drew from him, he simply lay back and allowed the moment to spin out. Wave after wave of pleasure ran through his body as her tongue swept the length of him.

Base to tip and back again. Deep, delicious curls of her tongue around the crown. Tender, firm strokes as she cupped the sensitive sacs beneath.

"Ilsa." Her name dragged from his lips on a low, breathless moan.

His heart pounded in heavy rhythm and sweat slicked over his skin, his body wholly and completely affected by her touch.

"Ilsa. Baby." He reached for her arms, intending to pull her closer. They were in this one together and no way was he spilling himself all over her. "Baby. Come here."

The incredible torture stopped as she lifted her head, a sultry smile spread across her face. "Are you asking me to stop, Kane Montague?"

"Gods, no! I just want you to come here. We'll finish together."

She sat back on her heels, her fingers tracing a tight path where her mouth had just been.

Another wave of pleasure swamped him, the muscles in his lower back tightening as his body prepared for release.

"Ilsa!"

Her voice slid over him like the finest liquor. "Do you remember what I told you last night?"

Kane opened his eyes, his breath heavy and his vision blurred as he took in the soft light of the room. "I'm not doing a great job of remembering much of anything right now, darling."

"Well, then," she purred, "let me remind you."

With one hand, she applied firm, tight pressure to the base of his cock, the sensations so strong he gritted his teeth to keep from going off right there.

And then she killed him. Decimated him into the ash of a thousand fires.

With her other hand, her thumb and forefinger tightened around the crown, applying a steady pressure that held him in check.

Mind-numbing pleasure assaulted every inch of his body, exploding through his brain like an oncoming freight train.

In a very good way.

With her expert strokes, she pulled another low moan from his chest, the pleasure so intense he was unable to keep silent.

When he took it as long as he could—took the pleasure and the desperate pain that came from holding his release—Kane pulled her toward him for a long, drugging kiss.

Shifting, he rolled them over, falling on top of her and embedding himself to the hilt.

She was so wet for him—so ready, so eager—and he let himself fall into the long, rhythmic strokes so incredibly necessary at that moment in time.

Ilsa met him thrust for thrust, her body in perfect harmony with his.

He knew the moment he was done for. His body exploded, the storm gathering from his very core. He buried himself deep inside of her and felt the telltale quiver of her muscles tightening around him in her own release.

The pleasure blinded him, but even in the darkness, he felt the light of love that filled him to bursting.

Kane reached for her, their fingers locking as the world exploded around them.

Chapter Twenty-three

Ilsa couldn't believe her eyes as she looked around. As someone who had spent nearly sixteen thousand years executing each and every task in her life on her own, the sight of other people porting alongside her was a heady feeling.

She was part of a team.

Four people accompanied her into MI6. Kane, Quinn, Drake and Emerson stood around her, assembled and ready to help.

Ilsa opened the door of an abandoned conference room they'd used for the port. Although it was nearly impossible to escape the all-seeing eye of a camera, no one thought to focus on the far corner of a conference room for security purposes. She'd used this corner more than once, on any late-night visits into the building.

She made a directional motion with her head, her voice a whisper. "It's down here."

They'd ported in small groups. She had taken Quinn earlier to give him a sense of location; then they left separately to retrieve Kane, Drake and Emerson.

"Shit, that's quite a ride." Emerson's excited whisper floated toward her as they filed out of the conference room.

They'd agreed ahead of time on clothing. The cameras would capture their every move and it was decided the hassle of trying to override them could be counterbalanced by acting the part and appearing to have the appropriate badges posted on the body.

Ilsa couldn't help but smile at Emerson and her enthusiasm, taking in the rather prim-and-proper beige suit that now covered her pixie-sized frame.

With a quick motion, Ilsa pointed toward the far end of the hallway. "The last door on the right."

If they'd had any doubt about bringing her along, Emerson absolutely proved her worth when they reached the door. Drake had a set of lock picks in his hand, when she waved her hands over the door, a steady chant on her lips.

A soft snick announced the door was unlocked.

"How'd you manage that?"

Emerson smiled broadly, her white teeth flashing in the dull lighting of the hallway. "Let's just say I got bored easily as a child. I liked finding new ways to use my gifts."

They filed into the room, the glass walls reflecting a beautiful view of London. Quinn swept the room with one of the many devices he used to check for paranormal activity. "You work for this guy, Monte?"

Kane's voice was ripe with the dark tinges of anger. "Did work. It sounds like the St. Giles I knew is long gone."

Ilsa glanced toward Kane as he searched a wood credenza, the grief unmistakable in his words. Anguish in the knowledge St. Giles had been killed by Emmett.

Even though she didn't know all the specifics, Emerson had been clear in her explanation that removing Emmett from the body wouldn't bring St. Giles back.

Sadly, the man was long gone.

Ilsa returned her attention to Quinn. She'd been fascinated earlier when the Taurus had held up a small handheld device that lit up like a video game. He claimed it could sense paranormal activity of any sort.

Although Ilsa had her doubts, who was she to argue. Instead, she gestured Quinn toward the desk. "Try over there. I think he keeps it in the desk."

The lights on the device played out her theory that the drawer held something important and she moved along behind the Taurus as he approached the desk. Kane stepped away from his hunt through the credenza to join them as well.

"Emerson's getting something over here, too." Drake gestured toward a filing cabinet Emerson stood before, her hands stretched in front of her as she ran them in front of the metal.

Quinn played with the small computer, punching in various buttons. With a nod, he gestured toward the far side of the desk. "The reading's coming off the top drawer."

"Quinn," Drake called, "get over here. I think you're going to get something off of this, too."

Kane stood with her over the desk.

"I'll get it." Kane reached for the handle, but Ilsa stopped him. "You don't know what's in there."

"My blood's in there."

"Yes, but what if he rigged it?"

"Rigged it with what? He gave up his powers to release the poison inside of me."

"You still don't know, Kane. You don't know what he's capable of."

"It's balance. His power for mine. We established that three hundred years ago." Without waiting another second, Kane pulled open the drawer.

Ilsa recognized the small vial immediately. She should. She'd been the one to fill it.

Some prescient thought pulled her forward and before Kane could argue about who would pick it up, Ilsa took matters into her own hands.

She'd gotten them into this mess by stealing his blood in the first place.

She'd take the hit.

As her fingers closed over the vial, a loud rushing of air flew through her, centered around the tear in her soul. The scream rose in her throat, but before she could open her mouth, everything went black.

"Son of a bitch!" Kane hollered, Ilsa's body a deadweight in his arms.

"What the fuck happened?" Quinn's dumb-ass computer was lit up like Christmas as he, Emerson and Drake ran across the room.

Emerson shook her head. "Oh shit. Shit, shit, shit. I should have known. How could I have been so shortsighted?"

"What?" Kane demanded. "What is it?"

Before Emerson could respond, Drake was reaching for the ground. "This must have fallen when Ilsa picked up the vial." As the Pisces had touched the paper, he yelped, the cry escaping his lips on a loud sigh.

"What the hell's the matter?" Quinn demanded.

"Paper's hot as an oven." Drake lifted the paper gingerly at the very edge with the tips of his fingers.

"Read it." Kane glanced down at Ilsa's still form in his arms. "Hurry."

Quinn, Emerson and Drake huddled around the desk, reading the copy of the note, until Emerson spoke up. "It's a letter from Emmett. Informing us of what we just opened."

Kane had lost his patience for guessing games. Ilsa continued to thrash in his arms and the urgent need to get her back to New York was overwhelming. "Hurry up."

"It says the poison has been unleashed."

"What? How?" Drake and Quinn both barked at Emerson in unison as Kane stood stock-still, taking it all in.

Increasingly frustrated, Kane shifted his attentions off his brothers and onto Emerson. "I don't need a fucking book report. Give me the highlights."

"Apparently, he's going to make it 'easy on us,' " Emerson said, glancing again at the note before leveling her stormy gray gaze at him. "The poison has now been unleashed in London, possibly in two different places. The London Eye and the zoo. We have exactly one hour to see that it's brought under control."

"How the hell are we supposed to control it?" Quinn snapped.

In unison, Quinn, Drake and Kane all shifted their focus to Emerson. It definitely helped to have a witch on your side.

Kane rocked Ilsa in his arms as they ported to the zoo. He could only assume the zoo was the place. The poison was tied to his scorpion—an animal. Of course, he couldn't stop the anxiety that the poison was actually at the Eye. Hundreds of innocent people. That would be enough to get Emmett's juices flowing.

They'd agreed in advance that Drake and Quinn needed to port. Kane wouldn't leave Ilsa so he carried her wherever they went. Emerson was the variable.

They needed her at both locations pending the outcome.

"I'm telling you, it's the zoo."

"The Eye's more high-profile." Quinn's voice boomed

so loud through Drake's cell phone none of them missed the conversation.

Or his opinion.

"We have to divide and conquer, Quinn. We're searching here and will call you back. Go make yourself useful. Kane thinks it's the zoo, which is why we have Emerson. If you get different intel, I'll port her there right away." With that, Drake hung up the phone and turned back toward the assembled group. "Where to first?"

"The scorpions," Kane and Emerson said in unison.

They took off for that section of the zoo, purpose filling each step. Kane worried over Ilsa—she'd gone completely still in his arms.

He couldn't ignore his fears as he felt his own strength waning. The deadweight of Ilsa's body, combined with the increasing pains now shooting like fireworks off the length of his spinal cord, had Kane almost staggering by the time they reached the scorpion exhibit.

"Let me take her." Drake held out his arms. "You're dead on your feet, Monte."

"I can handle it."

"Actually, you can't. Hand her over. All we need is you falling all over these fine families here. It's bad enough we're drawing attention carrying a woman who looks like she went on a three-day bender."

Kane handed Ilsa to Drake, who repositioned her into a more upright position next to him. Although anyone who looked would know Ilsa needed help, it wasn't quite so obvious as when he'd held her.

Emerson had found a spot on some benches and they settled in to wait.

"You feel anything?" Kane grilled her the moment he took his seat. The pain was nearly unbearable now, the nerves along his spinal cord shooting sparks down both legs. Sitting didn't help the pain, but it at least kept the possibility of falling at bay.

"No." Emerson shook her head. "Nothing at all."

"It's got to be here."

"Why?" Emerson's voice was direct. "He gave us two very large targets. We're selecting the most obvious places in hopes he went for predictable in the vain effort to see if we could diffuse his work in time."

"You think?" Kane looked up at her, where she paced the ground in front of him.

"What other reason could there be? There's a part of him that can only be validated if he gets caught. Can only show he won if we suffer. What's he going to do? Put it in the middle of the skunks?"

"Eye," Ilsa whispered.

"What?" Kane's gaze swung around to Ilsa, where she lay propped against Drake's shoulder. Her eyelids were so heavy they were nearly closed, but her words were clear. "London Eye. That was the site of St. Giles's last mission. Bet you ten to one Emmett's got a sentimental streak."

Kane was dead on his feet two hours later when Drake finally ported him and Ilsa to New York. Where she'd been doing better earlier, whatever toxin that had wrapped around the poison still held her in its grip.

As he laid Ilsa on the couch, he held her down, holding tight to her arms. "Get Callie."

Emerson stood at the head of the couch where he had Ilsa spread out. Kane longed to curl up and try to grab whatever rest he could find, but he needed to see Callie. Needed her to tell him Ilsa would be fine. "Tell me exactly what happened. Each step."

"Wait, wait, wait," Callie hollered as she came into the room. "Tell it once. I need to know."

Kane took them both through it, from Quinn's computer readings all the way to when Ilsa touched the vial and Quinn's subsequent adventures with the London Eye.

Emerson had been the real heroine, following Quinn through the attraction and diffusing each and every area where the poison potentially lurked. She now moved to kneel next to the couch, holding Ilsa's hands still with one of her own while singing various chants.

Soon Callie joined in and added her voice.

More incantations. More chanting. More hand movements.

In the end, Emerson's determination served her well.

Kane watched as Callie burst back into the room. "What happened?"

Callie had a book in her hands, the same one she'd held earlier before suggesting they contact Emerson.

Ilsa's body had grown deathly still. Panic twisted Kane's stomach muscles, along with the bone-deep fear of losing her.

And what would he do then?

Gritting his teeth against the pain of that image, Kane focused on Emerson. On her expertise. "What did he do to her?"

"It's a protection spell. And it's designed to punish."

The pain was centered in her abdomen. The hole where the scientists broke through her soul the epicenter of the pain.

Great, crashing waves of it poured through her body, forcing Ilsa into a doubled-over position where she sat on a hard bench seat.

Struggling for breath, she lifted herself slowly and looked around, dimly registering she'd been here before.

To this place of darkness and pain, sadness and woe.

The River Acheron.

Charon spoke to her as he rowed the boat, his movements practiced over millennia of steering the ferry.

"You sacrificed much for the Warrior."

"Charon?"

"Aye. It is me."

"But why am I here?"

His scaly hands stayed firm on his ferryman's stick, rowing them steadily onward. "They think I don't hear. That I don't understand. But I hear it all."

"Where are you taking me?"

"To Hades. He doesn't want you to wait on the banks of the river to hear your fate. Nay, he wants to give it to you now."

"But I'm not dead." The pain in her stomach spread out, morphing into a seeping mass of panic that beat in her chest with the ferocity of an out-of-control train.

"Aren't you?"

"Hardly. I'm alive." She struggled to a full sitting position, ignoring the pain and the panic at the little demon's words. "I'm an immortal, Charon, just as you are."

"Your soul is damaged. Your choices are set. You shall go to see Hades."

"Turn the boat around."

"I shall not, Nemesis." He stretched out the word, dragging out the first syllable of her name. "How the mighty have fallen, Nemmmm . . . esis. Your fate is sealed, Nemmmm . . . esis."

The heat of the river rose up to swamp her senses, and

then, without warning, the coldest of colds assailed her nerve endings as the scenery changed.

Charon's scaly face morphed into something else as another vision gripped her.

Something that looked like a large human male.

Zeus.

He stood over her, his booming voice delivering his harsh edict as his parting anger replayed before her eyes.

As she did so many lifetimes ago, she whispered her plea.

"I have protected you, as I gave my word I would do. Your mother asked me to hide you. To keep you safe. I have done my duty, Zeus."

"There will be nothing for you!" Zeus swept his arm in a bold arc, light flowing like a river from the end of his lightning bolt. "You will have what is coming to you, Adrasteia. Forever."

Another scream.

Another anguished cry.

On a wild, soul-searing shriek, she clutched at her stomach, desperate to stop the pain.

And prayed it would all go away.

Callie and Emerson worked over Ilsa. They'd chanted for what felt like a lifetime, but in reality Kane knew it hadn't been more than about an hour.

It was endless.

Ilsa screamed as she let out dark, desperate moans. Once he even swore she begged for death.

"What's wrong with her?"

Emerson broke her chant, but continued her elaborate hand motions. "The punishment built into the spell has attacked the weakest part of her body."

Realization dawned bright and clear. "The hole."

"Hole?" Callie looked up. "What hole are you talking about?"

"There's a tear in her soul. She sustained it on the journey to Hades. It took too long for us to get there. This happened along the way."

Quinn stepped forward. "What happened?"

Kane grit his teeth, bit back the anguish and pain, when all he really wanted to do was let his scorpion off the leash so they could both go postal on everyone.

"The scientists she carried figured out a way to escape their bonds." Kane gave them all a quick update, hitting the high points and avoiding a treatise on particle physics.

Concern etched Quinn's features, his eyes downcast. "I shouldn't be here." With stiff movements, he left the room. Kane watched him go, but refused to follow.

The bull could wallow by himself.

"Why isn't anything working?" Kane paced the length of the room again, the poison in his own veins tap-dancing on his lungs to a merry tune only it heard.

Emerson walked around the room, chanting as she went, seeming to pull energy from the air. Kane turned to Callie with questing eyes, but her shoulders only rose on a note of confusion.

Unwilling to keep his gaze off of her for more than a few seconds, Kane turned back toward Ilsa. Her skin grew increasingly pale, her lips taking on a faint, bluish tinge.

She was an immortal, damn it! An immortal with her head firmly intact.

There had to be a solution.

An antidote.

Something.

"Kane, I have an idea." Callie beckoned him over. "Here.

Stand at her head and keep contact with her. I want her to feel the warmth of human touch. Don't let go of her."

"Where are you going?"

"Just try it."

Callie ran from the room, leaving Kane to his thoughts. Quinn had already left and Brody and Ava were in the upstairs library, researching whatever they could find on dark spells. Callie had put Drake to work in the kitchen, watching over a pot of soup she had on.

Although the Pisces had complained at first at being relegated to an inactive job, at Callie's urging—and wise words—he'd come around. "She'll need fortification when she awakes."

The low, quiet chants from Emerson were the only thing to fill the room besides his increasingly dismal thoughts.

Callie burst back into the room, a gold lyre filling her hands.

"Music?" Kane spat the word. What the fuck was this? Playtime at day care? "You think that's going to help her?"

Callie's gaze was direct, her tone even more so. "You have any better ideas?"

What was it about the woman that she could incite remorse in an instant? "No." On a deep breath, Kane tried a different tact. "What prompted this idea?"

Callie positioned herself on an opposite chair, settling the instrument in her lap. "I don't know why I didn't think of it before. This is a golden lyre. Although I'm not nearly as adept as Orpheus, I can play a bit of music."

"You really think this will help Ilsa?"

"Orpheus was able to cheat death in the Underworld by playing his lyre. Between her association with Hades and her innate strength as an immortal, perhaps the music will aid her body in knitting itself back together."

Kane ran over the last several days in his mind. "Close the hole? But the scientists told us that was impossible."

"At this point, my goal is to remove the ravages of the spell. Because this is the weakest part of her body, it's the root of her suffering." Callie held the instrument aloft and plucked several strings in a series of chords. "We'll worry about trying to repair the hole later."

With exquisite care, Callie played several more rounds of scales, before moving into a soothing, stirring song. The notes hung in the air from each pluck on the strings, then seemed to hold there for a few moments, the quality of the music so beautiful—so pure—it seemed they had extra weight.

Kane maintained his touch, but shifted between watching Ilsa for any signs of life and Callie as she played, her eyes closed as the music absorbed her.

Was it possible? Were Ilsa's lips less blue than before?

Emerson moved to the foot of the couch, her hand on Ilsa's leg as she continued chanting. And as they sat there, everyone else in the house found their way back to the living room.

Brody held Ava in his arms as they took a place on the end of the couch. Drake came back and took a seat next to Emerson.

Even Quinn returned, although he maintained a spot at the doorway, unwilling to come into the room.

"Kane," Emerson breathed on an exhale. "Look. There's color in her cheeks."

Emerson was right. Color filled Ilsa's face and the pain that etched her brow was receding.

When he glanced at Callie, his gaze met hers, her round eyes full of understanding before she closed them again and turned herself over to the music.

They sat there for a long while.

Callie never stopped playing the beautiful music that filled up the house with sound. Eventually Emerson reached for Drake's hand and held it tight as they waited. Brody and Ava sat wrapped around each other, their gazes focused on Ilsa.

Through it all, Quinn never left the doorway. He stood statue-still, but Kane saw the emotion that roiled in his eyes. The concern stamped on his forehead. The weight of his conscience that rode his shoulders.

Kane returned his focus to Ilsa and watched as her breathing came easier. As her cheeks continued to pinken.

And then she opened her eyes.

That piercing blue gaze penetrated straight through to his soul. With a raspy voice, Ilsa smiled. "Does she take requests?"

Chapter Twenty-four

"**K**ane. We can't miss the meet." Ilsa swiveled on a stool in the kitchen, a steaming mug of tea in front of her. Or a tisane, as Emerson had informed her a short while ago. She felt surprisingly strong considering the nightmarish trip through her memories.

Or was it real?

Although the moments with Zeus felt like a real memory, she hesitated to say the same about her boat ride with Charon. Had she truly been that close to death?

A slight shiver ran the length of her spine.

It didn't bear thinking about.

Kane pointed to Drake. "Will you help me talk some sense into her? Nothing good can come of this."

Ilsa interrupted before Drake could answer. "And nothing good can come if we don't. It's time to end this once and for all. If Emmett wants a meet on Mount Ida, then we'll give it to him. But"—she glanced into her mug and swirled the contents with a spoon—"I need to go alone. I can't drag all of you into this."

Kane's reaction was even faster than she'd expected.

"Absolutely not. I don't even want you going there. I'm sure as hell not going to let you go alone."

"We're in this now." Emerson's gray gaze was clear and full of promise. "All of us."

Ilsa struggled against the wellspring of hope that bloomed in her chest at the words of solidarity. "But how can you say that? You weren't even a part of this yesterday. How can you want to do this?"

Emerson's eerily luminescent gray eyes took on a slightly dreamy look. "I've spent my life hoping for something like this. Something to make my gifts matter."

"Of course they matter," Drake added. "Look at what you can do."

"No. I mean *really* matter. Use my gifts to truly help others. All of you have the power to change lives. My grandmother told me about you all years ago. The Warriors, vested in another age and tasked to protect humanity. This is the chance I've been waiting for."

Quinn stepped into the room from where he'd taken up position in the doorframe. "You're not going alone, Ilsa. We're going with you. Or at least I am. We leave at three, for whoever else is in."

And then he did the oddest thing.

Ilsa saw Quinn come closer, saw his head bend down— and still, his actions didn't register.

Until he planted a soft kiss on her cheek.

Stepping back, the bull turned and walked right back out the door.

Had that really just happened?

Wonder filled Ilsa as she looked around at the remaining faces in the kitchen, all of whom peered right back at her. The same feeling she'd had when they entered MI6 came rushing back to her in a flood.

She had people to stand for her.

With her.

She had friends.

With a glance at Kane, she acknowledged she had more than friends. She had a man she loved.

For the moment, at least, it was more than enough.

"Let's walk through this one more time. Emmett wants a meet on Mount Ida." Kane repeated the meager facts he already knew. "With what agenda?"

"So we can renegotiate our bargain."

"Of which you have told him you're willing to *become* a part of the bargain?"

Ilsa nodded. "Yes."

"And the venue? His idea?"

"Yes."

A distinct unease ran the length of Kane's spine. He knew he should take some comfort in his surroundings, but even the proof of more than ten millennia of victories didn't make him feel any better about the impending trip to Greece.

The basement of the brownstone where he and Ilsa stood housed endless rolls of ancient scrolls, several large maps and quite a few reinforced rooms they used for battle planning. Although the entire house was relatively safe, existing on both the human plane as well as Mount Olympus, its basic structure was still rooted firmly in a bed of Manhattan asphalt.

Because the foundation existed on the human plane, they needed extra precautions in the case of damage or even possible attack. The basement had several fireproof rooms they could house their ancient texts in and the walls were structurally fortified to cave in on themselves, forming a sort of cocoon around those items that were most precious.

One look at Ilsa and Kane wished he could wrap her in a cocoon. A magic bubble where nothing could touch her.

Especially not the fucking rat bastard sorcerer who had it in for all of them.

Frustration rode him hard as he dug through their cases of ceremonial swords. Although the Xiphos was an outstanding weapon for hand-to-hand combat and for eliminating Destroyers, it wasn't of as much use in a larger battle. As basic protection, it hid easily on the body and served a purpose.

But for serious ass-kicking?

Kane's gaze ran in hungry waves over the heavy battle swords in their arsenal. His personal favorite—a claymore—shined back up at him in all its glory.

With a quick lift, he tested its grip, the exquisite proportions of the sword ensuring it fit his hand with the ease of a glove.

Just a few feet . . . that's all he needed. To get within a few feet of Emmett and finish what began three hundred years ago.

"Kane, please tell me you understand why I have to do this."

He turned to find Ilsa, her eyes wide with unshed tears, staring from his face to the sword and back again.

"Honestly, no. I don't."

Ilsa moved toward him, reaching for his hand that held the sword and pressing on his arm to lower it. "Because I need to put my previous life behind me if I hope to have any future with you."

"He tried to kill you, Ilsa. The trap on the vial of blood. It would have killed you if Callie hadn't remembered the power of the lyre."

"And it would have killed you instantaneously had you

touched it. It targets weakness and right now, the poison has you in its grip."

Rage. Pure, undiluted, frustrated rage swelled in his gut. Despite the urge to scream, Kane held himself back, his voice a harsh, quiet whisper. "I hate it when my brothers start in with their worrying bullshit and make me feel like a helpless little fawn. But from you?"

Kane stepped back and laid the claymore into its velvet keep. "When it's from you? I can't be the person I am called to be if I can't protect you."

"Oh, Kane, I'm not —"

He held up a hand. "No. Let me finish. All my life, I've been disinterested in any permanent connection with a woman. Women are for fun. I respect women—I love women—but I'm never sad to see one go. Even all those years ago. Yeah, I was besotted with Emmett's sister, but that was all. I haven't spent the centuries mourning her."

"But that's because she betrayed you. You might have felt differently if she'd returned your love."

A harsh laugh bubbled from his chest. "Don't you fucking get it? I'm in love with you! Great, fucking, gooey, embarrassingly mushy, I-want-to-write-a-freaking-poem, heart-wrenching love for you."

At Ilsa's wide-eyed stare, he continued. "I feel like a fucking lunatic. I'm a mess. A wimp-shit, fear-filled ass hat who is so in love with you I am in physical pain. And it's not the poison. And it's not Emmett. It's you."

He ran a hand through his hair, dragging the short strands into spikes as he went. "It's you."

Ilsa stepped up and laid her hand on his chest. The heat of her palms seeped into his skin, directly over the pounding beats of his heart.

"I love you too. Great, fucking, gooey, embarrassingly

mushy, I-want-to-write-a-freaking-poem, heart-wrenching love. And that's why I have to do this. Because in all my life, I've never felt that. For anyone. And I'm not starting a life with you with all my baggage still intact."

"Emmett is a danger."

"It's more dangerous to leave him alone, lingering in our lives. I need to do this, Kane. I need to come to you whole. I can live without a piece of my soul that was stolen from me. But I can't live without you."

Kane pulled her into his arms.

Because really, how did you argue with logic like that?

Ilsa heard the drumbeats of the Corybants in the distance and a wave of nostalgia assailed her. Could she really feel any sense of softness for this place?

Was it even possible she had any room for good memories?

Apparently so.

Shaking it off, she pointed to a spot in the distance. "Mount Ida is at the top of this next precipice."

"This is really the place?" Awe filled Emerson's voice as they stood five across in a row. Ilsa, Kane, Quinn, Drake and Emerson. "Where are those drums coming from?"

"It's the Corybants. They dance in armor, protecting the mountain. They're the reason Zeus and I stayed undetected all those years ago. Every time Cronus tried to find us, the beating of the drums and the crashing of cymbals hid the baby's cries."

"The Lord of the Dance for the Stone Age crowd," Drake added dryly.

Ilsa couldn't stop the giggle that rose up at the thought. "I suppose so."

"Game faces, people. Come on." Kane's harsh bark quieted them, but Ilsa couldn't resist shooting a quick smile at Drake.

While she wasn't exactly looking forward to this excursion, it was time to put an end to this situation once and for all.

"What if Emmett's set another trap?" Drake's smile vanished as he stared at the cave that rose up in the distance.

"We've got Brody and Ava in position in Crete, should Emmett find a way to flee the cave." Quinn said, his sword already in hand. "Add to the fact he doesn't have the ability to port and we should be able to manage him between us."

"And if we can't?" Kane probed.

Quinn nodded. "Then we'll go after him until we catch him. By the laws of balance, he violated his agreement with Ilsa. He used her for purposes that weren't explained in advance and he betrayed the scientists by posing as a double agent and a person he wasn't. We have a right to deal with him."

"Damn straight we do," Kane muttered.

Ilsa took a deep breath and tried to get the raging river of anxiety that drove her pulse into some semblance of order. Deep breath in. Deep breath out. In. Out.

The urge to smile vanished. "It's time to go in. I'm going first." Ilsa pointed to the mouth of the cave. "We need the element of surprise on our side and I want him to think I'm alone. I need you all to stay down here until I go in. Then stand to the side of the cave entrance as you listen for my signal."

"We'll be waiting, ready to enter at a moment's notice," Kane added. "How far between the mouth and the main room?"

Ilsa brought up a mental picture of the cave. The steps she'd taken for so many years. The steps she walked as she sought to soothe a crying baby. "It's about ten feet from the mouth of the cave to the inner chamber. You'll be close enough to hear us. Remember. When I say, 'Emmett, I'm ready to deal,' that's when you all come in."

"Men. Remember your mark. Quinn and Drake, flank the far sides. Brody's covering the rear and will come in on our signal. Emmett's mine."

"You can kill him? Even if he looks like St. Giles when you do?" Ilsa probed.

Kane drew her to him, his hand at the back of her neck as he pulled her close for a hard, welcoming kiss.

"Yes." Kane nodded.

"Wait." Ilsa pulled him close once more, and mimicked his movements with her hand on the back of his neck. The kiss was hard and unyielding at first, quickly giving way to something softer. Slightly desperate. And altogether wonderful.

Fortifying.

Ilsa nodded and smoothed the skirt at her waist. "Okay. Now it's time." Although the pants she hated would have been more practical, she didn't want to deviate from her usual look.

Emmett was used to seeing her in skirts.

She wasn't going to give him any visual clues all wasn't as it seemed.

With one final glance at Kane, she whispered the words that filled her heart to bursting. "I love you."

And then she turned and moved on ahead, her blood pumping in thick, heavy beats.

The gravel-strewn path up to the mouth of the cave looked as she remembered it. How was it possible? Sixteen thousand years of life had passed, yet she remembered this as if it had happened only yesterday. Last week. Last year.

How had time passed so quickly? And what had she done with all of it?

The question struck her like a slap, because she knew what she'd done with all her time. All the millions of days of her life that had passed since then.

She'd lived them with vengeance and anger, retaliation and hate.

But no more.

For a brief moment, Ilsa hesitated at the mouth of the cave. And then she stepped through.

Bold.

Confident.

Prepared.

Only to have all of it come crashing down in a pile of burning cinders.

What greeted her was something out of her worst nightmare.

Brody and Ava were attached to two guillotines. Flat on their stomachs, tied to the cross-board with heavy industrial chains. Callie stood in the center of the room, teetering on a chair, a hangman's noose around her neck.

Emmett turned to greet her from where he stood next to the guillotine that held Brody, fiddling with a pulley system that held the blade aloft. To her horror, it appeared to tie in some fashion to the second guillotine blade that hovered over Ava's neck. "Welcome, Ilsa. I'm so glad you've finally arrived."

A second voice echoed through the chamber. As Ilsa spun around toward the direction of the sound, a tall woman clad in fine robes stepped out of the shadows.

"Well, well, well. If it isn't the sainted woman that hid

my father for all those years. I'm so delighted to meet you."
The woman's long, slender fingers extended in welcome.
"I'm Enyo. And you must be Nemesis."

"I don't like this. She's been in there for a while and we
still haven't heard anything. Haven't heard her signal." Kane
whispered so only his intended target—Quinn—could hear
him.

The bull nodded, his own reply nearly silent. "Patience."

Fuck patience.

And why had he listened to her?

Why wasn't he in there himself instead of out here,
sweating his ass off as the poison threatened to overwhelm
him.

The venom had grown harsher over the last day, as they
made plans for the final encounter with Emmett. Each night,
Antares crept ever closer to its zenith. And with it, the poison's strength grew.

Harder to ignore. Harder to hold out against.

Kane refused to tell anyone about it. He simply worked
to ignore it—like tuning out a dripping faucet or a static-
filled radio station—but he was losing his patience.

"Why hasn't she given us the signal?"

On top of the poison, the damned Corybants were rattling around like those parade people he saw on New Year's
Day, dressed in costume and beating drums in a semidrunk
fashion. They made so much noise, the voices from the cave
were muted and hard to hear.

Could this place get any weirder? And did he dare enter
the mouth of the cave?

Shit.

The stories of his ancestors—hiding babies from their

parents and sending said parents to perpetual prison in the Underworld—had always read with a fair degree of inanity.

But to actually be here at the site of it all?

Surreal didn't even begin to describe it.

He glanced back at Quinn again, then on down the line to Drake and Emerson.

Kane calculated the risks. Shift away toward Quinn, Drake and Emerson to have a brief discussion and miss hearing Ilsa give the signal. Or have the conversation and reset their plans.

As the drumming rose in ever-increasing cycles of beats, Kane made a decision.

And moved away from the mouth of the cave to discuss a regroup.

"You have no business with them." Ilsa flicked a hand at Brody, Ava and Callie. "They mean nothing to me. But if you harm them, you will unleash the wrath of Themis."

The corners of Emmett's mouth twisted up in a cruel smile, and a matching one lit up Enyo's face.

"Such brave words from one who has nothing to bargain with." Enyo moved closer, her steps measured. "Did you really think you'd get away with simply changing your bargain with Emmett? That a quick 'Never mind. I'm no longer interested' was all it would take?"

Ilsa pressed haughty and arrogant into her tone, even as she wanted to fall to the ground and beg for mercy. Beg them to let her friends go. And her sister. The woman she didn't have a relationship with and now never would if Emmett had his way. "Hardly. I offered myself."

Enyo leaned in and whispered, her words holding all the warmth of pythons as they slithered over Ilsa's skin.

"Did you really think you were worth more than a Warrior? Hades's humble servant girl for a Warrior of Themis?"

Ilsa felt the goddess's cold, calculating gaze traveling over her body and desperately yearned for sunshine.

On an inhale, Ilsa forced the bravado yet again. Leveling her own stare directly at Enyo, she nodded. "Frankly, yes, I did."

Enyo leaned in closer, her voice a breathy whisper. "Then you thought wrong."

Maintaining a steady, unwavering gaze, Ilsa thought through all she knew. Took stock of all she possessed as an immortal in her own right. As her mind whirled with ideas, each one discarded in turn, she had to acknowledge two facts.

This wasn't the first sticky situation she'd gotten herself into.

But it was the first where her friends were in danger.

And that made all the difference.

"She's been in there too long. Something's wrong."

"Monte. You have to calm down. It hasn't been that long." Quinn held up a hand. "I know it's not easy, but you have to have a little patience. She knows what she's doing. She's not a mortal."

"I don't care if she's immortal." Kane pointed to the cave. "She's in there all alone."

Drake stepped in, his voice low, but pointed. "Quinn's right. Ilsa's spent sixteen thousand years in service to Hades. I'm sure she's learned a few tricks over the years."

"I'm telling you"—Kane shook his head—"something's not right."

Quinn mumbled something and reached for his BlackBerry. Flicking a quick glance at it, he did a double take and handed the phone to Kane. "Shit."

"What?" Drake and Emerson asked in unison as Kane read the readout on the screen.

CAPTRD.

Captured.

Kane handed the device back to Quinn. "We're going in. He's got Brody and Ava in there, too."

Ilsa purposely ignored the others as Enyo spoke to her, in hopes her unwillingness to look at them would be perceived as lack of interest.

"Now, Nemesis," Enyo said, adding subtle pressure on her back to lead her farther into the cave. "There's a little something I'd like to show you."

Ilsa shook off the touch. She'd captured enough souls over the years to know how to dominate someone and she sure as hell wasn't going to let Enyo have the upper hand physically.

She clearly had it psychologically.

Ilsa saw a large table come into view as they moved toward the back of the cave. Try as she might, she was unable to avert her gaze from Ava as she walked past.

The frightened look in her brown eyes was all Ilsa needed to renew herself against the despair. She would find a way out of this. For all of them.

She'd die before letting any of them suffer for her mistakes.

An odd mix of items sat on the table, but it wasn't until they got closer that Ilsa could make sense of them.

A large glowing object that resembled a very thick spear.

A crown of gold.

A small wadded-up baby blanket.

Enyo picked up each in turn, playing with them, turning them over in her hands. One by one, she picked up each object, strategically embedding them with her prisoners.

The baby blanket lay at Callie's feet, where she still teetered on the stool.

The crown of gold was placed on Ava's head.

And the thick spear—nay, *Zeus's thunderbolt*—was placed on the ground next to Brody.

As Ilsa watched Enyo carefully position each object, she realized their significance. Their horrifying, terrible significance.

Each of the items belonged to Zeus. And when he found out they were missing, his punishment would know no bounds.

Chapter Twenty-five

"**T**his is your great idea?" More forced bravado fell from her lips, but Ilsa found the attitude increasingly difficult to maintain. "A baby blanket?"

Enyo stood next to Brody's prone form and finished positioning the thunderbolt with her foot. "Now. What was it we were talking about before? Oh yes. Why you really don't matter to me. Why you're just a means to an end."

Keep her talking. That was the only thing Ilsa could think to do. There was no way she was uttering the words Kane waited for outside. No way she'd invite any more of them into the psychotic play that was unraveling within the walls of the cave.

Emmett roamed the cave like a restless cat, his avaricious gaze on Zeus's belongings each time he made his circular path past the items.

As Ilsa watched him and the calculating gleam that lit his eyes, she wondered if he might be the answer to getting them out of this horrible mess.

Could she use his greed against him?

Shifting so she could keep an eye on Emmett with her

peripheral vision, Ilsa turned her attention toward Enyo. "I'll repeat it. This is your great idea? A baby blanket?"

"Not just any baby blanket. The blanket you wrapped my father in when he was an infant. The blanket you spirited him away in. That blanket has power. The power of immortal protection for any who possesses it. It's why he keeps it locked up with his other protected items."

"And you just waltzed in and stole all of it."

"My father is the one who made that stupid bargain with Themis." Enyo spat the words, each laced with the most spiteful venom. "But I'm the one who has to answer to it. When he finds out these are missing—and clearly in the possession of Themis's Warriors—his willingness to maintain his bargain with that bitch won't last."

Ilsa shrugged, delighted to see Emmett edge closer to the blanket where it lay at Callie's feet. "Awfully complicated, if you ask me. What if he doesn't buy it?"

Emmett looked up at that. "Of course he'll buy it. Won't he, Enyo? You promised when we arrived here that you had it all taken care of."

"And I do. Don't worry yourself, Emmett." Enyo ran a hand over Brody's upper back and biceps. "I've got it all figured out."

Emmett's face—crinkled forehead, slashed lips and hunched back—suggested he wasn't nearly as convinced as Enyo. Ilsa had read people for far too long not to know the signs.

Nope.

The sorcerer had "rat leaving a sinking ship" written all over him.

Add in the pure greed that swam in his eyes, and Emmett really might create the diversion she needed all on his own.

With slow, shifting movements, Ilsa kept up her conversation with Enyo while she positioned herself to port toward Brody and Ava.

The elaborate pulley system rigged on the guillotines, while appearing detrimental to both parties if either moved, might actually work in her favor. Because the rope that held each blade was strung together, all she needed was to port in between the two of them to grab the rope.

The fear she couldn't get there in time was real, but at least she was positioned to try if the very worst happened.

Ilsa tuned back in to Enyo's ire, the goddess's continued pontification on her father's shitty negotiation skills clearly a topic on which she felt strongly.

Is that what she'd sounded like for all these years? Ugly and unpleasant and *whiny*?

"It's my turn to get what I want." The finality of Enyo's statement firmly pulled Ilsa from her thoughts.

"Well, then." Ilsa pointed across the room, where Emmett had his hands on the blanket, fingering it with deliberate strokes. "You might want to bring him to heel, or he'll be out of here with that blanket faster than you can say the word 'warrior.'"

"What?"

The diversion was all she needed, especially as Emmett was doing his level best to take off with the blanket. Enyo bent over to grab the thunderbolt, aiming it at Emmett and firing off a round.

As Enyo focused on dealing with the sorcerer, Ilsa ported across the room to position herself between Brody and Ava, hoisting the pulley upward to ensure the blades locked in place. While she couldn't ignore the fear in Callie's eyes, the precarious angle of the blades ensured she needed to start with the Leo and his wife.

As she worked, the drama between Enyo and Emmett played out.

"I did as you asked!" the sorcerer screamed as his pant leg burned with flames.

"You were going to steal the blanket."

"Not steal it. Bring it to you, my queen."

Enyo fired off another shot, this one hitting Emmett at the knee and dropping him to the ground in a wail. "Do not lie to me. Do you think I can't see what you are?"

Emmett still held the blanket tight in his grip, his eyes blazing with fury, his focus fully on Enyo. Before the goddess could react, he had the edges in his hands and spread the blanket out in front of him like a shield, ensuring Enyo would have to destroy the blanket in order to punish him with the thunderbolt. "Then you must be looking at yourself."

Although oddly fascinating, she couldn't spend much time watching as the fight between the two allowed Ilsa to continue working on Brody and Ava's bonds.

"Underneath. They didn't lock them, just slipped them into place," Brody whispered. "Get Ava's first."

Ilsa reached down to unhook the chains where they wrapped under the board Ava lay on, then did the same for Brody.

"Get Callie," Brody whispered urgently as he used his free hands to unhinge the head lock and leap off the board. "I'll finish helping Ava."

Ilsa was coming out of the port to Callie's side when light flashed in the small space, flaring from the edge of the thunderbolt Enyo wielded. Emmett's brief scream rent the air and then the distinct odor of brimstone filled the enclosed space. Where Emmett once stood there was now a heap of ash, a few feet from the stool where Callie still stood, her eyes wide with fear.

Kane, Quinn and Drake burst through the cave opening, followed on their heels by Emerson.

As the four of them reached the entrance to the room, all stopped short, taking in the scene before them. Without another glance for Emmett, Enyo hefted the thunderbolt and pointed it at Callie.

"Ah. The cavalry arrives. And it's just the horsemen I've been waiting for."

Kane took in the sight—Brody and Ava struggling out of bonds where they lay strapped on matched guillotines, Callie hovering precariously on a stool with a noose around her neck and Enyo pointing the business end of a very old, very powerful weapon—and had the fleeting thought that things couldn't get any worse.

Big mistake.

The poison reached up and grabbed on to him, choking him from the inside out. The sensation of being unable to catch his breath, like after a long sprint, gripped his lungs, preventing him from taking in any air.

With swift, brutal kicks, the disease that lived under his skin began the process of decimating him.

Organ by organ, limb by limb, nerve ending by nerve ending. Agonizing waves of pain lashed his body. As Kane fought for breath, he reached for his head, desperately trying to keep it from rending in half.

Zeus ported into the room, a crack of thunder greeting his arrival, the sound deafening as it echoed off the thick walls of the cave. It echoed through Kane's already-inflamed senses.

Zeus's gaze took in the room in a heartbeat, his voice implacable. "What is the meaning of this?"

"Oh, Daddy. I'm so glad you're here." Enyo ran to him, the thunderbolt in her hands. "They stole your things. I thought you'd never come."

Without hesitation, she handed the thunderbolt to her father and then pointed around the room.

"It's Adrasteia, Daddy. She made a bargain with the Warriors to steal your things. In vengeance against you."

Every muscle in Kane's body quivered as he writhed on the floor, helpless to go to Ilsa. Helpless to stand by her side as Zeus walked toward her. Callie still teetered precariously, but he saw Ilsa move up to support her with a firm hand under her thigh, holding her still and ensuring her neck wouldn't break if something happened to the stool.

"Adrasteia."

Ilsa nodded, her eyes direct on the fierce god. "That is no longer my name. And your daughter tells you only lies."

"You dare impertinence?"

"What of it? I've changed your soiled linens and held your hands as you took your first steps. You've no power over me. And if you don't pay close attention, your daughter's manipulations will bring down all you've built. Will force a real war with Themis and her Warriors."

Zeus cocked his head, a slight sneer on his face. "And how is that, little nymph? You think I spend my days worried about Themis's Warriors?"

"You think about Themis far more than you let on. And you know the bargain with her limits your ability to interfere. However, I'm sure if you thought your prized possessions had been stolen by a Warrior, you'd call off those barely held controls."

"What nonsense you speak."

"It's the very nonsense your daughter wishes you to believe."

Zeus's gaze darted to his daughter before coming back to rest firmly on Ilsa's face. "I have all the power over you. Wasn't it I who sentenced you to this cave?"

"And it was your brother who saw to it that I could leave."

Confusion etched firm lines through Zeus's craggy face as he reached up to stroke his beard. Although he had the look of an elder statesman, his body was a fine specimen, resembling a fit human in the prime of his life.

"My brother?"

"Hades rescued me. Gave me work. Gave me a new name. Gave me a life."

"And what name is this?"

Ilsa smiled again and Kane saw her gaze dart toward him ever so briefly. "I don't use that one any longer, either."

Zeus's voice boomed off the cave walls. "Games. Silly games and silly nonsense. If you choose to withhold it, I shall call you by the name I know. Adrasteia."

"Then I shall not answer."

Kane heard Quinn's sharp intake of breath behind him. The woman dared much in her dealings with the god.

His woman dared much.

Ilsa followed the cheeky comment with further taunts. "Come now. Do you seriously believe I took your things?"

"It's obvious you did," Enyo chimed in. "You betrayed him all those years ago and you've attempted it again. It's a good thing we got here before you could do any real damage."

Ilsa's calm demeanor shifted into something far more

potent. Far more dangerous. "Since you were the one who just decimated the baby blanket, I think you might want to reassess that opinion."

"Enough!" Zeus shifted his focus and Kane felt the glacial attention as it came to center on him, Drake and Quinn. "And you. Themis's Warriors. Do you do as my daughter says? Did you align yourselves with Adrasteia to steal the power of my thunderbolt and crown?"

Kane staggered to his feet, his patience at an end. Ilsa had suffered too long. His scorpion twitched to life on his shoulder, the tattoo's agitation at the internal and external battles being waged almost too much to keep it in line. The best and worst of his gifts, both locked inside of him.

Protector and foe.

Both pulsed with life.

Kane gritted his teeth against the feral pain of the poison and focused on the threat to his woman and how to eliminate it. "You will not speak to her this way. The theft of your possessions lies with your daughter. Not with Ilsa."

"Ilsa, is it?" A sneer formed on Zeus's lips, his tone an audible match for it. "She thinks a name will change what she is? What she did?"

Kane pressed on, unconcerned with consequence. With punishment. He wouldn't leave Ilsa to do this alone. To fight this battle alone. "She protected you and you repaid her with scorn. With punishment!"

"She kept me from fulfilling my destiny!"

"You seem to be doing just fine from my vantage point."

Kane knew it the moment he overstepped. The barely banked fury written on Zeus's face shifted from anger to action. The god leaped, his attack swift as his body forced Kane to the ground.

Kane pressed against the god, but in his weakened state,

he felt the strength in his arms slip almost immediately. Zeus lifted his arm, preparing to strike, when . . .

Light filled the cave, followed immediately by rolling claps of thunder.

In unison, all of them turned toward the epicenter of the light.

And found Enyo wielding the thunderbolt aloft, waving it wildly at all of them.

"Enyo!" Zeus's bellowing voice rivaled the claps of thunder that had sounded earlier. "Lay that down."

"No, Daddy. I will not. It is my turn to rise up. My turn to wield power."

"You have no right!"

"I have every right. You entered me into a bargain I didn't want, dictating the terms of the agreement. Well, Daddy, the terms are changing." She swung the bolt in a wide arc, the wild display of power erratic and out of control.

"She doesn't like her job?" Drake whispered. "Could have fooled me."

Zeus marched toward his daughter, only to be pressed back by a bolt of lightning straight to his chest. Although clearly alive, the bolt threw him across the cave to land on his back, lying there like a stunned turtle in an overturned shell.

"Clearly no one's done that to him in a really long time," Drake added.

"Or ever," Emerson finished for him.

Any sense of humor between them vanished as Zeus came to his feet with the finesse of a raging wounded animal.

"Over there." Drake nodded at Emerson, gesturing with his head to the far side of the cave, near the exit. "Get over there and prepare to run if things get bad in here."

"I don't need—"

"You're not an immortal. Do as I say." Before Emerson could argue further, Drake bent over and pressed a hard kiss to her lips. "Now."

Kane shot a quick glance toward Quinn, their thoughts telegraphed as clearly as if they'd spoken them. *Well, that was unexpected.*

Kane then watched as Brody settled Ava beside Callie, her grip on the woman's thigh matched in support to where Ilsa stood on the other side. Brody then continued on, flanking the rest of the Warriors.

"Can we take a direct hit from the bolt?" Kane whispered to his brothers.

"Maybe. Maybe not. You?" Quinn shook his head. "No way. The poison is too close. That bolt is designed to cut straight through a threat and destroy."

Sit and wait.

You're not strong enough.

The poison is too strong.

Scorpios acted. They were decisive and strong. And they protected what was theirs.

He could wait no longer.

With a battle cry, Kane gripped his claymore and took off for Enyo. His scorpion unfolded and rode high on his shoulder, that lethal tail swinging in deadly arcs.

Quinn screamed from behind him, but Kane ignored him.

Ilsa screamed from her position next to Callie, but Kane ignored her.

Enyo lifted her arm, aiming for his chest, but Kane ignored her.

With a last, final leap toward the goddess of war, he allowed his scorpion full extension within his aura, the large animal landing as he did, their combined force pushing Enyo off balance and landing so that the thunderbolt skittered from her grip.

The scorpion dropped its tail, the motion pinning her to the ground as Zeus stalked toward them.

His brothers stood in a half circle around them as Ava and Ilsa helped Callie to the ground, the women having already dealt with the noose.

As Enyo lay on the ground, she stared up toward Kane, a mutiny of the coldest evil alight in her eyes. The heavy black tail of his scorpion lay on her chest, holding her in place, but the air quivered with her anger.

Her fury.

"Let my daughter up." Zeus's voice thundered in Kane's ear.

Kane didn't move; instead, he questioned the order directly. "Do you believe we didn't do this?"

The god's tone had quieted, but his words indicated he wasn't ready to acquiesce. "I must evaluate further."

"Then I'm afraid I can't let her up."

A red flush crept up Zeus's cheeks, but his tone remained consistent. "Let my daughter up. I shall deal with her."

"So you acknowledge Ilsa is innocent in this deception? That the Warriors in service to Themis are innocent?"

Zeus's features remained implacable. "As I said, I must evaluate further."

Before Kane could respond, he felt movement against his scorpion, coming from the direction of the tail.

Enyo applied the force of direct pressure, coupled with the power of a goddess, and snapped the edge of his scorpion's tail. There was no pain, but the loss of a portion of his tail altered the animal's balance, allowing Enyo to wiggle free.

As she leaped away, she slid unerringly toward the discarded thunderbolt and once again lifted it.

"Mine."

Ilsa leaped toward Enyo, unwilling to allow the bitch to take the thunderbolt twice.

The move worked, her forward momentum knocking Enyo off balance as they wrestled each other to the floor.

Although Enyo had several inches of height on her, Ilsa managed to get a strong leg lock, ensuring the fight remained contained as neither could use their feet.

The large thunderbolt juggled between their arms as they fought. Ilsa felt the hard, jagged length of it slice at her inner arm and used the pain to fuel her anger.

Pulling back, she threw a direct hit at Enyo, satisfied when she heard a grunt of pain on contact. Ilsa shifted to try the move again when light blasted through the cave.

Enyo renewed her assault as the unexpected light faded and it was only as they rolled a few feet further that Ilsa realized the light suffusing the cave was different.

It filled the air with a warm golden light, soft and welcoming. Beckoning all to come closer.

Both Ilsa and Enyo stopped struggling to look at the source. Although neither loosened her grip, they did divert their attention to the woman that had materialized in the cave.

"Do you see what your daughter has wrought?"

Themis.

Ilsa looked with amazement at the sheer power the woman

wielded. Her slender form was clad in long white robes and her Titan red hair hung in warm waves over her back.

"My daughter has wrought nothing," Zeus spat back. "Your Warriors thought to gain the upper hand. Betray our agreement."

"My Warriors did no such thing, but your idiotic belief they did is why I'm forced to arrive here today."

"They had help." Ilsa felt the point of Zeus's finger with the same swiftness he launched thunderbolts. "Adrasteia."

Themis shook her head. "Why are you so blind when it comes to her? She raised you. Loved you. And you repaid her with scorn."

"She betrayed me! She kept me here, locked away while my father ruled in his glory. It was my job to punish him and she kept me from that."

"She protected you."

"She kept me from my destiny. You know that. It was you, all those years ago, who spoke of balance."

Themis shook her head, the lush waves of her hair a beautiful red waterfall about her face. "I spoke of the balance of our lives. Not that it should be based in vengeance. In hate. You took my words and twisted them to fit your version of strength and honor and manhood."

Ilsa listened to the goddess's words. Was it possible? Was Themis truly blameless?

Zeus's face remained stubbornly mulish. "You said that it is essential to seek balance."

"Aye. I most certainly did. You were a young buck, recently off your victory over your father and you thought yourself invincible. I tried to explain to you the price you'd pay if you didn't understand the balance required in our universe. The balance required by victory."

"I punished her."

Themis nodded, then shifted her gaze. Ilsa felt the warmth of her approval and—was that a sense of sadness?—for what had been lost.

"You punished her without cause. It is only through the mercy of your brother that she's even had some semblance of a life."

Zeus turned his gaze as well and Ilsa saw something there. Not quite shame. Not quite apology.

But perhaps a sense of regret.

Shifting her own gaze, Ilsa stared at Kane. As she met those endlessly deep, dark eyes, the final piece fell into place.

What came before truly didn't matter.

It was what came next that would give her life meaning. Fulfillment.

Truth.

Desperate to be with Kane, Ilsa let go of Enyo and rolled away. As she shifted to gain her feet, Enyo lifted the thunderbolt.

Ilsa felt the shot of cold fire at the center of her body as Enyo hit her target with unerring precision.

The hole in her soul that sat under her heart, just outside her rib cage, filled with the searing heat of the bolt.

All action in the cave happened at once.

Kane leaped across the room toward Ilsa as Quinn, Drake and Brody made a phalanx around him.

Zeus flew toward his daughter, tackling her to the ground and removing the thunderbolt from her grasp.

Callie, Ava and Emerson followed on the heels of the Warriors to close the circle around Kane and Ilsa as he lay on the ground holding her body.

"Ilsa." Kane rocked her, holding her to his chest. "Ilsa!"

High-pitched screams pierced the cave as Zeus dragged Enyo away, but they all ignored it. Everyone concentrated on Ilsa.

"Kane, let me have her." Themis hovered over him, her smile gentle.

"I can't let her go."

"Please. Let me have her. I can help her."

"You saw it. Nothing can help her. The bolt hit her chest."

"Kane." He looked up into eyes full of understanding and wisdom. "Allow me to have her."

Lifting his arms, Kane placed Ilsa in Themis's grasp.

They followed as Themis walked across the room toward a carpet that lay in front of the fire pit.

Themis turned to all of them after laying Ilsa on the rug. "She will be fine."

Silence greeted her proclamation.

With slow, graceful movements, Themis sank to the ground, her robes billowing out in gentle waves. With tender, probing fingers, she ran her hands over Ilsa's body, stopping when she reached the area where the tear was.

Themis turned her face up, her question direct. "Kane, is this it? Is this the site of the tear?"

"Yes."

"Come here. All of you." Themis beckoned them forward, instructing all but Kane and Callie into a circle.

"Kane. I want you here. On this side." Themis had him sit, replacing her at Ilsa's side. "Callie. I'd like you to match his position on the other side."

Callie quickly took her seat.

"Lay your hands upon her, over her heart."

Kane did as he was told; he saw Callie follow suit.

Themis stood to her full height and inquired of Quinn, "Your Xiphos. Please."

Quinn scrambled to pull the instrument from where it sat strapped to his thigh, then handed it over, handle first.

With deliberate movements, Themis lifted her arms, allowing the sleeves of her robes to fall to her elbows. Extending her left arm, she positioned herself over Ilsa's body. With the Xiphos in her other hand, Themis executed a quick slashing motion, blood immediately welling on her inner arm.

As she turned her arm over, allowing the blood to drip onto Ilsa's chest, Themis chanted.

> *Blood in strife.*
> *Blood for life.*
> *Souls do bleed.*
> *Souls in need.*
> *By my hand, feel my power.*
> *Take my strength, in your darkest hour.*

Warm waves of light filled the room, coming from the cut in Themis's arm.

Kane felt the change under his hands. Felt the pulse beat with increasing steadiness in Ilsa's chest and the color fill her cheeks to a bright pink.

Still, Themis chanted, over and over, as her blood slowly dripped onto Ilsa's chest.

With each drop of blood, Ilsa's body grew stronger, her breaths more full.

Until . . . she woke.

As simple as that, and equally wondrous.

Those beautiful blue eyes opened and stared up into his.

"Ilsa?"

"Yes?"

"Are you back with us?"

She smiled. "Yes. I'm back. What happened?"

Callie reached over and smoothed the hair from her sister's brow. "Themis saved you."

Themis shook her head as she readjusted the sleeves of her robe. "Ilsa saved herself. She chose life and she chose love. I simply ensured she was intact again to finally enjoy all those things."

"Intact?" Kane looked up at his goddess in wonderment. "Her soul?"

Themis smiled gently, and Kane felt her innate goodness wash over him as she pressed her cheek to his. "Aye. It is intact."

"You can do that?"

"I can do many things, my Scorpio. When the price is a fair one, I can do many things."

Kane leaned in, pressing his lips to her ear. "Thank you. With everything I am, thank you."

Themis pressed a light kiss of her own, then stepped back. A distinct twinkle filled her eyes. "Does the poison ravage you any longer?"

Her words registered and Kane focused on his own body.

The poison wasn't gone, but it was more of a nuisance than a threat. His muscles felt strong and vibrant and his stomach was free of nausea.

"It's at bay."

"And that's where it will stay. A small reminder of humility, but no longer a threat to your well-being."

"But how?" Kane marveled at the renewed vigor in his body, the pain that had filled his muscle fibers receding with each passing second.

"The one who bound you is no more. His dark magic will leave a mark—it is why you'll never be fully rid of the poison—but it no longer has the power to take your life."

With that, Themis smiled more broadly. Arms outstretched, she reached for Ilsa's hand and joined it with Kane's. "And now, all is as it should be."

The light shimmered and the air whistled around them as Themis ported out of the room.

Turning toward Ilsa, Kane looked down at their joined hands. "I think she meant something with this."

Ilsa smiled up at him. "You're a perceptive one, my Scorpio."

"I think I'd like to take it one step further."

In one fluid movement, Kane dropped to his knee.

"Ilsa. Love of my life and the keeper of my heart. Marry me. Live with me. Be my wife."

Ilsa stared down at him, love shining from her eyes with the brightness of a thousand suns. "Always and forever."

Kane stood and pulled her into his arms, crushing his mouth to hers.

With a whispered promise against her lips, he repeated her words back to her before taking her lips in a soul-searing kiss.

"Always and forever."

AQUARIUS/SCORPIO STAR CHART

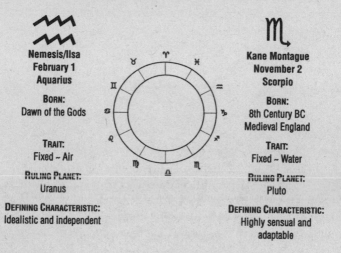

Nemesis/Ilsa
February 1
Aquarius

BORN:
Dawn of the Gods

TRAIT:
Fixed ~ Air

RULING PLANET:
Uranus

DEFINING CHARACTERISTIC:
Idealistic and independent

Kane Montague
November 2
Scorpio

BORN:
8th Century BC
Medieval England

TRAIT:
Fixed ~ Water

RULING PLANET:
Pluto

DEFINING CHARACTERISTIC:
Highly sensual and
adaptable

Attraction may be strained when sensual Scorpio meets independent Aquarius.

Although the Aquarius woman takes issue with the sometimes dictatorial nature of her Scorpio, his innate sensuality, magnetic personality and deep convictions will win her over. The Scorpio man is fiercely protective of his mate and will guard her to the end of his days.

Our sexy Scorpio seeks a woman who is his match in every way, not easily cowed by his sharp sting. Scorpios are sincere and honest and expect the same in return.

Although the road will be undoubtedly full of twists and turns for Kane and Ilsa, if the two can get beyond the battles each wage within their souls—and learn to trust the other with their deepest secrets—their love can overcome any obstacle placed in their path.

GLOSSARY

Ages of Man—the stages of human existence, as identified by the Greek writer Hesiod. Most often associated with metals, the Ages—Gold, Silver, Bronze, Heroic and Iron—reflect the increasing toil and drudgery humans live in. The world only thinks the ages are myth. . . .

Cardinal—a sign *quality*, Cardinal signs (Aries, Cancer, Libra, Capricorn) mark the start of each season. Those born under Cardinal signs are considered dynamic and, like each season, forceful in its beginnings. Cardinal Warriors are equally dynamic, forcing change with their impatient natures and independent spirits.

Chimera—with the body and head of a lion, the tail of a snake and the head of a goat extending from the center of its back, the chimera is one of the eleven monsters of Mount Olympus. Created by the goddess Echidna—the Mother of all Monsters—her menagerie is a favorite resource of terror for Deimos and Phobos.

Corybants—legendary male dancers, clothed in armor and playing drums. Their loud, rhythmic playing was said to drown out the cries of the baby Zeus so he wouldn't be discovered in his hiding place on Mount Ida.

Deimos—the son of Ares and Aphrodite, he is the god of dread. He is the brother of Phobos.

Destroyer—a soulless creature created by Enyo from an emotionally damaged human. They take on the appearance of men, but their bodies are nothing but husks, filled with a superconductive life force. They can be slowed and hurt, but quickly recover. The only way to kill a Destroyer is by removing his head. Each Destroyer Enyo creates takes some of her power, an innate balance agreed to during the creation of the Great Agreement.

Element—just as all signs are Cardinal, Fixed or Mutable, each sign also possesses an elemental quality of Fire, Earth, Air or Water. Each Warrior has an elemental nature to his sign, allowing for additional powers for those who have learned to develop them. These elemental qualities exist beyond those granted to all Warriors—immortality, the ability to port, rapid healing and above-average strength—and have begun to express themselves as the Warriors have grown more comfortable in their abilities and better understand the full range of their skills.

Enyo—the goddess of war, Enyo is the daughter of Zeus and Hera. Equipped with the ability to create anarchy and death wherever she goes, Zeus offered Enyo up to Themis for their Great Agreement. Before Zeus allowed Themis to create the Sons of the Zodiac, she had to agree to a counterbalance to the Warriors' power. Enyo provides the balance, at constant war with Themis's Warriors. For each battle Enyo wins, her power grows. As such, for each she loses, her power is diminished.

Equinox—a nightclub owned by Grey Bennett, Aries Warrior. Each Warrior has a role within the whole and Grey's is to keep an eye on the underbelly of New York for Enyo's likely crop of new Destroyers. What none of the Warriors knows is that Grey carries a secret—one that will lead him to his destiny or to his doom. . . .

Fixed—a sign *quality*, Fixed signs (Taurus, Leo, Scorpio, Aquarius) mark the middle of each season. Those born under Fixed signs are considered quite stubborn and persistent. Fixed Warriors are equally stubborn and persistent, unwilling to yield to their enemies.

Great Agreement—an agreement entered into during the Iron Age (the Fifth Age of Man) by Zeus and Themis. Fearful that her beloved humans had no protection from the trials of life, Themis entered into an agreement with Zeus that created the Sons of the Zodiac. The Sons of the Zodiac are Warriors modeled after the circular perfection of the heavens and each Warrior carries the immutable qualities of his sign. Under the Great Agreement, the immortal Warriors will battle Zeus's daughter Enyo, the goddess of war, for the ultimate protection, quality and survival of humanity.

Hera—wife of Zeus and mother of Enyo.

Iron Age—the Fifth Age of Man, generally thought to be about ten thousand years ago, where humans toil in abject misery. Brothers fight brothers, children turn against their fathers and anarchy is the rule of the land. During this age the gods have forsaken humanity. It is during this time that Themis—desperate to alter the course of human existence—goes to Zeus and enters into the Great Agreement. During this age, the Sons of the Zodiac are created.

Hades—god of the Underworld and brother to Zeus and Poseidon.

MI6—the British government's foreign intelligence service, also known as the Secret Intelligence Service (SIS).

Mount Ida—the legendary site in Crete where Rhea hid her son, Zeus, as a baby from his father, Cronus.

Mutable—a sign *quality*, Mutable signs (Gemini, Virgo, Sagittarius, Pisces) mark the end of each season. Those born under Mutable signs are the most comfortable with change, making them easily adaptable and resourceful. Mutable Warriors are the first to see the big picture, able to adapt and shift their battle plans at a moment's notice. Their ability to see issues from multiple angles make them strong Warriors and a comfort to have watching your back.

Nemesis—the Greek goddess of divine retribution. The name Nemesis means "to give what is due."

Phobos—the son of Ares and Aphrodite, he is the god of fear. He is the brother of Deimos.

Port—shortened form of teleport, the Warriors and Destroyers both have the ability to move through space and time at will. Porting will diminish power.

Prophecy of Thutmose III—a prophecy, carved on the walls of Thutmose III's tomb and not discovered until the early twenty-first century. The Prophecy outlines the power of the Summoning Stones of Egypt, for those who are chosen by them.

Sons of the Zodiac—created by Themis, the goddess of justice, upon her Great Agreement with Zeus. The Great Agreement stipulates for a race of Warriors—156 in total—

that will have the traits of their zodiac sign. Tasked to protect humanity, they are at war with Enyo. A Warrior is immortal, although he may be killed with a death blow to the neck. Removal of a Warrior's head is the only way to kill him. The Warriors' strength may be reduced from extended time in battle, multiple ports and little food. A Warrior's strength will be replaced with food, sleep or sexual orgasm. Each Warrior has a tattoo of added protection that lives within his aura.

Stregheria—an ancient Italian practice of witchcraft, which formed the basis for Emmett the Sorcerer's poisonous spell placed upon Kane Montague, Scorpio Warrior.

Summoning Stones of Egypt—the five Summoning Stones of Egypt were crafted during the reign of Thutmose III. For those who are chosen—and there will be a Chosen One in each age—the Stones give the user the power to control the universe. Each of the five stones represent a different element—death, life, love, sexuality, and infinity.

Tartarus—a prisonlike pit that lives under the Underworld. Zeus's father, Cronus, is housed in Tartarus at Zeus's hand.

Themis—one of the twelve Titans, Themis is the goddess of justice. Disheartened that her beloved humans toiled in misery and abject drudgery, she petitioned Zeus to allow her to intercede. With Zeus she entered into the Great Agreement, which provided for the creation of the Sons of the Zodiac, 156 Warriors embodied with the traits of their signs. Originally she envisioned twelve of twelve—but upon reaching her agreement with Zeus gained an additional twelve Warriors so Gemini might have his twin. Themis's Warriors live across the globe, battling Enyo and keeping humanity safe.

Titans—the original twelve children born of Uranus (Father Sky) and Gaia (Earth). Themis is one of the Titans, as is Cronus, Zeus's father.

Warrior's Tattoo—the Warrior's Tattoo is inked on his body, generally on his upper shoulder blade (right or left). The tattoo lives within the Warrior's aura and, when the Warrior is in danger the tattoo will expand as an additional form of protection. The tattoo is never separate; rather, it provides additional protection through the Warrior's life force.

Xiphos—an ancient Greek weapon, the Xiphos is a double-edged blade less than a foot in length. The Warriors each carry one, strapped on their calves. Although a Warrior may deliver a death blow to a Destroyer's neck when in close range, the Xiphos provides them with an additional tool in battle. Although a Warrior may use any Xiphos—or any weapon—when necessary, each Warrior was granted a Xiphos at his turning. Although nothing more than metal, many Warriors find a personal connection with their Xiphos through millennia of battle.

Zeus—the king of the gods and ruler over Mount Olympus. Zeus is married to Hera. Zeus's first wife was Themis, the goddess of justice and one of the Titans. Zeus entered the Great Agreement with Themis, which resulted in the protectors for humanity—the Sons of the Zodiac.

Turn the page for a preview of
the next powerful romance in
Addison Fox's Sons of the Zodiac series,

WARRIOR BETRAYED

Coming from Signet Eclipse in May 2011.

Quinn Tanner reveled in the night air as it whipped around his body, battering him with the force of an on-coming subway train. The October night was unexpectedly chilly, the blustery air a clear indication that winter was on its way.

He wended his way up Fifth Avenue, the heavy foot traffic of Midtown giving way to a tonier look and feel as he crossed into the Upper East Side. Despite the evidence of increased wealth and more sedate foot traffic the farther north he walked, the vibe of the city wasn't completely lost.

Three teenagers in matching plaid school uniforms squealed in a huddled mass over the middle girl's cell phone.

A food deliveryman fought in a mix of English—and was that Italian?—with a doorman as he juggled a cardboard box of food on the handlebars of his bike.

Several taxis let up a cacophony of horns when a Ford Focus in the lead didn't move the moment the light turned green.

Gods, he loved New York.

He'd lived in nearly every major city in service as a

Taurus Warrior to Themis, the great goddess of justice. From ancient Rome to London during the Dark Ages to a brief stint helping to colonize Australia—and many more places that had blended into a mental soup of blurred memories. None came even remotely close to New York in the early-twenty-first century.

Wild energy pulsing with life.

As he crossed the next crosswalk, Quinn's gaze scanned the large apartment building that dominated the entire block. His mental tally counted four video cameras and an eagle-eyed doorman whose harsh, craggy face and hulking body screamed bodyguard far louder than it did "I accept packages and visitors."

Stepping into the ornate marble-arched doorway, where he noticed his own frame was about two inches larger than the doorman's, Quinn stated his business. "I'd like to see Ms. Montana Grant."

The doorman's face never flinched but his blue eyes went flinty and cold. "Ms. Grant doesn't accept visitors."

"Not even those with appointments?"

Again, not a flinch, nor did the man even glance at the calendar in front of him at his station. "Ms. Grant doesn't have any appointments today."

Quinn moved a few inches closer, tossing a pointed stare at the date book. "You didn't even check your book."

"I know."

Quinn was impressed with the man's stoicism. He had the exact qualities Quinn looked for in his staff—firm, harsh demeanor and a don't-fuck-with-me attitude that would keep most people from thinking twice about making trouble. Alas, Quinn wasn't on a hiring spree at the moment.

He was on a fact-finding mission.

The elevator doors opened across the lobby as an older

couple tottered out, the woman in a large fur that touched the floor and the man in a hat that had gone out of fashion sometime in the nineteen fifties. To the untrained eye, it would look as if Quinn were observing the couple, but what he really saw was the open elevator.

And as the lobby doors swished closed, Quinn knew he had what he needed. Now that he had an image of the inside of the elevator, he had the visual he required to port back to the apartment later that evening.

With a glance out at the crowded hotel ballroom, Montana Grant took a deep breath and smoothed the waistline of her evening gown, her fingers snagging on the heavy sequins of the bodice.

She hated these things.

Thousand-dollar rubber-chicken dinners with a side of lumpy mashed potatoes and a serving of vegetables that presumably grew out of a garden somewhere, yet often looked like they had been grown in the marshy grasslands of northern New Jersey.

Of course, the food was hardly the worst part. It was the obsequious fawning from the crowd, desperate to "get on her calendar" or "plan a lunch" or, worse, invite her to speak at the next one of these events.

How had her life turned into one gala after another?

A row of flashbulbs went off as she mounted the dais at the front of the room.

As she walked toward the podium, the clear screen of the teleprompter offered her a small moment of comfort. Although she could have probably given the speech in her sleep, Montana believed in always having backup.

At least professionally speaking.

Matthew Stone, the celebrity spokesperson for the environmental organization honoring her, held out his hand, a small flirty smile on his face. She took his hand as soon as she was within arm's length of him, then tilted her head up to place a small peck on his cheek. The action ensured the next round of popping flashbulbs would be tied to at least a half-dozen newspaper stories linking the two of them together in the morning.

The month prior, the borderless, worldwide goodwill organization now honoring her had contacted Grant Shipping. Peace talks had taken a decided turn for the worst between two North African nations, after a pirate attack off the southern coast of the smaller nation. The attack was seen as an act of aggression, and battle had nearly broken out before Grant Shipping stepped in and helped settle the dispute.

Even now, Montana couldn't understand how it had happened or why anyone thought her interference was worth honoring. While she'd fully believed in offering her help—Grant Shipping's vast, worldwide resources made it easy enough; her belief in being a citizen of the world made it necessary—the fact that she was being credited with averting war between two countries was a tough one to swallow.

Matt finished his remarks and stepped away from the podium to allow her access.

Another round of camera flashes, coupled with a standing ovation, greeted her as she said hello to the crowd. Montana held her remarks and fought to keep a serene smile pasted across her face. Despite her discomfort—or maybe because of it—the moment seemed to stretch on interminably. And with it, a small kernel of unease whispered up her exposed backbone.

"Thank you. Please—" She held up her hand when the crowd wouldn't quiet.

Another whisper-light frisson of apprehension followed

the last and she focused her gaze, seeking a clearer view of the audience standing before her.

Was someone out there?

Although Montana hated public speaking, it was a part of her job—a part of her life—and she accepted it as such. So why did she feel this weird, almost preternatural sense of discomfort?

The clapping slowed and the crowd began to take their seats. Montana took a deep breath, eyeing the clear tele-prompter screens that flanked either side of the podium. As she shifted to focus on the screen to her right, her gaze skated oh so briefly across the far end of the ballroom.

And into the dark, dark eyes of a man who embodied every sinful thought she'd ever had.

His frame was draped in the finest-cut tuxedo, clearly custom-made. The black fabric stretched across his shoulders, making them look enormous where he stood at attention against the ballroom wall. She followed the line of the suit, admiring the muscular look of his body and the long legs encased in black silk.

Wow, this guy was a piece of work.

Was he the reason for her unease?

Even as the thought flittered across her mind, she had to admit he didn't set off any internal warning bells.

Montana did a quick scroll through her mental Rolodex. Who was this guy? And why did she have a vague sense of the familiar, like she *should* know him, even as she knew with certainty they'd never met? And why was he standing up, looking as if he were guarding something?

She knew she'd never seen him before. That wasn't a body a woman forgot easily. Add in the thick wavy hair that was a luscious sable brown and the impressively corded neck that looked like a very nice place to grab on to and, well . . .

With a startled glance, Montana saw the videographer standing below the dais wave at her to begin.

Offering another quick thank-you, Montana shifted her focus toward the teleprompter and the opening lines of her speech. The words scrolled as she spoke, the visual a welcome distraction from her thoughts about the large man across the room. Switching to the cadence she reserved for public speaking, she vowed to ignore the mysterious stranger as she extolled the virtues of the organization that had invited her.

"The continued efforts of this organization to bring and keep peace the world over are to be commended."

A small bead of sweat ran the length of her spinal column. The unease that had gripped her upon taking the stage spread through her again, morphing distinctly into fear as it did a merry dance along her stomach lining. What was wrong with her this evening?

"Th-the belief in the equality of all humanity isn't simply a noble cause. It's a necessary one."

Montana made a pretense of pushing a lock of hair behind her ear as a way to wipe at the moisture covering her hairline. The move did little to make her feel better as the moments ticked by along with the words on her teleprompter. The normal rhythm that took over after her nerves calmed simply wouldn't materialize. Instead, the small waves of panic began to grow larger and more pronounced.

Feral.

Shifting her gaze from the teleprompter to scan the rest of the room, Montana fought to keep her voice even and level. The words of her speech were so practiced, they were virtually memorized, and she used that shift into mental autopilot to her advantage.

Quadrant by quadrant, she scanned the room, searching

for something out of the ordinary as she allowed the benign words about corporate responsibility and what it meant to be the world's largest shipping company float toward the audience. All that looked back at her was a sea of smiling faces, dressed to the nines and in various stages of happy, glowing, open-bar inebriation.

Even as she told herself this reaction was silly, Montana's gaze sought the corner where *he* had been. The tuxedoed man no longer stood against the wall, and for some reason, that small fact made the fear coursing through her system spike uncontrollably.

Without warning, unease morphed into a desperate need to get out.

The flicker of the teleprompter drew her attention brief moments before two things registered.

A loud scream pierced the air as the room went black and a wave of static electricity washed over her with harsh, piercing needles. Montana reached instinctively to protect herself, wrapping her arms around her midsection and bending at the waist to stop the jagged pain coursing through her.

Before she could even utter a sound, Montana felt large arms wrap around her just as her knees buckled from the pain. The last thing she felt before going utterly numb was the sensation of falling against a very large, broad chest as the man cushioned her suddenly lifeless limbs and dragged her to the ground.

"Shhh. Don't say a word."

Quinn felt the long, supple lines of the woman in his arms and—for the briefest of seconds—forgot the danger that surrounded Montana Grant like a haze of noxious smoke.

Her luscious breasts pressed against his chest and his

inner thigh lay against the taut lines of her outer leg where they sprawled as he'd fallen with her in his arms.

What the hell was this woman involved in?

Every instinct he possessed suggested she was anything but the peace-wielding, beloved-by-all heiress of Grant Shipping.

The static that had gripped her from head to toe when Quinn first touched her was gone. The effect of his body, as well as the room's sudden plunge into darkness, killed the field of view of her attacker. Almost immediately, she began to struggle, pushing at him, hissing in a dark, throaty voice still trying to recover from the unexpected electric charge. "Get off me!"

"Shhh, Heiress. Not yet."

"Who the fuck are you?" Her words spewed anger, but at least she could do no more than whisper them.

Quinn tightened his grip on her, well aware the he-man routine wasn't going to win him any points in the "trust me" department. "Your savior, unless you insist on struggling away from me."

"What do you want?"

"A really good corned-beef sandwich. An ice-cold beer. World peace. I'm relatively easy to please."

The hotel's generator kicked in and a dull grayish wash of light filled the room. Montana's bright blue eyes never left his, her long lashes framing a stubborn gaze. "Who *are* you?"

"Quinn Tanner, Emerald Security. At your service."

He shifted slightly, moving off of her but still keeping her body shielded from the ballroom. He suspected her attacker had moved on, but he wasn't taking any chances until he could check out the room himself.

Extending a hand and helping her into a sitting position, he couldn't resist adding, "I'm your new shadow, sweetheart."

THE FIRST NOVEL IN THE DRAGONFIRE SERIES

KISS OF FIRE
A Dragonfire Novel

by DEBORAH COOKE

For millennia, the shape-shifting dragon warriors known as the Pyr have commanded the four elements and guarded the earth's treasures. But now the final reckoning between the Pyr, who count humans among the earth's treasures, and the Slayers, who would eradicate both humans and the Pyr who protect them, is about to begin...

When Sara Keegan decides to settle down and run her quirky aunt's New Age bookstore, she's not looking for adventure. She doesn't believe in fate or the magic of the tarot—but when she's saved from a vicious attack by a man who has the ability to turn into a fire-breathing dragon, she questions whether she's losing her mind—or about to lose her heart...

Also Available
Kiss of Fury
Kiss of Fate
Winter Kiss

Available wherever books are sold or
at penguin.com

S0107